THE
WOLF'S FEAST
VIKING STORIES
AND SAGAS

THE
WOLF'S FEAST
VIKING STORIES
AND SAGAS

CHRISTINE MORGAN

WORD HORDE
PETALUMA, CA

First Edition

ISBN: 978-1-939905-58-1

A Word Horde Book
www.wordhorde.com

TABLE OF CONTENTS

To my daughter Becca, and her father Tim, who always encouraged (or at least put up with) all the Viking stuff.

With ongoing special thanks to Professor Michael D.C. Drout, authors Nancy Marie Brown and Bernard Cornwell, and the band Amon Amarth.

Then let us lay the raven's table
And spread the wolf his feast

WINTER WOLF

When the time comes, child, when the time comes
Fleet through the hoarfrost and swift through the snow
The night ever-longer, never-longer, never-ending
In the brittle black crystal so star-pierced, relentless
Sleigh-skids through deep drifts spinning up skirls
Skate-skims on ice-sheets etch-scratch stark white
Freya's veils skein the skies, silken shift and shimmer
And I run with you, child, ravenous fate close behind.

On we go, on we go, field and fjord, farm and forest
Such a weight you are in my arms, such a burden
Clinging to me, your small hands, clutching tight
Seeking safety, seeking comfort, warmth and love
Why should you not? It is what you have known
All you have known; nothing of pain, want, and fear
Nothing of the wolf at our heels, hunger chasing.

Now it is dark, child, dark and darkest, it is cold
Now the frigid wind whistles, winter's bitterest bite
And the beast blowing the white rime of its breath
Paws and claws, teeth and jaws, the maw ever-wide
With each stride loping relentless on powerful legs
Bunched haunches, strong sinews, thick-bristling fur
The breadth of its chest, the black pit of its gullet

Eyes gleaming dull silver, dead silver corpse-shine
Upon unearthed treasure, lost barrow-grave goods
Scattered in bone and chill ashes of forgotten kings.

Harder I run now, harder, heart-pounding, feet numb
Joints aching, limbs weakened, so aged, so frail
Blood thin as water, skin like parchment and pale
The knots of my knuckles, the hunch of my spine
Crone-lines and crow-tracks the tale of my face
A year-saga, gnarled and seamed, a tree's rough bark
But oh, I was young once, child, young once like you.

Young and fair, young and strong, oh yes, I once was
Plump and life-ripe, rich in health, rich in beauty
The whole world all before me in all of its promise
I played in the spring-time, as you too should play
Buds to blossom, lambing, shoots greening the earth
I dallied my summer, dallied, laughing, and lazed
Meadow-flowers, lakes sparkling, sweetest fruit
And harvest would come, the butcher, the plenty
Feasting like lords, growing fat, growing merry
While already the winter's long shadow drew near.

And now it looms larger, child, now the end closes in
Giving chase, the fell hunter, pursuing its tender prey
However fast I might run, the wolf comes on faster
Nearer than ever, an inescapable, inexorable doom
Foam-spewing frost-fangs snap the hem of my cloak
Ready to snag and drag and bring down, rend and rip
Oh, my old bones creak brittle, my feeble heart burns.

When I stumble and falter, which I will, which I must
When at last the dread killing-cold dark overpowers
My throat laid open, guts savaged, my red blood spilt

When this aged body collapses to the hard-frozen earth
In my final moments, with my final gasps of breath
I will with my ragged corpse-flesh curl around you
Protecting in my death your precious renewal of life.

To pass through the black shadow, survive, and endure
Be reborn with the morn in the dawn of the day
Rise and arise, eyes shining bright and warm-smiling
In all fair promise, through the ages, year upon year
My daughter, my darling, my golden-haired Yul.

BLADES OF ICE
AND IVORY

Freylinde clung hard with both hands to the longship's oar-bench, uttering silent prayers to Thor the thunderer, and Odin All-Father, and Njord who ruled the sea's dark depths, that the storm's wrath would spare them.

She prayed that the wolf-howling wind, whipping white sleet and wave-spray in equally cold and harsh measures, would ease, no longer lashing their faces, blind-stinging their eyes, flaying their numb-frozen skin. That the water could calm, the grey whale-road of the ocean settling from turmoil and upheaval, before its surging fury smashed apart the hull-planking to send them splashing to a lonely and ignoble death.

She prayed that the thick clouds which churned low and sodden in the sky, like clumps of uncombed wet wool, would part and disperse... revealing perhaps the high stars gleaming and glinting like jewels in the blackness... or the shifting skeins of light, blue and violet and green, Freya's Veils, rippling from the north... or the pale shine of the moon upon the rocky shore of some island where they might put in to seek shelter...

If her prayers were heard, the gods ignored or laughed at them.

Already, her father and his crew had been forced to cut the ropes that held their fishing-nets, spilling the rich catch of cod and herring their settlement so desperately needed. Already, two men had

been lost, washed over the side—two men at least, two men Freylinde knew of; there may have been more gone since. In the deafening tumult of water and wind, she discerned no other voices or
shouts.

Lightning leaped behind the clouds in great vast flaring sheets.
Thunder rolled. Hail-stones pelted the ship in a merciless barrage.

Shivers wracked her body, shivers born as much of fear as of
cold, and she was *not* a cowardly girl. She was Freylinde Ravisdot-
tir, whose family was of strong and fierce bloodlines! They had been
Vikings, explorers and warriors! They had braved the long journeys!
First to Iceland, and then to Grunland and beyond!

These thoughts warmed anew her pride, but could do little for
the rest of her desperate situation. Her garments—heavy winter
clothing made of wool, fur and leather—were soaked through.
Her teeth chattered, clattering and rattling helplessly despite her
clenched jaw.

She had bound herself to the oar-bench with a stout length of
rope, not trusting alone to the grip of her arms to hold on. In their
seal-skin mittens, her hands had cramped into claws, so robbed of
sensation that she could no longer feel them. Likewise her feet; it
was as if chunks of frozen clay replaced flesh and bone below the
ankles.

Her very bones ached. The frost from her breath's moisture caked
on her hood's fox-fur trim. She blinked rapidly against the storm's
bitter onslaught but dared not press her eyes tightly shut, lest the
lashes be sealed together on a rime of sleet and tears.

Did Ravi, her father, yet live?

Did anyone besides herself?

For that matter, did *she*?

Niflheim, Hel's realm of the dead, was said to be bleak and grey,
cheerless and cold. A place without warmth, light, or hope... but
also without particular suffering.

This, then, could not be Niflheim. It was *too* cold for that, and
the suffering was severe.

The longship tilted and dipped and gave a sickening lurch. Its deck-planking shuddered. Its hull-planking groaned. Water sloshed in, icy and briny, flooding the oar-benches. Freylinde gasped for air. She coughed on salt and sea-foam. The pressure tugged at her, and if not for the binding rope she might have been swept away.

Someone else proved less fortunate. A man's body tumbled past her, limbs flailing, grasping madly for anything to save him but finding no purchase. She did not see his face, could not recognize him. A heartbeat later, he was gone.

Her mother had not wanted her to go out fishing with her father. Not for any premonition of bad weather, or other misgivings, not at all… Freyna thought her daughter's time would be better spent at home, on spinning and weaving and more womanly tasks. But Ravi, who had no sons, treated Freylinde almost as if she'd been born a boy. He'd taught her to fish, and to hunt, and to fight. And Freylinde, for her part, was just as glad to escape the incessant pestering of her five younger sisters.

At the moment, however, she would have given a great deal to be with them again, to have them pulling at her arms and clamoring for attention, asking her to braid hair and tell stories and play games.

Would that they were *all* home, snug and safe in the sod-walled houses! With fires in the hearth-pits, with hot broth simmering and bread baking on the flat stones! With dry clothes… and warm furs and fleeces heaped high on the sleeping-platforms!

Even through the wave-crash and storm-roar, she heard a despairing shriek as another of the men lost his grip. Him, she saw clearly and knew—Arnulf, who at fifteen was not much older than herself, with fair hair and moss-green eyes now made wide in terror. A cresting swell carried him off, his arms frantically waving.

Then—

An immense white shape burst up from the waves.

It was long and supple, a writhing sinuousness of muscular coils many times longer than the longship and far thicker than the thickest tree-trunk ever used for a mast.

A serpent.

The serpent?

But, no—even as Freylinde added her shriek to Arnulf's, she knew it could not be *the* serpent, not world-encircling Jormun-gandr, the Midgard Serpent. Huge though it was, it was not *that* huge… yet more than huge enough.

The force of its rising lifted Arnulf ahead of its gaping maw. Its bone-white head looked the size of a feast-hall, and aptly so for a feast-hall of sorts it was. Water sluiced out the sides of its mouth, streaming between myriad teeth like sword-blades made of ice.

Those teeth, those blades of ice, snapped shut with a clash and a torrential wet spray. A wet spray of foaming sea-water and bubbling red blood. The bite engulfed Arnulf from the collarbones down; his head and uppermost portion—arms still waving, eyes still wide with terror, mouth still voicing his now-voiceless shriek—dropped onto the ship.

What was left of Arnulf landed with a splash upon the wave-swamped deck-planking amid the oar-benches. Even those of the crew who had not seen the serpent's initial attack had, by then, noticed… and could not miss this grisly remnant, flopping and twitching the way half a fish might if let fall severed from an eagle's beak.

Nor could they miss the immensity of the white serpent, tower-ing above them, regarding them with a pitiless, polished-obsidian gaze.

Scarlet froth dripped from its jaws. Bony spines ridged its head. Its nostrils slitted and unslitted, snorting gusts of salty mist. Along the serpent's back, plated rows of scales overlapped like white-painted shields in a battlefield shield-wall; along its underside, finer scales flexed and meshed like a well-made mail-coat.

It seemed to pause there a moment, to preen there, as if inviting them to admire it. Or to challenge it.

This, Ravi did.

Shouting his war-cry, he stood tall upon the rolling and pitching longship. The wind flung his hair in drenched locks and flapped the edges of his bearskin cloak. He wore no mail or helm, held no shield or spear or sword, but his eyes burned with a rage to rival Thor's own.

And he did hold a stout, short-handled hand-axe, which he hurled with all his strength.

The axe spun through the air with good aim. It struck the monstrous serpent full in the teeth, splitting one with a terrible crack. Sparks flew at the point of that violent meeting.

The serpent flicked its white head backward as if in surprise. Its shining-black gaze regarded them. Its fine-scaled snout wrinkled, curled back, seeming almost to sneer at this pitiful show of defiance.

Others of the men called out. But, warriors though they were, none released his death-grip to take a stand by Ravi's side on the tossing, pitching deck. While Ravi, who was known to dance the oar-poles when he had the humor, looked as steady upon his feet as he might have been on good solid earth.

More thunder slammed through the lightning-shot clouds. The sleet struck like flung fistfuls of stones. The wind blew and keened with an eerie, whistling chorus.

Ravi shouted his war-cry again, shouted it to the roiling seas and skies. With the axe thrown, he stood now armed only with his fish-knife; it could have gutted a man as well as it did a cod, but against a north-beast of the icy deep such as this, the weapon might have been a child's plaything.

Nonetheless, he shouted, brandishing the blade, challenging the serpent to try and take him as it had taken Arnulf.

It dove instead. Its scaled and undulant length traced a pale arc plunging into the dark, seething ocean. Tremendous swells erupted in its wake, once more dousing and dangerously tipping the already imperiled ship.

Last of all went its tail, tapering whip-thin to a wicked

scythe-bladed bony white claw more than twice Ravi's height from base to sharp-pointed tip. This tail-claw, as the serpent dove, it slashed at the ship's proud and up-curving prow, which had been skillfully carved into designs of knotwork and galloping horses.

The claw sheared through the wood much as the scythe it resembled might have sheared through dry hay-stalks. Splinters flew. The hungry sea-waves flooded in, rushing and gurgling.

A man screamed. It was Knut; the final flick of the diving serpent's tail had caught his arm, upraised in defense. The cut was so clean and so quick that they all had had a stunned moment to stare at the stump, at the sliced raw flesh and jut of severed bones below his elbow, before the red blood spouted in a torrent.

Knut fell back, screaming anew in agony, terror and shock. Bregar, who was nearest, fought to seize hold of him in hopes of staunching the gouting wound. The others scrambled about in a frantic clamor as the cold, briny waters continued pouring into their stricken, wallowing ship.

Freylinde bit the ends of her seal-skin mittens and yanked them off to let them swing by their wrist-cords. With numb hands and stiff-cramped fingers, she pried at the knots in the rope securing her to the oar-bench. It was to have been her life-line; now it might be her trap and her doom.

The ropes had swelled, the knots tightened. She saw, but did not feel, her fingernails split and crack as she struggled.

Ravi made his way toward her, calling her name. The wind gusted hard, its throat voicing a thousand strange, keening wails. Snow fell heavy and fast in spinning, whirling sheets.

A wave broke over the ship's side and slammed her father to his knees. He dragged himself closer, the fish-knife gripped in his teeth. The determination in his eyes helped Freylinde quell her panic. He would save her... and if he could not, they would at least die together.

She had never been so cold, her body never felt so dense and heavy.

The wind wailed, wailed, louder and closer, both shrill and strangely melodic, seeming to come from all directions at once.

The sea heaved again. Out from it erupted the white serpent, jaws gnashing, the ice-blades of its teeth devouring men in gory crimson splatters of entrails and limbs. Its tail whipped about to strike this time at the mast, which fared no better than the prow had done. Nor did the men who'd tried to take cover against it. Their heads plunked into the water like pebbles, leaving their upright and rigid corpses to slowly collapse.

A massive coil of muscle and scales dropped across the deck. The hull split apart under it like an eggshell. The longship was done for, its sleek lines fractured to ragged ruin, storm-tossed pieces of flotsam and wreckage.

The section to which Freylinde's oar-bench was attached—and her still with it—capsized with a splash. Freezing water immersed her. Just when she had thought it impossible to feel any colder, the black chill sucked away warmth she hadn't known she yet possessed.

Her eyes and nose stung. Her lungs throbbed in her chest. The sudden muffling of sound was worse than the deafening thunder. She kicked, legs entangled in the sodden embrace of her heavy clothing.

Somehow, she got her face above water. She coughed out salt-brine and gasped for a breath. The section with her oar-bench rolled, upending, dunking her under, submerging her. Once again, she struggled to the surface. Blinking to clear her eyes, she cast her gaze wildly about in search for her father.

He was there, not far from her, wrestling with the entanglements of his own heavy clothes, his leather boots and bearskin cloak. The fish-knife, he had managed to keep hold of, its blade in his teeth. He swam with clumsy, splashing strokes until he reached her, then grabbed the wood to steady it when it would have rolled yet again. He cut the rope, freeing her, then did let it roll so that it floated as best as it would and they could both cling to it.

They clung to each other, as well. It was for comfort more than warmth; there was no warmth to be had, no warmth anywhere. Only the cold, only the sea.

Broken planks and debris fumed in the blood-foam around them. The serpent's coils enwrapped what was left of the ship, crushing it to slivers. As they watched, it tossed a man cartwheeling into the air, then swallowed him whole in one ravenous gulp. Voices cried out, lost from sight in the storm, drowned out by the ever-stranger, ever-nearer wailing songs of the wind.

No... not the wind... not wailing songs but whale-songs, the low hoots and shrill whistles, hollow warbling notes interspersed with clicks and barks.

They approached from all sides, sleek but bulbous dark shapes gliding through the waves, dipping up and down. Their tails slapped. Their blowholes puffed steamy mist.

In the lightning-flashes, their wet hides glistened, and the slender spirals of their single horns gleamed like spears of polished ivory.

Freylinde saw her father's lips form the word, though she could not hear him. She recognized it nonetheless.

Narwhal, the corpse-whale, so called for how their mottled grey coloring resembled the skin of men dead and drowned.

She had only ever seen narwhal by the few and at a distance, bobbing amid the ice-floes or traversing channels the waters had shaped. The Grunlandr *skraeling*-folk hunted them for their meat and rich fat, as they hunted seal and walrus and larger whales. They'd lived off the wealth of the far-northern sea since well before her own people sailed in their longships to settle.

There had been disputes on occasion, but more often there was peace, and the *skraelings* proved not adverse to trading with the taller, leaner, fairer strangers. Among the goods they offered were seal-pelts and walrus-tusks, and slim, elegant twists of narwhal-horn. Freylinde's grandfather, who lived with her family, had been these past months making a set of game-pieces from just such a horn.

Narwhal. The corpse-whale.

Now, several of the creatures passed so near to her that she might have reached out to touch them.

In her wonder and amazement, she almost forgot the frigid numbness seeping into her bones.

They weren't always a favorable omen, as the silvery, leaping sight of porpoises would be. Nor were they necessarily a bad one, despite the grim likeness that gave them their name.

But, as they plunged by to converge on the sea-serpent, their furious intention unmistakable, she thought they were the best omen she had ever beheld in all the world.

Their noises seemed less song and more speech, calling back and forth with urgent orders and conversation. The largest of them, the biggest males with chipped horns and battle-scars from dueling to impress mates, bellowed what could only have been their own war-cries, offering challenge and insult and threat to their foe.

The serpent reared high, all seething coils and lashing tail. Its jaws gaped wider than ever. Light danced a deadly promise along the icy blades of its teeth. The last surviving men, paddling frantically in the wreckage, were forgotten.

If the serpent's scales had been like the overlapping shields of a shield-wall, then the rising and falling of the narwhal horns was like spears on the shoulders of an advancing army.

And, like the spears of an advancing army against the shields of a shield-wall, when they met, the clash was tremendous.

What came next was, if anything, even more astounding.

As the narwhals charged the serpent, harrying it from all sides... as their horns stabbed and pierced... as the serpent reared, striking snake-swift with its jaws... as it writhed, and slashed with its scythe-claw tail... as thicker scales cracked the ivory horn-points and thinner scales were punctured by impaling wounds... as slick mottled-grey hides were sliced and torn and tooth-savaged... as blood warm and blood cold spilled to mingle together with the roiling salt-sea waters...

As all this happened, Freylinde felt the firm nudge of a blunt snout press her ribs. A bulging head broke the surface. No horn jutted from it. Blowhole-breath exhaled in a gust. A dark eye gazed into hers. The mouth's curve resembled a quirked little grin.

It was a narwhal… a female, a cow… while the horned males, the bulls, waged fierce war on the enormous ice-serpent.

Her father's exclamation told her that he, too, had been nudged. The narwhals surrounded them, jostling and bumping, crowding close. Their actions reminded Freylinde of the settlement's sheep, which, when being ushered into the sheep-byre to shelter for the night, moved in a similar amiable, pushing, bleating herd.

Yet, at the same time, their manner was more that of the shepherd's dogs, gathering and guiding, collecting the stragglers together… while she, Ravi, and the other men who'd not yet drowned or been devoured were the sheep, needing a stern shove to set them in order and motion.

Porpoises were favorable omens, often credited with saving shipwrecked sailors from a gloomy death in Njord's vast and deep kingdom. The black and white wolf-whales, however, tended to have just the opposite reputation.

Whether they were being rounded up by the narwhal-cows to be saved, or to be saved for later, Freylinde could not guess.

Nor did she much care. With the freezing waters having all but leached every scrap of heat from her body, having no longer even the strength just to shiver, she willingly enough wrapped her numb arms around the narwhal that had nudged her, holding on just above the small protruding side-fins.

Ravi did likewise. So too did the others. Any fate seemed preferable to those which awaited them by means of the serpent or the sea.

The narwhal was less than warm to the touch, but the solid feel of it, the smooth flex of muscle beneath that mottled-grey hide, the inner thump of its heartbeat, these all gave Freylinde a sense of safety and comfort.

She looked back once to see the white serpent, shedding scarlet from many gouging horn-thrusts, dive under the waves. The scything claw-blade of its tail cleaved a bull-narwhal crossways in half as it went. Bellowing and with shrill, enraged whistles, the rest of the males dove as well and gave chase. The battle vanished from sight into the black depths below.

Above, the storm kept raging, but with diminished vigor. The wind howled less wildly. Lightning flashed further off; the thunder muttered and rumbled. The narwhals, even those bearing their unlikely passengers, well weathered the waves.

They swam as a group, the laden ones at the center. Smaller forms, calves and yearlings, clustered around, and other mature females made up the outermost ring. The fishy smell of fresh cod and herring wafted strongly from them.

Freylinde remembered the nets her father had cut, dumping their rich catch. Had the narwhals found and feasted upon that unexpected but welcome bounty? Had they followed the longship in hopes for more, and intervened as they did out of gratitude for such generous gift-giving? Did they attack the serpent for that reason, or as a hated foe and intruder upon their territory?

Once more, she decided that she did not much care. Whatever their reasons, she was thankful for them.

Her thankfulness grew greater yet when the snowfall eased, and enough of the clouds parted to let milk-thin moonlight shine through. Not far ahead was a low, craggy stretch of coast, the rocky shore of some island or spit of land. The narwhals brought them to it, to a sheltered cove where steaming springs welled up and overflowed to trickle in waterfalls into the sea.

It was all they could do to drag themselves up the rough, slippery stone surfaces. Hard-edged shells scraped and cut at their numb, pale-wrinkled hands. The steam of the hot-springs was strong and sulfur-smelling.

Careless of whether it scalded their skin, the men splashed eagerly into the pools, some wading, others jumping headlong. Freylinde, shivering anew, her teeth chattering so it felt they might shatter each other to chips and shards in her mouth, would have joined them, but Ravi first made her wait until he himself tested the water.

From this refuge, their frigid flesh finally thawing, they watched the narwhal-bulls returning from their brutal battle. They came wounded but victorious, the ivory spear-blades of their bloodied horns bobbing. The rest swam warbling joy-songs to meet them.

But then, far out in the black ocean, arose a monstrous swell, a wave, a god-wave that drew half the tide up into its mountainous cresting surge.

It loomed higher, and higher still, until it threatened to blot out the moon.

And at its white-capped frothing peak, a hundred ice-toothed serpents rode to war.

THE VIKING IN YELLOW

Gulls cried faint and unseen through a heavy morning mist that cast all the world in damp and dripping grey. Distant waves rushed foaming upon the pebbled shore, filling the cool air with scents of salt and brine. Here, where the river widened to meet the sea, the waters mixed in eddying whorls. Ripples lapped the muddy banks. Splashes sounded where fish leaped, or struggled in the nets and traps.

Wigleof led the way from one spot to the next. His little sons followed, lugging the baskets that would soon be filled with this day's rich catch. They whispered to each other, joking, teasing. They were good boys and dutiful, twins, sturdily built, curly-haired like their mother. He loved them well.

At their home, a small thatch-roofed hut walled in wattle and daub, Wigleof's sweet-natured wife Aelda would be hard at work, helped by their daughters and tending the baby. Perhaps later, she'd walk to the village by the abbey, to trade smoked fish for milk, eggs and honey.

Or she might send Aeldwyn, their eldest, who greatly admired the nuns—Sister Gehilde most of all—and spoke of joining their order. Wigleof had no objections to this, though he held a private measure of doubt for her reasons. If Aeldwyn thought the life of a nun was nothing but restful prayer, candle-making, clean robes of soft wool and hymn-singing, he suspected she might be in for a surprise.

He chuckled to himself as he hauled up the first wicker-woven fish traps. They were well-full with sleek silver-scaled bodies that flapped and flailed, gulping. The boys chattered eagerly as they opened and loaded the baskets.

Then they hushed, frowning.

"Father," said Leofric, his tone unusually subdued, "what happened to this one?"

Wigleof looked at what the boy held in his small hands. The fish did not flail, flap or gulp. "That one's dead," he said.

"But what happened to it?" Leofwald asked, his tone also subdued.

Expecting to find nothing out of the ordinary, Wigleof took the fish, and frowned himself. An odd oiliness sheened its skin, and its flesh felt strangely warm. He had never pulled a warm fish from the river, or from the sea. Its eyes bulged, yellow-white and murky, rather than shiny black. It might have already been partially stewed.

Upon a closer-yet inspection, he found that its fins and tail were tipped with fine barbs curved like cat's claws, and in its mouth were not teeth but stringy tendrils. Something about it struck him as altogether loathsome, unnatural, and vile.

Both boys gazed at him, solemn, waiting for him—their trusted father—to have all the answers. He found himself speechless. His mind was torn, half of it wanting to hurl the fish as far away as he could, the other half thinking to take it to the village as a curiosity.

It twitched in his grasp. He dropped it with a stifled cry of revulsion. Leofwald bent as if to reach for it and Wigleof drew him back. The three of them watched as the fish writhed and clenched.

"You said it was dead," Leofric said.

"I thought that it was."

"It's trying to burrow into the mud," said Leofwald.

"Father, I don't like it."

"No. Nor do I."

The frightened tremors in their voices decided him. Wigleof seized a nearby branch, snapping it off so that the end came to a rough point. He drove this down into the fish, puncturing it through the gills, nailing its body to the river bank. Thin blood oozed out, almost more yellowish than red. The fish thrashed a bit more, then fell still.

Silence held.

They watched it warily.

It did not move again.

Silence yet held, a silence that seeped into Wigleof's consciousness. The gulls, which had been shrieking their cries, had fallen mute. He could not hear the steady rush of the surf, a noise as constant and familiar to him as his own breathing. The moisture, which had been collecting on the leaves, making them glisten, dripping off in a soft wet patter, now made no sound. Nor did the water lapping along the shore, although he saw its regular ripples.

Each of his boys held him by an arm. He felt their touches, felt their trembling, felt them press close against his legs. They looked up at him with identical pleading expressions, but did not speak. Perhaps could not speak, just as he was unable to find his own voice to reassure them.

A stirring in the heavy, silent grey gloom caught his eye. Out on the river, a shadow appeared, mist-blurred and indistinct, then coalescing into a shape... a long, low, narrow shape that brought dread to his heart... a shape with graceful curves rising at prow and at stern, curves topped with carven beast's heads... a shape, a ship... a ship with a single mast, from which belled a striped sail of yellow and white... a ship with many slim oars jutting out to each side... oars dipping and stroking in unison... the oar-blades slicing without splashing... the hull gliding in utter silence, water parting ahead of it and sluicing together in pale roils in its wake...

Terror welled up within him.

He should have fled already, run for the village to warn them, run for his house, for his wife and daughters, to take what valuables they could and seek refuge, seek safety hiding in the woods and the hills.

A Viking ship, a longship, a ship of pagans and killers from the savage north! A raid! Fire and plunder, murder and rape!

He should have fled already.

Yet he was unable to so much as move. The boys clung to him, quaking.

The oars rose and fell, rose and fell. Upon its oar-benches sat men in mail-coats, men in leathers and furs. Their faces were pale, their hair fair and stirred by the same wind that filled the striped sail, though no wind rustled the leaves on the shore and no wind tugged at Wigleof's own hair or clothing.

A row of shields hung along the ship's side. Round shields of lime-wood, some with rims and bosses of iron. Shields painted... painted not with horses or ravens, dragons or wolves... painted with... symbols? letters?

Wigleof of course could not read, but he had seen some writings. And if these were letters, they were like none he had ever seen. They were...

They were hideous, those painted symbols, those yellow signs. Hideous and horrible. Loathsome to the eye, to the mind, in much the same way as the strange fish had been. Unnatural. Vile.

The ship glided on. The oarsmen never turned from their labor. If they noticed the fisherman and his sons on the river's bank with their fish-traps and baskets, they gave no indication.

At the stern, upon the steering-platform, stood a tall figure, wrapped in a long and tattered cloak of yellow leather trimmed with the jaundiced-looking fur of a far-northern bear. He wore a gilded helm with a lank yellow horse-tail for a plume, the coarse strands blowing about his shoulders in that same unfelt wind. His helm's visor was made from ivory or bone, its aspect pallid and inhuman.

He alone among the men turned his head as the ship passed by. His gaze sought and held the three of them, there on the shore. Through his visor, his eyes seemed to blaze as black as the stars.

...as black... as the stars?

How could that be? That could not be. That made no sense. No sense at all.

Rising and falling, the oars cut the water. The striped sail swelled full from the mast. The yellow-cloaked Viking kept a thin-fingered hand curled to the steering-oar. He tilted his helmed head ever-so-slightly in wry acknowledgment, then faced forward again, faced the carved prow, faced upriver in the direction of the unsuspecting village and abbey beyond.

Skeins of mist whirled and wafted about the longship's stern. It became shape again, shape and shadow. Then it was no more to be seen.

Wigleof blinked, as if one emerging from a dream. He glanced at the baskets and fish-traps, and saw that every last fish—even those not yet pulled to land—lay or floated lifeless.

Somewhere, very faint and very far, a lone gull cried a dirge. Rain began to patter on the leaves, in the mud.

The boys looked at their father. Both had soaked their breeches. Becoming aware of the clammy wetness at his crotch and thighs, Wigleof realized he had done the same.

The village. The abbey.

His house. Aelda and the girls, and the baby.

Raid, rape and plunder. Fire and murder and blood.

Those shields, painted with those yellow signs.

He crouched and put an arm around each of his sons. He hugged them tight to his sides, picked them up, held them to him. They twined their little arms around his neck, and buried their faces against his shoulders.

Neither of them struggled as he carried them into the river, wading deeper to the dark channel where a strong current swept toward the sea. Nor did they make a sound, even as the cold water closed over their heads.

***

The blinded monk had passed another bad night. His urgent word-less gurgles grew louder, into raving grunts and groans. Though his hands were swaddled in soft wool wrappings, he tugged at them, pulled at them with his teeth, until Sister Gehilde was forced to restrain his wrists with strong bonds.

At last, she'd been able to persuade him to drink a sleeping-draught, though the sleep into which he finally succumbed was shallow, and unrestful. His head tossed. Low, guttural mumbles issued from his sore-scabbed lips.

Only when the sky began to lighten and the fog gave way to rain did the monk sink into a true slumber. Gehilde, her own weariness weighing upon her, drew a blanket to his shoulders. The bandage about his face had come askew, and with a murmured prayer she adjusted the cloth over the weeping wounds where once were eyes.

She stretched. She sighed. She rubbed her brow, and temples. For a moment, the thought of her narrow bed beckoned, tempting her with its promise. But day had dawned, if damp and dreary. The morning business of Marymeade Abbey must be done.

It had been built about the remains of a stone fort of the old Romans, moss-grown ruins, tumbled walls and archways, a few intact inner chambers with floors of tiled mosaic. From a hilltop, it overlooked the winding ribbon of the river valley. Behind it, beehive-dotted flower meadows and orchards sloped away toward the green farms and grazing lands around the village.

The nuns kept the bees, collecting combs and honey, making candles and sticks of colored sealing-wax. This was their main sources of livelihood in addition to what they received from the church. They also brewed fruit-wine to sell and trade.

At any given time, some three dozen women called it home. Not all were sworn to holy vows; some were lay-sisters, widows and forsaken wives. Their father-monastery was St. Neot's of the Stave and Crook, located further inland and upriver, some days' ride away at Shepsbury. Twice monthly, or more often during holidays, priests would come from St. Neot's to lead services, and supervise the running of the abbey.

And, when one of their monks might fall injured or ill, Marymeade was where they were sent to be tended as they recovered.

Monks such as Brother Oston, this poor and damaged soul. And Brother Camden, to whose room Gehilde now went. She found her sister there—Gamyl, her sister by birth as well as in their holy order. Gamyl was the younger, and of slighter frame. Otherwise they much resembled one another, with fine features, fawn-brown hair beneath head-coverings of white linen, and eyes the blue of ripe bilberries.

"How does he fare?" Gehilde asked.

Gamyl glanced up from where she sat upon a stool at the monk's bedside. "He woke for a while, spoke for a while," she said. "But he still does not know me, or himself, where he came from or where he is."

Brother Camden, though gone to grey, had been a hale and hearty, vibrant man... jovial in his humor, stalwart in his faith. Now he lay stricken, the right side entire of his body gone feeble and frail. The right half of his face hung slack, those corners of eye and mouth drooping. Age seemed to have draped him in a sudden cloak of additional years. If not for the slow swelling of his chest with each breath, he might have been a corpse awaiting the shroud.

"He inquired again after someone called Silvia," Gamyl went on, "then wept a bit, bade me be sure to remember to feed the cat, and..." She trailed off with an expressive, hopeless gesture at the monk.

"Did he take any broth or gruel?"

"Not much, no."

They watched over him together a moment, each speculating on who this Silvia might be. Mother? Sister? Lost sweetheart from Brother Camden's youth, before taking his vows?

Then Gamyl spoke. "How fares Brother Oston? I heard him through the night."

The weariness settling onto her again, Gehilde nodded. "Worse than ever. I had to bind down his wrists for fear he'd do himself more harm."

"What could have caused—?"

"It is not for us to wonder," Gehilde interrupted sharply.

"But after Brother Rubert, sister, surely you must—"

"I must not, I do not, and neither shall you."

They crossed themselves at the mention of the unfortunate monk's name. He had come to their care from St. Neot's greatly troubled, greatly distraught. After a time, he'd begun to regain both his senses and spirits… then went missing and was found in the orchard, a length of rope 'round his neck.

As she and Gamyl shared this conversation, Gehilde remained attentive to the quiet and orderly bustle of Marymeade's morning routine. Now it was disrupted in a flurry of commotion. Voices rose in anxious queries. Footsteps slapped quick in the halls. Robes swished and rustled.

"Sister Gehilde!" That was Magrin, not a nun but a short and stocky widow who served as a kind of gruff but well-meaning mother-bear nursemaid to them all.

Gehilde hastened from the room, Gamyl close behind her. In the abbey's main chamber, which they used as their common space for dining and sitting, the tables had not yet been set for the fast-breaking. Nuns and lay-sisters crowded in, wide-eyed, looking alarmed and frightened.

And with good reason.

Vikings.

Vikings, pagan sea-raiders, attacking the village below.

Through the fog and rain, they could see nothing of it. But they heard the shouts and screams, and the brief clash of battle.

Aeldwyn, the fisherman's daughter, had brought the grim news when she fled her family's house down by the shore.

"Mother told me to run, to take Wigla and the baby and get far away," the girl said, gasping for breath. "She went to look for Father and the boys."

The baby, red with indignation, fussed and squalled in a bundle slung across Aeldwyn's back. Little Wigla, a pretty child with long curls and freckles, began to sob.

Everyone looked then to Gehilde, their abbess. Weary though she was, she cast it aside at once. She barked swift instructions to Sister Udela, bidding her fetch the treasures of their humble church—a silver crucifix, an ivory cup set with garnets that had been a gift from Alfred of Wessex, the bronze-inlaid reliquary containing a clump of straw from the manger in which Christ had slept, and their holy books—and for the others to gather only their most prized possessions.

"Meet by the well-stone," she told them. "There is a tunnel there, through the old Roman bath. It leads to the hut in the orchard. Magrin, you know the way."

"Yes, Sister."

"Go, then, and hurry! Aeldwyn, you and the children go with them."

"Our mother—"

"Would want you to be safe. Go with Magrin."

The rest scurried to obey. Their lives of humble piety and simplicity here meant that they had little in the way of belongings. It would not take them long.

"What about you?" Gamyl asked.

Gehilde shook her head. "Marymeade is in my charge. The monks are in my care, and they are in no fit state to be moved. I will plead for them."

"The Vikings will surely kill them where they lie!" Gamyl protested.

Remembering Brother Rubert, who had damned himself by taking his own life, Gehilde softly said, "If that is God's will, then so be it and let it be a mercy."

Gamyl raised her chin in a manner Gehilde knew all too well from their girlhood. "I am staying with you," she declared.

There would be no arguing. Gehilde smiled and squeezed her

hand.

Soon, the others had gone. The abbey was empty but for the four of them, the two ailing monks and the two sisters.

No more sounds of violence reached their ears from the direction of the village. They could make out a dull glow that might have been the smoldering fires of thatch-roofed houses, but nothing else.

Out of the grey fog and rain, the Vikings appeared. They came in a line, round shields held before them as if they expected to be met by armed men.

A wretched, despairing moan slid from Gamyl's lips. She covered her mouth, then murmured through her fingers. "Gehilde... their shields... do you see...?"

"I see," said Gehilde, touching the rosewood cross she wore on a cord around her neck and sending a silent prayer to the blessed Virgin.

"They are the same that Brother Oston would—"

"I know."

Brother Oston, however, had lacked yellow paint. Or indeed any paint or ink with which to inscribe the hellish symbols. It had not stopped him. Nor had the absence of his sight, just as the tearing out of his eyes had not stopped him from seeing the marks... the words. With gruel, or blood, or excrement, he'd etch them upon the walls. When prevented from doing that, he'd claw them into his own skin, gouging wounds and scars.

"Do not look," Gehilde added. "Do not look at their shields. Do not look at them."

The Vikings came closer, came to the abbey's very door. There, they stood and waited. Their faces were corpselike. Their eyes were empty, and dead.

Another emerged from the mists. This one did not wait at the door but crossed its threshold undaunted. He was tall, with a cloak of tattered yellow leather sweeping from his shoulders and a yellow horse-tail as the plume of his helm. The contours of a visor carved from ivory obscured his features with a pallid mask, but for glittering eyes like dark jewels, or shining black stars.

"You have three monks here," he said, in a voice that rasped, the voice of a dry desert wind. "I want them."

"We have only two," said Gehilde, straightening her spine. "And you may not have them."

"Two?"

"The third hanged himself."

"Pfah. He was weak."

"The others are ill," she said. "Ill unto death."

"They have done you no harm." Gamyl stepped up beside her, chin again defiantly raised. "And harming them will do you no good, whatever your evil intention."

"Leave them in peace," Gehilde said. "Leave this place in peace. This is a house of God, and you are not welcome here."

The man laughed, and it was the scrape of a spade upon stone, the grind of bones in a grave. "They have looked upon that which should not have been seen. It is for their own sake, and yours, that you stand aside."

"Looked upon something?" echoed Gamyl. "Are you saying that's what brought this misfortune on them? That's what left Brother Camden brain-stricken, what drove Brother Oston to his state, what made Brother Rubert take his own life?"

"As I said, he was weak. They are all weak. Cowardly, and mad."

Gehilde shook with anger. "You come here, nameless and face-hidden, and call them weak? Call them cowards? For shame! Take off your visor, then! Show yourself unmasked, if you have such strength and courage!"

"My visor?" He removed his helm with its horse-tail plume and met her gaze with his blazing black eyes. "As you see, I wear none."

Or perhaps it was not anger that shook her. Perhaps it was terror.

"No visor..." said Gamyl in a high, fainting whimper. Tears spilled down her cheeks. She clutched at Gehilde's sleeve. "Sister... he wears no visor..."

They put their arms around each other, held tight in a trembling embrace, as the tall man in the cloak of tattered yellow slowly advanced.

Gehilde kissed Gamyl's brow, then leaned her own against it.

"Pray, sister," she whispered. "Let us shut our eyes, and pray."

***

He stood atop a rise as the day waned, as the sun sank like a fiery bauble in the west. The rains of previous days had passed, leaving clear the skies now darkening to woad, indigo and violet. The first few stars—white, and sharp—glinted in the gloaming.

Before him was a scene that, upon first glance, looked both peaceful and pastoral. Sheep grazed across the hillsides. Geese waddled, honking, to and from ponds where a few swans sailed with necks arched regal. Smaller birds darted from the bushes and whirled above the trees. The town spread in amiable clusters in front of the monastery's gate, the tanneries set further off.

Sheep, yes, sheep, a great many of them… the wool and mutton secondary to the main industry here, which was the making of fine vellum from the sheepskins. The monks had endless need of vellum. And for goose-feather quills and pots of ink in many colors, for blotting dust, for sealing wax. They needed leather for bookbinding, gilt with which to emboss and stamp.

The monks. Yes, the monks. The monks of St. Neot's of the Stave and Crook.

The monks who busied themselves long hours, bent squinting by candle-light or the little flicker of tallow-oil lamps. Reading. Writing. Copying. Transcribing and translating. Adorning their calligraphy with glorious illumination and illustration.

Somehow, and to their sorrow, they had come by a tome of dire potency and power. Had the thief who'd stolen it sold it to them, unmindful of what it contained? Did they think to learn from it? To add its lore to the writings of their kings and saints?

Whatever their reasoning, they now paid the price.

Witness the monks who'd read from those pages. Who'd sought to make copies of the manuscript, perhaps to send to all their churches, add to their libraries.

Witness the one called Brother Oston, who had torn his own eyes from their wet sockets to spare himself having to see another word, only to find to his horror that he could not unsee them even then! How, in his madness, he'd shouted them, reciting passages until his fellow monks could bear hearing it no longer! They wrenched wide his jaws and severed his tongue at the root. But even then, blinded and dumb, he'd written the words, drawn the symbols and the signs.

Witness Brothers Camden and Rubert, one left shattered of mind and body, the other driven to the worst of sins.

And now, witness this scene... so pastoral and peaceful...

Upon first glance.

Further glances showed that all was not as it seemed or should have been.

The sheep roamed the hills unshepherded, at an evening hour when they belonged safely sheltered in their sheep-byres. The honking geese likewise went untended, nary a goose-girl to be seen.

In the town, light shone in but few windows, and smoke curled from fewer chimney-holes. No peasants trudged home from the fields, or from the woods with faggots bundled on their backs.

The monastery's belfry, a square structure of tarred timber and hewn logs, was silent. Its bell had not tolled for vespers. No robed and tonsured figures moved about within St. Neot's walls.

The tall man who stood upon the rise, the tall man in his tattered cloak of yellow and helm with horse-tail plume, nodded with grim satisfaction. He raised one pale, thin-fingered hand and gestured his warriors to follow.

They moved wraithlike through the town. Only frightened, snarling dogs opposed them, readily dispatched with a spear-thrust or swung axe-blade. The smith's forge held just a bed of ashes. The bread-ovens were dark and cold. Rats capered in the granaries.

Here and there were indications of looting and swift departure. Several of the buildings sat abandoned, empty and forlorn. Those that still seemed to harbor life did so with a furtive doom and resignation, as if the people within huddled behind barricaded doors, gripping useless weapons while they waited for the end.

Once, a haggard, naked crone spat curses from a doorway, then plunged a knife into her scrawny belly and ripped it sideways so that her entrails bulged out, glistening. They passed her by, and left her where she fell.

The gates of St. Neot's were open.

Crow-picked corpses littered the outer yard.

Fly-crawling corpses littered the inner halls and chambers.

Some, like Brother Rubert, had hanged themselves. Some had taken their own lives in other ways—veins cut so that the blood pooled thick, or with cups from which poison had been drunk still clutched in death-rigid hands.

Others had turned their violence outward. In the dormitories, several monks lay suffocated in their beds. One had been stuffed headfirst into the kitchen hearth, held there as he roasted. Another had been crucified and emasculated. There were bludgeonings and stabbings, drownings and strangulations.

A few yet lived, if such could be said to be living. They crawled, mad and cackling, mutilated. They rocked back and forth, slamming their heads into stone walls. They wept. They laughed. They wallowed in their filth, eating of it.

"Finish them," said the man in the tattered yellow cloak.

His warriors obliged.

It was no battle, merely butchery.

As they saw to their deadly business, he saw to his own.

He went from one room to the next until he came to the library with its long lines of desks. Ink pots had been spilled. Books were scattered. Most of the candles had burned down or gone out; one had tipped and it was a wonder that a fire hadn't started.

A sole dead monk sprawled on his back, eyes and mouth agape

in final shocked surprise. An *aestel*, meant for following a reader's place, had been put to different purpose... the slender wooden rod of its pointer had been driven into the monk's throat, the enamel and crystal handle jutting like a strange ornament.

And here... here were sheets of vellum, manuscript pages, copies and translations half-finished. He collected them, studying each, tossing aside those of no interest to him and keeping the rest.

He noted the beautiful work, the lavish illuminations of rich and brilliant color. He noted the cunning illustrations done along the margins—a crown of diamonds and gold, a corpse-cart pulled by dark horses, a pure white lily with a beam as of sunlight shining from its heart, black stars blazing in a dome of sky, a disheveled cat with a slim pink ribbon serving as collar, the towers of a city rising behind tormented moons.

Gathering them into a pile, he rolled the pages together, tying them with a length of yellow cord. This thick scroll, he tucked through his belt, and drew his cloak to conceal it.

Next he searched among the scattered books, indifferent to bibles and scriptures, gospels and homilies, the writings of the saints and disciples. At last, partly hidden by the dead monk's outflung arm, he found a slim volume bound in leather more ancient and tattered than that of his cloak.

His long, pale, thin fingers folded around it. He picked it up, turned it over. There on the front, stamped in gold, faded and worn, was a familiar sign... the same sign his men bore on their shields. He traced it with the pad of his thumb, dry skin hissing against skin even drier.

Summoned, his warriors returned, weapons dripping. They brought no other plunder, had not looted the monastery of its silver, just as they had not ransacked the village or town.

He thought briefly of the women, the two sisters, the nuns. So brave... strong and willful... the elder of the pair most of all. Perhaps he should not have spared them and left them to their abbey. Perhaps he should have brought them along.

They might have made fine queens.

But, no.

He had what he'd come for.

Soon the shields hung again along the ship's sides. Soon the oarsmen took up their oars and the striped sail belled in the wind. The carved beast's head at the prow faced away from the land, the one at the stern watching the shore recede.

A gradual, sighing mist engulfed them as they lost sight of the rocky coast, as the ship leaped and crashed in the waves over the cold grey sea.

Then the mist changed, changed and warmed, became steam. The water flattened, smooth as glass, burnished as a mirror.

Overhead, blazing black, shone the stars. The hot, fuming lake stretched out vast on all sides. Fish flickered in the depths, the barb-finned and hair-mouthed fish of Hali.

And the longship sailed on, toward the far horizon, where the towers and spires of a great city rose behind tormented moons.

CATS OF WAR

We emerge in darkness, doubly-blind, our eyes sealed
Our world limited to scent and sound, touch and taste
The warm weight and squirm of bodies, feebly mewing
Long licks of a tongue, firm and gentle, fur-smoothing
Familiar pulse-beat, familiar purring, familiar presence
Oh and there is milk, rich goodly milk from soft teats
Little paws kneading belly-fluff, tiny claws pricking
Our world, yes, our world, and we know we are small
But the blood of our ancestors flows strong in our veins
We are cats, fast and cunning, agile and clever, so fierce
We will be hunters, brave warriors, bringers of slaughter
Bane of birds, rats, and mice… their doom, their terror
When we are grown; for now, yes, we still are very small
Bigger, though, bigger and stronger with each passing day
Eyes opened to colors and shapes, the gold flicker of fire
The hearth and the hall beyond our sheltered birth-place
This mother-den seclusion under pelt-heaped platforms
But we are curious, eager to venture forth, and explore
If clumsily at first, unsteady of leg and wobbly a'foot
So much to see and experience in our new wider world!
Huge hounds come snuffling, noses wet and inquisitive
We hunch and hiss, ears low, backs bristling, tails puffed
Because we are cats, swift and battle-bold, cats of war!
Here, too, in the hall, are the people, tall and peculiar

Loud in their voices, their laughter and story-singing
Rough and boisterous, sparsely-furred, lacking claws
But they stroke us and cuddle, and, best of all, play
With strings to twitch and dangle, and feathers to chase
Soon, we drink not just mother's milk but other-milk
Milk from dishes and bowls, licks of butter and cream
Soon, we sample bone-broth and fish-scraps and meat
Our little tummies all round and full, comfortably fat
We sleep curled on laps or stretched out by hearth fire
Though we do not forget our trueborn duty, our purpose
When there are mice in the granaries, or rats in the hall
Our elders teach us how to stalk and hunt, pounce and kill
And they teach us the age-old sagas and lore of cat-kind
How, one day, we might leave the hall, become travelers
Perhaps to ride the grey whale-road aboard far-sailing ships
Bringing tooth-and-claw death to the rats of strange lands
We learn of the great tree and the god-things and creatures
Of the wise All-Father Odin with his wolves and his ravens
And the shining goddess, bright Freya, her chariot cat-drawn
Queen of cats, friend of cats, who gifted us with nine lives
Nine lives for nine worlds when most are gifted only one
Who gifted us with stealth and sight and our own seidr-magic
And, just as Odin sends forth Valkyries, choosers of the slain
To bring the worthiest warriors to high gold-roofed Valhalla
So too does Freya send forth her bravest, most faithful cats
To claim those full-half of the fallen that are hers by right
We listen well, and we learn, for although we may be small
We will grow big and strong, bold and fierce, cats of war.

FREYA'S VEIL

L jutvin wakes.

Not with the dawn, no. Not with the dawn for the dawn is far off, far and faint and fleeting in this, the dark cold of the year.

He wakes with the night, with the deepest hour of the night.

He wakes to the warmth of fleeces and furs holding the heat of slumbering bodies. He wakes to sighs and snores, sleep-talk, the fitful stir of an infant comforted by motherly drowsing murmurs.

In the low glow of banked firepit embers, the longhouse is shadow-draped. A cat's eyes glint and gleam from the rafters, prowling, on the hunt. Sprawled dogs give dream-chase to hares or hinds, paws rustling floor-rushes. The air wafts thick with smoke-smells and sweat-smells, bread and ale, leather, wet wool.

The night, the deepest hour of the night. In this, the dark cold of the year.

Cold indeed, winter's grip on the north lands relentless. Snow blankets the earth. Ice chokes the fjords. A bitter wind whistles its shrill and chill ceaseless cry. To go out into it, into that wind and cold, would be to have breath snatched in frost-plumes from the lips… to feel exposed skin sting as if thousandfold needle-pierced… eyes squinting in protest rimed by their own freezing tears… limbs going leaden, extremities numbed…

Against such ferocity, even the fiercest must seek shelter. Even the wolves and white bears would have taken refuge, curled in caves, in drift-burrows.

To go out into it would be foolishness. Foolishness at the very least. Foolishness, if not death.

Yet, he rises from his bed.

Quietly. Cautiously. Careful not to disturb Ingiryf beside him. His wife, and he supposes he cares for her as much as a man can for a woman not of his own choosing. He wonders, some times, if she thinks the same way of him.

It is no fault of hers. It is not of her doing. She is pretty enough, Ingiryf, she is capable and kind, hard-working, a fair cook, a skilled weaver. They provide each other occasional, if dutiful, attentions. Should children be the inevitable result, Ljutvin does not doubt she will raise them well.

He knows he has little reason to complain. Others in similar arrangements have fared far worse. His parents, both too prideful and stubborn to demand divorce, despised each other by the end; it had been considered something of a marvel their marriage hadn't ended in murder.

He does not despise Ingiryf. He suspects, had circumstance been different, he might have grown to love her.

Yet, instead, there is within him a resentment, a dissatisfaction.

And, on nights such as tonight, an urgency. A *need*.

So, he rises. Quietly. Cautiously. He dons shoes and leg-wraps, pulls a cloak around his shoulders. With the sure-footedness of familiarity, he makes his way through the hall. The cat's glinting gaze follows him. A hound whuffs once, tail thumping. No one else marks his passage.

The bitter wind, whistling.

Winter's grip. Ice and snow.

The deepest hour of the night.

Foolishness to go out into it.

Foolishness, if not death.

He goes out into it.

His breath, snatched in frost-plumes from his lips. His skin, stinging as if thousandfold needle-pierced.

His eyes squinting in protest against freezing-rime tears... then widening, awe-struck with yearning and strange, unbidden desire.

The night is clear, without trace of cloud, mist, or fog.

But the sky is not black.

The sky is alive, is alight.

The sky is skeins of emerald, violet, and gold. The sky is bright wonder, sheeting, a luminous undulant dance. Bluer than woad, greener than spring, fiery pink... no orderly bands of a rainbow-arch but rippling and shifting... whorls like flowing liquid... the melding trill of harpstrings...

Ljutvin's heart surges in his breast. It is more vivid than he's ever beheld it before, spanning from horizon to horizon, the inner curves of a vast inverted bowl sheened with streaks and swirls of oils, paints, and dyes. More vivid and more bright, bright enough to make him marvel how *anyone* could sleep, how the cocks in the henhouse do not mistake a false dawn.

So beautiful... has there ever been, could there ever be, anything so beautiful?

Freya's veil, as if the goddess in her finery, wheeling and twirling, spun and danced, trailing rare-silken colors across the skies.

He gasps, heedless of the chill rushing to fill his lungs. He weeps with joy, the tears streaming, glazing his cheeks with silvery ice-trails, freezing in his beard. Without thought, his feet carry him onward, feet already numb and cold as blocks hewn from stone. He struggles through snow to his knees, flounders in drifts to his thighs, falls headlong more than once, and pays it no mind.

Her veil, Freya's veil, floating and writhing, outshining the stars.

Shimmering, undulating, silent melody in unearthly motion. A dance of fluid light, as if to a song, as if to music he cannot hear. Oh, but what he would give to hear it! The god-music, the song-strains of Asgard! Sweeter than honey-wine, enticing, intoxicating! Like a kiss, a caress, from Freya herself!

All around him, the stark winter-white world is transformed, softened by jewel-hues into a magical aelfheim. Trees dripping with icicles become glorious queens, tall and regal, pine-gowned, resplendent in diamonds. A pond, frozen solid, is a glimmering mirror. Fence-posts become sentinels, garbed in polished mail-coats.

And, above him, the sky… the marvelous sky… the veil swirling, ever-changing… the goddess in her lissome dance… Freya, lovely Freya, of the Aesir and Vanir the loveliest… her beauty… her generous passions…

He falls again, headlong again, plowing face-first into the snow. It stuffs his nose, clogs his mouth, dashes cold in his eyes. Coughing and sputtering, he thrashes to turn himself over. His cloak hampers, ensnaring, entangling, and he fights free of it with a furious oath.

Finally, he lies splayed on his back. His lungs heave like a smith's bellows. Great clouds issue from his lips; his breath is the smoke, his chest the coal-filled forge, hot and seething, a deep inner burn-pain. His limbs are so heavy, weariness weighting his bones.

But, the sky… filled with light, filled with color… cool and smooth as rolling handfuls of glass beads… rare and wonderful beauty… Freya's fine-silken veil, more delicate than any cloth ever woven…

It fills the skies. Fills the world. Fills his rapt, dazzled eyes. They are open. Wide open, the lids ice-locked by his caked, frozen tears. He stares upward, stares skyward, lost and immersed. His arms rest slack by his sides. The frost-rime silvering his beard crackles, faint and brittle, when he smiles.

The clouds of his breath are clouds no longer. Only thin, misty tendrils. Pale wisps, swift to dissipate.

Her veil, Freya's veil, fills his eyes. Fills his senses, and his body, and his being, mind and soul.

***

Ingiryf woke to find herself once again alone.

Not alone in the longhouse; oh, no, far from it. The raised sleeping-platforms to either side of the hall's central fire-pit span were thick with the jarl's folk. Warriors and farmers, craftsmen and thralls, women and children, elders and babes-in-arm, all surrounded her in their slumber.

No, it was the place beside her, the sunken hollow in the straw-stuffed mattress, the emptiness beneath furs and fleeces where a husband should have been… it was that which made her once again alone.

Alone in their bed, the great bed with its carved wooden posts, their bride-gift from Ljutvin's uncle the jarl.

"Make good use of it," he'd told them at the wedding-feast. "Good use, and frequent!" Then he'd held aloft his mead-horn, bidding everyone drink their happy, fruitful health.

Good use and frequent, indeed.

Two summers ago, the wedding had been. A year and a half, still with no fruitfulness to show for it. Other wives were mothers twice over by now.

While she, Ingiryf, woke again to an empty bed.

At first, she'd thought he must have a lover, to whose side he went when he crept from hers on these dark winter nights. Secrets of the sort were hard to keep in a close hall rife with milk-gossip and loom-talk; surely a hint of rumor would have reached her ear. When none did, her speculations turned more worrisome—if he were proved to be what she'd heard called a 'sword-friend,' what would his uncle the jarl make of *that*?

Though it would, she knew, help to explain the reluctance with which Ljutvin had approached their marriage. In a way, a strange way, she might find it oddly consoling, should his disinterest not be due to some failing on her part.

For whatever value such consolation might be worth; a balm to her own stung feminine pride was hardly the equal of the resultant shame. He'd end up exiled, or worse. While she got bargained off to some *other* lord's son or jarl's nephew with whom her father hoped to strengthen alliance.

"Look at me!" he'd said, time after time with increasing aggravation. "I have nine daughters. *Nine!* What *else* am I to do?"

Ingiryf rolled onto her side, extending a hand in the darkness as if to encounter her husband merely situated near to the edge. To no avail, of course. Whatever warmth left by his body had seeped away, so long already had been his absence.

She rolled further, pressing her face into the folded fleece he used for a pillow to inhale his scent. A manly scent, strong and pleasant, if only in this lingering ghost.

How much better it would be to have his arm curled around her, to settle her head on his chest and hear the steady thump of his heart, to have his beard tickle her brow as he nuzzled her hair. How much better to feel welcome, and wanted, and safe.

Ljutvin, a sword-friend? Could it be?

Was she, Ingiryf, in fact or deed somehow *cursed?* Ingiryf the Unlucky, Ingiryf the Loveless… the fair-haired youth for whom she'd held a true girlish devotion had chosen one of her sisters instead… other prospective suitors went sea-claimed or fell in battle before oaths could be sworn… it began to seem she'd never be wed… or end up the wife of some aged lord or poor but loyal thane.

Then her father had at long last made this arrangement. And, to her folly, Ingiryf allowed herself hope. The handsome nephew of a powerful, war-famed jarl? Had her fortunes finally turned?

But now, here she was, alone in their bed. Waiting, as she had done on many long nights before, for him to return. Which he would do quietly, and cautiously, while she feigned deep sleep and he believed her none the wiser.

Should she rage in confrontation? Demand answers, and divorce? Take lovers of her own, despite the loom-talk and milk-gossip?

Or should she bend her neck to fate, in doleful acceptance? Hers was not a bad livelihood, here in this hall. None of the jarl's folk went hungry or shabbily dressed. There were, often of evenings, stories told and sagas sung. The other women were good company as they wove and cooked, spun and sewed.

A child to love and be loved by would ease her burden, but what if she were barren? What if she bore a child, and it died? She could not withstand the pain of having another wish granted only to see the gods snatch it cruelly away.

So thinking, she lay wakeful, listening to the wind.

Wakeful, and waiting.

As Ljutvin still did not come home.

***

Cold, but not cold.

This *body* is cold.

Cold and immobile, solid and stiff.

This body with its blood slow-coursing in its veins, thick, sluggish as sap let too soon from a tree. With its heart infrequently clenching… feeble, fitful, sporadic spasms. And its lungs drawing such slight sips of air… imperceptible… the broad chest unmoving… not even the thinnest of breath-threads escaping nostrils or lips.

This body with its deaf ears that hear every feather-soft sifting flake as new snow gently falls, and every creak of bough or twig weighted by ice.

With its blind eyes staring up into white-specked cloud-laden black skies, staring and blind, staring and seeing, seeing clouds and night snow through sheeting ripples of color and light.

Through inner-sight ripples of color and light.

This body, this *man*-body.

Flesh and bone, mortal form, vitality, *life*.

But cold, very cold. The flesh, frozen. The bones, heavy. Mortal forms frail and vitality fleeting.

Life to be seized, to be taken and held.

Held deep and sheltered, through the long hours as Midgard revolves.

Seeing with blind eyes, hearing with deaf ears.

Hearing the flutter-pulse sounds of small creatures curled in nested burrows, the mewl and squeak of new bear cubs birthed in their mother's hibernation, the leap-splash of a fish in a nearly ice-locked lake.

Hearing the frost-crust crunch beneath plodding feet and cavorting paws... hearing dogs chuff and snuffle and snort... hearing voice-sounds, speech-sounds, human-sounds, *language*. The language of *men*.

And seeing, in the rime-glazed blind eye's periphery, a different light. A light not sky-born, not space-born, not eerie and incandescent and fey; this is heat-light, man-light, tamed fire, torches. The torches of men, searching men, men in fur boots and cloaks.

The dogs catch a scent and come running, running and baying, the men close behind. It is a chaos of sensation now, an onslaught of stimuli. Steamy dog-breath and warm wet noses, shaggy coats snow-dusted, wide tongues molten with slobber... the torch-heat and torch-light, the smoke, a resinous spitting crackle... and the men, their voices a clamor, alarm and consternation, surrounding this body's stiff-solid form.

Voices and language. Man-speech. Language and *words*. Words and *meaning*.

"—found him, but—"

"—doing out here?"

"—mad fool chilled to death!"

Meaning, communication, comprehension.

"—how long he's been—"

"Look at his *eyes!*"

They peer down, then upward at the snow-shrouded skies, then down again. Baffled and uneasy, but also somehow entranced.

"What, by the gods—?"

"His eyes ..."

"A reflection?"

"Where is it coming from?"

A man bends face-over this body's blind seeing eyes, the eyes in question. Through their ever-shifting eternal, rippling hues, the man's skin appears milk-fair where not ruddied by cold, his beard and braided hair blond, his own eyes fjord-blue.

Fjord-blue, filled with fear. Fear for a friend, but also an uncanny terror.

Nonetheless, he leans down, face-over.

"Ljutvin!" he shouts. His tone is agony, desperation. He shouts it again, the word, the *name*. "Ljutvin!"

Hands grasp and shake this body's shoulders. Fingers press hard at the side of its neck. Another man sets his ear to this body's chest.

"He lives! Just barely, perhaps, but he lives!"

Next there is activity, commotion. Sturdy boughs are cord-lashed into the crude shape of a sledge. More hands grasp, grasp and grip strong, and lift. This body, stone-rigid, is heaved from its cold drift-bed tomb. The dogs leap and caper. They bark. One of them utters a low, rumbling growl… then yips as a man swats its furry haunch.

Lifted. Lowered onto the sledge. Men take the pole-ends and the burden is awkwardly half-carried, half-dragged.

Ljutvin.

The word-sound that is this body's name.

This now-being's name.

Ljutvin.

It will do.

***

They brought him back in the manner of Sleipnir, Odin's eight-legged steed, warhorse of the dead. Four of them, each with the end of a pole hefted onto his shoulder, so that slung between them was the rough makeshift litter upon which Ljutvin lay.

A wail burst from Ingirif's throat as they carried her husband into the hall. She had been hard-pressed enough to convince them to go searching, as if none of them wanted to interfere. In the end, the jarl himself had bade them do it, for the sake of the peace of the hall if nothing else.

And so, they had gone, while within the longhouse the matters of morning began. Goats were milked and eggs gathered. The fires were built high, with bread put to bake and meat set to boil. Women shook out the furs and fleeces. Men hauled wood and water. Children raked the floor-rushes.

Ingiryf did her share, though in a distraction of waiting. Each opening of the doors made her turn, hope burgeoning. They would find him, she knew. Perhaps drunk, perhaps shame-faced, perhaps even injured... but they would find him.

That they would find him like this...

She wailed at the sight of her husband's stiff-frozen, motionless form. As she ran to him, she thought of others who'd perished in the merciless cold, locked in such wretched contortions that they had to be thawed so their limbs might be unbent, their bodies made fit for burial or pyre. Ljutvin had not, it seemed, been similarly afflicted. He lay straight as a plank board, arms at his sides.

Oh, but he was corpse-pale, his flesh ice, his skin blue-grey, the gold of his hair and beard age-silvered white by frost.

Well-meaning fingers caught at her as she passed, seeking to restrain her, to comfort her in her grief. Ingiryf shook them off. Then one of the men—Thurulf—took hold of her by the upper arms when she would have flung herself onto the litter.

"Ingiryf, he lives," Thurulf said. "He is not yet dead."

He explained how they had heard Ljutvin's heart beating, slowly, but beating nonetheless. He explained how the faintest whisper of chill breath could be felt at his lips.

"But, his eyes ..." At this, Thurulf shook his head, gave a slight shudder, and touched the luck-rune amulet he wore 'round his neck. "His eyes have gone strange."

Nothing would do but that she see for herself. The moment she did, she gasped.

Everyone did.

Gone strange? To say the least; they *shone*. Wide open, almost bulging, they raced and swam and whirled with bright colors. She could barely make out the familiar—if fixed, and staring—structures of Ljutvin's own actual eyes behind these twin glossy and glassy ever-changing surfaces.

The other folk of the hall crowded and clamored. Some spoke of sorcery, evil spells. Some spoke of plague, madness, or disease. Mothers whisked away curious children. Elders uttered grim portents of superstition and doom. Arguments were made to take him outside, return him to where he'd been found. Counter-arguments urged his immediate destruction—pierce a spear through his heart, cut off his head, burn him to ashes.

"This is no wraith!" Ingiryf cried, rounding on them with a ferocity surprising to them all. "This is no death-wight, no draugr! This is *Ljutvin*! Your kinsman! Your jarl's nephew! My husband!"

The jarl nodded. "That he is, and I will hear no more such talk. See him tended to, warmed. Have old Unna fetch her potions and salves. Make whatever use necessary of the resources of my hall."

"But, lord, his eyes—"

"And ready some horses. Thurulf, take a few fast riders to seek counsel from the skalds at Gods' Stone."

The discussion continued, but Ingiryf paid little more mind. Once Ljutvin had been moved from the litter to their bed, she took strong charge of his care. Never before had she so readily given orders and instructions; now it came easily as anything.

Under her direction, they undressed him, peeling away crackling layers of icy-stiff wool and sodden flax-cloth, making sure none of it adhered to and ripped loose his skin. The cold, solid, rigidity of his body made it difficult work; more than once, as they turned him, Ingiryf could not help but imagine him crashing to the floor, shattering to pieces.

They were, of course, well-accustomed to the maladies of winter, the injuries and perils of exposure. But they found upon Ljutvin's flesh no marks of frost-bite, no blackening or sloughing. Not even on his toes and fingertips, or nose and ears.

"Bring hot stones from the hearth-pits," Ingiryf instructed, once Ljutvin had been washed head to foot with warm water and rubbed with Unna's medicinal salves. "Wrap them in cloth, tuck them amid the bed-furs and fleeces around him."

"So he bakes evenly, like a loaf," one of the younger women giggled to her sisters, and Ingiryf did not dispute her.

They piled spare blankets and cloaks until the bed was a mound from which only Ljutvin's face emerged—his face, still so very pale... and those eerie, light-sheened, staring eyes.

Frightening, otherworldly, inhuman, terrible.

Yet, strangely fascinating. Strangely beautiful, in a way.

And, whatever else, he remained Ljutvin, her husband.

Or... *did* he?

She peered down into his eyes, wondering who, if anyone, peered up into hers.

***

A tumult of sensations, overwhelming, a piercing cacophonous barrage. Sights and sounds, smells and textures. Voices, language, words. Life, mortal life everywhere, rushing and bustling, frenetic in motion.

This body, this man-body, this *Ljutvin*-body.

The name-word, called again and again. Called with urgency, with desperation. Pleading, beseeching. A woman-form.

"Ljutvin, it's Ingiryf, Ingiryf, your wife. Can you hear me?"

They move so easily, their upright bone-frames, their agile and supple bending limbs!

They speak, they all speak! They communicate and cooperate and understand! Each of them, mind-brain filled, mind-brain brimming! Capable of complexity, coordination, intricacies beyond raw instinct and impulse. They do this, effortlessly, with such ease and skill.

It is too much.

"You're home now. You're safe." The woman-form again, tone strained with nuances, nuanced with strains, layered twinings of emotion. They do this as well, with that same effortless ease and skill, just as they keep constant knowledge, memory, identity, imagination, and thought.

How?

To balance and manage so much simultaneous function, of flesh-form and mind-brain, to experience and learn, convey, adapt... with casual mastery... *how*? When each and every stimulus is its own new shock, its own daunting challenge?

These increasing, intensifying tactile impressions as this man-body's nerves begin regaining some function... as they strip off the cold and wet outer cloth-wrappings... as they scrub with damp rags... as they smear on thick substances, pungent and greasy, rendered lard steeped with herbs, stinging scents of bitter green astringency... chills and tingling... the galvanic prickle of tiny hairs attempting to stand on end.

Then dryness, and the muffling weight of lush furs and soft fleeces... warmth, a growing warmth... a loosening...

The shallow sips of breath drawing more fully... the slow, clenching beats of the heart gaining strength, pulsing redder-hotter blood through the veins... autonomic, involuntary... the myriad functions of organs, of cells, on their own... the simple purpose of living things.

"Oh, Ljutvin, what's happened to you? What's done this?"

Ingiryf. The woman-form.

The wife-body. Ljutvin's wife-body.

His *wife*.

***

The others, having done all they could, went back to their own chores and pursuits, leaving Ingiryf to watch over her stricken husband.

His skin had begun to soften and thaw, regaining more of a healthier hue. He felt more like living flesh to the touch, less like frozen meat. The false silver aging of hoarfroast had melted; she dried and combed smooth his hair and his beard.

And gazed, with that strange fascination, into the terrible other-worldly light of his eyes.

Like Freya's veil, she thought. Freya's sky-veil, which sometimes drifted in colorful whorls and shimmering bands across night's crystalline blackness... casting their rippling un-shadows onto white snow and ice.

Ingiryf looked up, expecting despite herself to see the skies danc-ing with their glow... a glow mirrored, only *mirrored*, in Ljutvin's eyes. But, of course, she saw only the roof-beams of the hall, only planking and thatch.

Further, it was by now day-time, or what passed for it so far north, when the sun breached the horizon like a leaping whale, tracing a low arc before sinking again. Further yet, it was, accord-ing to those who'd been out-of-doors, steadily snowing. It could therefore, thrice-circumstance, *not* be the mirroring of Freya's veil so casting an eerie effect upon him.

What, then, could it be? What, and how could it seem to ema-nate *from*, which should in all ways be impossible?

Her musings brought her no answers, and little comfort. She sat by him, holding his cold hand in both of hers, as the longhouse's daily routines went on around her. Now and then, folk paused to make inquiries or reassurances, to bring fresh hearth-stones when the previous ones had cooled, to urge food and drink.

"He cannot eat in this state," Ingiryf said.

"*You* can," old Unna replied. "Which you will and you must, to keep your strength. As for him, if he does not wake soon, we might try broth or warmed goat's milk, or a wet-mash of gruel."

Ljutvin's uncle the jarl sat with her a while, patting her arm, speaking with confidence that Thurulf and the riders he'd sent to

Gods' Stone would return swiftly. "There are lore-keepers there," he told her, "omen-readers, rune-witches, and wise skalds. Someone will know what to do."

It was, however, a far distance to travel even under the best of summer-weather conditions, which these decidedly were not... omen-reading and rune-casting took time... the wisest of lore-keepers and skalds loved nothing better than to debate amongst themselves, arguing obscurities... this swift return the jarl hoped for might be long in coming.

Eventually, even the most superstitious of mothers relented, allowing their curious children a wondering look. Only the beasts of the hall seemed perturbed; dogs paced and cats glared. A faithful old hound known to Ljutvin since boyhood hung, fretfully whining, well back from the bed.

The evening meal—boiled meat, a stew of root vegetables and dried berries, bread, honey-mead, and cheese—was readied and eaten. With Unna's help, Ingiryf did spoon some broth into Ljutvin's slack mouth. His throat seemed at first to balk at the swallowing, but he did not cough or choke, and more dribbled into his gullet than into his beard. After, everyone gathered around the hearth-pits for story-telling and riddles and singing of sagas—not that hands were, during this, idle, not with wool to be spun or needlework done, not with wood and ivory to be artfully carved.

The wind howled like wolves in the eaves. Ice dashed in fistfuls of pebbles against the longhouse's log walls. The fires were let to burn low, the rush-lamps and candles extinguished, and folk retired to the sleeping-platforms.

Ingiryf unpinned her brooches and shed her wool outer dress, then crept under the mounded furs and fleeces beside Ljutvin. Lingering heat from the wrapped stones left the bed almost too warm, a near-incredulous thought in these depths of winter.

She slid over and reached for him, to assure herself he was still there. Her fingers found his skin likewise warm, his limbs thawed and pliable... if heavy deadweight beset by occasional twitching spasms. Yet, twitching spasms had to be better than no movement at all, portending some sort of recovery, rather than paralysis, when he finally woke.

If he woke.

He would. He *must*. He'd wake whole and healthy. Not crippled or lame, not addled, not oblivious to who and where he was. He'd wake, she would not be widowed or left half a wife… no more so than his disinterest had already made her.

In the darkness, Ljutvin's wide-open eyes stared blindly upward, while rippling bands of violet and amber and luminous green wavered across their rounded surfaces.

Beautiful, so beautiful, but so very strange… and a vivid reminder that this was no ordinary ailment besetting him, but something else, something *other*, something for which all the skalds and lorekeepers in the world might have no answer.

Unable to bear the sight any longer, she settled her head on his bare shoulder and turned her face against the side of his neck. Here was his scent, his manly scent, strong and pleasant, if also mixed with Unna's medicinal salves. Here was the tickle of his soft beard on her cheek. Her palm rested upon his breastbone, feeling the steady beat of his heart.

The usual night-noises went on. Someone began snoring. A baby fussed. Men and women did what men and women do. Ingiryf sighed—not in *envy*, not quite—and closed her eyes, and let her fingers brush gently through the modest pelt of Ljutvin's chest as she attempted to seek solace of sleep.

***

This body, this man-body, this impossibly complicated form… its innards contort, its nerves and muscles twitch.

These contorting innards, this is hunger, this is thirst. Needs of the mortal body. Needs and demands. Sustenance to sustain life. A physical vibrancy, physical requirements and rewards. Relief from discomfort, avoidance of pain. Sensory satisfactions.

Food, and drink. Warmth. Pleasure.

The hot spill of rich broth-liquid, the *flavor!* Meat, and salt, and onion. Deliciousness, while that only the simplest invalid's fare! The tantalizing aromas... which belongs to bread, to mead, to cheese? What are their tastes?

What it is to be *alive!*

This body has potential, potential for motion. But, motion without precision, without control... crude and violent, clumsy. The jerk and flail of limbs. The incomprehension of uprightness, of balance. Agility. Somehow, they stand, they walk. They move and manipulate objects, they affect their surroundings.

This body has potential for word-sounds as well. For language, communication. Potential, but the knowledge... the memory... these are absent. How *are* the word-sounds shaped? How *does* a voice, in tone, in song-noise, in such infinite variations? To speak now would be incoherence, of less meaning than the screaming of the wind. Even barking dogs and bleating goats make *meaning;* even a crying infant expresses desire and distress.

To live, to live, to be alive!

To be as them, one with them, the experience of vitality and sensation!

But, like this? Lacking mastery of speech? Unable to sit or stand or walk, unable to eat or drink without help, unable to perform the most basic of functions? Even if, over time, and by way of painstaking effort, such things might be learned... these people know this man. This Ljutvin. His history, his person and being and self.

They would soon know, too, an imposter. A semblance, a pretense wearing Ljutvin's flesh and form. A phantasm with his face. Already, some suspect or fear. If they judge this taken-body to be *not*-Ljutvin, there will be pain. Suffering and torture. Perhaps death.

To be *alive*, yes. But, to die?

It is, undoubtedly, the ultimate of mortal experience ...only that which lives may die... yet all living creatures, from earthworm grubs to human-kind, strove fervently to avoid it.

Better to abandon? Slip free and rise, returning to the high and distant light-sheened skies? Forsake the vibrant physicality, the sensations?

Another chance like this might never come. A fluke, a whim of fate gave rare opportunity.

Somehow, somehow... *somehow* there *must* be a way.

The Ingiryf-wife, so close beside. Touching. Softness, plumpness, curves. Skin and flesh and sighing breath. A resting head. A stroking hand.

And this body, this Ljutvin-body, this *man*-body with its involuntary impulses and reflex...

Responds.

***

Ingiryf woke to find herself not alone.

She woke to the warmth and scent of Ljutvin, to his even breathing in her ear. To the feel of their skin, molded slightly sweat-sticky beneath the piled bed-covers. To the weight of his arm draped over her in slumbering embrace.

And to the fond recollection of what they had done in the night.

It seemed a dubious matter, when first she realized the effect elicited by her idle caresses. But when she let her hand slide from his chest to his navel, then lower still, to his loins... the rising tension she found there...

Her whispered queries drew no reply, neither of encouragement or objection. She'd hesitated, uncertain. Still, she was his wife, and he her husband, and the unmistakable eagerness with which that part of him surged in her grasp enticed her to carry on.

The quiet coupling that followed proved slow and sweet. Ljutvin took no active part, which she found unsettling, yet strangely emboldening. Only the roll of her own hips set the pace, sending wave upon wave of pleasure sweeping through her, until a shudder shook him and he spilled forth, and she collapsed atop him, quivering and quaking.

At some point, it vaguely occurred to her that something was different, something had changed. In her drowsy, sated state, she could not be bothered to think, and so relaxed again at Ljutvin's side, the final delicious tremors diminishing to a pleasant glow.

And at some point even later, as they slept, they both must have managed to turn, ending up curled together with her back to his belly... his arm draped over, his hand loosely cupping a breast through the thin flax-cloth of the undershift bunched to her waist. Ingiryf murmured contentedly, wordlessly; it was indeed a welcoming manner in which to wake. She stretched, feeling languid and lazy.

Judging by the sounds from the longhouse, folk were beginning to stir for the day. Although reluctant to move from the comfortable bed, she supposed she should get up, wash and dress—

Ljutvin's arm tightened around her. The hand which had been loosely cupping gave a gentle, curious squeeze. His face nuzzled into her hair and her neck. "Ingiryf?" he said, sleepily.

She gasped, twisting to look at him. "Ljutvin! Ljutvin, are you all right?"

He frowned with puzzlement. "Shouldn't I be?" His eyes, though bleary, were otherwise clear, their color once again the same fine and fair blue.

"You were ..." Her words failed her. Ill? Stricken? "What do you remember?"

Again, he frowned. "Standing, outside, in the snow," he said. "And something about the sky, but... nothing else until waking just now." It must have come to his notice he was naked, and she mostly so, not to mention the fact of his hand on her breast or other telltale indications. He coughed, clearing his throat. "Although I did have the strangest of dreams; I was as a ship, an empty ship without oarsmen or sail, floating lost and adrift in endless dark waters."

***

This.

This is better, *much* better.

Let it be this, gradual, kept hidden.

Yes, this will do. This will do nicely.

***

She told him what had happened, how they had found him and brought him back to the hall, how they had tended him, how riders had gone to seek the counsel of the skalds at Gods' Stone. His brow furrowed as he listened, but he did not doubt or dispute.

"I am parched, and half-ravenous," Ljutvin said, as they rose from their bed, donning clothes. He soon proved it by breaking his fast with wolfish appetite, devouring a cold joint of boiled pork left over from the previous evening's meal, following it with rough-hewn slabs of bread and a great hunk of cheese.

Ingiryf watched him move about the longhouse, saw him speak to his uncle, and old Unna, and others. She saw him approach the faithful hound who, last night, had shied away whining… but who now, after a tentative sniff, rushed to him tail-wagging.

When he returned to her, he clasped her hands in his, looking solemn. "I have been unfair to you, unkind, my good Ingiryf, a poor sort of husband."

"Ljutvin—"

"No, it is truth. I see that now, like a veil has been drawn from my eyes. You have my apologies. And you have my oath to do better, if you will accept it."

"Neither oath nor apologies are needed," she said. "What matters is, you are here, whole and well."

He smiled then, a warm and wonderful beaming smile, a smile just for her. He touched her face as if he'd never fully seen her before. He bent, and kissed her, then swept her up, laughing, into his arms.

***

For sight, there is nothing, only a deep reddish darkness.

Sound is muffled and distant, awash in the rhythmic thump of heartbeat, the liquid rush of blood.

The sensations are of encompassment, a warm and wet fleshy cradling.

This is the way.

There is time, time to adapt, and develop, and grow.

Time to learn. To understand.

To become *alive*.

***

Days later, Thurulf and his riders returned from Gods' Stone. They came in disgruntled, all but stomping with frustration, then shouted in surprise and amazement to find Ljutvin on his feet, none the worse for wear.

A feast was held, the hearth-fires built high, the golden mead flowing richly. As the folk of the hall gathered, the jarl inquired as to what had brought them home in such grim spirits.

"The skalds," Thurulf said, scornfully snorting. "Lore-keepers and omen-readers, oh so very wise… we rode all that way in the chill depths of winter, and all they would give us were riddles and cryptic replies."

"Nonetheless," said the jarl, "you went at once without complaint, and for that I thank you." So saying, he presented to each of them a cloak-pin of worked silver.

"While here," added one of the other men, lifting his drinking-bowl, "hale as ever, sits our friend Ljutvin, with no harm done."

To that, they all drank, voices raised in approbation, a glad rousing cheer to the roof-beams.

"What *did* the skalds tell you?" asked Ingiryf when it subsided, comfortable beside Ljutvin with his arm close around her. "What manner of riddles? What cryptic replies?"

Thurulf shrugged, holding out his bowl to be refilled. "The greatest wealth," he said. "Jewels and treasure, shining gems, playmates and playthings for Freya's fair child."

***

In the warm, wet and fleshy reddish darkness...

Awash in the rush-sounds of heart-pumped blood...

Hearing the dim, distant, muffled sounds of singing and laughter and speaking voices...

Cradled there, tiny but gradually growing... gradually changing and developing...

Waiting, and learning.

Waiting for bright eyes to open, for bone and skin and flesh and form.

Learning... what it is to be *alive*.

HER FATHER'S SKIN

She gives chase through the snow, through the night, through the wind. Darkness howls and sleet stings. Shadows loom and reach, bare branches raking like claws. Ice cracks underfoot as she crosses a stream, and the water, not frozen, feels even colder in its sudden splash.

Somewhere ahead, her quarry stumbles and blunders, too old for this exertion, too weak and too frail. Only a mad desperation drives him onward, drives him deeper into the forest. Where he thinks he is bound, she knows not, only that she must catch him.

Her legs are stronger. Her breath gusts in clouds of frost-steam. Twigs that, to him, snag and catch and hinder, snap in brittle splinters of dead winter wood as her larger body bursts through the brush without slowing.

He falters. He falls. He flails and wails in a snow-drift. Blood shed from cuts, scrapes and scratches makes a scatter of stains on the unblemished white. His thin form quakes and trembles. He is stick-thin and scrawny, scarred, skin and bones and scant meat.

Cautious now, she approaches, wary of what he might do in his final, cornered extremity. He struggles to rise, fails, and falls again. His head turns. He sees her with eyes gone wide and wild.

She sinks to a knee and rests a hand on his shoulder.

"Father," she says.

***

In the great hall at Bjornsberg, many fires blazed their heat from earth-sunken rings of hearth-stones. Folk filled the mead-benches, feasting and drinking, voices raised in hearty laughter. There were warriors and farmers, fishermen, women, children, and thralls. All the household had gathered, and guests come besides.

At the high table sat Ullar Bjornsson, earl in all but name. The men looked to him as their lord and war-leader. He was not yet thirty, fit of arm for the sword and the shield, fair-haired and handsome, his chest broad, his gaze as steady as stone. His reputation was known to be proud but just; what he may have lacked in wisdom, he made up for in generosity.

His wife and young sons sat to his right, his brother and his sister to his left.

His mother, the true lady of the hall, had long since—if not quite ungrudgingly—deferred both her place and her duties to her daughter-in-law. When the day did come when her son was earl in name as well, no one doubted but that Ulla would remarry; in the mid-forties of her years, she had kept a fine figure and was muchly admired by widowed suitors. Meanwhile, however, she bided her time in a dim corner, tending to her ancient and ailing husband.

Earl Bjorn, or the white-bearded husk of the man he'd once been, slumped with head lolling. Straps of leather held him to his chair, preventing him from falling to the floor-rushes. He muttered and mumbled, half his face twitching. Spoon-fed broth and grain-mash dribbled from the corners of his toothless mouth.

Few at the feast remembered him any other way. Even were he not stricken by illness and infirmity, he would have been the eldest among them by far. His age-mates and battle-companions had all long since died. His marriage to Ulla was his second, done less for love than for politics, and he had been an old man already when their children were born.

It was said that, in his youth, Bjorn fought alongside the famed king Hrolf-Kraki, but many made similar claims about their ancestors. They likewise made claims of dragon-slayers, giants and trolls, sorceresses, monsters, dwarfs and dark-elfs. Myth and legend, god-talk... such was the stuff stories and sagas were made of, the embellished telling of tales to enliven cold northern nights.

The mead-bowls passed hand to hand. Thralls brought in more platters of roasted fish and stewed pork. To prove to their guests the wealth of the hall, Ullar distributed gifts of fleeces and furs, combs carved from ivory, cloak-clasps and belt-buckles, and other small treasures. In return, their guests uttered loud and effusive praises of Bjornberg's hospitality, stating that never yet in their journey had they until now received so welcoming a reception.

They had arrived on horseback soon before dusk, six men under the peace-banner of the new young boy king. Who was, it was said, a great-grandson of Hrolf-Kraki, very enamored of the old sagas and tales.

Farulf, who led them, wore two arm-rings of silver and another of gold. His woolen tunic was dyed deepest green, trimmed at cuffs and collar and hem with wolf's fur. His grey-streaked black beard was trimmed neatly short, and he spoke with the honey-dipped tongue of a poet.

Whatever their message or business, of course, Ullar had bidden it wait until later. They had traveled far and must be weary; let them rest and refresh, let their horses be seen to, let them bathe in the hot-springs if it was their desire. After they had done so, and been properly sated on food and drink, he would be only too glad to hear them.

And so, it was done as Ullar instructed.

Now, Farulf stepped forth and again gave great flattery and thanks. "It is not much to offer to repay such generosity," he said, "but my nephew rides with us, Rannulf, son of my sister, and he is reputed to be of reasonable skill at the harp. Would you permit him to play and sing, before we must talk of more serious matters?"

Ullar could hardly, and would hardly, refuse. An eager hush spread through the hall, until all was silent but for the crackle of flames, the hoot of wind in the chimney-holes, and the ceaseless vague mutterings from old Bjorn's dim corner.

Rannulf stood and bowed, then took his harp from its case. It was a well-wrought instrument, the wood polished to a shine, the strings bright as stars. When he struck it, the notes rippled water-pure in the smoky air. He took a place before the high table, nod-ded his respects to Ullar and his family, and then—in a gesture that did cause Ullar's lips to tighten—turned to nod to Bjorn and Ulla as well.

The ancient earl took no notice, drooling and mumbling into his beard. But, as Rannulf's clear voice rose in song, even Bjorn quieted, seeming to listen.

***

"Father," she says, her hand on his shoulder. Her voice is a sob, thick in her throat as she speaks. "Father, what's happened to you?"

He stares with a blank fright, as if he does not know her. Snow powders his white hair and beard even whiter. It cakes the thin linen long-shirt in which he'd been sleeping. Below its tattered hem, his bare legs poke crooked like gnarled branches. His feet look frost-grey and bloodless. His body shivers violently.

How he has done this, she cannot imagine. How he has come so far from the hall, so far into the forest, when most days he can hardly cross from his chair to his bed without help.

Yet, here he is, he has come so far, and so fast she was hard-pressed to follow.

"Where are you going?" she asks as she lifts him. "There's nothing out here but the old charcoaler's hut."

And, possibly, she thinks—although the thought is unwel-come—dangers beyond that of the winter night's cold. The woods are a feared place, feared with good reason. The woods are home to bears and wolves. They might be the refuge of murderers, outlaws, escaped slaves and thieves.

She braces him against a tree while she reaches for her cloak-clasp, intending to wrap him in the garment to carry him home. The moment she lets go of him, he does not fall again but darts away like a hare, ducking and springing, evading her grasp.

Then he is running again, running despite the numb and frozen state of his feet.

"Father!"

He does not stop. She gives chase once more, at first calling after him and then sparing her breath for pursuit. The land slopes upward in rugged tangles of stumps and undergrowth, blackly treacherous. A root, rock or hole might end this race without warning.

Ahead, the woods open to a hillside clearing, the pale-blanketed expanse offering welcome visibility. She glimpses at the edge of it the old charcoaler's hut, years abandoned, its roof half-collapsed.

Her father pauses midway in the clearing. He turns this way and that as if searching for something. She gains several strides on him before he utters a strange cry of mingled despair and relief, and sets off at a rapid stagger.

A stark ridge of granite juts up at an angle. The wind has scoured the snow from its barren back, but rows of ice-fangs and ice-fingers cover its lee-side. It seems this is what he's been seeking; he makes for it and begins scrabbling along the ground at its base.

This time, she does not bother approaching with caution. She removes her cloak and swing-tosses it like a fisherman casting a net. The heavy fleece-lined wool drops over him. He grunts in surprise, knocked flat, but she is already on him. She wraps him the way she might swaddle an infant, though he struggles. He works one arm free to claw and scrape at the snow.

As she hauls him up, she sees the pile of mossy stones his scrabblings and scrapings have exposed. It is no natural arrangement, she realizes, but something deliberately made. Those stones have been placed there, stacked there, as a marker.

Or as a cairn.

The thought sends a worse chill through her than does the

sleet-laden night air.

She has seen cairns before, of course, burial mounds with stones piled atop them to prevent animal scavengers from unearthing and eating the dead, or deter robbers from stealing grave-goods.

But this cairn, so far from anything, out here in the woods...

This cairn, so small, much too small for a proper grave... made long enough ago to now be moss-encrusted...

She looks at her father, mind clamoring questions. She finds, to her astonishment, that he meets her gaze with one of plaintive urgency. His bunched, tremulous hand wavers as it indicates the cairn. His eyes brim. A terrible effort tries and fails to bring words to his lips.

"I'll dig," she tells him. "If that's what you want, what you must have, then I'll dig."

***

Hear me! For so it was in the days of the heroes
Powerful war-lords and warriors, the best of men
That King Hrolf-Kraki, born of love and deceit
Assembled an army to avenge his father's death
Among them were twelve surpassing all others
The king's close companions, brothers-at-arms
God-granted by Odin the gift of shape-changing
When the battle-lust seized them, the wild war-fury
The violent kill-hunger, the wrath and the rage
A red mist descended on them, a frenzy for blood
They would cast aside their mail-coats and leather
Throw down their weapons, their helms and shields
The clothes from their bodies would be ripped asunder
Fierce beasts becoming, unleashing savage slaughter
The *Ulfhednar*, wolf-pelted with fast, flashing fangs
And the *Berserker*, strongest of all in their bear-skins
Unstoppable in combat, life-takers, slayers of foes

Howls, roars and bellows their dreaded war-cries
A raging of claws, teeth and sinew, a bestial thunder
Unhurt by iron spear-points, by axe-blades and swords
Fearing neither fire nor steel, fearing not even death
But striking terror to the marrow of all in their path
So that brave men pissed and cowered, fainted and fled
Across the field where the rats and ravens harvest
A great crop of death grew, a gluttonous bounty
Flesh torn and bones broken, an agony of screams
Limbs ham-strung at knee-back or ankle-tendon
The thigh's thick crimson river overflooded its banks
Skulls cracked like eggshells in the crush of bear-jaws
Breastbones smashed and shattered, ribs sprung agape
Guts glistened in glaring war-light, organs exposed
As bloodied wolf-muzzles burrowed deep, snarling
Seeking soft throats and pulsating, still-beating hearts
Carnage strewn over the churned earth, the battle done
The enemy's shield-walls dashed, their army in ruins
The dying-song and war-cries, the wailing of wives
Glorious to the ears of Hrolf-Kraki, declaring victory
That night in the mead-hall the warriors gathered
Ulfhednar and *Berserker* most honored among them
Removed now of their wolf-pelts and bear-skins
Men once more, the king's guard, his war-brothers
The harps silver-stringed, the drinking horns flowing
Skalds and poets recounted the day's great deeds
Names ever-remembered, long-lasting reputations
Hrolf-Kraki bestowed upon them generous gifts
Arm-rings and neck-torcs and brooches of gold
Jeweled bowls and goblets, a rich treasure-hoard
And prized above all their lord's love and acclaim
Hear me! For so it was in the days of the heroes.

***

The ground under the cairn-stones is cold and hard, but she digs.

The sleet turns to a rain that soaks her clothes from the outside even as sweat soaks them from within, but she digs.

She has only her hands, and a stick, and her trusty belt-knife, but she digs.

Her digging calms him, the old man, her father. He sits huddled on a log, wrapped in her cloak, and watches. He seems heedless of his bare feet, and by now the frost-grey is darkening to black blotches; he will be lucky not to lose toes, though she supposes that such a loss would hardly much hinder him, all considered.

What she finds is not a grave, but a small wooden chest. It is weathered but well-made, the fitted lid carved with intricate, beautiful workmanship. The style reminds her of the designs decorating the door-posts of the hall; they could have been made by the same hand. If so, it would have been well before her time. Those posts had been set when the hall was first built.

Her father groans when she lifts the chest from the earth. His expression is equal parts longing and loathing. He shudders, groans again, and averts his face.

The wood proves damp-warped, the lid swelled shut. Opening it will, she decides, have to come later. The weight is not such that suggests hoarded silver or gold. She can carry it as well as her father, if she needs to. She is strong-built, stout-limbed and sturdy.

As she starts to rise, her gaze catches a faint glint at the bottom of the hole… not the hole she dug, but a smaller hole yet deeper beneath it.

She reaches down. Her fingers, stiff and numb though they are, find a piece of metal, an amulet of silver in the shape of the world-tree. A silver chain trails from it, snagged on something below.

In the smaller hole is a blanket-wrapped bundle, and she understands now that the cairn did mark a grave after all. A child's grave. The rotted cloth crumbles wetly away at her touch, revealing pale, delicate bones.

When she looks at her father, his face is no longer averted. His eyes are fixed on the sad and fragile remains. Tears trickle over his wrinkled cheeks to his beard. He weeps, and in that moment she both understands... and does not.

That she and her brothers are the products of his second marriage, she has always known. Just as she has always known his second marriage was rather less than a love-match. His first wife, the wife of his youth and his heart, had given him one son who died in infancy. The soft-sleep, the cradle-death, claimed him after less than a year, to their great devastation.

Her mother maintains this is why he never warmed to her brothers. Why he had not wished them named for himself, and kept them at more of an arm's length indifference. A girl-child, however, held no threat to those cherished memories. He could have affection for a daughter without feeling it a betrayal of his firstborn.

But how can this be that same poor, dead babe? Buried out here in the woods, marked by a plain cairn of stones, instead of at the barrow-hill mound with its mother and kin?

How can this be that same poor, dead babe, when its bones show a far grimmer fate than the silent cradle-death? The fine, fragile dome of skull alone says enough, punctured through as it is in several places.

She, having seen her share of slain lambs and animal-bites, would all but swear these marks had been made by the jaws of a beast.

***

The harp-strains and words faded, Rannulf finishing his song-saga to great loud acclaim from the folk of the hall. Even the old earl, in his dim corner, thumped approbation on his chair's armrests.

At the high table, Ullar's wife and his mother wore disapproving looks, not caring for such tales of battlefield carnage. As for Ullar himself, his eyes somewhat narrowed, but he praised his guest's performance and tossed him a ring set with amber as reward.

The mead-bowls were refilled and passed around again, and with them went plates heaped with cakes slathered in boiled bilberries and cream. Farulf then once more stepped forward, for the time had come to address the business of his visit.

He reminded them that, as of course they all knew, Helgi, their wise and noble king, had died the previous year, leaving the care of the land to a half-grown son. This son, Hrugr by name, had been raised by his uncles on stories of Hrolf-Kraki, and now wished to make for himself a similar court. To this end, the boy-king had sent out emissaries, including Farulf's very company, to seek them among the earls and the lords.

"Why?" asked Ullar, his scowl returning. "Does he not have brave men enough at his hall already?"

These words caused a few of his visitors some hesitation, as they wondered if the meaning of them was flattery or insult. Farulf merely smiled… or at least showed the white flash of teeth through his beard in a wolf's grin.

"He does, and many," he said, "but he wishes more, an honor guard of bold champions, famed warriors as in the legends. As in the days of magic and heroes."

"Days of superstition," said Ullar, "which have long passed. You cannot mean to tell me that our king would surround himself with men claiming to be *Ulfhednar* and *Berserker*. What next? Giants and trolls? We have laws now, and peace."

"We have also our history. Men of Bjornsberg were among King Hrolf-Kraki's armies, were they not?" Farulf inclined his head in a respectful nod toward the old earl, who had begun to become agitated. "Indeed, just as my own grandfather was, was not *your* father—?"

A wordless cry burst from Bjorn's throat. He struggled against the straps of his chair. His gnarled fists thumped the armrests with increased vigor. Ulla rushed to him, hissing at him to be calm and behave, that he was making a spectacle before the whole hall and their guests. If he heard her, he ignored her, struggling all the harder and voicing louder, though still inarticulate, cries.

Ullar, face reddening, gestured to some thralls. They hastened to lift the chair entire, Bjorn still in it, and bore it swiftly into the smaller private family chambers beyond. Ulla followed, so embarrassed she could not meet the eyes of even her own children.

As the sounds of his distress continued unabated, an awkwardness overtook everyone upon the mead-benches. Gazes shifted in search of any distraction, then found it as Ullar turned back to Farulf with thunder upon his brow.

"If the kingdom has need of armies," he said, "I can bring five hundred men with mail-coats, horses, swords and shields. If raiding is wanted, I command four dragon-ships. But I will *not* caper in a bear-skin at the whim of a child."

***

When he does not object, she gently enfolds the bones in the cloth and replaces the tiny bundle into its lonesome grave. She is shivering by then from the cold but covers it with earth and piles over it the mossy stones.

The carved wooden chest, she does not leave behind. She tucks it under one arm, bracing its weight on her hip. In the other arm, she hefts her father, wrapped in her cloak. Though the combined burden is not too heavy for her strength, the weariness of her exertions makes her consider the journey to the hall with despair.

Better the old charcoaler's shed, she decides. It is not far. They will be less than comfortable, but should safely pass the rest of the night.

It proves better shelter than she had surmised. The roof may be half-collapsed but the walls are intact, and the wood left in the woodbin is dry. There is a cot upon which she settles her father. He sinks down into either unconsciousness or sleep.

Soon, she has a small fire kindled. She strips off her wet shoes and leggings, her dress and her shift. Naked, she crouches by the flames, rubbing her limbs, wringing the rain from her hair. The shivers ebb. Her teeth cease their chattering.

She checks her father and finds him breathing in slow, deep dream-mumbles. It will be a gods'-mercy if he does not catch the damp lung, and she is certain he'll see the loss of some toes. If, that is, he lives long enough for it to matter.

Her heart wrenches with sorrow. How she wishes she could have known the man that he was, the man who had gone into battle alongside Hrolf-Kraki. Not this frail shell, this husk impaired of both body and mind. This is no way to be, not for a warrior, not for anyone.

Sighing, she tucks the cloak more snugly around him. She takes the wooden chest to the fire and examines it more closely. This is what brought her father raving out into the forest, and she must have answers. Using her knife-blade with care, she pries at the lid until the warped wood squeals open.

Inside, she finds three items, the first two smaller and atop the third. One is a length of cord, twisted from sinews. The other is a pot of salve, somehow still supple, not solidified into a crust. She sniffs it. The scent is strange, a mix of tallow and bonemeal and blood and ash. The pot itself is painted with faded, flaking runes.

The third and largest item, at the bottom, is a folded fur. A thick pelt, a bear-skin, and when she lifts it out she sees that it is cut in the crude shape of an over-tunic with sides unstitched. It is also rent and torn in many places, as if pierced by arrows or spear-points, hewn by axe-blades and swords.

The thoughts in her mind cannot possibly be true.

Can they?

The stories… the sagas… the song Rannulf sang… Hrolf-Kraki's champions, the *Ulfhednar* and *Berserker*… her father's agitation, driving him on this mad errand…

She looks at the ragged pelt. She looks at the sinew and salve. She looks at the sleeping old man, drooling into his beard.

Her fingers scoop into the greasy substance. It melts oily and pungent as she smears it onto her arm. She feels a faint tingling, not at all unpleasant. The more she scoops from the pot, the level of the salve does not seem to change.

When her entire body is covered, glistening in the firelight, she draws the bear-skin over her head and belts it with the cord of twisted sinews.

Nothing happens, and she nearly laughs aloud at her own foolishness. Ullar must never hear of this, she tells herself.

Then the tingling of the salve becomes a spreading rush of heat that sinks into her flesh. The bear-skin adheres to hers like something alive. Her joints burn. Her bones seem to pop, her gristle to grind and her tendons to stretch.

The sensation is that of a cracked stubborn knuckle or a cricked stiff neck, a mix of brief agony and satisfying relief, and it wracks her from head to foot. She drops to her knees, then to all fours. Fur bristles, rippling, along her limbs and torso. Dark thick claws sprout from her fingers and toes.

She is the bear.

***

Ullar's declaration brought the evening to an abrupt, uncomfortable end. Farulf laughed it off, but it was clear the time for feasting and drinking was over. Not long thereafter, the tables were put aside. On the sleeping-platforms, furs and blankets were spread. Sounds of slumber soon arose.

The earl's family retired to their rooms at the rear of the hall. It was there, some hours later, Bjorndis Bjornsdottir woke to find her mother torn between anger and tears.

"That old madman, your father, has run away!" Ulla said.

"Run?" she asked, fully astounded. "Father? How?"

"The gods alone can say." Ulla flung exasperated hands in the air. "It took us ages to quiet him after his outburst earlier, but then he somehow got from his bed, out the side door, and escaped."

"He'll freeze to death!"

"Dolt of a girl, do you think I don't know that? Now I must wake your brothers, and when Ullar hears, how furious he'll be! He'll have to rouse the household, and our guests, and send out searchers—"

"Let me go after him," Bjorndis said as she pulled on her dress and her shoes. "He can't have gone far, not in his state. I'll find him and bring him back. No one need be the wiser."

Ulla contemplated briefly, then nodded. "Wear your cloak, girl, and don't forget your belt-knife. There might be beasts in the woods."

***

The bear's shoulder easily pushes open the shed door. The bear's paws crunch in the snow. The bear's moist black nose tests the air, detecting the tang of winterberries, the sting of evermint.

The bear's ears follow a swift gurgle of white-water to a creek tumbling over rocks between icy banks. Fish flick and dart silver in the deeper pools. A swipe of claws snags one, slaps it ashore where it flips its fins and thrashes its tail.

The bear's teeth rip through fine scales to the fresh, pale, cold meat. Thin blood flows and thin fish-bones splinter. The fish is half-devoured before it fully dies.

It is delicious. Bjorndis has never tasted anything so succulent and sweet. Her every sense seems more keen. Her pelt is warm, her body powerful, her spirit racing with exhilaration.

This, she realizes, is what her father lost. What her father gave up.

Her previous understanding is at last clear. Perhaps the echoes of memories linger in the bear-skin, the way strong scents or flavors linger long after the source is gone. Perhaps some pains are too great to be let go.

He had so loved the child, his little son. The moon could have risen and set for the child's delight. A bold boy, curious, sturdy, cheerful, and fearless. Bright laughter like golden bells… tiny trusting hands that clutched with equal affection at a father's beard or a bear's shaggy fur…

Until the day, that most terrible day, when those tiny hands tugged too hard, yanking out tufts.

The sudden rage overtook the bear for a moment, only a moment. But, a moment was enough.

Some pains are too great to let go. Some griefs are too great to be borne.

As are some shames.

They told no one the truth. Cradle-death, they said, and buried their son in secret, while a wrapped stone took his place on the barrow-hill.

His dear wife forgave him. In a way, that was worst of all. Her forgiveness cut sharper than would have her hatred. Her forgiveness, and then her gradual, despairing decline.

Bjorndis, in bear-shape, returns to the charcoaler's shed. The door still hangs open, askew on one hinge. Inside, the fire has burned low but not extinguished. Much the same can be said of her father.

As she comes in, a draft of fresh air makes the flames briefly leap to new life. And, again, much the same can be said of her father. He sits up, her cloak falling from him.

She tries to speak, but of course she cannot. A guttural growl is the closest she comes.

He springs from the cot, again with startling spryness for a man of his age and ill health. He snatches up from the cold dirt floor the stick she'd used to unearth the chest and the grave. He brandishes it at her.

A sour stink of sick-sweat surrounds him, sick-sweat and madness. His shout is as unintelligible as her bear's-growl, his face hectic and wild. He swings the stick.

It glances from her thick fur-covered skull. Bjorndis recoils. He swings it again and the stick strikes the bear's tender black snout a hard, smarting blow.

Before she knows what is happening to her, the red mist roils over her. She roars full-throated, shaking the shed's flimsy walls. A lunge, and a swipe of her huge paw, knocks the old man sprawling. He lands with a brittle snap of bones. His hip breaks with a pop like a pine-knot in the fire.

He screams, but he continues swinging and jabbing with the stick, battering at her face, gouging its end into her shaggy neck and chest.

Her forelegs pin him, frail ribs giving way beneath the bear's immense crushing weight. Her jaws gape in another bellowing roar.

In the instant before she rips the life from him, Bjorndis returns to herself in a clarity of horror.

But she sees, in her father's eyes, a different kind of clarity.

She sees that he *knows* her, that he has known all along. That this is what he wanted and craved. To see his long-dead son's murder avenged, and to be released from his own wretched torment.

To be granted a warrior's violent end.

And she, loving her father, wearing his skin, cannot refuse.

A NEW WORLD

At wide world's end where the wild waves break
Slate-grey sea dashing hard upon slate-grey stone
Crashing up hollow echoes from crevice and cave
White foam and froth leaping, the brisk salt spray
Driftwood, sand beaches, pebbles tumbled smooth
This rugged place, rain-dampened, cloud-cloaked
Rivers rushing white rapids between rocky banks
Secret creeks whisper while hidden springs well
Mist-bathed forests tower dark, dense, and deep
Tall, ancient trees of thick shag-barked immensity
Their trunks moss-draped, roots sunk in rich loam
Standing silent sentinel, oh watchful wood-giants
As fallen logs and cleft stumps slowly, softly decay
Up sprout corpse-mushrooms, pallid and strange
Waxen-fleshed yellow, spindle-stemmed, spotted
Upon their plump caps, raindrops bead like blood
To touch them draws blisters, to taste them is death
From feathery fern-fronds, tiny star-flowers bloom
Pale-petaled, sweet-scented, nectar at their hearts
Thin-twigged low bushes hang heavy, berry-laden
Clusters the color of garnets and king-purple gems
A green land, not Greenland, not Vinland, or is it?
How far to have traveled to reach this distant shore
A green land, a grey land, untouched and unowned

So it seemed when they came there in the long ships
By oar and striped sail, carved dragon's heads rising
Round shields slung at the sides, men on the benches
With women and children, wise elders, babes-in-arms
Huddled among livestock, crates and casks of supplies
For no Viking war-raid this, no quick-striking attack
Neither is trade the goal, but settlement, exploration
Across the wide seas where fish leap and whales sing
Beneath cold stormy skies, driving wind, freezing rain
Seeking a new home to claim and keep as their own
This grey-and-green land, both strange and familiar
Mysterious, promising, offering wealth and danger
And they have set ashore, those ships that survived
Some lost to the dark depths in the perilous crossing
Some swept far astray by uncertain, indifferent fate
They will be remembered, honored in rune and tale
Once the needs of the living have been safely secured
It has been a hardship, this long and perilous journey
Often seeming hopeless, heaving waves without end
But, at last, land! Land is sighted, forests and coves
Shallow hulls sliding over wet salt mud and grey sand
Leather boots on the beach, the firm earthen solidity
Smooth pebbles picked up, pale driftwood examined
The sight of a great brown bear river-fishing an omen
Haunting gull-cries in the air, and the barking of seals
The hard work begins, the unloading, the construction
Fresh water fetched, firewood gathered and fires lit
Shelters erected from ship's framing and sturdy sails
Huts for the chickens, pens for cows, sheep, and pigs
Now and then the clouds part, yellow sun beaming
Followed by sweeping rain-squalls in silvery veils
Chill dusk and dark night a world of black shadow
Until in rolls the fog, thick as fleece, ghostly-white
A damp blanket obscuring, its scent salt-sea and death

Suggestions of shapes writhing and wraithing within
Muffling silence descends… then come the screams.

DREAMS OF FIRE

She burns.

She burns, and she feels everything.

Every moment of it.

The heat. The searing flame-touch.

Her hair gone, disintegrated in a bright tinder-flare.

Her skin crisping and blackening, crackling and splitting. Charred scraps of it curling off, peeling away, wafting up, floating in the rising smoke. Drifting with ash-flakes and the fleeting wink of ember-sparks.

And oh, how she burns, how she burns, in great agony.

The bacon-sizzle, the loose and liquid run of melting fat, the hiss of boiling blood-steam. The smell of spit-roasted meat, overdone, as her flesh cooks to the bone.

Her wounds sear and seal shut, cauterized around the piercing metal points embedded deep.

Each breath brings blisters to her throat and lungs. Her vital organs simmer in their own seething juices.

Her eyes rupture and burst, blinding her in uttermost fact when she had already been blinded by scalding smoke-tears and heat-ripples. Blinding her so that she can no longer see the cruel faces that surround her.

In her ears is only the blaze-roar; she is deaf now to their voices, to their insults and taunts, to their laughter and demands. She is deaf now even to her own screams, torn choking and gasping from the depths of her blistered lungs.

She burns.

The long bones of her body, marrow-filled, crack lengthwise. The finer ones scorch and splinter. Her sinews contract, drawing her limbs tight, twisting her neck. She feels pieces of herself sloughing, dropping into the fire.

Burns, oh, she burns.

She burns, and she dies.

She feels them drag her smoldering black husk from the cinders.

Burnt. Burnt and dead.

But, somehow, she still lives.

So they do it all again… and she feels everything… as she burns…

***

Renate thrashed her way to a struggling, sweat-drenched wakefulness. Her parched mouth tasted of salt and ashes.

Hot… choking… on fire all over…

She fought free of the blankets and sat up, half-expecting to be met by suffocating smoke and flickering flames.

Instead, she was met only by undisturbed darkness.

Murky recollections of the previous evening swam below her mind's surface, partly visible as blurs and shadows, gradually taking form.

The noise, the thunder-clangor and lusty voices bellowing… the violent press and lunge of bodies… wild hair and beards, leather and chain, hammer amulets gleaming against bared chests… boots and belts and studded arm-bands… torn denim, piercings, tattoos… and black tee-shirts.

So, so many black tee-shirts. Viking imagery on the front—runes, dragonship prows, axes, shields, gods, giants, monsters. Cities and dates printed on the backs.

The crowd. The audience. The fans. Their loud and lusty cheers.

"… give it up for Frygga!"

Which, in announcer-speak, was "FUH-*RYGG*-UH!"

Greeted by a tumultuous roar; let the head-banging and hair-flailing commence. Hardcore metalheads, fantasy roleplaying geeks, history enthusiasts, bikers, feminists, folklorists... a near-50/50 mix of men and women... covering a wide range of ages, shapes and sizes. Some people brought kids, even babies, dressed up in little crocheted helmets or costumes, waving toy weapons.

Sure, the baseline fan was still your typical scruffy young adult male, but the appeal of folk and Viking metal tended to attract a more varied audience. Especially an all-female band, like Frygga.

An all-female band *not* made up of pop-tarts and divas. They, too, covered a wide range of ages, shapes and sizes, from Bera's 'full-figured' roundness, to stick-thin Stefya, from early-twenties to closing on fifty. Real women. Not cheesecake pinups in chainmail bikinis or armor designed by Vallejo and Frazetta. Ingebjorna, six feet and two-fifty of padded muscular curves, had more admirers than model-gorgeous Aud.

Female empowerment, fuck yeah.

Their songs centered on those themes. Goddesses and giantesses. Valkyries, Norns, shield-maids and queens. Norsewomen. Ladies of legend. Not as victims or prizes, helpless damsels in distress, but fearless, powerful, and fierce.

Fuck yeah.

Badass and beautiful. Strong and sexy.

Glass ceiling? Marte would smash it with her fist or forehead if she had to. Same for any knuckle-dragger who started in with the crap about how girls couldn't rock, make me a sammich, tits or GTFO. The suits and execs might buy into that garbage, but over-all, they had solid respect from their peers and their fans.

A packed house. The show. The concert. Last gig of the *Mists of Helheim* tour.

Followed by an all-out blow-out party.

Mead and beer and wine.

So, so much mead and beer and wine.

Was she hung over? She couldn't put it away like Marte did—their tough-chick guitarist routinely drank the biggest and burliest Viking guys under the table—but she'd had a few.

Not enough to give her a hangover, surely. And, though there'd been a pervasive, warm hemp-haze, she hadn't indulged in anything stronger. Leave that to Stefya, on another of her quests for omens or visions.

Besides, no headache, no nausea, and when Renate went into the bathroom and switched on the lights, her eyes did not rupture and burst the way they had in the dream, going dribbling down her cheekbones like runny poached eggs. She was just overheated, sweaty, achy, and thirstier than she'd ever been in her entire life.

That dream, what the fuck had been up with that? Being burned alive? Ugh.

To smite two birds with one stone, she stepped into the tub and stood open-mouthed under the showerhead as cool water rained down. Gulp after refreshing gulp seemed to permeate her from the inside out. The salty, ashy taste washed away. So did the sticky second-skin of sweat.

Maybe she should have learned from Bera's example and turned in early. The bass player could shriek and fling her amber-and-ivory-beaded braids around with the best of them, but ultimately preferred quiet evenings on Skype with her husband and kids to partying with rowdy fans.

Or maybe she should have stayed up, ridden it out, partied 'til dawn, and conked out on the plane. That was what Marte and Aud did. They probably hadn't even gone to bed yet.

Unlike Ingebjorna, who surely *had* gone to bed… the only question being with whom and how many this time. Lately, it seemed she favored slim elfin youths and curvy brunettes, in various combinations.

Stefya, now, Stefya would have been all over such a weird dream, trying to decipher its hidden meanings. If Bera was their earth-mother, Marte their valkyrie, Aud their wish-maiden and

Ingebjorna their warrior-queen, then Stefya was their crone and wise-woman as well as their drummer.

As for Renate herself, she wasn't sure quite where she fit in terms of archetype and role. Besides at the keyboard, that was. She certainly didn't sing; except for when war-cries or a shrieking chorus was called for, the rest of them mostly left the vocals to Ingebjorna... or Aud, if the song required a higher and purer note than Ingebjorna's husky she-bear contralto.

She got out of the shower and dried off. By then, she was shivering, goosebumps rising on her skin.

And still hot, still sweating, still feeling like she was being burned alive.

The hotel room didn't seem particularly hot and stifling. Checking the thermostat anyway, she found it was not set too high for comfort. The bed didn't have an electric blanket that she could have been unknowingly broiling herself under, either.

"Better not be getting sick," she warned herself.

If she was, if she had to, at least it had the decency to wait until the end of the tour. She pressed the inside of her wrist to her forehead. No fever that she could detect.

She'd gotten badly sunburned once, during a gig at a Ren Faire, but didn't think that could be the cause of her discomfort this time. Between long flights and indoor venues, she hadn't been out in the sunshine for ages.

What did that leave?

Spontaneous human combustion?

Fucking *menopause*? For Stefya, maybe, but Renate was nowhere near that old!

She turned toward the bed, intending to flip through the available television channels since sleep seemed unlikely. As she reached to pick up the remote, sudden pain slammed into her hip.

Shot? Stabbed?

Another pain struck her in the side. Like a lightning bolt, like a hammer blow.

Then her stomach.

Then blackness.

***

She burns.

They lower her again into the flames. Hold her there, pinned, speared, spitted like a yearling boar.

Once, she was golden.

Once, she was fair.

Now she is this.

This silently-screaming lump of burnt flesh and cracked bone.

Her blood baked to a thick black crust.

Her skin in flakes and ashes.

She dies, but she lives.

And, oh, how she burns!

***

Her first thought was of bedsprings, ends jabbing through a worn-thin mattress... that shabby, wretched apartment she'd shared with three other girls just out of college, all of them broke, working shit jobs and living on ramen.

Her second was of camping trips, roughing it, trying to sleep on rocks and roots. Aching already from the day's hike, unable to get comfortable, sure that she'd wake up stiff and sore, covered in bruises.

Her third thought was that she could do without this 'Princess and the Pea' routine, and then Renate opened her eyes.

When she did so, things made even less sense.

No hotel room.

A stony cave-floor, strewn with pebbles, illuminated by flickering pale-gold light. The cool air smelled of earth and minerals. Shadows lurked in the upper recesses and danced over the irregular contours of the walls. Set about the cave, on ledges and protrusions, were hosts of white candles, dribbling wax.

Renate, groaning, pushed herself to her hands and knees. She brushed away the pebbles that had stuck to her and found that she was still naked. Her hair still hung in damp tangles from the shower. The towel with which she'd wrapped it lay crumpled nearby.

Pain throbbed in her hip, in her stomach and side. Piercing pains… like sharp metal… grinding deeper, scraping against bone, puncturing organs.

But there were no wounds. There was no blood. If she had been shot or stabbed, she should have sported some sign of the injuries.

As she stood, she picked up the towel and tucked it around her body. More pebbles dug into the bare soles of her feet. The hotel logo, embroidered in the corner, rasped faintly against her skin.

What the fuck was this? Another dream? It seemed so vivid… too vivid to be anything but real… but how could it be real?

The cave chamber was oblong, tapering toward a narrower passage at one end. The rows of candles led that way. Beckoning.

A lure, a trick, a trap… but it didn't matter… she saw no other ways out. Taking hold of a hefty grapefruit-sized rock, she cautiously followed the candle-lined passage. It descended in a gentle, sloping corkscrew spiral. A faint breeze, or the stirring caused by Renate's own movements, made the myriad flames waver and sway.

At the bottom, where the passageway leveled, another cave-chamber opened before her. This one was larger, an immense stone cavern, a soaring subterranean hall. More candles filled it, candles by the thousands. The ends of lit torches were wedged into cracks and crevices in the walls. Small fires blazed in basins of hewn stone, basins with their edges rune-etched. At the center of the chamber was a huge stone trough, made of engraved slabs resting upon supports carved to resemble Nordic beast-heads—horses and wolves, boars and stags, dragons. A long bed of coals in the trough shimmered red-gold.

"What the fuck *is* this?" Renate said, this time aloud.

"They burned me."

Renate, who hadn't actually been expecting an answer, gasped. She whirled, clutching the rock, ready to crack it against someone's skull or into someone's face, send teeth skittering like chips of ivory—

But the voice had come from everywhere... and nowhere. It was whispery, yet resonant. Feminine, but inhuman.

"Who's there?" Renate called. "Who are you?"

"They burned me," the voice repeated. "Spear-struck, they held me, they put me to the flames!"

Flames sputtered and guttered as the strange voice, still whispery, rose into a roar.

Something tall toppled toward Renate. She sprang aside with a cry. A length of ash-wood, the height and girth of a ship's mast, clattered to the cave-floor where she'd been standing. The iron spear-point, corroded with rust and blood, rang like a gong on the stone. The mysterious pain in her hip gave a vicious, twisting throb.

"They demanded of me the secret truths that I could not then tell, I did not then know, I had not then seen!"

Another spear fell, clatter-clanging across the first. Renate doubled over, clutching her stomach. Every cramp she'd ever had in her life hit her at once. It was all she could do not to collapse in tears.

"I burned!" roared the voice. "I burned and I died, but when they took me from the fire, I lived! So they burned me *again*!"

The third spear landed atop the other two, making a pattern like cast rune-sticks or bones. Renate stifled a shriek as more pain, invisible but real, unseen but far from unfelt, plunged into her side. It ground between her ribs, scraping with a hideous vibration.

"Thrice they burned me and thrice was I reborn—"

Howling through a haze of agony, Renate blindly hurled the rock in her hand. It plowed into candles, scattering them like ninepins, spraying molten wax. A torch, dislodged from its crevice, rolled back and forth in a clumsy, trundling arc.

The brutal pains faded. But for the crackle of flames, silence fell. Renate straightened, drawing a shuddering breath.

Then she saw what was there, and she screamed.

It was a woman.

Or, it was what must have once been a woman, this char-blackened husk, a corpse snatched from the pyre or crematorium when the job was only half-done. As she lifted one wizened, scorched hand, her joints creaked and a fine dusting of burnt skin-ashes sifted down.

"They burned me," this half-cremated thing said, the seared scabs of lips splitting to show baked-brown nubs of teeth. "In the fires of Odin's hall, they burned me for gold-greed, for the secrets I did not then know."

Renate only stared, stared into the crisp-edged hollow sockets that, somehow, horrendously, stared back. Their empty gaze bored into her.

"They paid no *wergild* for my murder, no death-price, no compensation," the burned woman went on. "And so, there was war. The Aesir, gods of Asgard, and the Vanir, gods of old, brought down terrible slaughter upon each other."

"Who are you?" Renate asked in a whisper.

"My name was Gullveig."

"Gullveig…" It sounded vaguely familiar, only vaguely, and Renate frowned, wracking her brains.

"You see? I have been all but forgotten. There is a single mention of me in the lore that survives, and even that—even that one mention!—the scholars dismiss. They attribute my hard-won gift to that bitch Freya instead. Is it not enough she be revered as a goddess of fertility and love? Is it not enough that Odin cedes to her half of those best of men, those warriors slain in battle? Is it not enough that she and her brother have name-claim to a week-day, centuries later? Must she be given credit for *seidr* as well?"

"Magic?"

"That discovery was mine!" Gullveig shrieked, and the force of her fury was such that it cracked deep dry fissures into her skin and flesh. Pieces fell off with an awful, gritty noise. "Mine! Earned by my death thrice-over in the fires of the hall, so that when I was for the third time reborn I was remade anew as well!"

She began to tear at her own body with the charred stumps of her fingers. Yet more skin and flesh ripped away, revealing paleness beneath. A soot-cloud arose. Renate covered her mouth and nose, not wishing to inhale any of the ashy black powder.

Gullveig continued ripping and tearing, peeling, violently shedding and stripping herself of all that was burnt.

And when she had finished, she stood transformed.

"I emerged from the embers as a *völva*, a sorceress," she said, extending her white and unblemished arms. "Heidr, they called me from that moment on."

She was beautiful. Shining and fair. Her hair was as a river of gold, and gold gleamed bright in her eyes.

Other objects fell in a sudden rattling hail from thin air, as the three spears had done. Renate crossed her arms over her head in a defensive gesture. Flat, hard surfaces slapped her forearms, stinging, smarting.

She looked at the scattered items at her feet and reeled. As bizarre as the rest of this had already been—the candles, the spears, Gullveig herself... or Heidr now, she was Heidr—it was somehow ten times weirder to see a litter of CD cases on the cave-floor.

The cover art, and the titles, were familiar.

Choosing the Slain... Across the Cold Sea... Where Norns Gather... The All-Mother... On Raven's Wings... Hearth-Iron... Mists of Helheim... Disir Arise...

Their albums.

Every album Frygga had done, including the live concert one with the bonus DVD extra, and the two-disc *God-Thunder* collection featuring hits by Viking metal bands.

"Whereas you," Heidr said, "you and your skald-sisters, have made many songs for the others. For Freya, that bitch. For Sif of the dwarf-forged hair. For Frigg, of course. For even the dark gloom-queen, Hel, and Sigyn who catches the poison that spills onto Loki's face. You have sung of the giantesses Skadi, and Angrboda, and Gerdr. You have sung of the Valkyries, the Disir and the Norns. You sing of battle-maidens and queens, of mothers and wives, strong daughters, proud Norse-women all."

"But we have not sung of you," finished Renate. "That's what you want. That's why I'm here."

"I would be remembered. I would have my name honored and my story told. I would have song-justice. You will see it done. You will write me sagas, and songs, and epics of my own."

"Me? But I can't… I don't compose, I don't write lyrics, I just play the—"

The three great spears flew up from the floor then, hurtling toward Renate. They plunged into her body—hip, stomach and side. She shrieked. Blood gushed. Iron grated on bone. Something punctured in her guts like a wet, meaty water balloon.

"You can, and you will," she heard Heidr say, though the words were nearly lost in the terrible wrenching torment of being hoisted aloft by the spear-points impaling her flesh. "The gift is within you, Renate, as it was within me."

In the long stone trough, on its carved beast-head supports, the glowing banked bed of coals flared. Flames, rekindled, leaped high.

"It needs only be refined, smelted from you… like gold."

And the spears thrust her into the heart of the blaze.

***

She burns.

She feels everything.

The towel wrapped around her steams and smolders, then ignites.

Burning alive. Lungs blistering, fluids boiling, the sear and char and crackling, the sizzle, the stench of hair and skin.

Tempered by fire. Consumed and destroyed.

She dies. She burns and she dies.

The spears lift her corpse from the pyre.

She is dead, but she lives. She feels everything, and still lives.

As it happens once, then twice, then thrice again.

***

Her eyes opened to scorched carpeting, the nylon fibers shrunken and curled. A few scraps of towel—edges and corners, mostly, and the embroidered hotel logo—still gave off thin wisps of smoke.

Renate got up, not sure if she should be glad or disturbed by the fact that the fire alarms hadn't gone off. She looked at the black patch on the floor. It outlined the shape of her body like chalk at a crime scene. But, beyond that and the remains of the towel, the fire had not spread.

Downstairs, in the dining room, roadies and crew thronged the breakfast buffet for coffee, donuts, and plates heaped with greasy protein.

One by one, the band members themselves put in their appearances. Bera alone seemed well-rested; Ingebjorna wore her familiar expression of sleepy satiation, Stefya was more haggard than usual on the downside of some drug or other, Aud shuffled bleary-eyed and yawning, and Marte's talk-to-me-and-DIE glower would have made Thor take a step back.

If they were surprised to see Renate already awake, it didn't show, or was lost in the larger surprise of finding her surrounded by sheets of paper, feverishly scribbling. They were more surprised yet when, on closer inspection, they found the pages covered with song titles and lyrics.

"The hell is all this?" asked Marte. "You always said you couldn't write."

"This 'Magic-Bringer' one is really, really good," said Aud, roused from tiredness as she read.

"So's this one," Ingebjorna said. "'She Burns'… kick ass!"

"There's an entire album's worth here," Stefya said, shuffling through the stack. "If they're all that good."

"And check this out." Marte showed them a rough sketch of a woman, spear-pierced but with hands raised in exultation, wreathed by flames. *Dreams of Fire* was scrawled at the top, under their band logo. "She draws, too. Been holding out on us."

"You must have been up half the night," Bera said to Renate, with a mix of admiration and motherly concern. "Aren't you exhausted?"

Renate, smiling, shook her head. "Far from it," she said. "I feel... reborn."

ARM-RINGS
AND HACK-SILVER

At the height of the feasting, when the golden mead flowed, King Ragnar discovered his own sons had betrayed him.

He had the chest brought forth, intricately carved, so heavy that two strong thralls were needed to carry it. Men cheered at its passage through the feast-hall. They banged their fists on the long tables laden with roast meats, and lifted high their drinking horns.

The best warriors of Ragnar's kingdom had gathered, a dozen jarls and their men, heroes of the sword and the shield-wall. They came to celebrate victory, having driven invaders from their shores, saved their lands and villages, and won many battles.

Now was the time when their king, old and venerable, much-loved, would reward their loyalty with generous gifts.

He rose from his chair at the head of the hall. A fur mantle draped his shoulders, stooped now from age but still broad. His hair and beard gleamed silver-gilt in the firelight. A simple band of hammered bronze circled his brow.

The thralls lowered the chest to the rush-strewn floor before him and stepped back. King Ragnar lifted the lid to reveal—

Ingots of tin and scraps of iron and rough chunks of stone.

A puzzled hush fell over all those there assembled.

This was not what they'd expected, not treasure at all.

No arm-rings, no brooches, no buckles and cloak-clasps of gold. No necklaces of black jet and honey-amber, no ivory combs or glass spice-jars. No coins from far lands, no garnet and jade. No hack-silver cut from cups, crucifixes, candlesticks and chains.

There should have been ransom sent for lords captured in battle. There should have been plunder seized from enemy ships now soot-smoldered burnt husks on the sand beaches. There should have been wealth enough that each man here left pleased, honored and well-gifted.

Instead of gold, Fafnir's bed, Freya's tears, the showers of Draupnir and leaves from the grove Glasir... instead of bright silver... instead of jewels of all the colors of Bifrost the rainbow-bridge...

Instead, there was only stone, tin and iron.

A near-worthless hoard.

"What ill-made joke is this?" asked the old king, looking up, his gaze sharp and voice sharper. "Where are my sons, who choose a poor time to have their amusement? Ragnald? Ragvyn? Speak up, give answer for yourselves!"

But the princes, whom their father had entrusted with the task of filling the chest with rich wealth, gave no answer. They were not in the hall. No one remembered having seen them since late in the day.

A search was done, but they were nowhere to be found.

Their belongings were gone... their mail coats and weapons, their horses and helms. The same proved true of Einar, their most disreputable henchman. Lynd, Ragnald's woman, was missing as well.

The dark truth and knowledge spread like a swift plague.

King Ragnar, stricken by shock and by shame, fell senseless and had to be borne to his bed. A grieving tumult went up. The jarls and lords raged in outcry.

Some would have ridden out that very moment, in pursuit of such treacherous sons who would rob and lay low their noble father. Others swore by their swords that Ragnald and Ragvyn would have no respite, but be hounded to the ends of the earth, wherever the dragon-prowed longships could sail.

Then Ragnis stood forth and called for their silence.

Ragnis, the king's daughter, was tall but not fair, a long-faced and plain-featured girl, unmarried. Her brown hair hung coarse as a mare's-tail. But her words rang strong from the roof-timbers, her bearing was that of a war-queen or battle-maid, and Thor's fury seemed to blaze from her eyes.

"I will go," she declared. "On my oath, on my life, for my father's good name, I will find my brothers."

***

There was, of course, protest and arguments made. Ragnis held firm.

"If you confront them by force of arms," she told the jarls, "they will fight."

"But they are two," Jarl Ivar said, "and we are dozens."

"Then you will kill them, the sons of your king? You will pay the wergild for princes, or risk blood-price for blood?"

At that, Ivar hesitated, and was not alone in his uncertainty.

King Ragnar, it was known, loved his sons despite their faults. He turned a blind eye to their laziness and greed. He had forgiven many transgressions before. He might do so again, once wakened from this low-brought state.

And if he did *not* wake...

If he did not wake, in the absence of his sons, this plain-featured girl might next rule Ragnar's land.

"This is my burden," said Ragnis. "If I cannot persuade them to return, I will have them named out-law, unprotected."

So it was decided, and so it was agreed.

Ragnis set aside her linen frock and long tunic, donning instead woolen trousers cloth-wrapped to the knee. She braided her brown hair straight down her back and put over it a leather cap, with a leather coat to match. Boots and belt she wore, and a seax-blade at her waist, and a bronze horse-head amulet on a cord around her neck.

Then she went to the king's bedside, where he lay unconscious, watched over and tended by the hall's women.

"Be well, Father," she said, and bent to kiss his ashen cheek.

She returned to the jarls in the hall, bringing an oaken coffer inlaid with mother-of-pearl. This, she set down on the table in front of her father's chair, and opened. Within was her *heiman fylgia*, her dowry-portion, consisting of money and what jewelry she had—hair-ornaments and combs, bracelets and brooches, a belt-chain of silver links and a head-circlet of fine golden wire.

"If *I* do not return," she said to Jarl Ivar, who, after the king was the most powerful of the lords, "take this and divide it fairly among you as some compensation, and let none here hold grievance against good Ragnar for the misdeeds of his sons."

He nodded, and it seemed to Ragnis that he looked on her now as if having never seen her before.

One servant went with her, Ynna, a clever old slave-woman who'd belonged to Ragnar's wife. Ynna was as small of stature as Ragnis was tall, her body twisted and her back hunched, her gait a spider-like scurry deceptively swift. She possessed Mimir's uncanny gift for imitating the sounds of birds and beasts, and the speech of men.

They rode under a milk-pale moon, its shine bright upon patches of unmelted snow. Their breath and that of their mounts made frosty clouds in the cold air.

"You know where they are, you know where they've gone," Ynna said, as statement, not question, when they had left the hall well behind them.

"I have a suspicion," Ragnis replied.

For, even princes as children like to play at being kings. She had often enough followed along, the vexsome young sister, when Ragnald and Ragvyr made up their games.

Years ago, they'd found a farmstead, abandoned, its fields overgrown, its cattle-byre collapsed, half the sod roof of its house fallen in… this, they'd claimed and named as their own great hall. It became where they would hide from their mother's displeasure when they'd gotten into trouble for shirking their chores.

Ynna cackled approvingly at this information. "And have you a suspicion how we're to sway that wicked pair, your brothers?"

"The beginnings of one," she said. "Do you remember the stories you taught me of Otter's Ransom?"

Which, of course, the old woman did, and they spoke it back and forth together in turns.

***

Ynna began. "The gods, on a journey, came to a river, and there saw an otter with a fresh-caught fish. A cast stone slew the otter and the gods made much congratulation to themselves for taking two prizes with one throw."

"Then Otter's father, Hreidmar," Ragnis said, going on with the tale, "a man of great magic, demanded they pay him for the death of his son."

"And so the gods went to Svaltarfheim, the dwarf-land, to fetch enough gold—"

Ragnis waved off that part, with the otter-skin bag and the gold ring and the dwarf Andvari's curse. "So Hreidmar accepted the payment, the blood-price. When Regin and Fafnir, Otter's brothers, demanded a share, Hriedmar refused and Fafnir stabbed him as he slept."

"But when Regin asked Fafnir to divide the wealth equally, Fafnir claimed it all for his own, and threatened Regin with their father's same fate. Then, going away, Fafnir made a lair high on a heath. He changed himself to a dragon and lay down upon the gold."

"Meanwhile," Ragnis said, "Regin fled to a far land and became a king's smith. There, he forged the sword Gram, so sharp that a skein of wool carried against it by a stream's current would be sliced in half."

"There as well, he met Sigurd, who even as a youth was above all men in strength and in courage. Regin became as a friend to him, a foster-father. One day, he told Sigurd of the shining treasure, the dragon Fafnir's bed. Sigurd thought this a fine deed for a hero. On Regin's advice, he dug a pit in the path Fafnir used, and hid in it."

"So that when the dragon passed over him, he drove up Gram's sharp steel tooth and skewered Fafnir through the guts. As Fafnir was slow to die, they exchanged many words, but that, too, we may skip over."

"With his last breaths the dragon gave warning that Regin should not be trusted," Ynna said. "And when Regin arrived, he hailed Sigurd as among the least cowardly of men, thanks in large part to the sword *he* had forged. To which Sigurd retorted that it was indeed some bold talk from the one who'd not by his own hand reddened the blade."

"Then Regin told Sigurd whose own brother Fafnir had been, and claimed Sigurd owed him compensation," the girl said. "He bade Sigurd cut out the dragon's heart to roast over a fire, intending to eat it. While Sigurd did this, Regin slept in the heather and plotted further revenge."

"The heart cooked until blood-juices ran from it," Ynna went on. "Sigurd poked it to see if it was ready, and found it so hot that his finger was burned. When he stuck it into his mouth to ease the pain, the heart-blood of Fafnir spilled onto his tongue."

"Which gave him," said Ragnis, "the understanding of bird-speech, and he heard the nuthatches twittering in the trees. Their wise counsel was that Sigurd should eat the whole dragon's heart for himself, that he should strike Regin's head from his neck before Regin betrayed him, and that the great golden hoard should be his."

"All of this, Sigurd did, and the nuthatches told him—"

Again, Ragnis waved off the rest of the saga, saying they did not need to relate how Sigurd then rode to the place where the valkyrie Brynhild slept, and the woes and troubles that would go on to befall them.

"You asked me," she said to Ynna, "how we might sway my brothers, that wicked and selfish pair. I think I now know how it can best be done."

***

In a grove at the base of a hill, they tethered their horses and continued on foot. They skirted snow-patches and puddles of dirty, frozen mud-ice. They took care in their passage to snap no twigs or branches, but moved with caution and stealth until they crested the hill.

Below was the farmstead, overgrown and abandoned, still looking much as Ragnis remembered. She saw at once that she'd been correct in her guess.

The pale moonlight showed recent tracks. Other horses were tethered near the broken fence by the collapsed cattle-byre, dozing and snorting, grazing at tall weed-grass.

Someone slept there too, leaning against a log, wrapped in a fur cloak. This was Einar, Ragnald and Ragvyn's henchman. Some said he gambled, others called him a thief, and rumors whispered he'd once killed a man in a drunken brawl but avoided wergild as well as the noose.

A dull ember-glow shone through gaps in the walls of the ruined old house, where her brothers and Lynd must have taken shelter.

"You know what to do?" Ragnis asked Ynna.

The clever crone grinned. "Nuthatches," she said, and crept ahead with her low, scurrying gait.

Ragnis followed, hiding herself to listen.

First, Ynna nickered and blew, making the sounds of a nervous horse. So adept was her mimicry that the rest of the beasts tossed their heads, their hooves shifting, troubled but not yet alarmed.

They settled again, but the disturbance was enough to stir Einar halfway to wakefulness, at which point the old woman began to speak in two voices.

A shiver prickled the nape of Ragnis's neck. For all she'd expected this, for all it had been her suggestion and plan, for all she *knew* it was Ynna, the gooseflesh spread over her entire skin.

The voices were those of her brothers, Ragnald and Ragvyn, unmistakable in a low, hushed conversation.

With her gnarled hands cupped oddly over her mouth, Ynna made it seem that the words came from the direction of the house.

Einar stretched, glancing briefly that way. He drew his cloak more snugly around his shoulders as if to settle back into more comfortable sleep.

"… about Einar?" said Ynna, in Ragnald's voice. "Will you do it?"

At that, the henchman stiffened, and sat straight upright. Even from where she hid, Ragnis thought she saw his eyes widen, his ears almost twitch.

"But he is *my* better friend." Ragvyn's voice whined from Ynna's lips.

"Which is why you should do it," Ynna-Ragnald retorted. "He trusts you more than me. He would not see it coming."

"That much is true…"

Expression disbelieving, Einar slowly got up. He took a few soft steps toward the shelter, listening keenly.

"And you know that he would do the same thing to us."

Ynna imitated Ragvyn's petulant scoff. "For far less a fortune, of that I am sure. But when?"

"The sooner the better. Best by surprise."

"Yes. I would not wish to face him in a fair fight."

"Shh," said Ynna in the Ragnald-voice. "I thought I heard something. Feign sleep, now, brother, and wait."

She fell silent.

There were then only the normal night-noises to hear, but to Einar they must have seemed forced and false.

He went back to the place where he'd let his fur cloak fall. Before he pulled it over himself again, he eased from a belt-sheath a long narrow blade that gleamed quicksilver under the moon. He arranged himself so that it would be concealed but ready at hand, and tipped his chin down to feign sleep of his own.

***

Ragnis peered in through a crack.

Ragnald and his woman shared blankets to one side of the hearth-pit where the red embers glowed. Ragvyn, to the other side, slept alone under a thick fleece.

Nearby were the saddles and saddlebags, and the sacks filled with treasure. They bulged lumpy and heavy, their ends tied with twine.

At the sight of her brothers and this proof of their crime, she felt both rage and despair. That they could have done this... shamed their own dear father who'd never been anything but generous and kind...

If she woke them, and told them how the theft left him stricken, how it had felled him and sent him senseless to his bed, would they realize their misdeed? Would they return and beg Ragnar's forgiveness?

Her heart sank at the answer it already knew.

She gestured to Ynna, pointing. The old woman moved quietly along the outside wall until she'd come to a place closest to where Lynd's head rested.

Ynna made a snuffling and hot, breathy puffing. She scraped at the earth with a thin stone. She uttered a grunting, rumbling growl.

Lynd, who had a great terror of bears, woke with a gasp. "Ragnald!"

He groaned, rolling over to burrow his face into the crook of his arm.

"Ragnald!" This time she nudged him hard in the ribs.

"What?" he asked in a mutter.

"There's something outside," said Lynd. "I think it must be a bear!"

"It's nothing."

"I heard it!"

They argued in whispers until her frantic pleading turned tear-ful. At that Ragnald, though reluctant, relented. He pulled on his boots.

"Only the horses," he told Lynd, "or some harmless animal, or Einar moving about. He'd warn us of any danger. But if it will get me some peace, I'll go make sure of it."

So saying, he picked up an axe and ducked through the door.

What happened next was as inevitable as fate.

And exactly as planned.

Einar, still feigning sleep but alert, saw Ragnald step out from the house and make what must have seemed a pretense to look about. He saw the axe's curved edge catch the moon with its shine. Perhaps, in the shadows, he mistook Ragnald for his brother; they were not twins but the resemblance between them was strong.

Ragnald most likely meant just to shake Einar awake, and ask him if he had noticed anything unusual. But Einar, expecting murder-ous treachery, held motionless and waiting as Ragnald approached.

When Ragnald bent over him, Einar struck like a snake. He flung back the cloak and the long blade thrust upward between Ragnald's ribs.

A loud cry burst from Ragnald's throat. His blood gushed black in the moonlight, pouring over Einar's hand, wrist and arm.

His reaction was instinct, war-reflex more than thought. The axe, which had been at his side, swept high and came down. Its edge chopped into Einar where the neck met the shoulder. His collar-bone split. Another gush of black-looking blood sprayed forth.

Both men now were screaming, in anger and pain. The horses reared with panic, heads tossing, hooves flailing. Lynd shrieked Ragnald's name. Ragvyn plunged into view, sword drawn, in time to see Einar yank his blade from Ragnald's chest.

The axe swung again, cleaving Einar's skull from crown to nose-bone. It made a terrible sound, part sharp crack, part wet crunch.

The henchman's body jittered. His legs kicked. His bowels loosed. Then he went limp, and fell dead on the ground.

***

A great tumult followed.

Ragnis and Ynna retreated to the trees until matters had calmed. They waited, watched and listened.

Ragnald lived, though sorely wounded. He rested bandage-swathed in the shelter. His breath wheezed and made a red spatter when he coughed. Though the fire had been built high again, he shook uncontrollably, unable to get warm.

He insisted that Einar had attacked him with no provocation. This made no sense to Ragvyn but could not much be denied.

"Perhaps you startled him from sleep…" he ventured, and gave up on that reasoning before he finished his words.

Lynd was in hysterics. She blamed herself for urging Ragnald to go out, then began a wild speculation that they'd come under a curse.

"You have taken the sagas too much to heart," Ragvyn said.

"Gold *is* the metal of strife! You stole from your father—"

"We took what was ours by right!" Ragnald pressed a cloth to his lips to catch the blood that flew from them. He slumped, eyes shut, too hurt to continue.

Ragvyn continued for him. "Should we have done nothing as that old fool handed out our inheritance to those greedy carrion-ravens? They've picked at his carcass long enough already!"

"But see what misfortune it's brought on us already!" she cried.

"So you wish no more part of it?" Ragvyn slashed the twine tying shut the nearest bulging sack. He spilled out a shining heap of treasure, arm-rings and hack-silver, golden brooches and beads.

She gazed speechless with longing at the glittering wealth.

His smile lacked amusement, as if he'd expected no less. "Now go fetch more firewood—"

"Why can't you?" she cut in.

He cuffed her cheek, back-handed. Lynd gaped at him in shock. Even Ragnald made an effort to lift his head.

"You hit my woman?"

"*You* killed my friend!"

"And he killed me."

"You're not dead yet," Ragvyn told him.

Ragnald struggled to smile. "True enough. But why must she go for wood?"

"Because I have to bury Einar's skull-cleaved corpse before it brings down wolves on us, and the least your woman can do is make herself useful!"

"Give me… my sword then, before you go," Ragnald said. "If… Odin's mail-clad maidens come for me, I want to be ready."

They did as he asked, then went out, leaving Ragnald alone.

Ynna went to work once more with Mimir's gift, borrowing the voices of Ragvyn and Lynd.

"You didn't have to strike me," she said, imitating Lynd's sulking tone. "Or speak to me in such a way."

"Would you sooner have him guess at the truth of us?"

Ragnis saw Ragnald's expression at these overheard words.

"No… but you swore it'd be easy, you swore it'd be quick!"

"How is that my fault?" Ynna-as-Ragvyn spoke with bristling irritation.

"Einar was *your* man!"

"Yes, but *you* sent Ragnald searching for bears with an axe in his fist!"

"Don't be cross with me, Ragvyn," said the Lynd-voice, wheedling and placatory.

"I never can stay that way for long."

Ynna made the slow and moist sound of lovers sharing a kiss. Ragnald's grip tightened on the sword-hilt at his side.

"Now what are we to do?" Ynna-Lynd asked.

"He was stabbed through the lung. He'll die before dawn."

"What if he doesn't? You know how strong he is!"

"He'll die before dawn," Ynna repeated in the Ragvyn-voice. "One way or another, he'll die before dawn."

***

Meanwhile, of course, the two had neither said nor done anything of the sort.

Lynd, frightened of bears but more frightened of Ragvyn's wrath, went to fetch more firewood as he'd instructed. She gathered up armfuls of sticks from beneath the nearest trees, jumping at shadows and at each strange noise.

Ragnis, from her hiding-place, watched the woman return.

Ragnald watched too, through half-lidded eyes.

After setting her burden down near the hearth-pit, Lynd knelt by his side. He looked at her and she must have seen something odd in that look, something that gave her hesitation.

"What is the matter?" she asked. "Ragnald? Are you in much pain?"

"Not enough."

She blinked, frowning at that remark. Ragnald averted his gaze. He studied the treasure, spilled and strewn from its sack.

"So much wealth," he said.

"Yes."

"I told you I'd drape you in gold like a queen."

"You did."

He opened his arm to invite her into a careful embrace. She leaned against him, her head on his shoulder, her palm resting on the unbandaged half of his chest.

"Drape you in gold, and dress you in silver," he said.

"With a fine house," Lynd said, "full of servants and slaves."

His arm folded around her. His hand stroked her sleep-tangled long locks. "We'd feast well every night."

"And sleep beneath blankets woven from softest white wool."

"So much wealth," he said again.

"Yes," she murmured.

"Too much wealth to share."

"Ragnald—?"

Ragnald's arm tightened. His fist clenched in Lynd's hair.

"Whore!" His voice was ragged, his breathing blood-choked. "And with my own brother?"

Then with one hard-yanking snap, he broke her neck like a branch.

***

By the collapsed cattle-byre where the horses stood tethered, Ragvyn undertook the grim process of preparing Einar for the grave. Or the cairn, in this case, for they had not brought shovels and the earth was still too winter-frozen for digging.

It seemed to Ragnis that her brother avoided as best as he could the sight of Einar's blood-soaked face, or the way his brains leaked from the cleft-open skull.

"A pity to leave these in the mud of this desolate place," Ragvyn said to the corpse as he stripped off the arm-rings that Einar had worn. Two were of bronze, one ivory and one silver.

He also in this raven-robbing pried off a golden ring from Einar's finger, took his bronze buckle, and a silver-handled mug he kept hung from his belt. A pouch heavy with coins, Ragvyn tucked inside his shirt.

Finally, the cloak-bundled body was decently covered with planks from the fence and byre, held down with stones. The moon had set. Fish-scale clouds scudded over the sky. The night had grown colder and the air smelled of rain.

Ragvyn, despite the chill, sweated from his labors. He wiped his brow.

"Thief," said Einar's voice, hollow and ghostly, the words seeming to drift up from the earth. "Thief and traitor."

As Ragvyn stood shock-stilled with horror, staring at the cairn he had built, Ragnis stepped up behind him and sank her seax-blade into his back.

***

Mist dripped from the pine-needles. All the world was damp beneath watery grey morning light.

Ragnis had never in her life been so weary.

The bodies of her brothers had been slung over their horses. Lynd, too, hair hanging, arms limp. The saddlebags were fat with the sacks of treasure.

Even Ynna was too exhausted to speak.

They rode on. They rode home.

Word of their return spread swiftly. A crowd came to meet them, making much exclamation. Jarl Ivar pushed his way to the front.

"My father?" asked Ragnis as the jarl helped her down from her steed.

He brought her into the room where King Ragnar rested in his bed, looking frail and ancient, sickly, but unmistakably alive.

"Father?"

His eyelids twitched open. "Ragnis? Your... your brothers... did they...?"

"Yes," she said.

He winced as if heart-pierced.

"Your sons did betray you," said Jarl Ivar, not without compassion. "But your wise and brave daughter has restored the full honor of your hall."

The old king nodded weakly. He reached out with one trembling hand. Ragnis took it, and kissed it, and held it to her face.

"Be... the gift giver," Ragnar told her. "Distribute it... generously... to these... good, faithful men."

"I will," Ragnis promised.

But already he'd surrendered again, sighing, to sleep.

***

Another feast was held that evening as King Ragnar rested.

Much meat was eaten and much mead eagerly drunk. Songs were sung, stories told, and sagas recited. Ynna was called time and again to recount the tale of their cleverness in bringing the treacherous princes to fall.

Ragnis, dressed once more in linen frock and long tunic, did just as her father requested. She gave out arm-rings and bracelets, hack-silver and gold, until the precious hoard was depleted and the guests greatly pleased.

Only later did she realize one jarl had not come forth. She went to where he was sitting.

"You have not claimed your gift, lord," Ragnis said.

He touched the lid of the coffer she'd left in his care, tracing with a fingertip its inlaid decoration. "I would rather keep this," he said, "and all that goes with it."

"But that is my…"

"Bride-price? I believe I can match it, if you'll have me."

She looked at him, dubious, and said, "I am not pretty."

Jarl Ivar smiled. "To my eyes, dear Ragnis, you are fairer than gold."

HAKON'S RAID

To the headland and highland, the rearing rocky crags
Rising grey and stern above crashing storm-tossed sea
The fortress broods defiant, a hall with walls of stone
A wealth of riches awaits us within, plunder's promise
And we come to it eagerly, never mind local legends
Guardian monsters? A clan of night warriors of stone?
Farmer-talk, peasant-tales, whispers from hut and hovel
Already folk have fled before us, desperate in terror
Seeking safety behind the high walls and great gates
To cower with their princess as soldiers stand the line
Shield and sword, spear and helm, bow and arrows
However brave they may be, defending this home
They have little hope to last long against our fury
For we are Hakon's war-band, from the cold north
Come a'viking to this far rugged Scotsland shore
To raid and slaughter, burn the heath and heather
Kings fall before us; what chance has a princess?
Or some monklike magus, robed and book-learned?
Hakon will see them begging for their useless lives
Our leader, gold-bearded, cruel as the wildest wolf
He assures us easy victory despite the setting sun
And, at first, it seems his words will be proven true
The gates break, the walls breach, to brutal battle!
The kill-frenzy fills our hearts, we sing its glory
Our mailcoats shining with day's last dying light

But the defenders rally with tenacious resistance
Around us, shadows lengthen, the sky grows dark
In this dusk and gloaming, a strange power stirs
Leering beasts of carven stone upon the ramparts
Winged and clawed, with dragon heads and tails
Suddenly, their grey skin cracks apart thin-shell
Suddenly, their eyes blaze, white and red torches
They move, they burst free to roaring raging life
And we, Hakon's raiders… falter for a moment
Shock-struck by such magic; what sorcery is this?
Among our number some nerves fail and men flee
These vicious inhuman foes, savage and stone-born
Sweeping down on us, leathery wings spread wide
Eyes aglow, fangs bared, tails lashing, claws sharp
Splitting our shields, snapping our blades, howling
Hurling us bodily, bone-jarringly, heels over head
Our courage unmanned, our war-band a shambles
Until there is no other choice but scattering retreat
Shamefully routed, a panic, each of us for himself
Thoughts of a bold death in battle quickly forgotten
Never mind the Valkyries and gold-shingled Valhalla
Odin All-Father's mead-benches, the fires and feast
Thinking no further than hoping of seeing the dawn
We regroup one by one at our forest encampment
In a stunned, shaken silence… we scared survivors
Then Hakon is with us, and shows his stained blade
With which he smote a wound to the mightiest beast
Telling us that which can bleed is that which can die
A truth we know well, a fate waiting even the gods
When, in world's twilight, they all will meet death
But Hakon has made a bargain, and has a new plan
For the wolf may be cruel, but can be also cunning
We'll return in daylight, when the guardians sleep
And with treachery as our ally, the fortress will fall.

SISTERS OF HAMMER
AND SWORD

The sea's grey flesh bled white foam, slashed wide by the ship's hull. Full rode the striped sail, wind-bellied, the ropes taut.

At the prow stood Sifthora, tall and bare-headed, blond braids blowing behind her as the salt-spray dashed her fair face. A torc gleamed gold on her throat; on her arms were thick rings worked of silver. She had not yet donned her war-gear over wool tunic and breeches, though wide strips of leather were stitched to her lower leg-wrappings and sturdy bracers guarded each wrist.

She laughed strong and clear as the ship cut the waves. With one hand, she gripped the carved neck of the high, curved beast's head—a dragon, fierce-eyed and with fanged jaws agape. In the other she held a drawn sword by the hilt. The blade shone in the sun with sharp brilliance. Sky-Strike, the weapon was named, a prize taken in battle, and she had made promise to it that they would greet the first sight of Daan Dwinnoch together.

And there, ahead of them, it appeared... the shore a darker smudge on the misty horizon, soon resolving into a rugged landscape of forests cresting behind rocky headlands. Gentle slopes formed a valley, through which a river flowed to the coast. The morning fog, dissipating, revealed more as they drew nearer. Sifthora saw fields marked by low, meandering walls of stacked rock. She saw growing crops, farmstead hovels, sheep being herded to hill-pastures.

Their ship—*Fear-Bringer,* it was called—surged ahead as if it, too, knew they had almost reached land, and as if it was just as eager for the slaughter and plunder to follow. They came from the east, out of the rising sun and sea-glare, and with the wind swift in their favor would be upon their foes with little warning.

Sifthora turned to grin back at her sister, upon the stern platform guiding the long steering-oar. They had sprung on the same day from their mother's womb, but many at first meeting would hardly guess such close kinship. Where Sifthora was lithe and slender, long-legged, Thorsifa was broad of shoulder and hip, stout of waist, with limbs burly-muscled.

Already, Thorsifa wore her mail-coat, the links glinting from beneath a reindeer-hide cloak pinned with a bronze brooch of boar's head design. Another bronze boar formed the crest of her helm, of which the eye-pieces and nasal also were decorative bronze. Mail-skirting hung from the helm's edges to her collar-bones, protecting her neck and face.

Thus garbed in her battle-readiness, she had been on occasion mistaken for a man… if only from the back. Frigg and Freya had been more than generous. Even with her formidable fullness constrained by quilted cloth and leather under her mail, the sight was impressive.

In part as a result of such over-ample endowment, Thorsifa was not one for the deft clash of sword-play that Sifthora so loved. No, the war-hammer was her weapon, fashioned after Thor's own Mjolnir, double-headed hard iron and rune-carved oak. Gods-Fist, as the punishing weapon was known, rested in a sling-socket against her back. She had, for a time, used an axe and with no less deadly effect, but some deep part of her nature preferred to crush and bludgeon, to crack skulls and break bones.

If she grinned in return, it was hidden by the helm, but a

head-gesture told Sifthora that her sister shared her anticipation. However unalike they might be in looks—Thorsifa's hair was dark and cropped short, her eyes green as pine-needles while Sifthora's were blue—they were warriors, hungry for the fight, hungry for silver and song-glory to be won.

So too were the crew, thirty men and a handful of women, who hastened to furl sail and put out the oars. Mail-coats were donned, sword-belts buckled.

"Soon," Sifthora told Sky-Strike, and kissed the bright steel. She tasted cold sea-spray, to be replaced by hot blood.

Then she stepped down from the prow to where Jurvik waited with her war-gear. The boy, a nephew, gangled at the crossroads of child and man, with youthful voice but the fine, flax-fair fuzz of a fledgling beard. He sheathed Sky-Strike for her as Sifthora pulled on a coat of mail, shrugging and shaking the jingling links into place.

Next came her cloak, black wool trimmed with fur, held with a chain between two silver dragon's-head clasps. Then her helm, a black horse-tail at its crest, and her wide belt with its Thor's-hammer buckle. On her right hip rode a seax, a short stabbing-blade. On her left, Sky-Strike felt as much a part of her as her own arm.

She looked again shore-ward. The oars dipped, cutting the water, driving *Fear-Bringer* ever closer. If any at Daan Dwinnoch had yet noticed their approach, they gave no sign.

It was not a large settlement, nor had it been in the past by reputation particularly rich. But that had been before the priests came, looking to convert this wild land's heathens and pagans to the light of their crucified Christ.

And where priests went, wealth followed.

Wealth, Sifthora knew, to be theirs for the taking.

A church of new timbers sat atop old stone foundations from some long-abandoned shrine to the gods of this place. A high wooden cross rose from its roof-post. It was a grand structure for this part of the world, surrounded by lesser ones to lodge the monks who prayed there. Other houses—these far lesser still, walls plastered with mud and dung, roofed with sod or thatch—huddled around the church like ugly piglets at the teats of an indolent sow.

A mossy, earthen embankment topped with a fence of logs and brambles defended the village, but only on the side facing the dangerous forest where many savage tribes dwelt. They had built with their backs to the sea, but what had been intended as protection would instead be their doom.

Jurvik lifted her round shield, the strap-side toward her. Sifthora slipped her arm through. It was lighter and plainer than the one her sister carried; Thorsifa's was covered with ox-hide, iron-rimmed, with a spiked boss. Upon hers, the only decoration was a black-painted design of interlocked knotwork.

"Let me go with you this time," Jurvik said. "Let me fight. I'm old enough, Aunt, and I'm ready!"

"Then who will stay with Hurstuld and Froni to guard the ship?" she asked. "I promised your father my brother I'd look after you."

"You also promised him to show me, and teach me," he argued. "Ingi can stay with Hurstuld and Froni. He's only seen eleven winters."

"While you've seen twelve."

"Almost thirteen!" His voice split on the last word, and he flushed, but held her gaze resolutely.

She studied him a moment longer, Tyrsten's son by a Saxon noblewoman who'd fallen in love with him when Tyrsten had served as a hostage during a truce. The lad did have a good leather coat, and a helm and sword of his own... he was tall for his age... and the battle should be easy. They went up against not soldiers and warriors but farmers and monks.

"If you stray off or disobey me, I'll cuff you cross-eyed," she said.

"I won't!"

"Then go fetch yourself a spare shield, and be quick about it."

He dashed toward the stern, coltish, almost capering in his excitement. The oarsmen smiled as he passed. Jurvik was a favorite

among them, spirited and pugnacious. If he grew up even half
so handsome as Tyrsten, no doubt he'd be as much of a favorite
among the girls.

Sifthora watched as he ran to give Ingi the news, which brought
a look of envy to the younger boy's face. Ingi immediately went to
Thorsifa, no doubt with the same request… which did not get the
same answer, and his look of envy became a pout of indignation.

A sudden cry, like the cry of a gull, pierced the air. It was joined
by another, and another, in screeching chorus. But they were not
gull-cries; several washer-women had taken their burdens to the
riverbank, and once the first of them glimpsed the dragon-headed
ship slicing the waves, her shriek alerted the others. They scattered,
not gulls now but hens, geese, overturning their baskets in spills of
linen and wool.

Fear-Bringer slid through the shallows and up onto the shore,
hull scraping a trough in the wet sand. The longship had barely
halted when Sifthora leapt to the beach. Sky-Strike sang from the
sheath, steel ringing, blade flashing.

"Now let us fight!" she called. "Now let this day be ours!"

Hurstuld, who was hale but must have been sixty, remained to
guard the ship. Froni, still mending from a thigh-wound taken in
their last raid, stayed with him. And so, sulking, did little Ingi, a
short spear clutched in both hands because he was not yet considered grown enough to be given a sword.

The rest of the crew raced to the attack, warriors armed and armored, near forty-strong.

A terror of confusion fell over the village. Dogs barked, men
shouted, women screamed, and goats bleated. Some folk ran into
their huts and hovels, seizing children or what possessions they
could. Others fled for the hills with no more than the clothes on
their backs. The church-bell began, belatedly, to clang.

Sifthora led the way, and it was Sky-Strike that tasted the day's
first shed blood. A man swung at her with a length of firewood; she
caught the blow with her shield and slashed open his belly. He fell,

howling with agony. She kicked him in the face.

Beside her came Jurvik, wide-eyed over the rim of his borrowed shield. It was painted yellow, with a wolf's head in red. When a woman—the wife of the belly-slashed man, Sifthora supposed—hurled a cooking-pot at them, the boy ducked behind the shield briefly, then popped up again like a stoat from a hole and hacked the woman's arm to the bone.

A stocky farmer in a muddy, loam-green tunic had rallied a small group of his neighbors; he brandished a heavy oaken stave while they wielded hatchets and cudgels, knives and sticks. They looked frightened, but grim and determined.

"Come on!" Sifthora clapped Jurvik on the shoulder, staggering him. "Time to earn your war-glory!"

The men faltered when they saw that their foes were a woman and a boy, but their hesitation did not last for long. Their leader, the farmer with the stave and the loam-green tunic, urged them to fight. "For our homes!" he said. The language was understandable enough, if spoken with strange accent and inflection. "Our families!"

So saying, he whirled the stave above his head. It whistled as it spun. Stocky, he might have been; slow, he was not. His boldness likewise emboldened the others. They charged.

Sifthora met them, intercepting the stave with her shield. Oak against limewood cracked like a thunderclap. She felt the shield-boards split and loosen; she shook the straps from her arm and let the ruined thing drop. The stave whirled again. It caught her a blow in the ribs, glancing but painful, certain to bruise. The farmer raged something at her, something about pagan devils, until Sky-Strike found his throat.

A hulking brute with a hatchet went after Jurvik. For a heartbeat, the boy froze, and Sifthora thought this was it, this was the end, she would have to go home to tell Tyrstan that his son was dead. But Jurvik at the last instant sprang nimbly aside. The hatchet-blade cut nothing but air. As the brute stumbled forward, unbalanced,

Jurvik's sword skewered him through the eye.

Then it was carnage and chaos in the dung-strewn dirt lanes all around them.

Three grubby children and a dog ran past going north, then an old woman with a huge cheese in her arms tottered past going south. Ulbryn and Ulleif her brother fought side by side. The rickety slats of a hen-coop got smashed apart into splinters, the hens escaping in a clucking flurry of feathers. Hodric laughed as his spear nailed a man to a post. Hamstrung, a swineherd thrashed in the mud-wallow among his own panicked pigs; they turned on him with squeals of fury.

From the church rushed a half-dozen men still struggling to finish arming themselves. Four had mail-coats, the other two leather, but all six wore helms. They carried shields, and each had a sword or a spear. It seemed there were more than monks and priests among them, after all. But not enough.

"Take them!" roared Thorsifa. "Make them cower, crawl, and die!"

The six men tried to form a tiny shield-wall. They were disorganized, out of practice at facing war-skilled foes. They were accustomed to wild forest-folk, savages who wore ragged furs and painted their bodies with charcoal and woad. Before they could do more than begin to get in a line, the sisters were upon them like hawks upon hares.

To the church's scant defenders, it must have been as if they were being beset by Odin's own daughters, fierce Valkyries fresh from the fields of the slain. One flung away his weapons and fled, though a thrown axe—Bjaldrim's work, as more of the *Fear-Bringer*'s warriors joined the fray—whickered and flashed and stuck with a meaty chop into his spine.

A fat priest stood in the church doorway, making signs of the cross as if warning off evil. Praying, no doubt, for his god to send angels or fire or heaven's wrath. Monks gathered behind him. Most were well-fed and soft-looking, with dark robes and sandals, and hair shorn into tonsures. Their pale faces peeked out anxiously as the combat raged.

A big man whose helm bore a face-plate fashioned like a snarling wolf lunged at Thorsifa. His sword cut a long slash in her reindeer-skin cloak, and the force of the blow sent her back a step, but her mail-coat stopped the blade's edge from reaching flesh. She, in return, shield-bashed him, but he met it with his own.

An underhand swing of Gods-Fist shattered his knee-cap. He screamed like a horse being gelded. Yet, even as he dropped, he stabbed wildly, piercing through mail to sink his sword-point into Thorsifa's hip, and it was her turn to scream.

Landing hard on his backside, the man tried to scramble away using his elbows and one good leg. Gods-Fist arced up and over, and the war-hammer's heavy iron head came down squarely on the crown of his helm. The sound was that of a blacksmith at work at the forge. Metal crumpled inward, denting deep enough to hold a mug's worth of ale.

For a moment, he sat there, unmoving. Then thick red trickles ran from the eye-holes of his face-plate, and from under its edge to rain dark on his mail-coat. He slowly slumped over and lay dead in the dust at Thorsifa's feet.

In all this time, Sifthora had herself not been idle. The battle-joy embraced her like a lover, and she opened herself gladly to it, welcomed it, let it fill and suffuse her. With each urgent thrust and each yielding of flesh, with each man's breathy grunt or groan of exertion, she cried out her delight.

Blade-locked with the last, she grinned up at him. He, older, grey-bearded, not inexperienced, had landed more than one telling blow. But, in the absence of her shield, her mail and leather had well served their purpose. She gripped the seax in her free hand and drove it between his ribs, metal grating on bone.

The fat priest from the doorway had vanished. Monks scampered like mice in every direction. Some hiked the skirts of their robes to their knees as they ran, showing pudgy white legs. Crosses bounced on their chests. A few carried books, as if those were more valuable than silver, and two bore between them a musty old hide that was presumably some sacred relic.

Presented with no more opposition, the sisters paused, panting, to look at each other. Thorsifa limped, her leg blood-stained but supporting her weight. Sifthora pressed an elbow to her aching ribs. They were sweaty, red-spattered and disheveled... but they smiled. They had won the church, and the village, and the day.

"Gather your plunder," said Thorsifa, raising her voice.

"What of the monks?" asked Ulleif, indicating the fleeing robed figures.

"Let them run," Sifthora said. "They won't get far."

She bent to the grey-bearded man's corpse. He wore no arm-rings, but the brooch pinning his cloak was silver, fashioned in some religious design. She also took from him a belt-buckle of bronze, his weapons, and an ivory crucifix.

The others conducted similar searches, stripping the dead of their valuables, grabbing whatever they could. They were quick about it—though unlikely, it was possible some of the survivors who'd escaped might return, perhaps even with help from a neighboring village or in alliance with the wild forest-folk against a common enemy.

From the church, they seized a small sack of silver, some candle-sticks, a cup set with garnets, and a cask of priest's wine. The fat priest himself, they found hiding by the altar; he told them his god would surely smite them with damnation, but they only scoffed, then broke his wrists and ankles and left him to bear witness to what had been done.

The ransacking of the rest of the village proved something of a disappointment. They came away with coins and trinkets, a few cook-pots, a ladle with a whalebone handle, three good wool blankets and five thick fleeces, and a carved wooden box with pieces of polished stone set into the lid. It contained beads of fired glass and glazed clay, beads of copper and tin, and an assortment of animal teeth and bird's claws with holes bored through them for stringing. Not bad finds, all in all, but hardly rich treasure.

Haffe and Bjaldrim dragged a weak-chinned, pleading man from his house and threw him to the ground. Clumps of moldy straw clung to his clothes and stuck in his thinning hair.

"He was hiding in the roof-thatch," Haffe told Sifthora, laughing as she braced her knee between the man's shoulderblades.

"Shoved this up there," Bjaldrim said, shaking a clinking pouch, "and thought he'd crawl in after it."

"Don't kill me, don't kill me!"

"Where's the rest of it?" Bjaldrim shook the sack again.

"That's all! That's all I have!"

A strand of flat, oblong pieces of smooth jet joined by copper links hung at his neck; Haffe curled it in her fist and twisted until he gagged, half-strangled. It was a seal-sound, and the way his frantic, flapping hands slapped the earth also made Sifthora think of the barking fish-eaters.

"That's all?" asked Haffe, giving another twist.

He gurgled something about the floor by his hearth. Bjaldrim went in and dug up a bundle of sail-cloth wrapped around six rough chunks of amber and a lump of silver ore, while Haffe broke off the jet necklace with a hard yank, then slit the man's throat.

The raid had not taken long; the morning sun was still climbing and the coast-fog had only just dissipated to show the sea wide and blue, sparkling as if scattered with flecks of gold. *Fear-Bringer* waited down on the beach, dragon-headed prow snarling at the sky.

Durvald picked up a crying baby from an overturned cradle, patted it, soothed it, and tucked it into the crook of his arm. "Winna's been wanting another boy," he explained with a shrug.

Sifthora saw that Arn and Hodric had each claimed a girl—they huddled together, weeping—while Ulbryn had an unconscious curly-haired young man slung over her shoulder. None of the other villagers seemed worth taking as slaves. A couple of the hovels had burned, and damp thatch smoldered, but the fires did not spread.

"You should see to your leg," Sifthora said to her sister, indicating Thorsifa's worsening limp.

She snorted. "A pin-prick; I'll see to it later. Where's Jurvik?"

"Over there, still looking for plunder." Observing that the boy was approaching the village's cold-shed, Sifthora smirked. "Or something to eat, which isn't the worst of ideas. I'll go help him."

The cold-shed had a latch on the outside of the door, a bar held in place with an iron peg on chain. Inside, she knew, would be blocks of ice, hewn from winter lakes or hauled down from snow-peaked mountains, packed with straw and sawdust to keep the chill.

"Hungry, nephew?" she asked as she neared him.

He glanced sheepishly at her. "I just thought there might be butter-crocks, mushrooms, or eggs."

The *Fear-Bringer* had been some days at sea, their meals consisting of hard cheese, harder bread, salted fish and dried apples. Jurvik was right, a change would be welcome.

He struggled with the peg, which had been jammed crookedly though its hasp as if shoved there in a hurry. Not only had the lad done well in the fighting, but she saw that he now sported a copper bracelet with the knobs at its ends shaped like serpent's heads and flecks of green glass set for the eyes, and a new knife with a hilt made of antler.

His father would be proud. His mother, perhaps less so; Tyrstan's Saxon woman still clung to notions of their son becoming a good Christian one day.

The peg scraped free from the hasp to dangle at the end of its chain. Jurvik pulled the door partway open. Through the gap wafted the scents of smoked meats, earthy mushrooms, butter, and pears.

Half a heartbeat later, Sifthora's hand flew to Sky-Strike as she sensed something moving in the shed. Her mouth opened to call a warning to Jurvik, but she was too late.

A shape burst from the shadows. A cudgel swung two-handed.

A small shape. A girl.

And no cudgel, but a joint of mutton.

Girl or not, small or not, mutton or not, she clouted Jurvik with it full in the face. There was a crunch as his nose broke, cartilage snapping. He yelped like a kicked hound and sat down hard, eyes watering, hands cupped, blood streaming.

The girl—she couldn't have been much more than ten winters of age, with nut-brown hair in a long braid and a dress of faded red wool—paused only long enough to kick him in the stomach with one leather shoe. Then she ran. She was fast, fast as a fawn, but Sifthora was faster.

Realizing this, the girl stopped and turned and set her back to the wall of one of the shabby hovels. She held the joint of smoked mutton in a defiant grip. Her eyes were the color of dark amber, freckles sprinkled her cheeks, and a colorful stone hung around her neck on a twisted cord.

She stared at Sifthora. "You're a woman," she said, in the strange Daan Dwinnoch accent.

"And you're quite the little warrior."

"Come one step nearer and I'll prove it!"

The attack, the yelp, and the chase had drawn much attention. So too did the sight of the child, mutton raised against Sifthora, who had not drawn Sky-Strike. And the sight of Jurvik, with his nose bent sideways.

Thorsifa inspected him. "The worst wound you've had all day."

"Has she spoiled our nephew's good looks?"

"No. He was too pretty before. Now he'll look more like a man."

There was laughter at that. Even Jurvik laughed, blushing and embarrassed though he was. The girl frowned, puzzled and wary. Her knuckles were white from clenching the mutton-bone.

Sifthora took off her helm. "What is your name?"

"Aelfrin," she said, cautiously, as if the question might be a trap.

"What were you doing in the shed? It was latched from outside."

Then anger flared in her dark-amber eyes, real anger, even hatred. "My step-mother," she said. "She pushed me in there, told me to hide while she fetched the boys—my half-brothers, her sons—but she shut the door and latched it, left me, and went away."

"Left her for us," said Thorsifa.

"Hoping she'd be taken or killed," Sifthora said. "And they call us devils."

"She hit me," Jurvik said through bloodied fingers, the words muffled and clogged.

"You were foolish," Thorsifa told him. "Lucky for you, it was only mutton."

"Where is your step-mother now?" Sifthora asked the girl.

Her thin shoulders hitched in a shrug. "I don't know... ran off, ran off with her sons."

"Your father?"

"Dead last year."

"Was he wealthy?" asked Ulleif.

When Aelfrin shook her head, he sighed, then chuckled resignedly and went with some of the others over to the cold-shed. They began hauling out hams, flitches of bacon, more smoked mutton, and the full butter-crocks and eggs for which Jurvik had been hoping. From a nearby store-house, they took sacks of grain, pots of honey, and jugs of ale. If they were not to fill *Fear-Bringer*'s belly with plunder, they might as well fill their own.

"Are you going to kill me?" Aelfrin asked Sifthora.

"I could," she said. "Should I? Seems wasteful to leave you here."

"You can't mean to bring her," protested Jurvik. He snuffled, spat, wiped his nose, and grimaced.

"Why not? I like her."

"She hit me!"

"Yes, she did, and if that's what she can do with a joint of mutton, imagine how she'll be with a sword."

"Or a hammer," said Thorsifa, touching Gods-Fist's haft.

"Or a *sword*." Sifthora winked at the child. "What do you say?"

"Go... go with you?" Aelfrin chewed at her lip.

"Learn to fight properly, wear a mail-coat, ride a war-horse, carry a banner into battle, bathe in silver and sleep on a bed made of gold."

Her brow creased dubiously. "I'd rather sleep on a bed made of fleeces."

"Fleeces it is, then. All the fleeces you could ever want."

"Whatever it is, fleeces or gold," Thorsifa said, "we'd best be on our way. We've stayed too long already."

Aelfrin regarded them for another speculative moment, then surrendered the joint of mutton to Sifthora. The men and women of the *Fear-Bringer* cheered. They cheered louder still when Sifthora in return unbuckled the sheathed seax from her belt and placed it in the girl's hands.

"We'll find you a real sword soon enough," she said, grinning.

"Or a hammer," Thorsifa repeated.

"Or a *sword*."

Laughing, laden with their plunder of weapons and foodstuff and silver, they went back to their ship. The hull was pushed easily back over the wet sand into the white foam and gold-sparkling surf. Out went the oars, the men turned about at their benches. The oar-blades bit the water. The sea beckoned, wide, blue, and open.

And Aelfrin stood by Sifthora, watching the green land recede, as they left the ravaged Daan Dwinnoch behind.

ONLY STONES

"We ride!" cried Kjarstan. "We ride for slaughter, for wealth, and for glory!"

His men shouted in answer, voicing great cheers. They rattled spear-shafts on shields in a drumming wooden thunder. Their banner, a white sword on a triangle of red, flapped from the pole Kjarstan's nephew held aloft.

"Our king has sent summons!" Kjarstan went on, his stallion's hard hooves striking up muddy splashes from the soft, thaw-soaked earth. "He has need of us, those good and loyal, oath-sworn! Need of our sword-might, our strength and our courage!"

Heartier still were the cheers to greet this. Even the humblest of peasant-horses, seized from plow's purpose, tossed their heads and snorted like proud battle-steeds.

"Shake from your limbs the weight of this long winter's weariness! Rouse your blood and war-fire! When we are old men, white-haired and wizened, we may sit by the hearth-stones... those of us not yet then gone to gold-shingled Valhalla! For now, there are foes to be cut down and plundered!"

Oh, but their blood and war-fire *were* roused. They'd struck at Pedham with the ending of autumn, when the harvest was in, the livestock butchered, the smoke-houses and granaries full. Once they had taken the village, there'd been little to do but wait. Wait, tend their weapons, gamble, and talk.

Under such circumstances, even the best of men would grow

restless. The simplest squabble, a dispute over dice or rivalry for a woman, an ill-spoken insult or ill-timed jest, could flare into violence as an ember into flame.

Now, though…

Kjarstan grinned, teeth a broad flash through his face-plate and a blond bristle of beard. His mail-coat, helm, and arm-rings gleamed in the morning's thin light. It was a grey day and clouded, the land wet from recent rain and snow-melt, and the wind off the sea carried a damp, heavy chill… but spring had come.

Spring had come, as had the summons.

The king's messenger went by ship around the headlands and along the coast, bringing word wherever allies could be found. But there were not ships enough to carry them all with their war-gear and horses. Kjarstan had sent Udr and Anbjorn, two of his own best warriors, back with the messenger as proof in good faith of his oath and intent; the others, almost sixty strong, would meet them again in a matter of days.

And then they would put an end to the armies of Gunnlief Guthnarsson. Gunnlief the outlaw, the traitor, the oath-breaker and kin-slayer.

"What say you?" Kjarstan asked his men now. "Are you rested and ready? Do your swords thirst and your axes hunger?"

Many throats as one bellowed back their affirmation.

"Will you see our foes flee before us, and fall to our fury?"

Again, they bellowed, and louder, so loud the skies shook.

"For Earl Kjarstan! Kjarstan and the king!"

"The king!"

"King Jorfyn!"

"For Thor, Tyr and Odin!"

"Death, death to Gunnlief and his craven piss-dogs!"

Yes, they were eager, they were rested and ready, and they would ride!

"We will have victory!" Kjarstan told them. "Victory and rich reward! Let us fatten our purses on Gunnlief's stolen silver! Let us earn generous gifts, our king's gratitude in gold! We'll drape our women in amber and jet, and bring jeweled trinkets as toys for our children!"

Further back, where hovels and thatch-houses huddled around a log-timbered hall, the surviving villagers looked on with dull, beaten eyes. They would be hungry in the weeks to come; Kjarstan and his men had feasted well from their larders, drained dry their ale-barrels, and depleted their stores.

But, such was their lot. They were farmers and swineherds, not warriors. Those who'd fought back had been slain. These remaining could count themselves lucky enough. They still had their lives, their homes were un-burned, and some even had their families intact.

If, of course, a few young widows and daughters would not be staying, preferring to follow those whose furs and fleeces they'd warmed through the cold nights...

If, perhaps, a promising youth or two had decided to forsake farm and field in hopes of proving his worth alongside the men from the north...

Well, such it was and so it would be.

"And," Kjarstan said, slowly drawing his blade from its scabbard with a scraping hiss of metal, "we will make name for ourselves!"

His men roared their approval.

"Make name by action and deed, such that the skalds will long sing of us and see us never forgotten! To honor our fathers and theirs before them; to leave lasting legacy of pride for our sons and their sons and their sons' sons after!" He swept his sword in a shining arc.

"Kjarstan! Kjarstan!"

"To battle and slaughter and glory!"

"We ride, my war-brothers..." He tugged on the reins so his horse reared up high, forehooves lashing the air. Then he kicked his heels into the beast's side and set off at a gallop. "We ride!"

***

On groaning hinges, the door opened. Its draft flickered the candlelight, and stirred dark wisps of hair escaped from the long plait hanging over Hreyth's mail-clad shoulder.

She glanced up from the table, where was spread a wolf's pelt with rune-marked bones scattered upon it. They were old, those bones. Time-worn and hand-worn, ivoried with age, shaped and polished. The runes set into them were blood-red, soot-black, and gold.

Egil stood in the doorway, his wide shape filling it. He was not a tall man, nor fat, but big just the same. Slab-thick with muscle, barrel-chested, brawny and strong. His leather coat seemed ever to strain at the seams.

"It's happened," he said. His voice was like that of millstones taught to speak—grinding and gritty, crushing the grains of thought into the flour of words.

Dread moved in her heart. Dread, but no surprise. "Where?"

"Along the high-hill river valley between Pedham and Langenvik."

Her fingers brushed through silver-soft fur as she swept up a handful of rune-bones and poured them, with brittle clicks and clatters, into their bag. The bag, she tied at her belt, which held also a sheathed seax, a short but sharp stabbing blade.

"How many?" she asked.

"Fifty."

"Fifty?" At that, surprise did come, flavoring the dread, enhancing it the way salt enhanced the taste of a broth.

"At least."

Hreyth touched the ash-wood amulet of Yggdrasil, the World-Tree, hanging around her neck on a cord.

Fifty at least.

She looked at Egil, the craggy outcrop of his nose, the knotted jut of his jaw, the broken expanse of his brow. His skull was bald, scar-gnarled, and misshapen. When he gave over to his battle-rage, there was no warrior more ferocious and feared, and his sword Life-Breaker had sent many men to the corpse-halls.

But his eyes, meeting hers, shared her unease.

"We must be quick," she said, and reached for her cloak.

***

Kjarstan's boldness and boasting, his promises of war-plunder and wealth as they brought death to their enemies, had carried them well through the first days of their ride. They talked and laughed, joked and sang. Every man of them, they knew, would win glory and fame.

Too long had they sat idle, wintering in their seized hall, feasting and fucking and throwing dice. Too long since they'd felt the crisp wind on their faces, heard the ring of steel and the clash of shield-walls. Too long since they'd slashed and stabbed, hewn and hacked, heard the screams of their enemies, smelled the blood-stink and shit-stink of gutted entrails.

Oh, there was joy in it, joy in war, joy in slaughter and carnage. A joy and a passion and a fire like nothing else. Whatever delights a man might take from riches, from meat and mead, or in the arms of a woman... only when he confronted death could he truly be most alive.

And if he should be struck down? If he should be pierced by sword-blades or spear-points, cut by axes, fall and be killed? A man could hope for no better end! Who would wish to die old and infirm, weak and feeble? To die of sickness, or drowning, or foolish mishap? A man must die well to earn his place at Odin's table!

Away from the sea, into the high country, they rode. The coastline fell away behind them. Creeks tumbled down rocky clefts. Vales lay open, bleak and muddy, but beginning to green. Twigs budded. New grass grew. Snow lingered in the lee-shadows of ridges, dirty ice-patches un-reached by the sun. Now and then, hares scampered or a scrawny deer stepped. Once, they glimpsed a bear, lean and hungry, but not so hungry as to dare menace men and horses.

They made camp by night, building fires, setting watches, sleeping bundled in blankets and cloaks. Jugs of sour barley-beer they'd brought with them, bread and hard cheese, smoked fish. To those who'd come from Pedham, the few youths and women never before gone far from home, it was both a frightening and exciting adventure.

Soon, they reached the high-hill river valley, long and slope-sided as if scooped in a trench from the earth. Above it rose rugged peaks, white-topped the year 'round. The river itself, fed by many more rushing creeks, flowed fast and full. Stones and boulders littered the ground, strewn like pebble-pieces of some giant's game.

Clouds drifted in. The day, not warm to begin with, cooled and grew damp. Mists whirled in ghostly skeins along the water. The horses' breath billowed steamy vapor. Men and women pulled their cloaks more tightly around their bodies. Beads like dew-drops collected on the fur trim of hoods.

The red banner hung limp and dispirited from its pole. Stefnir, Kjarstan's nephew, swiped moisture from his forehead and wrung it from his fair hair, then cursed as some trickled down the nape of his neck.

The talk, laughter, jokes and singing dwindled. Soon they went on in silence, a sodden silence broken only by the plodding squish of hooves, the creak of straps, and the faint jingle of mail.

The mists thickened. Or a fog rose. Or the clouds lowered. Or all of those, together and combined. The world turned to greyness, dreary and blurred. The snow-peaks vanished, the land lost its edges, the trees faded to suggestions, and the boulders became indistinct. The river, off to their left, was a liquid whisper more felt than heard or seen.

"Stay close," said Kjarstan, his voice both oddly loud and oddly muffled. "No one goes straying, no one gets separated."

So he said, but when each of them could only see a few

horse-lengths to either side, such words proved less than reassuring.

"It will clear soon," Kjarstan added. "If it does not, or this Hel's-gloom worsens, we'll stop for a while and wait it out."

The horses trudged on, heads low, manes and tails dripping. Everything smelled of wet wool and leather. Unwelcome thoughts insinuated their way into minds. Hel, as Kjarstan had mentioned… Hel, goddess in whose bleak realm resided the miserable dead who had not won their way to Valhalla…

Someone did try to bolster their spirits with another song, but the sound of it was a dirge and was soon let trail away. The silence returned.

Stefnir gripped the banner-pole with a half-numb, clammy hand. His other held the reins, though slackly, his horse following that of Rikolf, just ahead.

How suddenly their moods had changed… how distant in memory seemed the smoke and hearth-fires and cheer of the hall… or the fervor of riding to battle… how far and distant and impossible…

His horse stopped. Stefnir saw that Rikolf's had stopped as well, though he could barely make out more than its hindquarters. Not even Rikolf's red cloak was visible.

From somewhere behind him came a sudden low gasp, or cough. Stefnir turned his head, but only grey fog and vague shapes met his gaze. He opened his mouth to call a question—was everyone all right?—but his skin prickled with unaccountable gooseflesh before a single word passed his lips.

With his knees, he nudged his horse a few paces forward, meaning to bring himself up alongside of Rikolf. He would ask the older man before bleating like some frightened little lamb—

Rikolf's saddle was empty. His horse only stood there, head down, reins dangling.

A cry wavered out of the mist, a woman's cry, over almost as soon as it began. He heard a man's grunt, and a thump.

His nerves shrieked.

"What is it? Who's there?" he shouted.

No one answered.

"Kjarstan?"

There still was no answer.

"Anyone!?"

And still, no one answered.

The silence returned again.

The silence returned again, and was complete.

***

Kjarstan would not, would *never*, break his oath.

This, Udr Udarsson knew as well as he knew his own name, and the names of his father and grandfather before him. This, he knew as well as he knew his own heart.

The very implication was an insult, the kind of insult only answerable by blood. To suggest Kjarstan had not only broken his oath but utterly betrayed his king and kindred by joining with that yellow piss-dog, Gunnleif? For that, even blood would not suffice.

Yet, when the expected day of arrival came with no sign of his banner… when a second day passed the same, and a third… when possible explanations for delay wore thinner and thinner…

What else were men to think?

Udr and Anbjorn told them what to think.

"If Kjarstan is not yet come as promised," they'd said, "it is because some ill fate or fortune has befallen!"

They, two of Kjarstan's best and most loyal warriors, had accompanied King Jorfyn's messenger to Langenvik as proof of intent. Their earl—their *friend*, and war-brother!—would not lightly cast them aside as hostages.

"On my life, I so swear it," Udr had said. "On my life and my sword."

"Both of which," a dour old lord called Olla had retorted, "will fast be forfeit if you are proved false."

"It is that misbegotten whoreson Gunnleif you should give blame," Anbjorn said. "If his dogs struck Kjarstan by surprise in the hills—"

Back and forth, they had argued, Jorfyn's advisers voicing their doubts, Udr and Anbjorn their protestations. Finally, with harsh words about to turn to harsher blows, the king intervened. A small group of swift riders, he declared, would go out in search of Kjarstan's missing men. A dozen, no more. To seek sign or answer, and return with news.

"We will ride with them," Anbjorn had said.

"Madness!" cried Olla. "If they *are* to stand hostage against treachery, do not let them leave!"

"Do you say," asked Anbjorn, with a dangerous hush, "that we would turn against our own king?"

"I say," said the old lord, "that you would be loyal to your earl."

Anbjorn might then have struck him, respected elder or not, if Udr and Jorfyn's *skald* hadn't intervened.

Again, the arguments raged with much shouting, until the king decided *one* would go while the other stayed behind. It satisfied none, but mollified enough, and so the matter was settled. The king then had them draw lots. Udr was chosen to ride.

He rode with a handful of others selected by the earls and from the king's own guard. They set out for Pedham, back-tracking the route Kjarstan should most likely have taken. On rare occasion, they ran across spies or scouts from Gunnleif's army, dispatching them with ruthless efficiency of sword and spear.

Now, they had reached the high-hill river valley, and something was not at all right. A strange mood crept over them, a strange apprehension. Talk died away. Men tensed in their saddles and twitched alert at every bird-call or noise. More than one checked to see his blade rested loose in the scabbard, ready to be drawn.

Udr himself felt uncommonly jumpy, his sack tight, his skin crawling. Nothing he could see, hear, or smell gave any reason for such skittishness.

The valley ahead lay peaceful, dusted fine green from the new-growing grass. The river flowed smooth in its course, disturbed only by the silvery leap-flicker and splashing of fish rising to snap at skate-flies.

Still, his palms clutched, sweating, at the reins as he guided his horse through the random scatter of stones. He found himself wishing the lots had drawn differently, with him the one to stay behind at the war-camp where it was safe.

Which was no sort of thought for a warrior... a wrong sort of thought in more ways than one... and he could not say why.

Further on, one of Jorfyn's men gave a shout of discovery. When the others neared him, they saw he'd found a horse. Udr recognized it as one of the horses from Pedham, wandering saddled and bridled but riderless among tall grey standing stones, nosing at the tender green shoots to graze on the new grass.

"It bears no wounds, nor bloodstains," someone said. "Where is its rider?"

"Look, there's another, by the river there, drinking."

"Riderless as well, with panniers and packs untouched."

"Why would they abandon their horses yet laden?"

"They did not abandon their horses," Udr said. "They must have been attacked."

"Well, if they were, why would the attackers not have—?"

"Here!" called another man, amid a jumble of stones. "See this."

They rode to him as he stood over a bright splash of crimson that Udr first took for blood. Then he recognized it as a crumple of cloth, white on red. A white sword on a red field, attached to its pole but lying forsaken on the ground.

Udr sprang down and bent to it. "Stefnir never would have let drop his uncle's banner."

"Then where is he? Where are they?"

"Dismount. Spread out and search."

They did so, nervously, their former apprehension creeping again along their nerves.

"I see a shield." A man pointed. "And a spear beside it."

"Broken?"

"No, not broken, not so much as scratched."

Without any order given, they gathered together, forming a defensive circle as if in anticipation of attack. Udr shivered, and by no means was the only man to do so. The air had gained a sudden chill.

And when had the sunshine given way to this fog?

***

The war-camp of King Jorfyn consisted of tents and huts surrounded by trenches, thorn-brambles, and angled rows of stakes hewn to crude points. The banner of the king—three white serpents interlocked on a triangular green field—flew accompanied by the banners of other earls and battle-chieftains.

Njoth, Jorfyn's *skald*, brought Hreyth and Egil into the makeshift *wittan*-hall, where gathered the king and his advisers.

It was a small assembly, a half-dozen earls and war-lords seated on benches by a stone-ringed central hearth-fire. Apart from them stood a young man with a dark beard; he was unarmed and his posture declared his resentment of that fact.

The king himself—of middle years, greying but not wrinkled, hale and hearty—wore a tunic of green wool with white *wyrm*-work embroidery at collar, cuffs and hem. He held across his knees a scepter, a long whetstone below topped by a piece of whale-ivory carved into entwined serpents. His cautious, intelligent, war-weary gaze fell upon the newcomers.

Two other women were also in attendance. One, red-haired and curvaceous, sat near the king's side, nursing a babe at one plump, freckled breast.

The other, immense and imposing in shining battle-glory, stepped to block Hreyth's way. The sword strapped across her back must have measured four feet in the blade. Its grip-worn leather hilt proclaimed it was by no means just for show.

"I am Valhild," she said. Her helm hung on a strap at her side, leaving her bare-headed with myriad thin, close-woven blond braids. A scar sliced her chin. "First among the king's guard."

"Hreyth of the Grey Cloak."

"So, you are the rune-witch Njoth's been going on about?"

"I am."

"Hmf. I expected some haggard old crone."

"It seems we are both of a sort to defy expectations."

"True enough." Valhild's gaze swept Hreyth's mail-coat, and the sheathed seax at her hip. She grinned. "Mine's bigger."

Hreyth smiled, touching Rook-Talon. "Mine gets the job done."

Valhild roared a laugh and clapped her on the shoulder hard enough to stagger her on her feet. "I like this one," she told the king, then turned to Egil. She towered over him, but he did not back down. "And who's this?"

"Egil Einarsson," Hreyth said. "Or, Egil Splitbrow, as men call him."

"I can see why." She inspected the scarred, fissured dent at the front of his bald, lumpy skull. "You must have a hard head."

Egil looked up at her, mouth unsmiling, eyes flat. "It gets the job done."

Again, the big woman laughed, louder than ever. She slugged him on the arm. The sound was like that of a mattock meeting a bull's carcass. "I like this one as well," she said to King Jorfyn. "You'll do worse than to put your trust in them, I think."

With that, she stepped aside and let them pass into the circle, where spaces were made for them on the benches. Further introductions were made. The angry, resentful young man apart from the rest was called Anbjorn, who followed Kjarstan, the missing earl.

There had not been much in the way of serious confrontation between their armies as of yet this spring. The sides were too evenly matched, neither leader wanting to risk a direct assault, neither having the numbers to make a proper siege. So, they sat across the bay and tide-plain from each other, with occasional scout-parties and skirmishes, negotiations, insults, raids, and harassment.

"Fifty men more or less," said Jorfyn, "may not seem like much in a war. But these are Earl Kjarstan's men of which we speak. Among the best, each worth any three of Gunnleif's."

"Any *five*," Anbjorn said, earning him not a few glowers.

"And in battles such as we face here," the king continued, unde-terred, "every man counts. If Kjarstan had come as intended, we would have taken the town by now."

"But, if Kjarstan has joined Gunnleif," put in an old earl, Olla, he of the sourest expression, "those same fifty men, whether worth five or three, will slaughter us like wolves upon lambs."

Jorfyn raised a hand to forestall an argument. Or, rather, to forestall the rekindling of an argument that had already gone on far past its welcome—Anbjorn protesting his lord's loyalty, Olla doom-mongering, the others debating how those fifty men could turn the tide and which way, and so on.

"I cannot move against Gunnleif without knowing what's become of Kjarstan," the king said, addressing Hreyth and Egil directly. "I need him with me. More vitally still, I need him not against me."

"Your spies at the town?" asked Egil.

"Have heard nothing beyond that which we know."

"Would be hard to keep so many men secret."

"Agreed," Jorfyn said. "Regardless of where matters lie with his loyalty—which I have never before had reason to doubt—I cannot believe he could be with Gunnleif and we've no word of it."

"Nor would they have deserted," Valhild said, which brought fervent agreement from Anbjorn. "We're not speaking of Saxon farmers running back to their fields, or dirt-eating Britons skulking in the bushes."

"Then there's the matter of the riders we sent out," Jorfyn went on. "A dozen men, hand-chosen by myself and my earls."

"And Udr, my war-brother," Anbjorn said. He shot Olla a look like an arrow. "Unless you think Udr betrayed them, led them into a trap."

"They have not returned," said Olla, uplifting his palms as if that itself proved enough.

"I've told you, something happened to them. Something strange."

The old earl scoffed. "Armies of men don't just disappear. It isn't as if they were at sea, where they could have been sunk, lost, and drowned, ship and all."

"Folk do vanish," said Njoth, the *skald*. He was lamed, absent a leg at the knee, getting about on a stout wooden crutch. "Not only at sea."

"My grandmother would tell me of farmsteads, or villages, or whole halls abandoned," Jorfyn's wife said, lifting her babe and patting its back to draw up a milk-burp. "As if overnight, leaving work half-done on the loom and unfinished meals upon the feast-tables."

One of the other earls nodded. "Mine would tell me of travelers venturing into dark forests or over high passes, never to be seen again."

"But not," Olla said firmly, "whole armies out of thin air! Grandmothers' tales? We'll be talking of dark-elves and *seidr*-magic next!"

"Aren't we already?" Hreyth asked. She rose and moved near the glowing hearth, turning in a slow circle to let them all see the strangeness of her mis-matched eyes—one blue as the fjords, one amber-gold. "Is that not why I'm here? Your king's *skald*, in his wisdom, sent for me... because folk *do* disappear, or worse."

No one answered. Only a few—Valhild, Anbjorn, Njoth, and the king most among them—could long withstand her gaze.

"We may think we are mighty, with our kingdoms and oaths, our laws and law-speakers," she went on. "We forget there are older places, and things, of this world."

Njoth nodded vigorous support. "If they trespassed on a giant, a dwarf-cave, a troll-den... if they woke a dragon from its slumber... disturbed a grave-barrow..."

"There's no knowing what they might have unleashed," Hreyth

finished for him. "And whether it will be satisfied with whatever it's already done, or will come looking for more."

***

In the town was the army of Gunnleif Guthnarsson, whose banner—a snarling yellow dog on a triangle of black—waved from the top of the walls. Shields hung there as well, round shields painted half black and half yellow. Spears leaned ranked against the ramparts, an iron-tipped forest.

But no one came out to challenge or follow as their company of eight rode from Jorfyn's war-camp beside Langenvik's broad bay.

With Hreyth and Egil were Valhild, of course, and Anbjorn, and four other warriors chosen by the earls.

The day was brisk and clear, the wind off the sea sharp as a blade's edge. Eventually, as they rode amid idle conversations, a burly swordsman named Atli asked Egil what someone always seemed eventually to ask.

"Does she lay with you?" he whispered. "Is she your woman?"

He no doubt intended discretion, but Hreyth's ears were keen. She hid a smile as Egil made his usual growling reply.

"Ask such again, and my fist will give answer."

There was then a moment of cautious, considering silence. Then one of the others—called Thrunn—mentioned he'd heard it likely they'd see a rainy spring, and his friend Osig replied that a rainy spring meant a fair summer, and so the subject was safely changed.

Valhild, who'd also heard the exchange, grinned wryly at Hreyth and made more distance fall between their horses and those of the men. "Will *your* fist give answer if I ask you the same?"

"Oh? Have you an interest?"

She snorted. "Not in you. I only fight and drink like a man."

Hreyth's eyebrows rose.

"He seems tough," said Valhild, as if by way of explanation.

"The toughest."

"But that wasn't my question."

Hreyth released her reins with one hand, and made a fist—a rather small one. She looked at it, then looked at Valhild, and chuckled. "To what end, breaking my fingers?"

"You might land a lucky blow."

"I'll not chance it. As for the question beyond the question, Egil was brought orphan to the hall before I was born, and is as a brother to me."

Again, the big woman snorted. "*There's* a story told often enough. If I'd a sack of silver for each lovestruck fool I'd seen crying over his mead because of some girl who held him as brother or friend..."

"Tyr's truth in *that*," Hreyth agreed, rolling her eyes. "But, in this matter, it is as I say."

"Very well, then. How came he by his distinctive scar?"

"When he was brought orphan. His village fell under attack. His family was slaughtered, he himself injured and left for dead, only a child. My mother tended him, took him in. She was a healer... of sorts." She frowned. Speaking of her mother was not something she often did, or found pleasant.

Most folk, realizing as much, let it pass. Not so Valhild.

"Of sorts?"

"She brewed potions. Both helpful and... otherwise. They say she poisoned her husband."

"Did she?"

"I believe so. I was too young to know at the time. I remember he beat her, and they hated each other, and when he died, his kin accused her of murder."

"Your mother murdered your father?"

"No," she replied. "That's why her husband beat her."

"Ah," Valhild said, nodding in worldly-wise comprehension. "What of your true father, then?"

Hreyth shrugged. "Of him, I can say only what was told to me, and it sounds the most terrible arrogance."

"I like terrible arrogance."

"You would."

"Don't make *my* fist give answer!" Valhild hefted hers, the knuckles callused, a design of Thor's hammer marked into the skin with needle and ink.

They both laughed.

"As I was told it," Hreyth said, "during a long year when the men and their ships were away a'viking, a stranger visited the hall. A lone wanderer who wore a grey cloak and a strip of cloth bound over his lack of an eye. He sought to discuss *seidr*-magic with my mother, staying three days and three nights as her guest."

"And when he was gone…?" Valhild made a rounding gesture in front of her belly.

"And when he was gone." Hreyth mimicked the gesture.

"A one-eyed wanderer in a grey cloak, eh?" She whooped, drawing the attention of the others. "You're claiming Odin All-Wise himself—?"

"I do not claim so, only say as I was told, and I warned you it sounded a terrible arrogance."

Just then, Anbjorn signaled urgently. "Tracks," he said. "Hoof-prints. They must belong to Udr and those who rode with him."

"Let us investigate," said Valhild, testing how her great sword rested in its scabbard. She winked at Anbjorn. "Remember, if you're leading us to some trap or our doom, I'll cleave you from crown to crotch."

"I assure you," he told her earnestly, "I've not forgotten."

***

They crested a rise and beheld the broad river-valley, green and peaceful, dotted with dark, coarse boulders and smoother grey standing stones. No carrion-crows circled, no scavengers roved, no stench of decay reached them on the mild spring breeze.

All that moved was the rippling current of the water, shining like glass; a few fish leaped, a few birds flew. Here and there, horses grazed.

Horses... many still saddled and bridled... the buckles glinting in the sun... other glints and flashes of metal showed from the grass... as if from sword-blades or bright-polished helms.

"I see no corpses," Valhild said.

"I see no one at all," added Osig. "They aren't here."

"But they *were*," Anbjorn said. "I know these horses. I know this gear. That's Kjarstan's war-stallion! And, there, his banner, by those stones! Stefnir would never have let it fall so long as his arm held strength."

"Unless they fled," said Inglar.

"They did not flee!"

"What, then? Did they surrender? Were they taken, meekly, without a fight?"

"I'll give *you* a fight, you—"

"Come and try—"

Valhild nudged her horse between them, a one-woman shield-wall with a dangerous scowl. "Settle it later," she said. "Or *I'll* settle it now."

There were no corpses, no indications of struggle... only wandering, riderless horses... shields and spears and a banner-pole as if carelessly cast aside... dropped swords or cloaks... simply strewn here and there among the random scatters of stones...

"*Could* they have ..." Thrunn trailed off, as if unable to bring himself to utter the words.

"Vanished?" Egil suggested.

"Pff, vanished," muttered Inglar, then subsided as he caught Valhild's look.

"They *were* here," Thrunn said, in a slow but solid sort of reason. "Now they aren't. So, they must have gone somewhere."

"Then, Freya's tits, *where*?" Anbjorn flung up his arms in frustration.

They dismounted, one by one, warily. Hreyth last of all swung down from her steed. This was not what she had expected to find, no monster's slaughter-yard, no grave-barrows or rock-hewn giant's halls. Some other mischief seemed at work here, a subtler magic, *seidr* or sorcery.

"Someone lost a boot," Osig said.

Anbjorn held up a helm, undented, undamaged. "This is Udr's. He had it from his father. He wouldn't have left it, not while he lived."

Atli stooped to a twinkle in the grass and came up with a jeweled brooch in his hand. "And who, winning such a battle, would walk away without taking plunder?"

"This was no battle," Egil said. "There's no blood. Not a drop to be seen."

"The king sent skilled warriors," Inglar said. "Are we to believe none of them so much as wounded a foe?"

"Or fought foes that did not bleed," Anbjorn said.

Osig eyed him dubiously. "Every living thing bleeds. Man, beast, or monster."

"And men plunder," said Atli.

"Living *or* dead, men plunder," Egil agreed. "And beasts devour, and monsters do both."

"But, whatever did this, did neither." Valhild frowned, shaking her head. "I don't like it."

Hreyth unfastened her cloak as the others continued their search. She spread the heavy grey wool cloth on the ground and laid the wolf pelt upon it.

"It's as if they *did* vanish, plucked from their very saddles as they rode." Anbjorn turned his friend's helm over and over in his hands.

"And from their very boots?" Thrunn glanced uneasily around.

"While leaving the horses untouched?" Inglar added. He had not joined in the searching, but stayed near Hreyth, watching her.

For those questions, none of them could offer answer.

Onto the silver lushness of the wolf's fur, Hreyth cast a fistful of rune-marked bones from the bag at her belt. They landed with rattling clicks, some atop others, runes showing blood-red, soot-black, and gold. She studied them, the patterns of them, the arrangement they'd made, their meanings and messages.

Earth-Smoke-Man-Stone-Breath-Change-Theft-Danger.

She rose slowly, gaze sweeping over their surroundings. The peaceful river valley, green with new grass... its sloped sides curving up toward rugged, rocky peaks... the spring-blue sky overhead now gone pearly-pale... skeins of mist lingering in dark fissures and clefts, wafting in curls around the bases of the many tall and scattered standing stones...

The stones.

The standing stones, akin to those erected by the Old People of half-forgotten days, but these not towering huge and set in henges with altar-slabs and crosspiece lintels.

These, of smoother texture and lighter hue than the rocky peaks above or crag-ridges and dark boulders jutting from the earth... these were each at the most not much taller than a man, and of a random, straggling-line order... but for the cluster, almost a ring, near to where Anbjorn had found his war-brother's helm...

The stones.

An apprehensive silence had fallen, creeping with the same soft, insidious stealth as the fog seeping from the shadows. When she spoke—"The *stones!*"—her words came louder than intended, a sharp cutting of that silence. Everyone started, some gasped, and several hands went to hilts.

"By Odin, woman!" Inglar thumped a fist against his chest, as if to correct his heart in its cadence. "Are you trying to shock us to death?"

She turned her gaze upon him, and judging by the way he blanched, whatever Olla's man saw in her mis-matched eyes made him regret his choice of words.

"*Stanvaettir,*" she said.

"What?" he asked, scowling at her.

Egil's own eyes widened beneath his scar-creased brow. "Creatures of the deep earth."

"Breath-stealers," Hreyth said. "They draw out the life of men, transform them, and leave only stones in their place."

Another silence fell, this one filled with dread and understanding. Even Inglar, hand still held over his heart, showed a reluctant, dawning comprehension.

"Are you telling us," Anbjorn began at last, his voice low but shaking, "that these... these stones all around us... are... my earl, my war-brothers, my friends?"

Before she could reply, a whirring rain of arrows smote into their midst.

One struck Thrunn in the shoulder, piercing through his mailcoat. He shouted with mingled pain and surprise. Another nailed Inglar's wrist to his torso; he fell back, uttering a strangled cry. A third grazed Valhild's leg, slicing the leather and the skin beneath.

"Shields!" the big woman bellowed.

Egil raised his, stepping in front of Hreyth as another volley flew. Arrows thunked into heavy limewood or buried their iron heads in the grass.

Atli and Anbjorn raised their shields as well, overlapping their rounded edges, forming a line to either side of Valhild and Egil. Thrunn, swearing ferociously, ripped the arrow from his shoulder and joined them. Blood gushed from his wound, coursing over and dulling the shine of his mail and his bright silver arm-ring.

Blades sang from their scabbards. The nearest horses, no longer placid, whinnied and ran, stirring whorls and eddies in the low, rising ground-mist.

"Inglar?" called Valhild.

"Down but living," Osig said, crouching beside the wounded man, then seizing his other wrist as he reached for the protruding arrow-shaft. "Don't pull it! You'll just die all the sooner."

Inglar coughed. Red bubbles burst on his lips. He fumbled at an awkward angle with his left hand for a spear, unwilling to face death without a weapon in his grasp.

"Gunnleif's yellow-dog bastards!" Atli peered through a gap in their small shield-wall. "Behind the ridge by that broken boulder...

fifteen, maybe twenty."

"Outnumbered *and* they have archers," said Valhild. "The gods must have thought we needed more of a challenge." She eyed Thrunn's blood-soaked mail. "How's your arm?"

He grimaced. "Still attached, and it's only my left." In his right hand he held a short-handled axe with a wide, sharp double-blade.

"They'll be coming for us," she said, after another flurry of arrows struck their shields.

"Let them come."

"Then why aren't they?" asked Anbjorn. "They've stopped shooting."

"No sense wasting arrows on limewood," Osig said.

"Come on, you ass-sniffing curs!" Atli shouted at their foes. "Fatherless bitch-whelps! Come and fight! Come and die!"

"They're afraid," Egil said.

"They should be," said Thrunn.

"Not of us."

"They *should* be!" he repeated.

"They suspect something," Hreyth said. "They know something is wrong here."

From behind the ridge came a man's voice. "Drop your swords and surrender!"

"Fuck your sister!" Atli retorted.

"We want to talk!"

"*We* want to fight!"

Anbjorn nudged Atli with an elbow. "They might know what happened."

"They might shit amber, too, but I wouldn't bet on it."

"Enough," Valhild told them. She lowered her shield enough to poke her helmed head up over it. "Talk, then!"

"We're looking for some missing men."

"As are we, but there's no one, only horses."

"Do you take Ulfvir Sneasson for a fool? We know Earl Kjarstan was coming this way."

"We've not found him, either."

A pause followed, no doubt marked by hasty conference behind the ridge. Then the man—Ulfvir—spoke again. "But *we* have found *you*."

More bowstrings twanged, more arrows flew. So did a hurled spear, which struck, shaft quivering, in Valhild's shield.

"So," said Atli as they hunched behind their limewood wall. "We talked."

"You didn't tell them about the stones," Hreyth said.

"You didn't finish telling *us* about the stones," Anbjorn said. "*What* about the stones?"

"Forget the god-fucked *stones*!" Valhild ducked a second spear, then hefted her great sword, its long blade sheened silver in the fog-dimmed sunlight. "Stand ready!"

Gunnleif's men charged with their yellow-and-black shields held high, weapons drawn, uttering full-throated war-cries. As they came, Egil and Atli stepped forward and met the first two with a tremendous crack of wood and iron.

Then the battle was upon them.

Thrunn reared back and flung his axe; it spun whickering through the air and caught a brown-haired man squarely between the collar-bones. Valhild's sword swept in a deadly arc. Her foe shield-turned the blow, leaving his body exposed, and Anbjorn sank his blade deep into the man's belly.

Ulfvir, the leader of the enemy, the one who'd said he wanted to talk, wore the shaggy yellow-brown pelt of a dire-hound for a cape. Its forepaws were knotted at his neck and its head, still with skull and jawbone and muzzle of snarling teeth, jounced on his shoulder as if snapping to bite. He, like Thrunn, carried an axe. Unlike Thrunn, he did not throw it, but brought it down in a furious slash that cleaved Atli's shield into kindling—and Atli's arm at the elbow.

Atli screamed even as he thrust his sword at the dog-pelted man's face, but missed, and stumbled to a knee with his stump gouting crimson and the fingers on the severed portion twitching and clenching convulsively in the grass. Ulfvir again lifted his axe, meaning to take Atli's head, but Egil bashed his shield's boss into the man's chest, making him stagger.

A younger man, lean and lithe and quick, darted around his companions, perhaps thinking to get past Valhild and Anbjorn, and strike from behind. But Valhild, for all her size, was almost as quick as him. She side-kicked, shattering his kneecap, tripping him. He went sprawling near Hreyth, who gripped her seax two-handed and seated it hilt-deep in the small of his back, the blade's edge grating against his spine.

"You were right," Valhild said with a grin. "It does get the job done."

"We haven't time for this," Hreyth told her. "We'll disturb the *stanvaettir,* and end up stones ourselves!"

"You're the rune-witch!" Whirling, Valhild swung in another great slicing arc, shearing mail and leather like thin cloth, opening a foe's torso from shoulder to hip so that his entrails bulged obscenely from the gore-purple cut. "Think of something!"

The chaos and clangor filled the world. Sounds rang, echoing strangely in the gathering mist. War-cries and death-cries trembled the air. Osig fell with his thigh slashed to the bone, the blood a torrent. Anbjorn dodged a sword-thrust, then went reeling from a helm-cracking blow to the head.

Think of something. She was the rune-witch; she must think of something.

Inglar had somehow gotten to his feet, despite his right arm still arrow-pinned to his body. He'd shed his shield and picked up a spear in his left hand, and now ran at their enemies, shrieking like a *berserk* out of legend. He ran at Ulfvir, the dog-pelted leader, who'd retreated already from Egil's relentless defense of the stricken Atli; Ulfvir scrambled back further, his courage deserting him in the face of Inglar's ferocity.

Another of Gunnleif's men moved to meet Inglar's charge. The spear-point rammed through yellow-and-black painted wood, splintering both shield and shaft with loud cracks, fouling them entangled and useless. Still like a *berserk*, Inglar ignored the man's desperate sword-strokes. With another enraged shriek, he flung himself full on his foe. As they crashed together to the ground, Inglar tore free his arrow-pinned arm from his chest—the dark jet of heart's-blood leaped in a fountain—and buried the arrowhead in the other man's throat.

The mist roiled, the mist churned.

Hreyth ducked the wild swing of a black-bearded man's blade. She heard Egil shouting, and Valhild's war-cry as the big woman's great sword claimed another quick kill. She heard screams and insults, and Ulfvir demanding their deaths. She saw bodies writhing in pain amid motionless corpses.

She saw the mist, a thick fog now, not rolling in from the sea or river but issuing like cold smoke creeping and seething across the earth. Wisps flowed down from fissures in the rugged rock-ridges, and a billowing undulation from the broken boulder's wide rough-edged cleft.

Stanvaettir, she had thought, but she had been wrong.

The black-bearded man swung again, hilt-first for her temple as if meaning to stun her senseless. Hreyth caught the blow with her left forearm—she felt the snap reverberate all the way to her toes—and Rook-Talon's sharp, sturdy blade stabbed up through the man's beard and chin-underside, scraping teeth, cleaving tongue, to impale his brain through the roof of his mouth.

He collapsed in a violent, blood-vomiting gurgle. Hreyth wrenched Rook-Talon loose, the *seax* dripping. She tried to raise her left hand to swipe the scarlet mess from her face but it would not obey her. She blinked, shaking her head frantically, clearing her eyes.

With one, that of blue, she saw only what anyone would—the fog, wafting thick to surround them.

With the other, that of gold, she saw more.

Things *moved* in the mist, shapes and forms, lines and symbols, dancing like *wyrm*-work embroidery, a glow of strange colors pulsating the way embers waxed and waned through a coating of ash.

Not *stanvaettir*, no.

Something else. Something bigger, something more.

And it was coming, coming for them. Caring nothing for which lord, king, or earl they might serve.

The others, friend and foe alike, did not notice. Their sole concern was the battle, fiercely fought and costly on both sides.

Think of something, rune-witch, think of something!

Rune-witch.

She spun. There, undisturbed amid the combat and carnage, was her grey cloak, laid out on the ground with the wolf-pelt spread upon it. No one had trampled or trodden upon it. The rune-marked bones seemed faintly to flicker with their own inner light. The air above and around them was clear. Even as she watched, tendrils of eddying mist wafted near to the bones, then curled away.

"Gather!" Valhild bellowed, standing over Anbjorn—whether he was dead or merely unconscious, Hreyth couldn't say. "Gather, fall back, and shields!"

Those who could, did. Egil all but carried Atli, who had bled to a whey-water pallor from his severed arm. Thrunn came limping, fending off two warriors, many small wounds making him resemble a hound-harried boar near the end of the hunt.

For Osig and Inglar, there was no question; they had gone to the mead-benches of Odin's golden hall. Gone, but with glory, and far from alone. If Ulfvir had led twenty, he'd lost more than half. But he, and his remaining men, looked largely unhurt, and still outnumbered the paltry defense of Valhild, Egil, and Thrunn's three-shield wall.

Hreyth could have picked up Anbjorn's shield and joined them, for what little good it might have done. Instead, she ran for her cloak through the thickening mist. It swirled about her legs, made her mail-coat glisten silver, and cooled—chilled!—her flesh.

"I'll take your heads back to Gunnleif in a bag," snarled Ulfvir.

"We'll set them in a row and piss on them in turn."

"You'll have to come get them," Valhild replied.

"With pleasure," he said. Yet he and his men hung back, hesitant to again throw themselves against the formidable strength of Valhild's and Egil's swords.

"Hreyth?" Egil spoke with low urgency.

"I'm here."

For a terrible moment, she felt the fog congeal dense and heavy against her skin, weighing on her limbs like damp wool, and she thought she was too late. But another step brought her into the clearness. She bent and seized the edges of the wolf-pelt, scooping its contents into a bundle as best she could with one hand.

"What's happened to the sun?" someone asked, one of Gunnleif's men, anxious.

"Never mind the sun," Ulfvir told him. "Kill them, or I'll bring *your* heads back to Gunnleif!" He raised his sword, and howled. *"Kill them!"*

As they howled in return, emboldening their spirits to renew battle, Hreyth ran back to the close cluster of her companions. She let go an edge of the wolf-pelt, casting the rune-marked bones in an arc at their feet and hoping it would be enough.

Then Egil swept her behind him, and their small shield-wall braced for the overwhelming charge.

***

The overwhelming charge did not come. It ended in a dark whorl of mist, a chill breeze, a shiver, and a sudden hush.

Hreyth, who had closed her eyes in wincing anticipation, opened them. Valhild cautiously lowered her shield. The others did likewise.

At their feet lay the rune-marked bones. Around them, already, the mist was lifting, dispersing, giving way again to mild spring sun and clear blue sky.

In front of them, mere paces from their line, several tall grey shapes jutted from the earth at canted, slanted angles. By some, shields painted half yellow and half black had fallen. By some, swords and spears.

Crumpled at the base of the nearest was a dire-hound's shaggy pelt, knotted at the forepaws.

No one spoke. Their throats worked as they swallowed, their mouths faltered at forming words, but no one spoke.

The dead, those slain in the battle, were as they had been. Unaffected. So too were the horses, nosing in the grass. Atli barely clung to life, and Anbjorn was little better.

Of Ulfvir, and his men…

Only stones left in their place.

Valhild found her voice first, looking at Hreyth. "Your runes protected us?"

"I hoped they might."

A nod, and the firm squeeze of Valhild's big hand on Hreyth's mail-clad shoulder, conveyed her thanks. Then she stepped toward the group of stones, though made no move yet to touch.

"Wh-what happened to them?" stammered Thrunn.

"The *stanvaettir* stole their breath," Egil said.

"Not just *stanvaettir*," Hreyth said. "Another power."

"And it did this?" Valhild indicated the valley. "All this?"

"With each theft, growing stronger. Growing hungrier, more ravenous."

"How do we kill it?"

"Kill it?" Thrunn gaped. "How?"

"That's what I'm asking," she told him. "Can it be killed?"

"I don't know," Hreyth said. "Perhaps."

"If not?"

"If not," said Egil, "this valley won't contain it long."

Hreyth thought of farm-steads and villages… of Jorfyn's war-camp and Gunnleif's forces at the town… two armies, and more men arriving every day in answer to the summons of their earls.

"It emerged from those fissures in the rock, and that broken boulder's cleft," she said. "There must be something under us, underneath the ground. A cavern, pit, or tunnel."

"A lair," said Valhild with a grim smile.

"My runes stopped it once. If I can find where it came from, I might be able to block its way, and trap it in the earth."

The grim smile widened. "Well then, what are we waiting for? It's gorged itself and gone to rest; let's finish this before it wakes again."

Egil shook his head. "We cannot all go. We have injured men."

"And the king must be warned," Hreyth said. "Gunnleif, too, for that matter; they'll have greater worries if this evil descends."

"You heard them," Valhild said to Thrunn. "Get horses. Take our wounded, and the bodies of our dead, and ride for Langenvik."

***

Egil bound Hreyth's arm with two sticks, and strips cut from her cloak. "You're hurt," he said, tying more of the grey cloth into a sling. "Are you certain?"

The pain *was* considerable. It gnawed the way the wicked squirrel Ratatoskr gnawed the bark of Yggdrasil as he ran up and down its great ash trunk. But she could not let it dissuade her.

"I work the runes. It must be done."

Valhild approached, settling her helm securely in place. "Thrunn's off," she said. "Gods willing, Anbjorn and Atli survive the journey, and the tale be believed when they get there."

"Gods willing, we survive our journey as well." Egil donned his own helm and helped Hreyth to her feet.

"What a tale we'll have to tell if we do!" Valhild clapped him on the back. "Over mead-bowls in the king's feasting-hall! Hailed as heroes, shining with silver and gift-given gold, our names long remembered in saga and song."

"And if we don't survive?" asked Hreyth, clutching her bag of rune-marked bones in her sling-bound hand.

The big woman laughed. "Then I trust you'll put forth a good word to the All-Wise All-Father for us, so that even if we do not fall in battle, we'll still tell our tale over mead-bowls in *his* feasting-hall!"

They'd left their three horses loosely tethered with some that had belonged to Ulfvir and his men, and proceeded to the rocky ridge from behind which the first hail of arrows had come... and from fissures in which Hreyth had noticed the curling, coiling, issuing mists. The broken boulder reared there, cracked nearly in half to reveal a narrow crevice running throatlike into the earth.

Its wound looked recent, perhaps frost-made over the past winter, perhaps sundered by tremor-quakes as Ymir stirred in his giant-god sleep. Scree and shards gritted underfoot at each step, stone chips and flecks sifted loose as they passed.

"I go first," Egil said, in a tone brooking no argument.

Hreyth followed him, and Valhild brought up the rear. The way was narrow indeed and grew narrower still, until Valhild could not even have drawn her great blade. Her shoulders and Egil's scraped the rough passage walls. The air was cool, heavy with moisture. Thin shafts through the rock let in weak threads of sunlight; otherwise, they went in a deepening darkness.

Until Hreyth, with one of her mis-matched eyes, again glimpsed the waxing and waning strange glow, etching lines not unlike runes themselves in the misty shadows opening ahead.

Here was a roundish cave-chamber of tapering formations, joined columns, and shallow ridge-lipped pools where drips plinked and rippled. At the heart of it brimmed a well, a well rich with power, *seidr*-magic.

This, yes, this was the source of it. This cousin to Mimir's Well, where Odin had made sacrifice in exchange for knowledge. This well, which drank rather than quenched, which took rather than gave, which stole and consumed rather than bestowed.

Across its glass-black surface, images seemed to whirl and flow... images, visages, spirit-faces... bodies drifting, floating weightless as if in liquid, trailing hands and limbs and hair...

"Do you see them?" she whispered.

"I see only water," said Egil.

"As do I," Valhild agreed, adding, "What do *you* see?"

"Later. I'll begin setting the runes. Be ready."

"For what?" Valhild asked, eyebrows lifting.

"I wish I knew. But, if anything comes up from the well, hold your breath."

Their expressions suggested they found this scant comfort, and Hreyth felt the same. Held breath against a power such as this? A power that had drawn life from so many men, leaving only stones in their place? Dotting the river-valley with them, silent standing warnings of an incomprehensible danger... and she had come, a young rune-caster of uncertain parentage, armed with little more than her witch-queen mother's lore...

But she *had* come, and as she'd told Egil, it must be done.

She reached into her bag of rune-marked bones. Old and worn smooth, ivoried, rolling and clicking beneath her fingers. One by one, she brought them out and set them in a ring around the well's rim.

The spirit-fraught glassy surface heaved in a sudden, terrible bulge as her circle neared completion. Hreyth sprang back, gasping. Her heel caught on the lip of a shallow pool. The last rune-bone clattered to the cavern floor.

Mist plumed from the well, wreathed her hand, gloved it, wrapped her arm, and pulled. It was insubstantial yet solid, mist made iron, iron made mist. It had her to the elbow, to the shoulder, to the throat.

From somewhere sounding far away, she heard Egil call her name, and Valhild shout a battle-cry.

The gasp she'd taken, she held. Struggling to do so, locking jaw and mouth, lungs already throbbing with a burning ache. The mist engulfed her head and chest.

She felt a tug at her belt—Egil, anchoring her with one hand as he groped along the floor for the fallen rune-bone. His boots slid as he, too, was inexorably pulled toward the hungry well.

Then came a violent, striking crash—metal on stone, steel on stone, the steel of Valhild's great sword-blade, hewing and hacking at the cave ceiling's formations. Sparks flew. Again and again, the strong steel struck, until stone cracked and shattered. Huge fanglike chunks of rock, some broken off in pieces and some at the root, smashed down.

The solid mist released abruptly. Egil and Hreyth pitched backward. As his free arm flailed, she saw the rune-bone in his fist and grabbed for it.

A heap of rubble filled the well, mounded there like some crude and makeshift cairn. Valhild stood astride the pile with her sword-hilt in both hands and the blade poised for a downward thrust.

Around the well's rim, the rest of the rune-ring was—by god-miracle, praise Odin!—undisturbed. Hreyth slid the last bone into place. The rune upon it flashed an almost blinding gleam that raced around the circle in a line like fire.

The chamber's air changed with an odd, pressuring pop. The cave walls shook; more rock-chunks fell from the ceiling and water sloshed over the lips of the pools. There was, for a moment, the sense of a vast, gusty sigh, an exhalation from the very lungs of the world.

The sense of *seidr*-magic dwindled to a fading echo, then was gone.

She shakily released her long-held aching breath. Her gaze found Valhild's in the gloom, then the familiar crags and outcrops of Egil's scarred features beside her.

They had done it. They had lived. They had won.

Tales over mead-bowls, feasting-halls, hailed as heroes, shining with silver and gift-given gold, names long remembered in saga and song.

Through the half-collapsed passage, they picked their bruised and battered way back to surface and sunlight. The high river-valley spread green and peaceful before them, horses grazing in the new spring grass.

But, although the spell had been broken, it had not been un-made... and where so many brave men had once been, still re-mained only stones.

HEL'S ROAD

R ime-ice edges the rough stones, broken beneath a low, dull
sky
Clothes fall to rags around us; we stagger, haggard, wan and
naked
Our feet unfeeling, numb and bloodless, frozen flesh corpse-grey
Skin in shreds, brittle toes blackened, the white bones protruding
Frost crackling and joints creaking with our every onward step
We walk, we fall, we crawl and stumble, then we rise, and walk again
Far above, beyond our sight, arches the rainbow span of bridge
Where gallop the gold-shod war-steeds of the Choosers of the Slain
Valkyries bold and fierce and beautiful, Odin's terrible shield-maids
Bearing from the battlefields the bravest to their glorious reward
That is not to be our fate, those of us who walk on Helheim's road
We did not die as warriors, helmed and mail-clad, sword in hand
Ignoble illness claimed us, injuries and age; misfortune stole our lives
Man or woman, rich or poor, old or young, king or earl or slave
Fair-faced as elves or troll-foul in form and feature, no matter
In this bleak and barren landscape, we are now made all the same
Ahead of us, forever far, our wretched journey will reach its end
But there will still be no succor there, no surcease from our sorrows
At the ice-gate rise tall twin pillars burning with a cold blue fire
Guarded by the great hound Garm, sharp teeth and strong jaws stained
Beyond the gate stand vast mansions where dwell neither agony nor joy
In those halls the hearths give chill steam, damp ashes without warmth

Hunger heaps high the feasting-tables, the drink-bowls brim with thirst
The beds are made from restlessness, the blankets woven of discomfort
Lame and Lazy are the servants, the songs silent, the harps unstrung
Here is where the dead-queen rules, Loki's daughter, Hel herself
She sits silent upon her carven throne, robed in mists and gloom
Half pale and fair, half dark with decay, a god chained by her side
The sister of Wolf and Serpent works no other cruelties or tortures
There is no need; her pitiless indifference proves punishment enough
The one mercy she grants us is to forget who we once were
In gold-gleaming Valhalla the brave gather, and await the final call
To war against the giants in the twilight destruction of the world
But we, the dead of Helheim, will have our own part in that battle
To walk again, to march forth in our mindless, thronging thousands
To walk again, to fight and fall and falter, and finally to truly die.

MONKSHOOD

"**A**ll right, tell me," Ivarra said, plucking another tuft of carded wool from the basket at her feet. "You've been humming and smiling to yourself the whole morning. What is it? Or, rather, who is he?"

Svanna did not bother to try and dissemble, making no show of either innocence or bafflement. She smiled again, in a way that struck Ivarra as almost salacious. The tip of her tongue slipped along the underside of her upper lip.

"Mmm, oh my dear sister," she sighed. "If only you knew."

"So, you *have* met someone?"

They sat, spinning and sewing, in buttery sunshine dappled by elm-shade as a fair breeze blew. In the fields, peasants toiled and in the meadows, sheep and goats grazed. A bell tolled from the stone monastery beyond the orchard. The summer day was both warmer and milder than those they'd known before, as children back home in rugged Daneland before the ships of the Ragnarssons brought armies to Northumbria.

Though sisters, they did not much resemble each other. Svanna, a year the elder, was long-limbed and slender, as graceful as the swans for which she was named. Her hair hung fine and straight and red-gold to her waist. Ivarra, by contrast, was more plump and well-rounded, with dimpled cheeks and sky-blue eyes. Tousled curls the color of honeyed cream spilled over her shoulders.

Svanna glanced about, then leaned close over her sewing. "Just wait until you see him," she said. "A golden Dane, a warrior, tall and fair, beautiful enough to ride in Baldr's own company!"

Ivarra shushed her, making her own hasty glance around. "Our stepmother will have you to church in a heartbeat if she hears you invoking the *pagan* gods." This last word, she uttered in peevish, timid imitation of their father's pious new wife.

"Pff, I'm not afraid of her, the dumpy porridge-faced sow." Yet, at that, Svanna glanced about again to be sure they were still alone.

"The priests, then. Or Father."

"As if Father truly cares what the priests think."

"He did let them baptize him." Ivarra touched the circular amulet of silver she wore, depicting Yggdrasil the World-Tree with reaching roots and arching branches in intricate knotwork design. "And he'll have us baptized too, I've heard him say so."

"It's nothing," said Svanna with a dismissive wave of her hand. "A dunk and a splash to placate the Saxons." Dismissive or not, though, she made sure to keep her voice low as she said it, and cast another glance around.

"But never mind that... a warrior, a Dane? Who?"

"I don't know his name yet."

Ivarra sighed, exasperated, and picked up her spindle again. "So you haven't met someone. You're making it up."

"I've met him. We just... haven't spoken much." She purred like a contented cat by the hearth.

"You can't be suggesting..."

"I most certainly can."

"You haven't! You're teasing me, and I don't find it funny."

"Twice now he's visited me, my golden and glorious Dane." Svanna pressed her folded hands to her bosom. "Oh, sister, he is the most magnificent of men! He has eyes like the fjords, and his teeth are so straight and so white! His beard feels like rabbit's fur, and his kisses—"

"Svanna!"

"I swear by Frigg and Freya, it's true."

"I'm to believe that you have a lover? Who's visited you? When? And how? Your bed is in the same room as mine."

"Do you remember the potion old Hilga told us of?"

Ivarra scoffed. "Old Hilga's always going on about this potion or that spell. I'm surprised Father tolerates it. She'll be lucky if the priests don't decide to burn her for a witch."

"But," Svanna pressed, "do you remember, or not?"

"What potion?"

"The one brewed from monkshood. The one that she said would show us, in dreams and omens, our future husbands."

"Silly superstition and nonsense. You didn't believe her, I should hope?"

"I did and I do. And, Ivarra, it works!"

"*That's* what this is?" she cried, and it was Svanna's turn to shush her. She dropped her voice to a whisper that was almost a hiss. "A dream? Only a dream?"

"Never before have my dreams seemed so real. It's as if he's there... I can see him and hear him... smell him... taste the mead on his lips and the salt on his skin... feel his touch..." She flushed at the recollection, shifting upon the stool. Her tongue slid over her lips again. "Oh, and the way he touches me... the way he kisses me... like I've never been touched or kissed before... like none of these ham-handed Saxon louts, and certainly like none of the clumsy, groping boys we knew back home. My golden Dane is a *man*, dear sister, a man from head to toe."

"A dream-man, a dream-Dane. Listen to yourself. It's shameful."

"What if it *is* an omen, a vision, just as Hilga said? A foretelling of who my husband will be? What if he *is* real?"

"He's still not sneaking into your room at night."

"No? Then explain these marks." Svanna unpinned the bronze brooches that pinned her wool over-dress, and tugged down the collar of her linen under-shift to reveal reddish blotches on the white slopes of her breasts.

"Am I to think those are love-bites?" asked Ivarra, letting the scorn drip from her tone. "You've caught a rash, is all."

"I've not caught a rash! They're from him!"

"They might be from this potion of yours, that I grant you," Ivarra said. "Isn't monkshood poisonous?"

"If improperly used, but I prepared it just as Hilga said, and I drank it when I went to bed, and I dreamed of him, the same man, my golden Dane, both nights." She crossed her arms defiantly, giving Ivarra a challenging stare.

Which mood of defiance and challenge, Ivarra ruined by a sudden spate of snickering. "Put those away before someone sees you. Our stepmother would have fits, and if any of the priests came up from the village, they might burst into flames."

Looking down, Svanna saw how her pose and her lowered undershift did make for a rather prominent jutting, and she too began to laugh. "A fine thing," she said as she fixed her brooches, "when my own sister doesn't believe me."

"I believe some of it. Most of it, even. I believe you made the potion and drank it, and I believe you dreamed lewd dreams of some handsome, imaginary Dane. But I'll sit wakeful all night and watch over you if it'll prove that no strange men are visiting you."

"Or you could try the potion, and see for yourself."

"What if he liked *me* better?" Ivarra smoothed the front of her own dress over her more ample curves, then fluffed the tumbled masses of her hair.

Svanna uttered a gasp of mock outrage and indignation. "Why you little man-stealing bitch! Keep away from my Dane!" They laughed again together, bending back to their tasks with spindle and needle.

When they had done for the day, Svanna persuaded Ivarra to help her gather fresh monkshood to brew another draught of the potion. They went together, past the village, gossiping and giggling, until they came to the place where the monkshood grew, along the crumbling ruins of a rambling old rock wall. There, purple flowers nodded at the ends of tall, sparsely-leafed stems. The topmost petal of each formed a large cowl-shape over the others. It did, Ivarra noticed, give the plant a vague likeness to the bowed head of a robed, praying priest.

Once Svanna had carefully gathered as much as she needed, they made their way back to the house that their father had gained by way of his marriage to the widow of a Northumbrian lord. Weary of war, he'd chosen to settle and make peace with his conquered foes, sending home for his daughters and servants and the rest of his folk. Now, his beard greying, he was jolly and complacent, living the good life.

The house was not a long hall as the sisters remembered from when they were children, but a large and sprawling manse of many rooms. Earl Ivar himself was away, attending a council-mote of the men of the Danelaw. Had he been present, their stepmother no doubt would have been at him again with her urgings to see the sisters baptized, church-taught, and respectably wedded. In his absence, however, she did her best to ignore and avoid them.

They, for their part, were just as glad to ignore and avoid her as well. The evening meal eaten, they went to the bathing-chamber and then to the room that they shared. Two of its walls were stone, cut-and-mortared, with woven wall-hangings to fend off the damp chill. Here were stout frames of wood through which ropes were laced to hold straw-stuffed mattresses, piled with blankets. Once, not so long ago, they'd shared the same sleeping-platforms as their parents and kin, to either side of the long hall, under fleeces and furs. But that practice, said their stepmother, was indecent and pagan, so now each of them had her own bed.

"Do you still intend to sit up all night, waiting and watching?" asked Svanna as she stirred the clay bowl in which the potion had steeped and was cooling.

"There's no man visiting you," Ivarra said. "Only your dream-Dane."

"Explain the marks, then."

"I did explain them, I told you, a rash."

"Pff." Svanna drank off the bowl's contents and got into bed.

Ivarra, shaking her head, blew out the soapstone oil lamp's flame and got into her own. She drew the blankets to her chin, closing her eyes.

She woke some time later to the sound of her sister's sleep-mumblings, and the rustle of mattress-straw, as if Svanna tossed and turned, restless, upon it. She then heard the mumblings become murmurs and sighs, and a drowsy moan.

"Oh... mmm, yes..." Svanna sighed. "Yes, my love, yes... ooooh yes..."

So, the potion did bring lewd dreams after all, did it? Ivarra smirked to herself, rolling to a more comfortable position on her side. But, as she was on the verge of sinking back into her own rest, she became aware of something that was not quite right.

The room had been in darkness; she'd blown out the oil lamp herself. The windows were small enough to admit little in the way of sunshine even by day, and shuttered now against the night. Yet there was a faint glow along the seams of her eyelids, as if a dim candle were lit somewhere nearby.

Svanna caught her breath with a gasp and let it out in a soft, yearning cry.

Ivarra opened her eyes. There *was* a faint glow, a dusky twilight radiance quite unlike that of any candle or lamp that she knew. She blinked, unable to discern its source.

More rustlings came from the direction of Svanna's bed, and when she turned her gaze that way, Ivarra forgot all about anything else. A startled exclamation lodged in her throat, leaving her voiceless. She stared in helpless and dumbstruck astonishment at the sight that met her shocked eyes.

Her sister was no longer alone. Another figure was with her, a larger figure, whose muffled words were indistinguishable but whose deep chuckle was decidedly male. Ducked as he was beneath the blankets, Ivarra saw only the shape of him moving lower, and heard the moist noises of him presumably kissing his way down from Svanna's breasts to her belly… and lower still.

"Ah!" Svanna writhed and squirmed. Her long hair tangled in fine skeins across the mattress. With her eyes shut, she remained unaware or uncaring of Ivarra's gaze. Her hands clutched at the blankets, between her upraised knees, in the vicinity of where the man's head must have been. She bit her lip. "Mmm… oh! Oh!"

Whoever he was and whatever he was doing, it clearly gave Svanna no end of pleasure. She moaned, quivering, quaking. Ivarra had witnessed love-making often enough, and was no stranger to it herself, but she had never heard or seen a woman so overcome with ecstasy.

She could not look away. A fascination held her as if spellbound. A flush suffused her cheeks. She felt a slippery warmth kindling in her loins and was suddenly eager for a man's touch, eager and even jealous, envying the skill with which Svanna's mysterious lover brought her again and again to impassioned heights.

He reared up then, shedding the blanket from his shoulders. There, in the strange glow, was—

Ivarra's mind reeled.

This was no glorious golden Dane, no warrior.

This was no man at all!

What knelt above her sister's nakedness was a creature of nightmare. Something gaunt and twisted, hideous… its skin violet mottled with grey… something that seemed made of bone and leather and cold, dark, seething smoke.

She only found she could move when she passed a shaky, horrified hand over her eyes. But, after she blinked and her sight cleared…

It *was* a man.

A glorious golden Dane, beautiful enough to ride with Baldr's own company.

His eyes like the fjords, his teeth so white and straight as he smiled… his full beard looking soft as rabbit's fur… his muscular torso, flat stomach, lean hips and strong thighs… the lush blond expanse of hair on his chest tapering to a line that ran from his navel to his...

Then it was the nightmare creature again, and Svanna reached for it, imploring, needful, whimpering with wanton lust... she did not *see*, did not *know*... as it fell upon her and she wailed such a cry of delight it was a wonder the whole house didn't hear...

And then it was the man, the golden Dane as Svanna saw him...

...then the creature...

...the man, firm buttocks flexing...

...the creature, bony wings unfurling, whip-thin tail lashing and snapping...

...the man, sweat gleaming on his back...

...and Svanna, oblivious to the changing flesh, sobbing desperate exhortations for more, more, harder, faster...

...and the creature obliging with fervor, features contorted in leering lust...

...the slick sounds of their quickening coupling...

The world swam and spun dizzying grey around Ivarra. Her last thought was the realization that she must be fainting.

She woke to her sister's voice again, to Svanna singing a love-song as she brushed out her long hair until it shone. As Ivarra sat up, Svanna turned to smile. The smile faded at once into an expression of concern.

"Ivarra?"

"I... I saw. Last night." She nodded toward Svanna's bed.

"Did you?" Svanna brightened again. "I told you he was real!"

"Svanna, no... it wasn't a man, not a man at all... it was something else... a monster, a..."

"What *are* you babbling about?"

The story spilled from her, describing in faltering phrases what she'd witnessed. Rather than grow alarmed, Svanna swiftly grew angry. Then furious.

"Why would you make up such ugly and hateful lies?" She slapped down her brush and stormed from the room.

Ivarra went after her, but could not placate her. Svanna refused to listen to another word.

Yet something must be done, Ivarra knew that much. Her sister might be in danger. Something must be done.

With their father away and their mother dead, she was not sure where to go for wise counsel. Not their stepmother, certainly. She considered seeking Hilga's advice, but Hilga had told them of the potion to begin with... what if the old woman truly *was* a witch?

Most of the day, she passed in fretful indecision, stung anew each time Svanna's indignant glare fell upon her. They had always been close. They had always been friends as well as sisters. She did not want hurt feelings between them. But neither could she ignore what had happened.

At last, the tolling of the monastery's bell gave her an idea. The priests often bragged of their powerful god. They kept relics. They spoke of miracles and angels and saints. Perhaps they would know what to do.

She set off as if intending to go to the village on some errand or other. No one questioned her, or objected that she went alone. Once there, however, she circled around to the orchard, its trees laden with ripening apples and plums.

Apprehension crept through her. It felt deceitful to do this, deceitful and dishonest, after all her mocking of their stepmother's piety and their father's baptism. She tucked the silver amulet of Yggdrasil well into her collar as she approached the stone church-buildings.

The closer she got, the more Ivarra wondered what in the world she would say to the priests. How could she broach the subject of her sister's dream-Dane nightmare lover to churchmen who might be quick to judge and condemn? They all seemed, in her experience, to be either old, frail and fussy; pink, pompous and well-fed; or scowlingly stern with pinched disapproval.

For that matter, she wasn't sure how to address them. A priest was called 'father' and a monk 'brother,' but which was which? Or was it the other way around?

The orchard was empty. So too were the gardens. The bell had ceased tolling and the monastery sat draped in thick silence. Not a monk, a priest, or a churchman in sight.

Were they all at prayer, or whatever they did? Would she further offend them by interrupting?

Ivarra was on the verge of giving up when she finally saw someone reading in the privacy of a low-walled alcove. He wore a hooded robe of black wool belted with a braided cord. An ivory crucifix rested against his chest and a book rested open upon his knees. His hands were, she noticed, soft and white, uncallused, long-fingered and fine. Not hands accustomed to hard work or weapons.

As she stood there, hesitating, uncertain, he somehow became aware of her presence and raised his bowed head. In the shadows of the cowl was a face both pale and youthful, beardless, yet strikingly handsome.

He started at the sight of her. Ivarra stammered an apology, which he demurred with a gesture. He closed the book, setting it aside on a bench, and pushed back his hood. Dark hair fell over his brow, cut short but not shaved in that bald-pated manner. His eyes were dark as well, dark and expressive.

"Aren't you Lord Ivar's daughter?" he asked.

"Ivarra," she said.

"I am Brother Gregor," he said. "But... what brings you here?"

She opened her mouth, still without knowing just what she might say. As had happened that morning with Svanna, she found the whole story spilling from her.

Unlike Svanna, however, Brother Gregor did not grow angry or indignant. He showed discomfort at the tale but not disbelief. When she finished, he agreed that something must indeed be done.

He showed yet more discomfort at the prospect of hiding that night in the room she and Svanna shared, but Ivarra was far less concerned with priestly propriety than with her sister's safety. If he could vanquish the evil spirit himself, so much the better... and if not, he'd need the proof of his own eyes before he could bring it to the attention of his superiors in the church.

Ivarra led him into the house during the bustling spate of activity before the evening meal, concealing him on a stool behind the wall-hangings next to her bed. Then she went to eat—though she had little appetite, and less with Svanna continuing to snub her. She hoped that when this was over, when the monkshood potion's spell was broken, Svanna would forgive her.

Only as she was returning to the room after her visit to the bathing-chamber did it occur to her that she wore nothing but a thin linen sleep-shift under her fur wrap. Should she have worn something heavier and more modest to bed, for the sake of the poor flustered monk hidden behind the hangings? If she had, though, might not Svanna have questioned it?

And she had to admit, if only in the secretive back of her mind, that it sent a tingle of excitement through her nerves. To think that Brother Gregor could be watching her as she slid the wrap from her shoulders... that his gaze, with chaste but tormented yearning, lingered on the fullness of her breasts... the nipples poked like tight little buds against the fine cloth...

Why was a man so young and vital and darkly handsome being wasted on the church? Those soft hands of his, with their long and elegant fingers, were not made for the coarsening toils of hard labor, but did that mean they were meant solely for ink and parchment and book-bindings? Should a mouth so sensual, so finely formed, be devoted to prayers and hymns instead of sweet kisses?

She'd hastened through her bath so as to be already in bed and feigning sleep by the time her sister came in. It proved difficult, her pulse fluttering, her every sense seemingly all too aware of the presence of the monk sitting concealed behind the wall-hangings but a scant arm's reach from her bed.

Svanna did come in, and for all the notice she gave Ivarra, the feigned sleep might not have been necessary. Without a word, without so much as a glance, Svanna blew out the lamp and got into bed.

Some time passed in quiet darkness.

Ivarra twice caught herself on the verge of dozing, and twice stirred herself wakeful again. The third time, she must in fact have slept, because she woke with a twitch and a stifled gasp.

The dusk-purple glow, from no visible source, once again illuminated the room. From the other bed came the rustling of the straw-stuffed mattress, the murmurs and whispers of low voices. There then commenced the faint but rhythmic creaking of ropes and wooden bed-frame.

Quietly, cautiously, Ivarra slid from beneath the blankets, on the side of her bed nearest the wall-hangings. She edged them aside and found Brother Gregor asleep, slumped on the stool with his shoulder pressed to the wall and his head lolling, a pale hand draped over the holy book upon his lap.

It lent him an even younger look, an innocence and vulnerability that transcended handsomeness into beauty... the fall of his hair across his white brow... the inviting curve of his slightly parted lips... thick lashes fringed dark against his cheeks... and how smooth his skin looked... how smooth it would feel if she brushed her fingertips ever-so-softly along...

She touched his knee instead, tapping it through the woolen robe. He stirred, licked his lips—Ivarra almost swooned—and opened his eyes. Such eyes... those warm and dark pools into which she could have willingly fallen.

Confusion held him for a moment, then cleared. He heard the sounds and blushed at their very clear meaning. He grasped the holy book as if for strength and nodded to Ivarra. With great stealth, she edged the wall-hanging aside again, revealing the scene to the monk's gaze.

Svanna knelt astride her lover, her spine arched, her head tipped back so that her hair fell shimmering to the cleft of her buttocks. As she moved, rising and falling, moaning her pleasure, the mingled scents of sweat and love-musk filled the air.

The creature ran its leathery hands over Svanna's breasts, her waist, her belly. It leered up at her, mottled lips peeled back from sharp teeth like crooked black thorns.

Brother Gregor made a choked, strangled sound in his throat. His eyes went so wide they appeared about to tumble from their sockets. His lips formed silent words—prayers, Ivarra supposed— and a hectic crimson flush colored his fair complexion.

Ivarra flushed as well, feeling that slippery heat of envy and desire kindling again in her loins. She saw that, below the braided cord he wore for a belt, the front of Gregor's dark wool robe protruded in a rather substantial bulge. Overwhelmed by her own lustfulness, she reached over. He jumped, gasping, but his hips pushed forward in an involuntary surge and the firm flesh seemed to leap at her touch.

Gregor caught her wrist but his fingers were strengthless and trailed away with no further resistance. He groaned under his breath. She squeezed, and rubbed, and he trembled all over.

Across the room, Svanna's movements quickened into urgency. Her moans turned to fevered whimpers, almost frantic. The figure below her had the Dane's visage now, muscles rippling in his chest and flat stomach as he matched Svanna's pace.

Ivarra watched almost without seeing. So too did Brother Gregor, who clasped weakly at the ivory crucifix he wore with his right hand while his left dropped as of its own volition behind her to fondle her plump backside. After a moment's fumbling at the cloth, he'd gathered up the hem of her sleep-shift enough to caress her bare skin, and Ivarra's legs went weak.

His robe and loose knee-length linen drawers proved scant obstacle to her, and he groaned again as if in welcome agony or delicious damnation when she stroked him unimpeded. He made bolder exploration of her rump and thighs, fingertips probing, sliding in slow circles.

She felt as if she were melting, as if she were falling, as if she were liquid fire that simultaneously burned and quenched.

Then there was nothing else for it but to have him, to have him fully and deeply, in desperate passion. She stepped in front of him and bent forward just enough, and guided him. Gregor uttered a low cry, as of one suffering tormented damnation, but did not hesitate at completing their fleshly, urgent joining with eagerness and vigor.

Ecstasy rolled over her like waves endless upon the shore, and coursed through her with a storm's power as it gathered... and crested... and broke in a crashing turbulence more overwhelming than she'd ever known.

Again and again, that sweet storm broke. She was conscious only of the bed when they fell upon it, groping, kissing, struggling the rest of the way free from their garments. Again and again, he pleasured and plundered to the very depths of her body, and again and again she brought him to renewed readiness for more.

At last, when time had for Ivarra lost any or all meaning, they collapsed into exhausted slumber in each other's arms.

Morning was already well on toward noon when she revived, aching all over in the most delicious of ways. She stretched, smiling for a moment, before being struck by a sudden and terrible trepidation.

Brother Gregor was gone. Had he been able to sneak away, unseen and unnoticed? Or had he been caught? And if so, what troubles would there be? For that matter, even had he not been caught, what must he think? What might he do? In his mind, they must have committed the most woeful of sins.

She could not bear the thought of him being punished. Worse still, of him deciding he must punish himself.

Ivarra leaped from her bed, dressed with fumble-fingered haste, dragged a brush through the wild bed-tangles of her tousled honey-cream hair, and rushed from the room still affixing her belt and her brooches. She passed her stepmother without pause, ignoring that the woman was scolding at her for sleeping so late.

Svanna turned toward her when she came to the house's main hall. The hint of a smirking, knowing smile had only barely begun to form on Svanna's face as Ivarra dashed by.

Her sister called after her, but Ivarra did not pause. She ran on, out of the house, through the yard, down the lane toward the village and the orchard and the stone-walled monastery beyond.

Continuing to call out, Svanna gave chase. On any other day, with her long and lean legs, she should have swiftly outpaced Ivarra, but alarm lent Ivarra the far greater speed.

A dozen or so monks, clad in brown robes and hoods, made a silent and worshipful circle as an ancient priest of the frail and palsied variety droned on in some stuffy, unfamiliar language. When she burst into their midst, it was like a fox startling a flock of complacent fowl. They clucked and flapped in an uproar, regarding her the way they might have regarded a madwoman.

"I must speak to Brother Gregor," Ivarra said to the frail, ancient priest.

He blinked at her, wrinkled brow creasing further as he frowned in confusion. "Brother Gregor?" he echoed. "We have none here by that name."

"But…"

Svanna, having reached her by then, took hold of Ivarra's elbow. "Please pardon my sister," she told the churchmen, pulling Ivarra by the arm.

"What are you doing?" asked Ivarra.

"Come away, you goose," Svanna said.

Determinedly, she marched Ivarra back through the orchard. Only when the monastery was well behind them did she start to giggle, then laugh.

"A monk? A *monk*, little sister?"

Memory made Ivarra's face burn red-hot. "You saw, didn't you? You know what we…"

"Ah-ha-ha, you lewd and wicked girl! I mixed some of the potion into your drinking cup."

This time, memory made Ivarra's blood run ice-cold as she thought of the creature she'd seen with Svanna… whip-tailed and leathery, mottled, leering and dark.

Could that…? No, not Gregor, not her youthful and beautiful Gregor…

"Do you mean to tell me that he… wasn't real?"

"As real as my glorious, golden Dane," Svanna replied. "Now, hurry, let us go gather more monkshood, so we may summon them to us, again, tonight."

KVASIR'S BLOOD

In Jarl Thorvald's longhouse, fires blazed hot in the hearths and smoke hung heavy in the air. The feast-tables groaned beneath the weight of beef and pork, bread, cheese, butter, and nut-cakes sweet with boiled fruit. Great bowls brimmed with ale and barley-beer. From high-raised drinking horns, the honey-mead flowed golden.

In Jarl Thorvald's longhouse, drums thumped and harpstrings rang. Men boasted and jested and joked. Girls squealed and giggled, women uttered throaty laughs. Tales were told, songs sung and sagas said. Voices roared hearty approbation.

In Jarl Thorvald's longhouse, agate-carved game-pieces sat ready upon whalebone-inlaid boards and ivory dice clattered in wooden dice-cups. Dogs nosed through the floor-rushes for scraps. Children played with toy dolls and horses, with mock swords and shields.

In Jarl Thorvald's longhouse, the old jarl himself bestowed rich rewards on those who most pleased him. He was wise and wealthy, a generous gift-giver. At his side rested a chest of treasures: coins and hack-silver, brooches, bracelets, arm-rings and amber.

And Ofradr Ulfradsson, who should long since have been there, was not.

The squirrel-fur trim of his hood dripped sleet into his eyes. His wool cloak clung, thick and sodden, over his shoulders. Each plodding hoof-fall of his horse's slow, swaying gait struck up splashes from the puddles lining the muddy lane.

Lining it? Making it more river than road at this rate.

Ofradr squinted into the wet, grey gloom. How he hoped for the welcoming glow of the longhouse, torches beckoning!

But he saw only more rocky hills and stubby trees with their gnarled boughs rain-bent. Low clouds encroached close, obscuring the rest. For all he could tell of the landscape, they might have crossed this same stretch of lane time and again, going in circles and making no progress at all.

He swiped his wet brow with an equally wet sleeve and glared at the thrall who led his horse by the reins.

"You told me you knew these lands," Ofradr said. He'd meant to sound accusatory, but the words emerged sulky and petulant.

The thrall—a stout-bodied man, grubby, sparse-bearded, shabbily dressed—groveled. "I do, lord!"

"Then why are we not yet to Jarl Thorvald's hall?"

"We should be soon, lord!"

Ofradr groaned. There was no use in arguing, no use in further scolding. He needed to preserve his voice for the contests ahead. Already, he'd put it in peril, being out here so long in such wretched weather.

His nose trickled, running freely. He blotted it on the back of his hand, wincing at how raw and tender the rims of his nostrils felt. And was that a coarseness, a scratchiness forming in his throat? The soft tissues growing swollen, beginning to ache?

He prodded with his fingertips under the shelf of his jaw, pressing the flesh, testing for signs of pain. He swallowed thickly. A cough, now… a hoarse rasping cough… would be the end of his chances.

The rain worsened. The damp chill seeped into his bones. Ofradr tried to comfort himself with the prospect of a hot fire, a hot meal, a bowl of mulled mead heady with honey and spices. That liquid warm balm coursing down his sore throat… the sweet steam of it easing his nose and lungs… its kindling heat pooling in his belly, spreading through him to thaw his marrow… his heart lightened, his spirits lifted, the cares washed from his mind…

Yes, a bowl of mulled mead would set everything right in the world.

"Lord?" ventured the thrall, sounding fearful and more abject than ever. "I seem to have brought us the wrong way, lord."

"What?" Ofradr looked up.

"This creek, lord, with these split logs laid across… and that stone, the moss-covered one… I recognize this place, and we have come far from Jarl Thorvald's longhouse."

"How far?"

"Far, lord. Even if we turned now, we would not reach it by night-fall."

"*If* we turned?" echoed Ofradr. "What else would you have us do, if not turn?"

"There are, or were, some farm-steads not much further. If we sought shelter—"

"What do you mean, were? When I hired you to guide me, you assured me you'd grown up here."

"It has been years, lord. I was a boy. But I do remember. We are bound to find some welcome. Some food and a fire, someplace to sleep, and then we'll make for the jarl's hall at first light of morning."

Ofradr put his face in his fur-gloved hands. The prospect of a night spent in a farm-stead hovel… sleeping on a cot if he was lucky and a straw pallet if he was not, instead of on stout sleeping-platforms heaped with fleeces and pelts… dining on gruel and sour beer rather than boiled beef and mulled mead…

Then again, the prospect of a night spent huddled in his wet cloak beneath a tree, with only what wizened apples and cheese-rinds remained in his pack…

"Take us there, then," he said to the thrall. "Anything to get out of this rain and cold."

"Yes, lord!"

On they went, crossing the creek on the bridge-ford of split logs, passing the moss-covered stone, descending a rough slope toward a rugged country of valley folds sprawled around the base of a mountain.

The first farm-stead they reached was little more than a few char-blackened timbers leaning askew near a collapsed and abandoned sheep-byre, but the second looked to still be inhabited. The cottage had sod-and-stick walls plastered with daub, and a roof of dank thatch. Desultory smoke curled from the chimney-hole and faint light flickered through a crack in the door. To one side was a crooked fence around a mud-yard and a shed, where a goat eyed them dully while chewing a wad of hay.

The thrall hailed the house and an old woman answered. She was large-bodied but flabby, her skin loose in sags and wrinkles, hair straggling from under a kerchief, her mouth toothless and her features falling just short of crone-like. But she greeted them readily enough, bidding Ofradr come in to warm himself while the thrall settled the horse in the shed.

He needed no second invitation. Moments later, he huddled close to the small fire, holding his hands over it. The old woman bustled about, draping his cloak on a bench, lighting a fish-oil lantern that gave off a greasy, sputtering flame, and setting out two more clay bowls on her rickety table.

Her name, she told him, was Lodunng. She lived alone, with no near neighbors and few far ones, and it had been long since she'd had visitors.

"What brings such a fine youth to such a miserable place as this?" she asked as she ladled up broth from a pot.

"I am Ofradr Ulfradsson," he said. "Do you know Jarl Thorvald?"

"I know of him, to be sure," old Lodunng said. "This is his land. He sends his men out each spring and autumn to collect what is due. But, the jarl himself, I have not met, no."

The broth, when she passed him the bowl, Ofradr found to be a thin, watery concoction made from onions and dried fish. The accompanying bread was flat and lumpy, stone-baked, coarse-ground, hard, and tough to chew even for one who still had all his teeth.

"Jarl Thorvald is holding a feast and contest," Ofradr said. "He has need of a new skald for his hall, a poet and tale-teller, a singer of sagas and songs."

"Ah, and you are a skald?" Lodunng scrutinized him, then cackled. "So you must be, so fair and graceful, and with such a voice!"

At that, Ofradr permitted himself to preen a bit, smiling. Sometimes, remarks of that sort seemed to hide barbed insults within, as if obvious he certainly could be no kind of warrior, not him, slim as a girl and almost as pretty.

"Like sweetest honey, strained pure gold from the comb," she went on, marveling in admiration.

She spoke in reference, of course, to his voice. Which must not have yet been adversely affected by his ordeal, he was gladdened to know.

The thrall came in, stamping mud, and squatted by the fire with his bowl and his bread. The old woman poured them each a cup of beer as well. It was the sour stuff Ofradr had dismally imagined, its aftertaste a scum that made him think of stale sweat and feet.

"A skald," Lodunng said, with evident admiration. "At my fire."

"Yes, well," said Ofradr. "Thank you for your hospitality. We meant to be at the jarl's hall by now, but *he*—" here, with a jerk of his chin at the thrall, "—led us astray."

Mumbling apologies, the thrall gulped down the sour beer.

"Will you miss the contest?" Lodunng asked.

"It spans several days." Ofradr smiled again. "And even were I the last to arrive, I'm bound to win. There is no better singer in all the North-Lands."

"Are you so confident?"

"You yourself said my voice is like sweetest honey, strained pure gold from the comb."

"Yes, but there may be others who know all the sagas, or compose their own poetry, or are captivating tellers of tales."

"When *I* sing," he said, "men hush and women swoon. The

very birds go pale with envy. The gods themselves, in high Asgard, would weep to hear… and the dead in bleak grey Niflheim would, for that time, forget their sorrows."

Lodunng sat back and blinked at him, duly impressed. "Well, you *have* tasted of the skaldic mead, haven't you?"

He grimaced into the cup. "Do not speak to me of mead, when *this* is what you offer."

"The *skaldic* mead," she repeated. "Kvasir's blood, Odin's gift… oh, but surely you must know the kennings."

"Kvasir's blood? Odin's gift? Your words are of no sense, old woman," he said, waving a hand in a bored gesture. "Enough. The hour grows late and I am weary."

"Will you favor me with a song, then? Before you sleep?"

"No, I must not," he said. "I must preserve my voice at its best for tomorrow."

"Very well. But let me instead tell you a tale, one which I think might be well for you to hear. An old tale, of dwarfs and giants, and the gods…"

***

"That it should come to this," said Fjalar, to Gjalar, his brother. "That we two so cunning, the cleverest of dwarfs, must be brought so low."

Gjalar nodded. "To think we once took our ease in the feast-halls of kings."

"Eating from golden plates and drinking from golden horns."

"We, who worked our ruses upon gods and giants and men…"

"And now, here we sit in dreary poverty."

"With no fortune and no prospects."

"With nothing left to our names."

"Except for these three vessels in which our mother made mead."

"And not even honey enough left to fill them again."

They both sighed together in their despair.

"How much better it was when the gods were at war," Gjalar said. "Oh, there was ample opportunity for trickery then, was there not, brother?"

"Tricks and schemes upon both sides, ah yes, and rich profit to be won."

"A curse upon the Aesir and Vanir, and their new-sworn peace." So saying, Gjalar kicked a stone.

"It would not be so bad, but for Kvasir, that man they created." Fjalar scowled.

"Kvasir the wise," sneered Gjalar. "Kvasir the knowledgeable, answerer of any questions posed to him. Quite the accomplishment for a man born from *spit*."

"God-spit."

"God-spit, but spit nonetheless. That they sealed their truce by spitting into a vat, fine, hardly unreasonable. But that they'd then think to fashion a living *man* of it!"

"A man who goes all about the land, teaching, spreading wisdom," added Fjalar. "To *our* sorrow and undoing."

"Indeed! How are we now to earn a livelihood? How will we keep body and soul together?"

"Learn a trade?"

"A trade!" Gjalar cried. "Would you have us hammer and tinker and make trinkets for the gods?"

"Well, we must think of something. We must use our wits."

"We have made our way all this *time* on our wits, and relying upon the foolishness of others. Our *wits* have not changed. It is *their* foolishness Kvasir ruins."

Fjalar rolled his eyes, and spoke with great sarcastic scorn. "Perhaps we should seek *his* advice."

The two dwarfs laughed, not unbitterly. Then, suddenly, they paused. Their gazes met. Their eyes first widened, then narrowed, then gleamed.

"Brother…" said Gjalar.

"Yes, brother?" Fjalar asked, grinning.

"There is, nowhere within Yggdrasil's reach, any so clever or cunning as you. Even Loki himself, Laufey's son, could not devise so brilliant a plan!"

"Let us hope you are right, for even Loki himself, Laufey's son, could not outsmart Kvasir while hiding from the gods."

This, Gjalar knew to be true, but they resolved to be more cautious than was Loki's usual wont. In guise of seekers of counsel, they sent invitation to Kvasir that he should visit and be their most honored guest. They had, they said, many difficult questions in need of answer, questions such that might challenge even *his* vast knowledge.

Kvasir, who was wise but honest and unsuspecting, agreed.

No sooner had he arrived than—

"Now, brother!" shouted Fjalar.

He and Gjalar fell upon Kvasir and killed him with swift blows.

"We must conceal this deed," Gjalar said, "or we may bring down Odin's wrath upon us."

"Hang him and press him," Fjalar replied. "Crush his flesh so the blood is all drained out."

"But we possess no other containers to catch it, only our mother's mead-making vessels."

"So be it; we will brew the blood with the honey."

They did, and found the mixture became a most potent drink, so powerful anyone who drank of it would be imbued with the skaldic gifts of poetry, tale-telling and the singing of sagas and songs. The scent alone of this heady mead inspired Fjalar and Gjalar to craft an ingenious explanation for how Kvasir had happened to die.

"His very intelligence and wisdom caused him such a burden that he suffocated of it," they told the gods. "None in Midgard were learned or educated enough to pose him further questions. He could bear it no longer."

And the Aesir believed them.

"Ha!" they exclaimed. "We have done it! Let this be an end to the spreading of knowledge and wisdom in the world!"

To put this to an easy test, they set out straightaway to the home of a neighboring giant, Gilling, known to be among the most foolish of beings. Gilling, whose sons were grown and gone, lived with his wife in a stone hall on the shores of a deep lake.

This in itself was proof enough of Gilling's foolishness, as he feared the cold waters and could not swim. Yet so much more foolish even than *that* was the giant, he owned a boat... and it was a matter of mere moments' persuasion for Fjalar and Gjalar to convince him to row with them out to the very center.

"You are not up to some trick or scheme, are you?" asked the giant as he rowed.

"Us?" said Fjalar.

"A trick?" said Gjalar.

"A scheme?" Fjalar went on. "Whatever for?"

"To rob me of my gold," Gilling said.

"Why, Gilling!" laughed Gjalar. "You are a giant, and we two are only dwarfs. See how much larger and stronger than us you are!"

"Both of us together could not hope to fight against you," Fjalar said.

"It had best be not so," Gilling said. "I heard Kvasir, the wisest of men, is visiting these lands. When he comes here, I mean to speak with him and gain his counsel. If I learn you deceived me, I will crack your skulls like nutshells in my fists."

"We would never want that," Gjalar assured him.

"Is this the deepest part of the lake?" asked Fjalar. "The water is so very dark below."

Gilling glanced over the side, and shivered despite his immense size. "Yes. It is so deep here, not even I could touch the bottom."

"What a terrible fate it would be if your boat were damaged," said Gjalar.

"If it leaked," Fjalar said.

"If the hull-plankings were splitting apart."

Which, of course, the brothers had already seen to doing. As Gilling saw the water pouring in, as he felt it lap and splash at his feet, he went into a thrashing frenzy of terror. His struggles broke the boat all to pieces. Fjalar and Gjalar clung to the scattering flotsam, but Gilling did not think of it and soon the giant went under.

"Well, *he* was still foolish," Fjalar said.

"Now let us see if his wife is any less so," Gjalar replied.

After paddling their way back ashore, Fjalar climbed by stealth to the roof of the stone hall. He waited above the door. When he was in readiness, Gjalar commenced a loud and woeful clamor of weeping and wailing.

"Ah, Gilling, brave Gilling, his boat is wrecked asunder! He is sunk to the depths of the lake and drowned! He is dead! Ah, alas!"

Hearing this, Gilling's wife—who *was* no less foolish than her husband—rushed forth, shrieking with grief. No sooner had she crossed the threshold than Fjalar pushed down a heavy stone. It struck her on the head and she died.

They returned to their home, wealthy again with the gold and jewels they'd taken from Gilling's house. This pleased them both greatly, or did so until one of the sons of the murdered giants heard of their fate, and came for his revenge.

Unlike his father and mother, the giant Suttungr was no fool. He seized the dwarfs, closing his ears to their entreaties and explanations. He took them not to the deep lake but to the stony sea-shore, where the cold waves crash and the foam leaps and the cries of the gulls sound like the screams of the dying.

Wading into the surf, Suttungr placed Fjalar upon one barren rock island and Gjalar upon another.

"Now you have no boats to break," he told them. "Now you have no flotsam to cling to. When the tide rises, we shall see how well *you* swim."

Then he sat on an outcrop with his great arms crossed, watching.

In came the tide, ever higher. The islands upon which Fjalar and Gjalar stood became smaller, and smaller still. They retreated to the loftiest spots, but still the tide came in. The bitter salt-water lapped at their toes. It lapped at their heels and at their ankles. It engulfed their feet. It wetted their knees.

The dwarfs, unable to paddle to safety, began begging the giant for their lives. They promised to return Gilling's treasure, every coin, every scrap.

"I will have *that* regardless," Suttungr said. "It is mine by right, mine and my brother's, our inheritance."

The water reached to their waists. A wave-surge nearly pushed them from their precarious perches.

"Be merciful!" cried Fjalar.

"Spare us!" cried Gjalar.

The sea-spray dashed into their faces, the salt stinging their eyes.

"We'll do anything!"

"We'll reward you!"

They slipped, their heads dunking under, and scrambled to regain their footing.

"We have mead!"

"Magic mead!"

Gjalar coughed and Fjalar choked. Their arms flailed, slapping and splashing.

"Mead made from the blood of Kvasir!"

"Wisest and most knowledgeable of men!"

The water rose to their necks, to their chins.

"It grants any who drink it—"

"—the gifts of a skald!"

The water rose to their lips as they strained on tip-toe.

"Poetry!" shrieked Gjalar.

"The mead of poetry!" shrieked Fjalar.

Another wave sluiced over them, engulfing them. But Suttungr lunged out with his long grasp, catching the dwarfs each by the scruff of his neck. He hauled them ashore in the last heartbeat before they surely would have drowned.

Soaking, chastened, and humbled, they trembled. They brought Suttungr to their cave, where they returned to him the gold and jewels they'd taken from his father's stone hall. They gave him the three vessels of mead.

No sooner had the first taste touched his tongue than the giant knew he had come by a rare treasure indeed. He knew also the dwarfs were sure to betray him despite their promises, that they would kill him the moment they had a chance.

Yet, *he* had promised to spare their lives… and he prided himself on being of more honor than the likes of Fjalar and Gjalar.

Another sip of the mead gave him the answer. He chained them together in iron neck-collars and dumped them at the very gates of Asgard, letting it be known that here were the murderers of wise Kvasir, to be punished.

Then he hid the three mead-vessels away in the heart of a mountain called Hnitbjorg, setting his daughter to keep watch. The only passage to the spot was of so twisting and turning a nature that no one who had not partaken of the mead could ever find it, and so, only Suttungr himself knew the way.

Odin the All-Father, however, was curious enough to question the dwarfs before punishing them—he had them transformed into roosters, one crimson and one blood-red, whose doom-crowing would herald the end of all things, that which men call Ragnarok. Upon hearing their full tale, the All-Father resolved he must drink of this mead—for Odin was ever a seeker of knowledge and wisdom, such that he'd made sacrifice of his own eye and hung nine days and nights from the tree by Mimir's well.

He went first to Suttungr's brother, a giant named Baugi, who kept nine slave-thralls as workers to tend his extensive hay-fields. Odin, disguised, showed to the slaves a whetstone that would sharpen their scythes to the keenest of edges, making quick and light work of their labors. Each of them wanted it, and in their squabbles they slit one another's throats with the blades.

Baugi, having now nobody to toil in his fields, feared he would not be able to bring in the hay that summer. So, Odin, still in disguise, approached him with the offer to do the work of nine men, in exchange for a drink of Suttungr's secret mead.

"Over such," said Baugi, "I have no say… my brother hid the mead-vessels deep within the mountain, where he keeps it all for himself, with his daughter standing guard. Much as I would like a taste of the mead myself, he refuses. He claims he shared with me half of our parents' wealth as rightful inheritance, but the mead was his own fair reward for seeking revenge."

"We shall ask him together, when winter comes," the disguised All-Father said. "And should he still refuse you, we may think of something."

When winter came, and Odin had done the work of nine men, he and Braugi went to speak with Suttungr. They did ask him together, and he did still refuse.

"Not a drop," he told them. "Not a sip."

"As you know," said Odin to Baugi as they left Suttungr's house, "I have a whetstone that hones any blade to the keenest of edges."

"Yes," Baugi said. "It has been much use to you in cutting the hay. But I hope you do not suggest malice against my brother."

"No, no," Odin was swift to assure him. "What I did wish to say was I have also an auger so strong it can bore holes through the hardest of stone, and suggest with this we pierce through to the heart of the mountain."

To Baugi, this seemed a clever plan, and, they set to work. Only when they had bored halfway into Hnitbjorg's side did he pause.

"How will this be of help to us?" he asked. "You are no small man, and I am a giant, and this auger bores a hole no wider than my thumb."

"Keep at it," said Odin. "I know what to do."

Not without some misgivings, Baugi did so. He'd no sooner begun to wonder if his hired man was up to some trick than the auger's tip broke through into the cavern at the mountain's heart. And then, no sooner had the auger been drawn out than did Odin transform himself to a snake, swiftly squirming into the hole.

Cursing at how he'd been tricked, Baugi grabbed for the serpent's tail, but he missed. He smote the mountain-side with the auger in his anger and snapped the bit off at the handle. This made him curse all the more fiercely, but by then the snake had slithered far beyond his reach.

Odin made his way to the heart of the mountain. There, he found the three vessels of mead. There, he found also Gunnlod, the daughter of Suttungr, keeping watch over them. Odin resumed his own godly form, proud-bearded and handsome, his brow shining with wisdom, his one good eye like a jewel. He soon won the favor of the giant's daughter, and they struck a bargain. For three nights, he would lay with her, giving her pleasure in all ways. In exchange, she would allow him three drinks of the mead.

This arrangement, Odin found very agreeable. But when the time came for him to have his drinks of the mead, he did not stop until each drink had drained one of the three vessels so they each were emptied.

Baugi, meanwhile, had gone to Suttungr and admitted all. Suttungr knew at once it must be one of the Aesir. And he suspected strongly which of them it was.

"Odin," he said. "Well, he will not steal from me! Go to the hole you bored into the mountain, Baugi. Stop it up, block it, that he has no escape. I shall wait for him at the hidden exit and seize him as he emerges!"

This they each did. But Odin, so glutted on mead he sloshed, anticipated Suttungr's trap. He took eagle's shape and flew from Hnitbjorg as fast as his wings would carry him. The giant, seeing this, likewise changed his form to an eagle and gave chase. But he, unburdened, was far faster.

Screeching in fury, Suttungr slashed with sharp talons, forcing Odin to flee in desperate flight. Back and forth they went, this way and that, diving and veering, flapping and soaring. Feathers tore from the All-Father's plumage, fluttering like dry leaves in the wind.

Each near-miss of the deadly claws gave Odin such terror mead sprayed squirting from under his tail. It rained down in soiled spatters across the earth; wherever the mead fell, men gained a semblance of its gift and thought themselves great poets.

From the gates of Asgard, the other gods heard the eagles screeching and saw this wild pursuit. Odin had told them of his intention, so Frigg's handmaidens rushed to set out vats in the courtyard. Ullr, Sif's son and the best archer among the Aesir, shot arrows at Suttungr to force him to turn from his course. Defeated, he had no choice but to return to his mountain.

Down swooped Odin. His beak gaped wide. Up from his gullet came a gushing regurgitation, spewing forth into the vats the rest of the mead he had drunk. This was the true skaldic mead, unsoiled and untainted. Odin shared it among the Aesir, and granted portions of it to those he deemed best deserving its gifts.

***

"And that is why poetry is called Kvasir's blood," Lodunng said. "Or Suttungr's mead, Odin's find or Odin's gift, the treasure of Hnitbjorg."

She smiled at Ofradr with her sunken, toothless mouth. He, despite his weariness, had listened raptly to her story as the cottage's small fire burned low to embers and ash.

"What few think to wonder is what became of those giants," she went on. "Of Suttungr's daughter, in particular, who betrayed her own father for three nights in Odin's arms."

"Only to have the god empty the vessels of every drop of mead," Ofradr said. "A devious trick."

"Some say she lived on in the shadow of the mountain, she and the son that was born to her. Each year, she sends her son out to find someone… a skald or poet, a tale-teller, a singer of sagas and songs. It is a simple enough matter to lure them with promises of a contest at a jarl's hall, then lead them to her door."

At that, Ofradr felt his marrow, which had finally thawed, again go chilled. "That is a poor jest," he said.

"It would be indeed, were I jesting."

He looked from her to the thrall. The thrall grinned a cruel, knowing grin.

"Jarl Thorvald—" Ofradr began.

"There is no such man."

"Then… why…?" His wits seemed to have deserted him, leaving him fumbling for words.

She pointed to the back wall of her cottage. Which, Ofradr now saw, had opened to reveal a passageway cut into the stone. It led to a cavern where three vessels waited, each half-filled.

"Each year, Suttungr's daughter brews a new batch of mead, in hopes of earning her father's forgiveness. To do so, however, requires something more than honey."

Before Ofradr could move more than a step toward the cottage door, the thrall seized him in an iron-strong grip.

"You are, of course, no Kvasir," Lodunng said—or, Gunnlod, as he now knew her to be—drawing forth a long sharp knife. "But you will do."

ODIN'S EAGLE

The blade, small but sharp, wicked-sharp, piercing. The blood welling, first in a dark bead, then a line as the knife slices, then overflowing in irregular trickles to form strange red runes.

The struggles, though limb-lashed. The screams, although gagged.

Drawing it down in a single long cut, as straight and as even as the struggles allow. The blade's sharp steel tip scraping and grating on bone, bumping over the rough vertebrae nubs.

The skin, slit nape to nethers, parting in a narrow gap like a slit curtain. Then, four more quick slashes, two to each side: the upper across the shoulders, the lower just above the waist.

Still struggling, straining against the tight bonds.

Still screaming, sobbing, shouting, swearing, into the muffling gag.

More blood, not just welling but flowing, coursing crimson. Not a flood, not deadly… not yet.

***

"Did he die well?" I asked, willing my voice not to break. It was not yet a man's voice, nor still a boy's; I had seen only thirteen summers and was beardless of cheek.

"Did he die well?" echoed the messenger who'd brought the grim news. He sounded incredulous at the very question.

I flushed for my foolishness. Of *course* he had died well, our father! Died bravely and boldly in battle, died a warrior's death with weapon in hand and the blood of his foes on the blade! How else could it have been? He was a big man, a strong man, a man who'd fought in the shield walls and ridden the wild whale's road, and come back with glory and plunder. True, that had been long ago, before he'd settled and wed and taken up the smith's trade, but his heart had ever belonged to Odin and Thor. And now, in the golden-roofed feast-hall—

"Did he die *well?*" the messenger repeated, then laughed, scoffed, and spat. "He died in the dirt like a dog, reeking of ale and of piss and of puke!"

I reeled on my feet. From behind me, where she knelt to comfort our mother, I heard my sister's harsh gasp. I heard my brother's pained groan; slow though he was, even Hjot understood those words, and the sneering tone of mockery in which they were uttered. The neighbors who'd gathered reacted in shock, whispering, murmuring, eyes wide with disbelief.

"How did it happen?" Despite my best intention, my voice did break then, into a shrill, shameful squeak.

Again, the messenger laughed. He had a well-bred look about him, wearing a good leather coat and a thick cloak of green wool, sporting a silver arm-ring and bracers of twisted horse-headed bronze. "Are you certain you wish to know, lad?"

"*I* wish to know," Hjot said, rising from his crouch.

My brother, my elder by some four years, took after our father in stature and size. He towered above most men of the village, broad of shoulder, thick of chest, a stout barrel on legs, brawny arms bulging with muscle. A half-wit, he might be—a tool pulled from the workbench when he was barely able to walk had struck him a bad blow to the head; to this day no hair grew in the deep-dimpled scar on his scalp—but give him hammer and anvil, give him fire and forge, and Hjot was well-able, a tireless worker.

Kjarte and I took much more after our mother, lean and

sharp-featured, almost elfin. At eleven, Kjarte in particular was a fey, feral thing, stick-thin and wiry, with a hawk's golden eyes.

The messenger looked at us. Looked at Hjot, looked at me. A flicker of what might have been pity or understanding crossed his face, before vanishing the way brief sunlight vanishes among cool and indifferent clouds.

"Your father," he said, shrugging, "made the mistake of offering insult to Jarl Urlstan."

It was not a name I knew, though indrawn gasps from some neighbors told me it was not, to them, unfamiliar. Through their curious crowd, I glimpsed our mother's cousin Otli approaching, hastening from his mill, clothes dusted with barley-flour. Like her, like us, he was not large, but lean, though he had of late developed a comfortable paunch.

"There was a fight?" Hjot inquired, forming each word with care.

"There was no fight," said the messenger. "Your father gave insult, Jarl Urlstan took exception, and then it was done."

"The jarl killed him?" My voice held steady that time, for which I was glad.

A nod, and another indifferent shrug, made his answer.

"Just killed him?" added Kjarte. "Just like that, for no reason?"

He favored her with a smirk. "I told you the reason, girl."

"Must've been some insult," someone muttered, though I did not see who.

Our mother pushed herself up, shaking off Kjarte's help. "Murder is what it is. Craven, honorless murder!"

"Woman—" the messenger began.

"Not a fair fight, no square made, no rules set?" She was as a sword then, slender and shining, bright but brittle. "Your lord struck down a good man—"

"A drunken man."

"—who likely meant no harm; drink makes many misspeak! My husband—"

"Hjothilde, enough." Otli reached us, gripping her shoulder.

He smiled a thin, placating smile at the messenger. "Pardon my cousin's emotion. I am certain Jarl Urlstan rightly felt provocation."

The glare Mother threw him would have boiled water. He ignored it.

"And the jarl, no doubt," Otli went on, "is bound by the law?" His tone and his eyebrows rose in hinting suggestion.

"No doubt," said the messenger. "A regrettable incident, to be sure, but the king prefers peace to dissent among his people, and would see this matter resolved without further begrudgment or violence."

My bones ached from holding myself rigidly still. Despite my youth, I understood the meaning of their words. The king did not want feuds and revenge. He did not want men of our family to hunt down this jarl, and repay him blood-for-blood. Our father had been cut down with no warning, with no chance to earn his way to Valhalla, perhaps without even knowing his death was upon him... his valor in the shield-walls and victories on the battlefield brushed aside... his courage on the grey seas dismissed... and we were simply to roll over and take it.

Hjot, at my left, steamed great breaths from his nostrils like a bull. Kjarte, on my right, gripped my forearm such that her ragged nails dug into my skin. Our mother had gone still as a stone.

"*Wergild*," she said. "You speak of *wergild*."

"Which Jarl Urlstan sends, in generous excess." The messenger pulled a sack from beneath his cloak, and tossed it to the ground at her feet. It clinked heavily, silver on silver.

Unsurprisingly, it was Otli who bent first to open the sack. He exhaled a low whistle, stirring the contents. "Generous indeed. There must be a full half-weight here."

"I have heard of Jarl Urlstan," Mother declared. "He is no stranger to the paying of *wergild*, is he not? How many has he killed? Not in battle, but in other such 'regrettable incidents'? Ten? A dozen? Twenty?"

"Hjothilde!" Otli nudged her.

Now she ignored him. "But he goes about as he pleases, with his quick temper and quicker blade, striking down men with impunity because his family has wealth!"

"Your cousin," the messenger said to Otli, "would do well to mind her tongue."

"She is distraught—"

"Wealth un-earned at that!" she continued with rising stridency. "Not even war-plunder, just found-money... a buried dwarf's horde or dragon-treasure, my eye! Likely, they stole it from some barrow-tomb or grave-mound—"

Otli sprang up, seizing her wrist. "Hjothilde! Think of your children."

Hjot rumbled low in his chest as he stood beside me. Kjarte quivered, her nails digging deeper into my skin.

The messenger's lips pressed a white line, no more pity in his expression. "She is distraught, as you said. Her words will not be held against her. The *wergild* has been paid. The body will be returned for proper burial. Let the matter therefore be considered resolved."

He turned, and strode to his horse, the neighbors parting a path for him. Some watched him go. Some gazed at us, and some at our mother, and some at the open sack where silver gleamed.

Wergild. The man-price. The cost of a life. This was to make up for the loss of our father. Of a good man, a big man, bearded and bearish, often booming with laughter. And yes, he drank; he loved his ale and his mead... but what of it? So too did many men. He'd loved us as well. Loved our mother, despite the other half-dozen babes that she'd lost, leaving them with only us. He'd loved Hjot, despite his slowness, teaching him the smith's craft and trade. He'd loved wild little Kjarte, never making her spin thread like other girls but letting her bend metal into link after link of shimmering mail.

He'd loved me, scrawny though I was. He'd called me clever, told me it was its own form of strength. If I might never grow to heft a shield, swing a sword or an axe... if I was not for the anvil and forge, or the sea… he took pride in my learning, my memory for the skald's stories and sagas.

Now he was dead, dead and gone—

"… *died in the dirt like a dog,"* resonated the messenger's words in my mind.

—and we were left with a pile of silver.

***

Now to pull. Now to peel back that curtain. Parting the skin in wide flaps, opening it, the way monks from the western islands were said to open their sacred books.

Skinning animals is different. So is dressing game. Those beasts are already dead when the cutting begins.

Even a sacrifice is different from this. A throat-slash, deep and sudden. The pain a flash, then and gone.

Not a slow, peeling agony. Not trembles and shudders and piteous moans.

The blood flows and trickles. It patters like rain onto the sodden earth. The raw flesh lies naked, wet and exposed. Here are rib-ridges in ivory curves, and the red-streaked length of spine.

And now the real work begins.

***

Sleep eluded me, eluded all three of us, as we rested beneath fleeces upon straw in the loft above our house-hall. Below, by the hearth, our mother sat with Otli late into the night. He made much wise counsel, but I heard his greed like a song through his speech.

She should, he advised, sell the smithy and its tools. Hjot could not manage the place on his own, and would be better served by having a new master. The house-hall, as well, would bring her a tidy sum. Combined with the *wergild*, she'd be comfortable for life.

"You must think of your children," he said. "Think of their future."

"Think of their home," she retorted. "Where would we live?"

"My mill-house is large, with room to spare since Ilke died and Ana and Otra each married. The other girls have always held you with fond regard. They'd be glad for the company."

By the flicker of firelight through the floor-slats, I saw Kjarte grimace. Ilke, Otli's wife, had given him nine living daughters, seven of which had not yet wed. That gaggle of girls, our next-cousins, concerned themselves mainly with gossip and clothes. They already teased Kjarte mercilessly, made fun of Hjot and of me, and would no doubt challenge our mother at every turn.

To live by the mill... to work for Otli, hauling grain-sacks and grind-stones... bad enough we'd lost our father, bad enough the loss was to be repaid by a rich man's casual silver... to then see that very silver go toward dresses, hair-ribbons, ivory combs, and trinkets for those giggling geese...

I shut my eyes and pressed my head to the pad of my pillow. Into that inner darkness came images, fancies forged from my mind, of places I had never been and faces I had never seen. I imagined the king's great fortress-city, high walls flapping with banners, the tall masts of longships a forest in the broad bay. I imagined the gathering-fair there, to which our father had gone. There would be jarls and thanes, war-chieftains, lords of the land. There would be travelers and merchants, swordsmen and spearmen, tradesmen and slaves. All doing business, making deals, gambling and feasting and whoring as well.

And drinking.

I imagined our father, who'd so loved his ale and his mead, and wondered how it was he could have possibly offered insult to anyone, no matter how drunk. He'd been a jovial man, friendly, no grudge-holder! Never angry, not even in battle! When the blood-lust and war-fury descended on other men, he'd always kept his wits and his humor.

Had it been an accident? A mistake? Some jest ill-timed or ill-taken? From what Otli had described, I envisioned this Jarl Urlstan as plump and petulant, a strutting cockerel, vain and soft-faced. The sort to take offense quickly, warranted or not.

A mere bump in passing, an ale-driven stumble, might have been enough to stoke such a man's wrath. His indignation, our father's good-natured slurs of apology, laughing it off… and Jarl Urlstan not finding it funny. Heated words flying like sparks, then the bright flash of a blade… the hot splash of blood.

I rolled, fitful, and opened my eyes. I'd not been able to shut my ears, anyway, as Otli kept up his persuasive talk.

"My father, your uncle," he was saying to her, "would urge you to be sensible, Hjothilde. For your sake, and theirs."

"Your father, my uncle," she retorted, "thought I should have married *you*."

Otli chortled. "Well, it's to think of; it's still not too late."

Kjarte grimaced again, and mimed gagging. She leaned toward me. "If *our* uncle were here …" she whispered.

"If our uncle were here," I whispered back, with a wistful pang, "he would have gone with Father, and Father would still be alive, and none of this would be happening."

She flung me a sour look. "That isn't what I meant, and you know it."

I sighed. "Truth; I do."

Our uncle, Eyrk, our father's younger brother, had not given up his warrior's ways. He raided and plundered, he'd sworn sword-oaths to kings, he'd sailed to strange lands at the far edges of the world. We'd not see him for years, sure he must have been dead, but then he would suddenly appear, laden with tales of adventure.

He'd bring us gifts—I yet carried the dagger he'd given me when I was no more than five winters old, a tiny thing but wickedly sharp and easily hidden, a stone of rune-carved jet set into the pommel. Squirrel-Tooth, he had named it, for Ratatoskr, the squirrel who scampered up and down Yggdrasil, gnawing and doing mischief and bearing news. Kjarte wore to this day a bronze amulet of a wide-winged eagle with eyes of polished amber. Hjot had a ring of real gold, which now fit snug only upon his smallest finger, in the shape of a ferocious boar's head.

Straw rustled as Hjot's big body shifted, turning him onto his side. "What, then?" he asked, also whispering. "Uncle Eyrk. What *would* he do?"

"He wouldn't take *wergild*, I'll tell you that." Kjarte nearly snarled, and I cautioned her to stay quiet.

"He'd have revenge," I said, heaving another sigh. "Blood for blood, like in the stories." My gaze caught Kjarte's amulet, the eagle's amber eyes glinting. "He'd find this Urlstan, and make him suffer."

"How?" Kjarte asked, savagely, her own eyes also glinting.

Still gazing at the bronze amulet, still thinking of the old stories, I said, "The eagle… he'd cut Odin's eagle into the murdering bastard's back. Cut his ribs and haul out his live, breathing, bleeding lungs… and let them flap there. As wings. Wings of pain, of agony and torment. Until death finally claimed him and sent him to Hel."

"Yesss," hissed my sister. She showed her teeth. Like those of Ratatoskr, they were tiny, but wickedly sharp.

Hjot shifted again. Boards creaked under his weight. Downstairs, the conversation ceased a moment. The three of us held our breath, making no further sounds.

Then we heard good Cousin Otli readying to take his leave, telling our mother to consider what he'd said, to hide well the *wergild-*silver—unless she'd rather him take it, to keep it safe at the mill?

She assured him it would indeed be well-hidden, thanked him for his counsel, and saw him to the door. They stood outside a while longer, their voices muffled, their words unclear.

"Would that help Father?" asked Hjot. "Odin's eagle? Would it… bring him back?"

"He won't come back." Kjarte snapped a piece of dry straw. "Oh, they'll return his body, as that… that… sneering goat-shit man said—"

I raised my eyebrows, but she was far from finished.

"—let *him* have a taste of it, too; what things to *say* to a man's grieving widow and children! I'd have *fed* him his sack of silver and hope he choked! To try and *buy* our father's life? To try and buy *honor?*"

"But the king—" Hjot began.

"The king can also choke on his silver for all that I care!"

Putting a hand on her narrow shoulder, I spoke past her to Hjot. "She's right, though. He won't come back. His body will, but his soul's gone on."

"To Valhalla? To drink and to feast and fight giants?"

The hope in his tone almost slew me on the spot. Hjot was the elder brother, but I felt the burden of a grown man's responsibility drop over me like a heavy cloak.

"He... he did not die in battle," I said, each word a difficulty. "He might not have had time to even lay hand on a weapon. He was just... just killed."

"Murdered," snarled our sister.

"Not to Valhalla, then?" Hjot's eyes welled with stricken tears.

So did mine. I reached across Kjarte to clasp his big hand. "We don't know," I said, swallowing a tightness in my throat. "We can't know."

"But you think not," Kjarte said. "Not without vengeance."

I thought of Eyrk, our uncle. I wondered where he was, if and when he'd return. Too far away, I supposed. Too long from now, if ever. "Not without vengeance," I admitted, as if I myself by my own words was dooming our father's soul to the drear greyness of chill Niflheim.

"Then, my brothers," said Kjarte, laying her small hand atop mine, atop Hjot's hand much larger, "vengeance is what we will seek."

***

The *sound* of it!

The crackle of gristle, the heavy crunch-snap of bone! A meaty tearing as muscles contract, as ligaments lengthen and tissues stretch!

As, one by one, down the left side and then the right…

Crack-crunch, crunch-snap, that meaty ripping and tearing!

No more screaming and sobbing; there's that much at least. A quivering wide-eyed wild-eyed shock has set in. Frantic breaths whistle through nostrils, bubbling with snot.

Oh, and the *stink* of it too, the slaughterhouse stench, sour terror-sweat, the helpless voiding of bladder and bowels! Blood flung in spatters and sprays, splashing hot and thick!

***

I tried to dissuade Kjarte. I did.

Not because she was the youngest, or because she was a girl, but because we should not *all* go. Someone, I argued, should stay with Mother, to explain the others' absence and purpose. To be here *for* Mother, lest the worst happened. She'd already lost her husband, and it was quite likely this mad mission would only lead to more deaths; she should be left with *one* of her children, at least.

Yes, I tried to dissuade her, but she would have none of it.

"We go together," Kjarte declared.

And I knew she was right. We'd each be needed were we to have any chance.

The next day, we gathered in secret supplies for our journey, hiding them in the smithy's back shed. That evening, when our mother went to dine at the mill-house with Otli's invitation—he wanted to discuss, he claimed, business and burial arrangements—we begged off. Mother, knowing our opinions of our next-cousins, allowed it. So, we watched her go, in her best blue wool dress, swathed in a reindeer-pelt cloak.

Then, feeling like thieves, we dug up the sack of silver from where she'd hidden it under one of the hearth-stones. By way of explanation, I had Hjot leave his gold boar's-head ring in its place, that she might know it was us who'd taken it, and not robbers.

In this season, the sun sailed a long, low slope across the sky, so we had fair light for a good while before full darkness fell. We fetched our supplies from the shed, slipped from the village, and made our way unchallenged and unquestioned into the sparse woods beyond the farm-fields.

I led the way, checking our path with a birchwood staff. It served as a good walking-stick, but I'd also trained with it as if it were a weapon. A true warrior armed with sword and with shield would make quick work of me, to be sure. Still, it was better than nothing. Against some robber or ruffian, I might hold my own. I was scrawny, but I was quick, and I could deliver smart blows that fell where I aimed them.

Kjarte walked behind me, ever alert. I'd loaned her Squirrel-Tooth, my small but wicked-sharp dagger. Behind her came Hjot, carrying the supplies and the silver. He had a heavy smith's hammer slung at his waist. Across his broad back rode an iron-cutter, its handles of stout oak, its biting head hardened soot-blackened steel.

Once, a wide-winged eagle soared high overhead, moving in the same direction that we were. I took this to be a sign, a good omen. Odin's approval of our journey and purpose. But we also passed a bare-branched tree where three black ravens cawed, and if that was also an omen, it could not be a good one.

We did not talk much as we went. I kept us close to the road, close enough to see and hear other travelers before they saw or heard us. My concern was that Mother—or worse, Cousin Otli—would send men after us from the village. Our meals were cold and simple: bread, cheese, smoked fish, plus whatever early fruits, nuts, and berries were there to be foraged. When night came, we piled thick beds of pine branches and slept huddled together, wrapped in our cloaks.

The weather held in our favor as we descended the long valley toward the fjord and the bay. There, sprawling greatly, was the king's fortress-city, with its high log walls and its halls. It was at once both grander and more squalid than I'd imagined. The houses crowded each other. The streets were dung-dotted mud. Smoke and grime hung in a dreary miasma.

Yet we saw also the bustling marketplaces, vast livestock pens, corrals of horses. We saw the forest of ship's masts on the broad, shining bay, the ships themselves sleek and swift. All around the log walls were irregular rings of ditches, and thorn-bush palisades, and the clustered tents of those attending the gathering-fair.

Hjot had been here with Father a few times before, and remembered well enough how to guide us to the tradesmen's quarter. Kjarte was agog with amazement. So was I, though I tried not to show it.

So many folk! So much noise! The sights and the sounds and the smells battered at our senses. Every turn brought new wonders— far-foreign faces speaking strange tongues, exotic goods, pungent spices. We passed legless beggars and jugglers up on tall stilts. We passed women selling honey-cakes, men selling sword-belts and leather coats. A crone wearing a ragged patchwork of mangy furs rattled rune-sticks at us and offered to tell our fates; I nearly had to drag Kjarte away.

"But we could find out if we—" she protested.

"Or we could find out that we'll fail," I said. "It's a terrible thing to know your own future!"

"Why?"

"Because you can't change it."

She frowned, glancing back at the crone. "Then you'd be warned."

"And doomed either way."

"Can we have honey-cakes?"

"No." It was a hard no to utter; the cakes were golden and glistening and my mouth watered for sweetness.

"Can we see the dancing bear?" she asked next, pointing at a tent where a man in a red robe beckoned and hectored.

At that, even Hjot turned with a wistful hope in his eyes. I hated to dash it, but had to.

"No," I said again. "They'd all want silver."

"We have—" Kjarte began.

I shushed her harshly. "Not to spend."

On we went, following Hjot, as the surroundings changed to rather more familiar. We'd reached the tradesmen's quarter, crammed with woodworkers and weavers and blacksmiths like our father. Amid the basking forge-heat and clang of hammers, we felt more at ease.

Although I'd said we didn't have silver to spend, I meant the *wer-gild*. I'd brought a few other scraps saved up from here and there. It wasn't much, but it bought us a space to sleep in an empty stall of a farrier's stable, and a warm meal of barley stew with mushrooms and lentil.

"Now what?" Kjarte asked, using a crust of bread to scrape every drop of stew from her bowl.

"Now we find Jarl Urlstan," I said.

Hjot nodded, and looked at me. "How?"

***

Again and again, the meaty crunch-snap of iron cutting through bone. Again and again, the blood-spray as another rib springs from its moorings. The back spreading apart, gaping, widening.

It does not particularly resemble eagle's wings.

It resembles a broken wicker fish-trap. A mangled butcher's jumble of pallid sticks and red flesh. The dripping, toothy maw of a ravenous ivory-fanged beast.

The bound limbs twitch and spasm. The gagged mouth no longer screams; only muffled whimpers emerge. The head droops, eyes shut, hair dangling.

Below, the earth has gone sodden with blood. Yet, the work is not done.

Again, with the knife, its blade small but wicked-sharp.

***

The largest nearby ale-house was both popular and boisterous. Men crowded it, talking, gambling, and drinking. Men and women, though Kjarte said most of the women were whores. Her worldliness and wisdom startled me, but we were both of us startled far more when one of the women recognized Hjot.

He blushed like we'd never seen him do before. I wondered what else had gone on during his trips here with Father. I wondered what Mother would say if she knew, not that I was about to tell her.

The woman, Ulthe, was plump, fair-haired, full-hipped, and extraordinarily buxom. She brought us a pot of water-weakened ale and a dish of boiled eggs, refusing payment for the food.

"Your father was a good man," she told us, after kissing Hjot's cheek and sitting down beside him. "Never mean, never sour. Always joking. He drank a lot, but, in this place, who doesn't? Terrible, it was, what happened to him. He deserved better."

"Is it true he made insult and started a fight?" I asked.

"Him?" Her earnest surprise gave us comfort. "Not hardly! He'd fallen down, that was all—the mead that night was very strong—and as he was laughing about it, the other man, the jarl, tripped over his legs and fell too."

"So, just an accident?"

"Well, the jarl, he'd been wearing a fine new fox-fur cloak, and it caught on a nail and tore. He also spilled a full horn of mead on himself. And, when your father went to help pull him up, the jarl farted."

I couldn't help snickering. Kjarte did too.

"Your father, of course, laughed. Rightly enough. We all did; it was quite the arse-thunder."

Kjarte and I snickered again.

"The jarl, though, denied doing it. Said it had been your father. No one believed him. Your father only laughed harder, claiming he'd love to take credit for such a mighty blast, but that just made the jarl all the more furious."

Kjarte stopped snickering. "Then he killed him? For a fart?"

Ulthe shrugged, the effect of which I must admit caused me no small distraction. "The fart, the spilled mead, the torn cloak, the laughter... any or all of it... he took offense."

I stopped snickering too. "Right then and there?" My gaze swept the room. "Where?"

"Oh, no, bunny-buck," she said, as if to console me. Leaning over, she patted my shoulder. Being called 'bunny-buck,' and the pat, made me feel like a child... but the sight as she leaned over was another matter. "It was later. It was outside. Your father had another drink, then stepped out for a piss. The jarl, who'd been sulking in a corner, followed."

"It was murder, then," Kjarte said. "In cold blood."

"Tell us how," Hjot said.

Ulthe hesitated. "I didn't see. I just heard from one of the other girls, later, after she'd been with one of the jarl's men."

"Tell us anyway," I urged.

She heaved a sigh and shrugged again, the effect no less impressive. "They say that the jarl found him stumbling and bumbling and only half-conscious, and drove a seax hilt-deep in his back." Patting my shoulder again, she added, "It was quick. So quick he probably never knew."

None of us found that much consolation. Our father, struck down without a chance to fight back, without a chance to prepare himself for impending death, without seeing the face of the man who had killed him. A cowardly blow from behind.

"I am sorry," she said, and repeated, "He was a good man. Sorry as well that you came all this way to fetch his body; you've wasted your trip. I think they sent it already by pony-cart."

"We're not here for that," said Hjot. "We're here for revenge."

Kjarte hissed him to shush, and I kicked his shin under the table. It was like kicking an oak. He looked at us, befuddled, then slow comprehension finally dawned.

Meanwhile, after a momentary widening of her eyes and a darting glance around the ale-house to see who else might have been listening, Ulthe managed with magnificent casualness to pretend Hjot hadn't spoken.

"I understand, though," she said, choosing her words deliberately, "that the king ordered a generous *wergild*. Jarl Urlstan's lucky he can afford it. He has many enemies. He's angered many folk. If someone were ever to refuse it and seek… other compensation… I suspect they would find a great deal of sympathy."

"Someone," I said, with equal deliberate care, "would have to know what he looks like. A man so wealthy probably doesn't go around undefended, either."

"Oh, true." She refilled our cups from the ale-pot. "I've never seen him without at least two or three men, though they're usually armed with nothing more than cudgels because of the king's peace."

"But the jarl carries a seax?" That was Kjarte, indignant.

"Bribes will do much," Ulthe said. "It's a shame he's such a bastard. With that long golden hair, and those leaf-green eyes, and the way he trims his beard to a tapered point, he *is* very handsome. Vain as a queen, perhaps, but very handsome."

"Does he come here often?" I asked.

My casualness was not so magnificent as hers, and for a moment she considered us as if truly seeing what we were: a simpleton, a scrawny youth, and a half-feral girl. Perhaps she pondered our mother, already grieving, and could not in pitying conscience send us to our own deaths.

Then Hjot, somehow sensing I needed the help, smiled his sweet, childish smile at her. "Does he?" he echoed, putting his big hand over hers.

She softened. Kjarte and I exchanged a look; we'd had no idea our slow-witted elder brother could be a charmer of women!

"Despite all his silver, he wears out his welcome at one ale-house after another in time," Ulthe said. "These past few nights, I think he's been doing his drinking at the brewer's yard by the bridge."

***

The meat of the back, slabs of raw-pink muscle, whitish ropes of tendon. Seeping and weeping with red beads of blood.

More cuts. Two more, deeper, but precise and careful. More flesh widely parted, slippery against bare skin, loathsomely warm and alive.

Reaching in, fingers sliding and sinking. Squelching. Probing. Finding the slick, thick, pulsating lung... heavy and strange, moving as if with its own life... maneuvering both hands around it, under it... grasping, gently and carefully lifting it, working it, birthing it free.

Birthing it, yes, a hideous unnatural birth... like they said sometimes happened to women when the babe would not emerge the normal way... like wolves opening the belly of a ewe to prise out the unborn lamb even as its mother bleats and squeals.

This, though, no birth-sac. This, a lung, and then the other. Its sibling. Its twin. Both of them eased from their cradling comfort, brought struggling and protesting into the light.

Breathing in unruly, desperate, great heaving gasps.

***

Finding Jarl Urlstan proved to be easy enough, thanks to Ulthe's description.

Oh, there were other men with long golden hair in the brew-yard by the bridge, other men with green eyes or taper-trimmed beards, to be sure. But only one who also wore a fine cloak of fox-fur, the color of autumn leaves set aflame. Only one who, for all he *was* handsome, was also as soft-faced and petulant as I'd imagined. Only one with a sheathed seax on his belt, and two surly-looking guards in constant attendance.

If we'd needed further confirmation, as we watched from the shadows beneath the bridge's span, we got it when a third companion joined him. Leather coat, green cloak, silver arm-rings; it was the messenger who'd come to our village.

They sat together a while in conversation, drinking jugs of mead, carving juicy slices from a roasted haunch of meat. The messenger seemed weary and exasperated, and when the jarl pressed upon him a weighty sack, I guessed why. Another *wergild* to deliver, another family to make stricken with grim and terrible news. Another murder, another life bought and paid for without a single care.

Beside me, Kjarte snarled, and I knew she understood too.

We waited. It was hard, but we waited.

The bridge spanned a white-rushing river tumbling toward the fjord, crashing noisily over the rocks. On the far bank were cattle byres and ox barns, and log-fenced paddocks where the big animals lowed and shuffled and mooed.

We waited. I thought again of the old stories… of trolls hiding to ambush travelers and passers-by.

The messenger finished his mead-jug and left, and if he'd crossed the bridge above us we might not have been able to resist the temptation. How satisfying it would have been to spring out and seize him! To do as Kjarte had suggested and force-feed him the *wergild*-silver piece by piece until he choked.

But, no. We waited.

The sun finally sank. Night flooded the valley like dark water rising. Fires and torches did little to hold it at bay. Folk retreated indoors. Soon, the brew-yard was all but empty.

Jarl Urlstan and his remaining two men were among the last to leave. The jarl looked smug and sated and pleased with himself; the guards, who wore leather and bore cudgels, still looked sullen. They also looked tired, and none too sober.

We followed, not yet with much of a plan. Kjarte and Hjot trusted me to come up with something. When I guessed the jarl's route would take him down a muddy alleyway between long large storehouses, I sent Hjot one way while Kjarte and I went the other.

At a place where alleys intersected, dimly lit by tall torches on distant walls, I scattered a handful of the *wergild* on the ground and had Kjarte kneel to scrabble at it as if trying to gather it up. I, meanwhile, leaned on my staff to feign lameness, scolding her for being clumsy, telling her to hasten before anyone came along.

But, of course, someone already was coming along. To the jarl and his men, the scene such presented must have been almost comic. Two scrawny children, a lamed youth berating a girl as she picked coins and scraps of silver from the mud... we may have appeared as beggars, or perhaps thieves... but we did not, to three grown men, appear dangerous.

"Well, what is this, what is this?" the jarl said, cruel mockery in his tone. "A pair of grubby little rats been in the granary, have you?"

Kjarte and I flinched, donning guilty expressions. I took a step back, letting my leg twist-drag so that I nearly stumbled, while she made a fumbling attempt to hide the silver.

"You'll be in quite a lot of trouble, I think," Urlstan continued. He grinned over his shoulder at his guards, swaggering, as if pushing *us* around made him a mighty war-lord. "Let's just see what you have there."

"It's nothing, lord," I stammered. This time, I willed my voice to break, and it readily obliged. The men laughed. "We found it, is all—"

"Oh, well, if you *found* it, I'm sure it can be returned to its rightful owners. And I'm sure they'll be lenient. Probably won't see you sold into slavery—"

"Not much use, that," snorted one of the guards. "Bring scant enough profit."

"True, very true." The jarl bent toward Kjarte, fox-fur cloak sweeping, golden hair spilling in shining sheaves. He smiled at her, and he *was* handsome, but his leaf-green eyes were cold. "Just a beating, most likely, to teach you a lesson—"

In a flash, she was on him, quick as a cat, all claws and all kicking, hissing her hate in his ear. Urlstan shouted, more in astonishment than pain. His two men drew up startled, then roared with mirth. Such a sight, their rich lord, beset by a wild stick of a girl, riding his shoulders and drumming at his head.

I darted up fast with my staff, and punched its end into the jarl's belly so that his breath coughed from his lungs. As he bent double, Kjarte flipped from his back, clutching in both fists fine locks of fair hair. She landed lithe on her feet, our swift sister, and still grasping blond fistfuls, yanked his head down toward her rising knee.

It was small, that knee, but hard and sharp, bony. Urlstan's nose shattered like a fresh red-yolked egg.

Springing sideways, I lashed the staff across his heel-tendons, and he dropped with a cry.

All this in a matter of heartbeats, his men looking on, their laughter stopped by shock, their eyes wide with surprise. One of them went for his cudgel, while the other only stared, and it mattered little either way because Hjot had come silently up behind them.

His huge hands, forge-callused, seized them each by the nape of the neck. He brought their skulls together. The sound was of stone-giants cracking enormous nuts. Then the two men collapsed, unmoving, in the alleyway mud.

***

The lungs heave and pulsate, fully exposed, not accustomed to open air on their outsides. Pinkish and purplish, fat-marbled, thickly veined. They heave and they gasp, puffing like a faulty smith's bellows, causing more cough-ash than blowing hot life into coals.

Each new shuddering, jerking inhalation is terrible. Each new sputtering, wheezing deflation is worse. Each *must* be the last, surely *must*, yet onward they labor. Onward in stubborn agony, drawing breath, loosing it, struggling to draw it again.

The pale rib-ends twitch. The body trembles.

And the red blood runs in slow, flooding rivers.

***

We had him. Thanks to Kjarte's deft knotwork, we bound him. Thanks to my quick thinking, we silenced his mouth with a gag. Thanks to Hjot's great strength, we bore him away from the spot where his men sprawled unconscious, and took him back to our hiding-place under the bridge.

There, I struck a rushlight, trusting its faint glow would not reach far, then turned to regard our furious captive.

His face was bruised, his nose broken and dripping. He snuffled through it in bubblings of blood and of snot. His leaf-green eyes mutely first raged at us, promising punishment, promising death.

I removed his sword-belt, to which the sheathed seax was buckled. I slid the steel partway free, looked at it, and then looked at him.

"It was with this that you murdered our father," I said.

The leaf-green eyes widened, sudden fear seeping into them. He fought not to show it, much as I fought to keep my voice from breaking, but it was there.

"And it was with this," said Kjarte, holding up the sack of silver, "that you tried to buy your way free and clear."

Other promises, as mute as his threats, filled his eyes. If the *wer-gild* wasn't enough, those looks assured us, he'd gladly pay more… he'd give us gold… land, horses… anything, anything we desired.

"We don't want your money," Hjot rumbled.

Kjarte spat contemptuously, spun, and hurled the heavy sack into the river. It came open as it flew, bits of silver twinkling like stars before vanishing.

His eyes implored us, pleaded for mercy, pleaded at least for a chance to explain. We ignored those pleas. We stripped him of his fine fox-fur cloak. Hjot slung him belly-down over a log washed up onto the bank and secured him so that he could not move. Kjarte, with Squirrel's-Tooth, slashed away his wool tunic, then the linen undershirt beneath, baring his back.

I crouched in front of him, holding Hjot's iron-cutter. Working the oak handles, I snapped the stout sharp-edged jaw-blades. They made an eager, hungry sound. I'd seen Hjot use them to shear through bars of metal, and had no doubt they'd go through rib-bones with ease.

Only desperate terror remained in Jarl Urlstan's eyes, a frantic and desperate terror bordering on madness.

But that was all right. Pain would join the terror soon enough.

We had him. And now, for our father, for our honor, we would make Odin's eagle and have our revenge.

A WARLORD'S FOREST FATE

For Michael Allen Rose and Sauda Namir

U pon the field of the fallen, dusk's shadows draw long
Clouds lower and mist rises, the world cloaked in grey
Already, the ravens gather, dark-winged and watchful
Already, the dogs skulk closer, snarling and hungry
A blood-bounty awaits them, axe-hewn and sword-cut

It was a grim battle, a dread day of betrayal and death
In the mud, once-bright banners crumpled and torn
Limewood shields splintered, spear-shafts snapped
The faces of men frozen, blank-eyed, mouths gaping
Mail-coats blade-pierced, guts spilled, limbs severed

Then, from the dead stillness, movement... a groan
A figure slowly rises, wounded, struggling through pain
His chest heaves for breath, he blinks at the carnage
Does no one else live? No one does, it soon seems
Friend or foe, all are equal, cold meat for the feast

With bloodied hand he draws and drops dented helm
Pushes back cloth-quilted coif beneath, bares his head

His high scalp smooth, war-stained by sweat and toil
His brow wise, beard kingly, aspect shaken but strong
Although injured, he stands steady, this lone survivor

There around him are his sword-brethren, closer than kin
Good men and bold, drinkers of the sweet honey-mead
Brave in the shield-wall, generous, of hearty reputation
Quick to laugh or to fight or to love, now pale and still
Fists clenched on weapons, defiant to death and beyond

He recalls through a dimness some strange memories
The thunder of hoofbeats as if from on high and afar
The glint of unearthly light on harness and spear-points
Windblown cloaks, long hair streaming, fierce beauty
Valhalla's shining war-maidens, choosers of the slain

But he had not been chosen, for he had not been slain
He lives, injured and alone... he lives, but how long?
Already, the ravens, caws and black feathers fluttering
Already, the dogs; their wild wolf-cousins soon after
And those beasts by far from the worst of his worries

Before long, he knows, greedier scavengers will come
Hungry not for butchered flesh but a different wealth
Corpse-pickers from hut and hovel, seeking plunder
Silver arm-rings, gold brooches, neck-torcs and buckles
Coins and gems, polished ivory, to peasants a fortune

This is not his own land, these will not be his people
When even trusted allies had turned and proved false
He will find no welcome among them, no mercy, no help
Instead, themselves like a dogpack they'll set upon him
With bludgeons and cudgels, curses, sticks and stones

Fight though he would and fight though he will, to his last
It shall be no true warrior's fate, death in valorous battle
No Valkyrie coming for him, no seat in Odin's highest hall
Only beat down where he stood, left to rot with the rest
If they do not take him prisoner, or worse, make him slave

No. He will not have it, will not surrender or succumb
Sheathing his sword and clutching his wounds, he turns
What horses came with the armies have long since fled
The field-valley spreads far and shadowed around him
Mountains loom, towering, ice-peaked, giants' country

And there is the forest, dark and grim, gloomy, forbidding
Saga-place of danger and mystery, secrets, a thousand perils
Home to trolls, home to bears, home to witches and elves
More feared than the icy vastness of the far northern seas
Yet it is the forest offering him his only refuge and escape

Beneath the tall trees thick-canopied, night has already fallen
Leaves and needles rustle, twigs and cones crunch underfoot
He makes his way with wary caution, limping, chills setting in
Hoping to find some form of shelter, some safety and warmth
Even an abandoned woodcamp or empty charcoaler's shack

No such salvation offers and the chills burrow bone-deep
He wonders how injured he truly is, how much blood lost
If he dies here in the forest, he might go forever unfound
No funeral-pyre or rocky cairn marked with runestones
No gravegoods, his name lost, his fate and fame forgotten

Or, in an even bleaker wondering, might he already be dead?
Had he shamed himself in battle and not been Valkyrie-chosen?
Had he been passed over, deemed not worthy, left behind?
Could this staggering, stumbling trek be just the beginning

Of the drear and endless walk of Hel's grey eternal road?

The prospect is soul-crushing and he forces it from his mind
He fought well, with skill and bravery, earning no disgrace
Two dozen men or more must have fallen to his thirsty blade
And hundreds before that; he was born and bred a warrior
There must and will be a place for him among the Einherjar!

By this true resolve sure-strengthened, he presses onward
Until daylight's last dregs are vanished and dark is absolute
With no found shelter, he huddles cloak-wrapped in a hollow
Half-roofed by unearthed roots below a massive leaning oak
His thoughts of hall and hearth as drizzling rain begins to fall

Noises awaken him, soft chirps and chittering, barking yips
His eyes open to a strange radiance, an amber-golden glow
Not morning sun, not torch or candle flame, but warming
As he sees around him a ring of foxes, their russet fur afire
Is he in fact awakened? Or still in some uncanny dream?

They look back at him, inquisitive, heads tilted, gazes bright
Larger than any fox he's seen, black-tipped ears pricked keenly
Fearless and intelligent, their cunning paws precisely placed
Each wearing a slim silken collar pinned with a shining gem
Yet most amazing of all are those lush, flowing fiery pelts!

In disbelief—he must be dreaming!—he slowly sits upright
The foxes do not disappear, do not retreat, do not flinch or shy
They croon and chirp and chitter as if encouraging his efforts
Their warmth permeates him; he basks in unexpected comfort
Weariness falls away, the ache of his wounds seems lessened

When they do move, they move as one, pausing, glancing back
He understands their urging, the foxes wish for him to follow

Sleek and fleet through the forest, a living river of fire and fur
And follow he does, deeper into the dense woods' darkness
Guided by their glow, apprehensive, uneasy, but not afraid

Then ahead shines a greater light, as of bonfires or beacons
The narrow tree-path opens onto a wider scene of wonder
An autumnal grove, a high-timbered hall roofed in boughs
Caged flames hang as lanterns, leaves twinkle, motes dance
Rich moss softer than thick fleeces carpets the earthen floor

From a wellspring crystal-clear wells cool crystal-clear water
Coursing clean and cool along a winding stone-lined creek
Natural wood forming furnishings, long tables and benches
Where gather not men but the birds and beasts of the forests
Deer and bears, wolves and owls, fierce boars, all in a peace

Here, though not harvest-time, a harvest feast has been laid
Freshest fruits and ripe berries, meaty nuts flawless in shell
Drink-bowls brimming sweet with mead and crisp apple-wine
Seed-cakes and honey-cakes, bread, savory porridge-grains
Mushrooms, river-fish cooked and crusted with wild herbs

As the fiery foxes flood in to take their own places at table
The warlord stands nearly spell-struck by the strange sights
Then the largest fox, silk collar emerald-pinned, leads him
And again, he follows, unafraid, his battle-senses quiescent
Either he truly is dreaming, or truly is in no danger here

To a side-chamber, he's taken, a leafy bower moss-draped
Where silent servants await, wooden folk brought to life
He lets them attend him and soon is washed and bathed
His wounds balmed and bandaged, beard neatly brushed
Clean clothes brought for him of gold-trimmed dark green

When he returns to the main hall, the feast is underway
These animals of the woodlands, predators and their prey
Eating and drinking together in hearty good fellowship
Regarding him with keen interest but utterly without fear
Welcoming him among them as if he's one of their own

Then a trill of bright birdsong thrills through the warm air
Feathered hosts sweep in swift, red-winged, yellow-crested
Dancing and darting in an intricate, glorious, aerial display
Sparks and embers rain from them, a glittering fire-shower
Hushing the hall as a figure of breathtaking beauty appears

Not so much woman as elf-queen, or a wild-wood goddess
Some daughter of the Vanir, Freya's kindred, fairest of fair
She stands tall and slender, shapely, lithe and long-limbed
Skin smooth and pale as moon-milk, creamy, unblemished
A gossamer gown brushing her curves like a lover's caress

Her hair is richest auburn and autumn, all garnets and gold
Curled and pinned, piled high, plaited, ringlets dangling
Crowned with a wreath of gilded leaves, twigs, and berries
Every step is a swaying gracefulness as she crosses the hall
To a throne of oak; the beasts bow their heads in her wake

Around her slim white throat is girded a thin silken band
Like those of the foxes, hers likewise is held with a jewel
Her features, too, seem foxlike—vulpine, sleek and clever
A wicked vixenness to be seen in the sly slant of her smile
The tilt of fine auburn brows, the glint of mysterious eyes

Seated upon oaken throne, she surveys this forest assembly
This harvest hallmote, this uncanny, unheard-of gathering
Where bear and wolf, boar and owl, fox and deer all dine
Her gaze reaches the warlord, and her smile turns winsome

With beckoning gesture of elegant hand, she summons him

He approaches, his heart beating hot and hard in his breast
Blood pounding, his throat dry, his knees nearly trembling
He has sworn oaths to earls and to kings, great gift-givers
He has faced armies in battle, fought the most terrible foes
Yet never before in his life has such nervousness held him

This fae creature, whether woman or goddess, witch or elf
Needs no sorcery to enchant and enthrall to the very soul
She is her own magic, mistress of herself and of this realm
Her scent woodsmoke, apple-wine, rainfall and rare spices
As he stands before her, he knows he is both lost and found

His mouth opens, but utterance fails him; words inadequate
She stops him with the press of a slender finger to his lips
Her touch startling in its shy gentleness and lingering heat
Those vixen's eyes twinkling, rosy color tinting fair cheek
Her hand trailing downward to stroke his fullness of beard

If words are inadequate, they are in this moment unneeded
He takes a slow knee, grasping the hilt of his trusty weapon
His sword strong and proud, worthy veteran of many battles
Its heft and weight and grip familiar, an extension of himself
Drawing it forth to lay naked blade upon the lady's fair lap

She, gliding delicate fingertips along sword's firm length
Tracing the patterns and runes in its finely-worked steel
Leans forward to once again press his lips, with her own
A warm kiss of autumn, harvest-time's ripe, rich promise
Suffusing him with magic and power and apple-wine light

Let other oaths and allegiances fall aside and be forgotten
Battles and kingdoms, silver and sea voyages, be no more

Even the Einherjar, the prospect of Valkyries and Valhalla
Here in the formerly dark and feared forest is a better fate
To be wood-lord, not warlord, here with his foxfire queen.

HIGH SCHOOL MYTHICAL: ASGARD

"Gimme a V!" yelled Brunhilde.

"V!" responded the squad, throwing their arms into the air.

"Gimme an A!"

"A!" Hands triangled together above their heads.

"Gimme an L!"

"L!" One arm straight up, the other straight out to the side.

"Gimme an H-A-double-L-A!" Brunhilde's pom-poms shook a metallic flurry of blood-red and gold in the stadium lights. "What's that spell?"

"Valhalla!"

"What's that spell?"

"*Valhalla!* Gooooooo, Vikings!"

Whooping and cheering, the Valkyries launched into an exuberant display of high-kicks, split-jumps, cartwheels and hand-springs. They wore shiny gold breastplates, pleated red and gold mail skirts, and headbands with upswept gold foil wings.

"And we're back," came a voice over the loudspeakers, Kvasir in the announcer's booth at the top of the bleachers, "for the fourth quarter in this thrilling contest between our own Asgard Vikings and the Midgard Serpents!"

The crowd roared. Pennants flapped. Horns blew. Down by

the 50-yard-line, a bunch of shirtless Einherjar body-painted the team colors bumped their muscular chests together, brandishing tankards that sloshed froth into the three rows behind them. Nobody objected. Fans waved homemade banners—GO VIKINGS, I (HEART) YOU SIGURD, STOMP THE SNAKES!

Kvasir went on to wax eloquent about the long-standing rivalry between the two team captains, quarterbacks Thor and Jormungandr. Theirs was a bitter grudge-match going back years, and would probably only end if and when they killed each other.

Over on the Midgard side of the stands, the scene was much the same, though done in dark green and silver, the banners read CRUSH THEM and SERPENTS RULE!, and the fashion statement of choice was big foam snake-heads complete with fangs.

The score was tied, injured players were regularly carted off the field. They'd be back on their feet the next day and raring to go like nothing had happened. Indulgent blind eyes were turned to the heavy wagering going on. Similar indulgence would be afforded later to the inevitable riots and wild parties.

From the line of scrimmage came loud war-shouts and the thunderous crash of battle. Helmed heads cracked together. Armored shoulders met like shield-walls. Spittle sprayed and hot breath grunted. The fallen tumbled, groaning, to the torn turf. Ravens wheeled above and wolves skulked, yellow-eyed, in the shadows beyond the goal posts.

Back and forth they went, in violent conflict. Then Thor, with a mighty hammer-blow that he'd named his signature move, drove Jormungandr heavily to the ground. Hrothgar passed to Beowulf, but the Dragon tackled him at the ten.

"Fumble!" Kvasir, even amplified, could barely be heard over the tumult. "Wiglaf for the recovery... he's at the five... the two... *touchdown*! Touchdown, Vikings! That was epic!"

As the spectators went wild, either in celebration or protest, Kvasir started relating the story everyone in the Nine Worlds already knew, about the infamous junior-varsity match when, after

Beowulf tackled Grendel, Grendel's mother charged onto the field to attack the team. People would be talking about *that* one for ages.

It proved the surge the Vikings needed. They scored three more times before the end of the game. Wagnerian music burst full-volume from the loudspeakers. Immediate fights broke out, jubilant Asgardians and outraged Midgardians, and others who just always enjoyed any excuse for a good brawl or drunken free-for-all.

Skadi waited a while, giving the evening's festivities a chance to get fully underway. A purpose far more serious than football had brought her hither from the mountains. Only an errand so grim could, in this season, lure her from the snowy slopes.

She came seeking not revelry, but revenge.

As she waited, she made ready for the upcoming challenge. She girded herself with underwire bra, hoisting high the proud mounds of her bosom. Fine mesh stockings encased her strong legs. Her sexiest, most stylish dress, she donned... silver and snug-fitting with a slit up the side. Onto her feet, she buckled absolutely kick-ass killer heels.

Thus attired, she adorned her lips and eyelids with cosmetics, and brushed out until it shone her long locks, until her fair hair shone like firelight.

Then she made her way to the best party, where all of the cool kids would be. Held, of course, at the home of Odin, Asgard High's student body president and all-around Big Man On Campus.

The scene was already much as she'd expected. A great bonfire blazed. Vikings and Valkyries frolicked in the pool and the steaming hot tub. The Einherjar guzzled and gorged. There were kegs of beer, vats of mead, jugs of wine. An entire boar turned on a spit, sizzling with grease and dripping with juices.

The house itself had many doors and a roof shingled in gold. From the open doors, and windows, throbbed a heavy, pounding beat.

As Skadi approached the front gate, heels crunching on rainbow-colored gravel, her gaze caught the glow of a cigarette ember in the shadows of a large ash tree. Glancing that way, she beheld a wicked grin, and felt her curves closely scrutinized from head to toe.

"*Hwaet*," he said by way of greeting, flicking his hair back from his brow. "Skadi, right? Jotunn High skiing champion?"

She nodded.

"I'm Loki."

"Oh, I know who you are, Loki, Laufey's son."

His eyebrows climbed, with a bit of a swagger. "Yeah?"

"Yeah. You used to go to Jotunn, too. But they kicked you out."

Loki looked wounded. "Kicked me out? No, no. I transferred to Asgard."

"Someone must have pulled some very long strings."

"So, they still talk about me over there?"

"They certainly do."

"Glad to hear it. That's what counts, isn't it?"

"You say that as if it's anything to be boasted about?"

"Why wouldn't it be?"

"Have you forgotten Angrboda?"

He raised both hands, palms out. "Now, *she* dumped *me*."

"She tells it differently."

"Yeah, well, she would."

"And what about the time you stole our mascot during the big game at Hrimthurs Wall?"

"You can't claim that's why your team lost. We were kicking your butts anyway. The mascot thing was only a… a prank."

A squirrel ran halfway down the tree trunk, chattered something obscene, then scampered to safety as Loki shot it a warning look.

Skadi watched it go, and did a mild double-take at the sight of several other animals up in the branches. An eagle with a hawk on its head, weird enough; but three or four stags? She shook her head, focused on the ground, and took a reflexive step back at the sight of a nest of snakes writhing around in the roots and puddles beside a leaking sprinkler head.

"Don't listen to that little snot," Loki said. "You want a drink or something? I'll introduce you around." He did the hair-flick again, and the grin, and Skadi did have to admit, he was far from unattractive.

She reminded herself that he was also nothing but trouble. He'd known who she was; could he also know why she was here? If she walked into a trap...

If she walked into a trap, then she walked into a trap. And on their dishonorable heads be the shame.

Loki stubbed out his smoke and tossed it into the rainbow gravel. "Come on in."

"Out of curiosity," Skadi said as they went through the gate, "how *did* you steal our mascot? That horse is a monster! Nobody can get near him."

"I... have my ways," Loki said, reddening.

"Tell me," she urged.

He coughed, rubbing fitfully at the nape of his neck. "Trust me, snow-bunny, you *don't* want to know."

Before she could further press the matter, two guys and a girl ambled around the corner of the house.

The girl was gorgeous in a carefree, natural way that put all Skadi's careful preparations to shame, with flowing hair, limpid eyes, a lush figure swaying unrestrained in a loose and gauzy gown. She wore chunky jewelry of amber and ivory, and not a bit of makeup. A fluffy cat, striped and indolent, nestled purring in her arms.

One of the guys resembled her enough to be her twin, complete with similar clunky jewelry and a shoulder-length wavy mane. Homespun cotton pants rested dangerously low on his hips and suggested rather strongly that he didn't bother with other, more restrictive garments either. Or shoes. His eyes smoldered half-lidded, his mouth was a ripe sensualist's, and—a cute little gold-bristled pot-bellied pig trotted snuffling at his bare heels.

Ah well, she'd seen stranger things, and had a feeling the night was far from over yet.

"Hi, Loki," said the girl. She had a whispery, half-sultry and half-dreamy voice.

"Yo, dude," the guy added, his voice the male equivalent of hers. "Who's the lady?"

"Freya, Freyr. This is Skadi."

Freya extended a slim hand, bracelets clinking. "Your aura is so blue... not just any blue but glacial... so clean, so clear."

"Nice to meet you. Real pleasure." Freyr also extended his hand.

"Thanks." Skadi briefly touched them both and felt a warm, almost dizzying, rush from each.

The other guy with them, some scrawny underclassman, stood there awkwardly with a basket of freshly unearthed mushrooms. Or maybe truffles.

Loki leaned in to inspect the basket's contents, then gave Freyr an approving thumbs-up. "Looks like Gullinbursti sniffed out a good crop, there."

"Only the best, dude. Only the best."

"Hey, is that a ship in your pocket, or are you just glad to see us?" Loki asked Freyr.

"Old joke, man," he said.

"But funny every time."

"So say you," said Freya, petting the cat. She smiled at Skadi. "Are Jotunn boys as shameless as these?"

"Pretty much—" Skadi said.

Freyr started, losing a portion of his lazy cool. "Jotunn? You go to Jotunn High? Whoa... oh wow... do you know Gerdr?"

"Yeah," Skadi replied. "Why?"

"Oh wow, oh man, dude." He swiped his hair back from his temples, where beadlets of sweat suddenly glistened.

Freya sighed, not unsympathetically, and touched her brother's wrist. "Would you just talk to her already? The crystals aren't going to get any more favorable."

"Talk to her?" For someone not wearing a shirt, Freyr did a good job of trying to loosen his collar, gulping. "I can't... I mean... I mean whoa… she's so, like… so foxy and…"

"Wait, wait, wait," said Loki. "What's this? Freyr has the jitters? Over a *girl*? Freyr? Freyr-the-*Playr*? You're kidding me. You've dated half the babes at Asgard, half of them at least."

"This time it's different," Freyr said. "Ever since I saw her, I just… dude… but whenever I think about trying to talk to her, I… whoa…"

"Well, you can't keep on gazing at her from afar, mooning and moping, driving past her house and following her to the mall," said Freya.

"Mmm, stalkery," Loki remarked.

Freyr groaned. "I know, I know. But what if she, like, shot me down? What if she's seeing someone? I don't know what I'd do. I'd… dude, die or something. I mean, it'd be a seriously major bummer."

"I don't think she is," Skadi said, not sure why she was feeling sorry for him or urged to help, though she also held no particular grudge against him. "Seeing anyone, that is."

Loki, marveling, shook his head. "I don't believe it. Freyr, struck love-stupid. What next? A wolf swallows the sun?"

"Want me to go?" the underclassman spoke up. "I could take her a message, maybe."

"You could?" Freyr blinked. "Wow, yeah, man, you could… that'd be all right… that way, if, she, like, wasn't interested, it'd soften the blow… and if she was, then—"

"Then you'd look like an insecure idiot," Loki began.

"Then all would be well," Freya interrupted.

"You'd do that for me, Skirnir? Be my, like, wing-man?"

"Sure. Glad to. Though… could I borrow your car?"

"My car? *My* car?"

"How's it going to look if I go on the bus?" Skirnir asked. "Seriously. I'll be careful. You know you say that car practically drives itself."

"This isn't going to go well," Loki said. "Trusting this junior varsity nobody with your wheels? What about the car show? Surt's been working on that hot-rod flame chariot of his all year."

"Hey man, whatever, I can deal with Surt. And if it gets me a chance with Gerdr, who cares?"

"Your funeral."

"Yeah, yeah."

Loki turned to Skadi again. "I can't bear to watch. Let's go get that drink."

"Later, dude," Freyr said absently, his full attention on Skirnir. "Okay, so, say that I did loan you my car ..."

"Stay out of trouble, Loki," Freya said.

"As if." He winked. "Don't forget, you promised to teach me that falcon trick."

They said their goodbyes, then Skadi followed him as he entered the house. The music was louder, and the party had spread through several rooms.

The band had set up in a center-most chamber. Across the bass drum was scrawled, in black runic lettering: *The Skalds*. The lead singer, spiked of hair and pierced of lip and eyebrow, wore ripped jeans and arm-rings of studded leather. He howled poetic sagas into a microphone.

"That's Bragi," Loki said. "He's pretty good. I don't have much of a talent for kennings, myself. Flytings and insults are more my speed. But you should hear him when he busts out his electric harp. He *shreds* on that baby."

"Idunn's boyfriend, isn't he? Is she here tonight?"

"Who, Idunn? Yeah, she's around somewhere, probably making sure everybody stays hydrated and healthy with her apple-a-day reminders. You know her, huh?"

"Heard of her." A rime-frost of ice crept into her tone, despite her efforts of nonchalance.

Crafty Loki was no doubt far from fooled. He'd recognized Skadi as Jotunn High's ski champion, after all; he must also be aware of her other connections. Maybe her presence here intrigued him, amused him. Maybe he just wanted to see what would happen next.

A great revelry of laughter rang from the feasting-hall, where the drinking was heaviest and mead-benches lined the walls. Two Einherjar attempted kegstands on a long table, and others guzzled mead in contest from horn-shaped funnels. Sigurd, with Brunhilde riding astride his shoulders, faced off against another Viking with Valkyrie astride; the girls, shrieking giggling war-cries, swatted each other with oversized foam-rubber axes.

Loudest among the laughter was a jovial, booming roar like mighty thunder. Loki rolled his eyes at the sound of it, reaching into a nearby cooler. "Thor, obviously."

"Obviously," Skadi said. She accepted the can of Heidrunn Lite he handed her, opened it, and took a sip as she surveyed the room.

Thor, in an Asgard High sweatshirt with the sleeves and collar torn away to expose his brawny arms to the shoulders and his powerful chest to the collarbones, was unmistakable even before she saw the hammer tattoos on each bicep. Mjolnir in ink, Mjolnir in duplicate. When he flexed, which he did at any opportunity, jagged bright lightning-bolts flashed around the hammers. Those standing near enough could even hear the rumble, and those standing too near might get a jolting static shock.

When he saw Loki, Thor's laughter didn't stop, but a baleful reddish light burned from beneath his thick brows.

"He looks like he wants to wring your neck," Skadi said. "What'd you do this time?"

"Ah, he always looks like that. Not my fault he doesn't have a very sophisticated sense of humor."

"Weren't you the one who talked him into wearing a wedding dress and a veil to crash our Homecoming pep rally?"

Loki snorted with mirth. "Yeah... awesome moment, truly epic... one of my best, if I do say so myself."

"No wonder he wants to wring your neck."

"Like I said, not a very sophisticated sense of humor. Sif, either. That time I cut all her hair off, that was a *joke*."

Sif, of course, was another Skadi recognized. Thor's girlfriend was not one of the Valkyrie cheerleaders, but Asgard's top female athlete in her own right, a track and field star. She stood tall and strong, poised and confident. A shining braid the color of ripe wheat had been coiled and pinned at the back of her head.

"You cut off her *hair*?"

"It was a *joke*," he repeated. "And I fixed it. See? You can hardly tell the difference anymore."

"Don't you ever think that, one of these days, they're going to get tired of your *jokes*?"

"Oh, they keep threatening that they'll... I don't know, pants me and tie me to the flagpole, or chain me to that big rock out in the quad. But I'm not worried. They'd have to catch me first."

The high chamber was smaller, and somewhat quieter, with conversational clusters and less chanting of, "Chug! Chug! Chug!" Loki made an exaggerated shushing gesture as he ushered Skadi in.

Odin, of course, she knew on sight and by reputation. Popular enough to win student body president in a landslide; cool enough to be in on the fun high school hijinks instead of an uptight hall monitor and prefect like Tyr; going steady with Frigg, the wholesome beauty queen who formed the center of the Asgardian social scene. Between her connections and Odin's own network of informants, nothing went on that they didn't know about.

The BMOC's attire was of a moderately prep-school style, with two white wolves embroidered on the breast of his polo shirt and the sleeves of a grey cashmere sweater loosely knotted at his neck so that it draped his back like a thick cloak.

"What's with the eyepatch?" Skadi asked in a murmur.

"Oh, that? The way I heard it, he really wanted to be class valedictorian, as if he didn't have enough going for him already. Said he'd hang upside down from a tree and give his left eye for straight A's. So, Mimir, the crazy old librarian, took him up on it."

"Ouch," Skadi said.

He shrugged. "Could be worse. Most guys would have said their left nut."

Two slim, quick youths with hair the glossy black of raven's feathers darted up to Odin, tapping him upon the shoulder. Odin tipped his head to listen to what the youths whispered into his ear, then turned to regard Loki and Skadi with the keen gaze of his remaining eye.

"Loki," Odin called, the effect silencing all within earshot. "Who is this you've invited to our party?"

"I didn't invite her," Loki said. "She just showed up on her own. You can't blame this one on me."

The set of Frigg's mouth conveyed her doubts on *that* account, but she said nothing. Instead, Asgard's queen bee studied Skadi, evaluating her on fashion, poise, posture and hairstyle. Skadi lifted her chin, knowing she had done well to garb herself in her wardrobe-glory for this confrontation.

"I am Skadi," she announced, taking a bold stride forward. "Skadi Thjazisdottir. I come with a grievance."

"I knew it." Loki smirked. "Oh yeah, this ought to be good."

"Well, well, well," Odin said, steepling his fingertips together. He didn't even have the decency to look concerned, let alone contrite, guilty or ashamed. "Suppose you tell us, then, what is this grievance you bring."

"I'm here on behalf of my father. When you and some of your friends were on one of your road trips, you stopped at his diner. The Ox and Eagle, do you recall it?"

"I may recall a restaurant by such name," Odin said. "We were only looking to get something to eat, after such a long journey."

"It was five minutes before closing time," Skadi said. "He'd already shut down the kitchen for the night, cleaned the grill. He offered to make you some sandwiches, instead, but you'd have none of it."

"As I further recall it," Odin said, "we invited him to sit down and join us for a meal. We said that we'd buy him dinner as well as our own, but what he did was serve us some cheap frozen burgers while making a thick slab of prime rib for himself, and charging us triple the price into the bargain."

"For which," Skadi said, "you ruffians, you bullies, you started trashing the place and roughing him up. Him, an old man, and outnumbered besides."

"That would hardly convey a positive image and glowing endorsement of our fine school," Tyr said. "I'm surprised this wasn't brought to the attention of the debate team or student council."

"Some drinking," admitted Odin, clearing his throat, "may have been involved."

"But, when the outnumbered old man didn't prove to be so easily beaten," Skadi went on, "when, in fact, he began giving *you* a sound thrashing instead, you begged him to let you go. You offered to bribe him. Then you threatened to blackmail him."

"We were only goofing around," Loki said. "Kids. Guys. Goofing around. Things got a little carried away, that's all."

"Goofing around?" cried Skadi. "By telling everyone he tried to kidnap Idunn? Like he was some sort of filthy pervert, chasing after high school girls?"

"Idunn had no idea," Frigg said. "She was very upset when she heard of it later."

"You Asgard hot-shots think you can go anywhere and do anything you like, without consequence," Skadi said. "You humiliated my father, nearly ruining his business and his reputation. What do you have to say for yourselves?"

"Go, Vikings?" snickered the trickster.

"Loki!" snapped Odin, Frigg and Tyr in unison.

"All in all, it was perhaps a regrettable incident," Odin continued. "We may, indeed, owe some manner of apology, compensation and atonement. Would you grant us a few moments to discuss it? In the meanwhile, Loki will be glad to entertain you."

"Get him to do his party piece," one of the slim, black-haired youths said. "I thought it hilarious. Remember, Muninn?"

The other nodded vigorously. "I certainly do, Huginn. When

he tied a cord strung between the beard of a nanny-goat and his own..."

"How about we save that for later?" Loki interjected. "I did promise Skadi I'd give her the tour, and we haven't finished yet."

"By all means, then," said Frigg. "Please do."

He swept with a flourish a most lavish bow, then ushered Skadi from the high chamber.

"So," he said, chortling. "Old Thjazi's your dad. Did he and your uncles really have to settle their inheritance with an eating contest?"

"Don't you take anything seriously?" Skadi asked, ignoring his question.

"Not really, no. Where's the fun in that? Oh, hey, check out the little weirdo in the corner. That's Heimdall. He's got nine moms. Don't ask."

"Nine moms?"

"I said, don't ask. And he's a band geek. I mean, he plays the *gjallarhorn*, for crying out loud. You probably saw him at halftime, marching around out there with the other unfortunates in their uniforms."

"I get the idea you don't like him very much."

"Why, just because I had a perfectly good prank in the works with Freya's favorite necklace, and he had to butt in and wreck it? He dances like the whitest white boy in the Nine Worlds; who knew he could swim like a seal? That's more Njord's department."

"Njord? The sea-god?"

"Sea-god, beach-bum, whatever you want to call it. He's over there, by the way. The one with the tan and the shaggy hair hanging down in his eyes."

"He's kind of cute," Skadi said, as much to irk Loki as anything else.

"If you're into mussel-shell jewelry and herring, maybe, I guess. Hey, you know, once, I caught an otter that had just caught a salmon. Two meals for the price of one. Let's see... who else is here? You saw Frigg, and Tyr, making sure nobody has too much fun.

Did you hear about the time he stuck his hand in a wolf's mouth?"

"Was that your doing, as well?"

"Only indirectly," Loki said. "In a round-about kind of way."

"Right. What about that girl?"

"What girl?"

"That one, there, the one who keeps staring at me."

He grinned again. "Not narrowing it down much, snow-bunny. You were getting a lot of attention before the word started going around. It'd be easier to spot who *isn't* staring at you."

"Glaring, then."

"Glaring?" He slid a subtle scan of the room this way and that. "Who, her? What's-her-name? Sigyn? Don't worry. She glares at everyone."

But the girl named Sigyn, Skadi noticed, did anything but glare when her gaze fell upon the handsome, wicked bad-boy. Then it went wistful and suffering, and Skadi understood.

She might as well have had the truth writ large on her face. I (HEART) LOKI, just as the fans had waved banners for Sigurd. Hers was the desperate hope that, some day, he'd notice her; and the glum soul's certainty that of course he never would.

To all of which, Loki passed in utter obliviousness or unconcern.

"Now, if you look to your right," he said, adopting a tour-guide tone, "you'll see more of the Asgard Nerd Squad... the blind-as-a-bat kid with the glasses is Hod, the one with the big stupid ortho-pedic boot is Vidr, those three busybody know-it-all told-you-so gossips are the Norn sisters, and..."

Skadi caught her breath. "Never mind them; who's *he*?"

Without even looking, Loki said dryly, "*He* must be Baldr the Beautiful, and don't get your hopes up, snow-bunny. He's out of your league. He's out of everyone's league."

"I heard that," Baldr said.

And he *was* beautiful, that was for certain. Male-model hand-some, flawless skin, perfect white teeth, better-dressed than any-one else in attendance but carrying himself in a way that conveyed comfortable assurance and ease. Skadi felt her wits freeze, then give way in the inexorable grandeur and slow-motion manner of glacial ice calving off to crash into the cold northern sea.

"Baldr! Buddy! Hi!" Loki said brightly, flashing his own teeth. They were as white, if not nearly as perfect, as Baldr's... and quite a bit sharper. "Any adventures under the mistletoe lately?"

"You'd be wise to watch your mouth, Loki. I'm still mad at you."

"From the Yule festival? I swear, it was an accident."

"Accident? You nearly got me killed, putting poor Hod up to throw that dart at me."

"Total fluke. Lucky shot. One in a million. He shouldn't have been able to hit the broad side of Midgard; there was no way I could've known. Besides, it didn't turn out all bad. You totally could have scored with that Goth chick."

"Hel?" Baldr's perfect, beautiful eyebrows made perfect, beautiful arches on his perfect, beautiful forehead. "She's hardly my type."

"I'm just saying."

"You're always just saying, and always just saying too much. Which is what *I* was just saying. Watch your mouth. It's going to get you in trouble."

"From you? Pfah." Loki scoffed. "What, and risk mussing your hair? Sure thing, pretty boy. I'll keep that in mind."

"Hi..." Skadi belatedly managed to say.

By then, however, Baldr had turned away with a sigh of impatience and disdain.

Loki gave her a smirk. "Told you that you were out of his league."

"Thanks a lot."

"But, if you're looking ..."

"Don't flatter yourself."

"I always flatter myself. It's part of my charm."

"I wouldn't go out with you if we were the only survivors of Ragnarok. I'd sooner hang a snake over my head while I slept. Or, better yet, over yours."

Loki drew back a step, feigning shock. "What did *I* do? Did I ask you out? Was I hitting on you? Ski-jumping to some conclusions, there, aren't you?"

"What did... you... my father... why I'm even *here*... ugh! You really *don't* take anything seriously!"

The black-haired freshman youths appeared beside them so suddenly it was as if the pair materialized out of thin air. "Odin would like to speak with you again, Skadi," Huginn said.

"Indeed, to everyone," said Muninn.

Just then, the Skalds ended their current number with a shriek of instruments that sounded like the scraping clash-clangor of many sword-blades. Bragi, with the microphone, requested the attention of the entire party, bidding them be summoned at once to the main hall.

It was soon done. The Asgardians gathered, some Vikings and Valkyries yet dripping from their frolics in the pool, others with their mouths grease-smeared from feasting or attempting to refasten their disarranged garments. Idunn stood with Frigg and gave Skadi a silent look of remorse for her unwitting part in the previous events. Freyr and Freya were there, though the underclassman Skirnir was not; presumably, Freyr had consented to loan him the car.

Odin, resplendent in his wolf-logo polo shirt and neck-knotted sweater of grey cashmere, took the stage. He held high a commanding hand. His lone eye held a stern, flinty shine. Coached by Bragi and Kvasir, who were both good with words, and advised by Tyr's law-lore and Frigg's social counsel, he spoke.

He told the assembly of what had happened on that ill-fated road-trip, how the bounds of fair hospitality had been disregarded. He told them how Thjazi had been misused, abused, wronged and maligned.

"This is not a shame that we want staining our honor and school pride," Odin said. "We must make amends to Thjazi. I say that we shall hold a fund-raiser, the proceeds to go toward rebuilding, repairing and restoring his business. And that, furthermore, we lend our own volunteer efforts to the cause."

The declaration was met with much acclaim and approval. Idunn offered to host a bake-sale of her prize-winning apple pies, and Bragi said on behalf of the Skalds they could conduct a benefit concert, and several other such suggestions were put forth.

"Will this satisfy your grievance, Skadi Thjazisdottir?" asked Odin.

"If you also let the truth be far-known," she said. "I would have my father's name cleared, and his reputation."

"It is only fair, right, and just," said Tyr. "I agree."

"Then let it be settled, unless any among us have further amendment to make."

Loki's arm shot immediately straight up over his head. "I think we owe Skadi a token of esteem and apology as well. She did a bold thing in coming here to speak for her father."

"What are you up to?" Skadi asked him, eyes narrowing.

"She did do that," Odin said. "What do you suggest?"

"Well, she's looking for a boyfriend."

Skadi gaped, gasped and sputtered. Mingled reactions, mostly of amusement and some of outrage or astonishment, swept the hall.

"Or maybe just a date," Loki went on. "The Idavoll dance is coming up, and I know plenty of guys here who don't have dates yet either. I say, we gather our most eligible bachelors and let her take her pick."

"Whatever you're playing at ..." Skadi began, still sputtering.

"No, sincerely," he said. "It's the least we can do. The Idavoll is *the* best dance of the year."

"He speaks the truth about that," said Frigg. "We'd be delighted to welcome you, and I'm sure you would have a wonderful time."

"And I'm just supposed to go to your dance with..." She waved her hand in an arc. "Someone here? Whoever I want?"

"As long as they're single," Brunhilde said, entwining Sigurd's arm in both of hers. Other Valkyries murmured in agreement.

"And as long as they're willing to stand forth in the first place,"

Sif said.

Freya purred a laugh. "For a date with fair Skadi? Look at her. I daresay we'll have no dearth of participants."

Odin glanced at Tyr, who shrugged in a helpless way that said it was well out of their hands now... the girls had seized eagerly upon Loki's idea and seemed ready to run with it.

"All right," said Asgard's BMOC. "How?"

"How," Loki cut in, "about we make it a little more interesting? They all stand behind a drape, with nothing showing but their—"

"Loki," Frigg warned.

"—feet, I was going to say feet anyway!" His sharp teeth flashed in their wide, wicked grin. "And then she must choose based only on what she can see."

"Fine," said Skadi. She jabbed a finger at him. "But *you* won't be among them, sly one."

He folded his hands to his chest. "Oh, Skadi. After all we've been through together, all we've meant to each other—"

"I *could* satisfy the rest of my grievance by demanding you do your party piece with the nanny-goat and the string!"

Loki winced. "Fair enough. I will not set myself, nor my feet, nor any other body parts, to this contest."

Freyr likewise begged off, for how would it look if Skirnir's errand to chat up Gerdr on his behalf was successful, only to have him then promised to go to the dance with someone else? Thor was spoken for, as were Odin and Bragi, and many of the Viking football players by their Valkyrie cheerleaders.

In the end, however, a group of unattached Asgardians were duly collected, while Skadi accompanied some of the girls to the restroom to powder their noses and chat. By the time they returned, benches had been set along the wall with a drape hung in front so that it fell to the ankles of those who stood bare-foot upon this makeshift platform.

Loki had not, Skadi saw, pulled some mischief of deceit. She supposed Sigyn, lurking near him with her sad, soulful eyes, would have found a way to interfere or make protest if he had. Or done something to assure Skadi chose anyone but him.

Not that Skadi would have had any intentions of doing so. She knew full well whose feet she wanted to select from those on display. Maybe Loki had thought he'd have a nice joke at her expense, throwing in that last-minute condition to make it a challenge… but he was not so crafty as he believed.

Those feet there, for example, could only belong to Vidr; they were mis-matched, one smaller and slightly twisted, looking weak and lop-sided without the built-up heel and sole of his special boot. And those, painstakingly neat and groomed but in other ways unremarkable, must be Tyr's. The pair with toes inward-turned and a nervous quaver, she guessed were the feet of Hod or Heimdall.

Some of the feet were, to be sure, quite well-formed and handsome. She might have had a difficult time deciding among them, did not one pair surpass even the rest.

Why, Baldr could not help but have feet as beautiful as the rest of him. Flawless feet and perfect, without blemish… free of any scar and smooth of any callus… strong toes and supple… the nails like polished crescents of moon-ivory. Lovely feet that might have been sculpted with all the best skill of a craftmaster's art.

"I choose these," she said, indicating the most beautiful pair of feet. "They look like they can dance."

Odin gestured. Huginn and Muninn drew back the drape. Skadi first saw that she'd been correct about Vidr and Tyr. She then saw that she had not been correct about Baldr.

His feet were handsome, yes, but not the most beautiful of all. Those, those belonged to another. Those belonged to fit, golden-tanned Njord.

"Congratulations!" Loki said, clapping Skadi cheerily on the back. "You two should make quite the couple. And now, I don't know about the rest of you, but I want another drink. Let's have some music! This party's only getting started."

"Music!" called Odin. "Mead and wine!"

Bragi sprang again to the stage, swung his electric harp into position, and raked his fingers over the glittering strings. He launched into an edgy rock version of *Heimskringl*. Kegs were tapped. The bonfire was rekindled so that flames leaped high, Valkyries and Vikings celebrating around it. Thor scooped up Sif and tried to throw her in the pool; she held on and toppled him in with her, sending up a great splash.

Amid it all, left to their own devices and largely unobserved, Skadi and Njord looked at each other.

"Hey," said Njord.

"Hey," Skadi replied.

There was a pause.

"You surf?" he asked.

"Ski."

"Water?"

"Downhill, slalom, cross-country."

There was another pause.

"How about wind-surfing? Sailing? Snorkelling?"

"Hiking, skating, ice-climbing."

"My family's got a beach house."

"Mine has a mountain lodge."

Yet another pause passed.

Njord exhaled a slow breath. "This isn't gonna work, is it?"

"Probably not."

"Want to give it a try anyway?"

"Sure," said Skadi, smiling. "Might as well."

She held out her hand to him, and Njord took it.

And so began the saga of the snow-bunny and the surf-bum.

WHEN PELE MET LOKI

O nce it was that sly Loki, child of giants
     Wolf-father, horse-mother, ever a prick
     Found it prudent to make quick departure
From Asgard's high halls where the gods dwell
Taking haste for he had, again, with his mischief
Most wickedly punked the red-bearded Thor
Mjolnir's bearer, known more for temper than wit
And Thor, in his humiliation, waxed wroth
Hwaet! Odin's son was most seriously pissed
With hammer in hand he set off smiting blows
Each striking lightning bright from the sky
As trickster fled fast and thunderer pursued
Until Loki, in falcon-form, took to flight
Swift over Bifrost, the bridge between worlds
Thor called for his chariot, goat-pulled, and gave chase
On raced cloven hooves, the iron wheels rumbling
On flew Loki through Norse-lands of ice and fjords
Through Saxony and Frisia, over hills and pine forests
In desperation, Thor close on his heels, Loki turned
Seaward the whale-road stretched vast before him
Its waves wide and endless, beyond reach of ship or of sail
Soon in fog and cloud-bank did Thor lose sight of his quarry
And turned back, satisfied he'd taught Loki his lesson,
With good cheer to Asgard, where golden mead-horns

And golden-haired Sif, his good wife, awaited
As Loki, who knew none of this, flew on with wings tiring
And heart beating fear that his ass would be kicked
Until, half-spent from exhaustion, he at last descended
Searching a safe haven to rest and recover his breath
He saw then below him such wonders as never imagined
The sun shining brilliant in tropical skies
The sea smooth as glass, blue-green and jewel-clear
Islands rose, archipelagos, a rocky profusion
Dense with lush foliage, and tall, strange, thin trees
On ivory-sand beaches rushed rolling surf-waves
Warm and white-foaming, tossing the shells
Fish filled the shallows and shadowed the depths
Here were folk living, brown of skin, black of hair
Wearing not furs and mail-coats but loincloths of leaves
Their women bare-breasted, blossom-bedecked
They had no dragon-ships, but sea-skimming canoes
No longhouse log-halls, but grass huts on high poles
Loki forsook falcon form for his own, and approached
How they marveled! For he was to them uncannily pale
Awestruck, they begged of him, was he mortal or god?
To which Loki, with immodest assent, claimed the latter
For when someone asks if you're a god, you say YES
They brought him to the sacred place of their idols
Where logs stood upright, carved like squat-bodied men
Faces war-painted, with feathered headdresses adorned
These, the folk said, were the Tiki, god-servants
Bringers of prosperity, good weather, and fortune
To prove his own power, Loki cleverly crafted a spell
And brought, to their wonder, the Tiki-idols to life
Drum-thumping and chanting enchanting tunes
Such a show as had thus been unknown to the world
(and, until nineteen-sixty-three, would be so again)
The amazed islander folk then showed him all honor

Offering succulent fruits, flowers, fishes fresh-caught,
Whole pigs sand-pit-roasted, meat falling tender from bone
Maidens were set to attend him, fanning with palm-fronds
While young men competed at sport and games for his pleasure
They strewed petals before him, hung garlands at his neck
Strong drink, they gave him, stronger than ale, mead or wine
In nut-hulls, hard and hairy, sipped through hollow reeds
Soon, Laufey's sly son was quite merry and contented
Contemplating not bothering to return to Asgard for a while
Now, there was here also a great smoking mountain
A fuming earth-cauldron, a volcano, deep-cratered
From its clefts would flow rivers of hot molten stone
From its peak, surging volleys of ash, flame, and death
This was home to a goddess, fierce fire-eyed Pele
The hungry, the vengeful, she who must be placated
And it so happened, in the fuss over Loki's arrival
The people had neglected to make their due sacrifice
Enraged, the goddess burst forth and descended
To punish and destroy them in her righteous ire
There, she beheld Loki, feasting and drinking, at his ease
She beheld the carved wooden idols, her own sacred Tiki
Transformed into capering animatronics
And fire-eyed Pele was, to say the least, not amused.
She appeared in a blazing and blistering heat
Flame-girdled, wreaths of fire alight on her brow
Black hair billowing, writhing like tendrils of smoke
Terrible in her beauty and glorious wrath
Abject island-folk threw themselves at her feet
Cowering and groveling, pleading for mercy
But this, she was most disinclined to bestow
She would have her revenge for her Tiki-idols
Of which had been made a dancing mockery
They turned from their antics, sprouting sharp claws
Embers kindling in their eyes, hot sparks spitting

Teeth bursting forth jagged in splintery rows
Fiery tongues licking and flicking from their jaws
And the Tiki, at Pele's bidding, commenced a slaughter.
In their attack, they were relentless, unstoppable foes
The islanders found their hunting-spears useless
Stone tips breaking brittle, thin shafts snapping
They fled for their lives and were cut down as they ran
Skin slashed to ribbons, the red blood wetly spraying
Bodies screaming in agony, guts spilled on the sand
Flesh sizzling, char-blackening, awash in fire-breath
Until, like sand-roasted pigs, meat fell tender from bone
The sweet stench in the sea-breeze wafting over the beach
As palm-trees became torches, and huts burned blazing
Then Pele turned to Loki, who yet stood unharmed
Alone now among the carnage and bloodshed and ruin
This pale stranger, who'd come uninvited to her land
While he looked with admiration upon the goddess
And with words of charm and flattery lavishly praised her
So that her anger gave way to passions of another kind
With which Loki was more than glad to comply
For three days and nights they made love with such vigor
That the islands trembled and the seas churned all around
On the fourth day of their bed-sport, every volcano erupted
With a lava-gouting, earth-shaking, shattering roar
Smoke, ash, and soot seething to darken the skies
So that in the farthest-off lands the tumult was noticed,
All asking each other, "What the fuck was that?"
Pele, smoldering and well-sated by Loki's attentions
Declared he should stay with her, as husband and king
To this, although flattered, he made quick demurral,
Admitting in fact he did have, already, a wife
Not to mention his several various children,
So he could not, in good conscience, commit to another
He was certain, however, Pele would understand—

Hwaet! No such luck, and indeed, far from it.
He'd thought Thor was pissed off? A mere trifle
Against the fury of a fire-goddess scorned
Her temper did not so much erupt as explode
Forget volcanoes; half the world split asunder
Landmasses cracked apart, broken to fragments
Whole continents sinking, doomed, into the sea
Waves awash, boiling, steam-scalding the rest
An obliterating cataclysm of epic proportions
A devastation almost to rival Ragnarok itself
And Loki? Be assured, he did not stick around
But took off as if his ass was on fire—which it was
When the smoke cleared, he was nowhere to be seen
Leaving Pele to simmer and stew in her molten anger
While he, again prudent, made haste home to Asgard after all.

FATE OF THE WORLD

"My fellow Heimlandrvolken... I stand before you now not only as your elected Lawspeaker but as a human being, mother, and citizen of the world.

"The purpose of this address is supposed to be for me to assure you that the state of the Althing is strong. To talk about the economy, our plans to reduce the tax burdens on the housecarl class, provide much-needed healthcare and jobs to those living in thralldom, and eliminate special-interest corruption among jarls.

"I could talk to you about foreign policy, military spending. I could placate you with platitudes, false hopes, gilded rings of tin disguised as gifts of gold.

"I could remind you of our struggles, our progress, and our triumphs through a thousand years of history, since our sea-going forefathers braved the icy waters of the north Atlantic to found a new land of freedom and opportunity upon these shores.

"I could seek to stir your spirits, your patriotism and pride. Divert, and distract you from the dangers that are so very, very real.

"My fellow Heimlandrvolken, you deserve better. You deserve honesty, and truth. You have entrusted me with this office. I am your thane. I owe you no less.

"But I speak not only to the people of this great nation. I speak also to our southern neighbors in the three proud empires of Quetzalcoata. I speak to our northern cousins of the Rus-Inuit territories.

I speak to our kindred and friends across Europe, Asia, Africa, and the Middle East. I speak to you, as I said at the beginning of this address, as a fellow human being and citizen of this world.

"And, as I also said, as a mother. If there has ever been one single drive and unifying force among us as a species, it is to build a better future for our children. We have fought for that common goal since first we took up tools and fire. Through wars, through plagues, through climate change, through disasters both natural and un-, we have persevered.

"We have even survived, and thrived, in the face of eldritch madness. We, who once slaughtered each other over petty differences of skin color and religion, came together, and held together as a race. The human race. Our intelligence, our inventiveness, our advances in science and technology, more than held their own against occultism and magic and creatures from beyond the realm of nightmares.

"That strength of will, that determination and tenacity, that sheer stubbornness, is what has kept us going. It is why we have not, and will not, surrender to our enemies. The atrocities in Carcosa… insurgents and extremists from Leng… the tyrannical sorcerous regimes of Eibon… we have stood fast against them all.

"We now face the greatest threat our world has ever known. Greater than global warming, greater than the last ice age, greater even than the cataclysmic events responsible for the mass extinctions of the dinosaurs.

"There is not a culture among us which hasn't portended a final apocalyptic doom, not merely for civilization or humanity, but on a total planetary scale. Whether you call it Ragnarok, Armageddon, B'Ak'Tun, or Judgment Day, we have long lived under the shadow of the end times.

"Which, I'm sorry to say, appear to be upon us.

"I am reliably informed by our top scientists that a rogue cometary dwarf star, designated X/1307616 2A but informally known as Grim-Ruin, is on a collision course to intersect its orbit with that of our solar system.

"To put it simply, it's going to hit. Not us directly, not our planet—the odds of that would be even more astronomical; a full presentation will be given following this address—but our sun, which is a much larger target with a much more powerful gravitational pull.

"If this were an ordinary comet, the effect would be like throwing a snowball into a bonfire. Grim-Ruin, however, is massive. Even a near miss would have catastrophic effects in terms of flares and radiation. A direct impact, such as projected…

"You may wonder why I am telling you this. If there is nothing we can do, if only utter obliteration awaits, wouldn't it be better to keep quiet, to let the world live out its last days in blissful ignorance? Rather than risk plunging us into another New Dark Age of panic and chaos?

"Some of my Wittan of advisers strongly advocated just that. But I, as I said, believe you deserve better. You deserve honesty. Not pap and pandering. We are not a nation—not a world!—of milksops. If we are to fall, I believe it is better to fall with eyes open, with hearts strong and spines straight, defiant to the last.

"And I do not believe there is nothing we can do. I refuse to believe that. We have taken on every challenge the cosmos has thrown at us. We have risen to meet them, overcome them, and won.

"I believe we can win this battle as well.

"But we cannot do it alone.

"To that end, I have taken the unprecedented step of opening diplomatic negotiations with R'lyeh.

"I have not forgotten, nor have any of us, nor will we ever, the numerous conflicts our countries have had before. I am not urging anyone else to forget, or forgive. The lives lost, the ships sunk and planes brought down, the terrible tragedies of the South Sea Islands, these memories will always be with us.

"However, if we are to have any chance at there being such an always, we must move past our history. We must move forward. We must work together. For the sake of us all, and the sake of our world. A world in which the R'lyehans, as well as humanity, have a substantial stake.

"Our science, technology, and military might alone cannot defeat a cosmic destructive force the likes of Grim-Ruin. Neither can the magic and esoteric arts of R'lyeh. A combined, cooperative effort is our only hope.

"Even now, an international think-tank of experts, the most brilliant minds from across the globe, is being assembled. It is their conviction that, with the assistance of R'lyeh, we can divert the cometary dwarf star from its course, if not destroy it outright. Thereby saving our sun… our solar system… and ourselves.

"The Wittan and I recently met with other world leaders. They have pledged their full support in this endeavor, but defer to Heimland as regards the establishing of diplomatic relations.

"I've also spoken privately over secure channels with Spawnpriest Cthlullan, who assures me that his government will gladly provide experts to contribute to the think-tank, and bring their full formidable magics and esoteric knowledge to bear on addressing the impending crisis.

"If, of course, we can agree on terms of truce and treaty.

"If our two nations can vouchsafe our honorable intentions, demonstrate good faith and goodwill, by a temporary custodial exchange.

"To be blunt, my fellow Heimlandrvolken, they have offered, and asked for, hostages.

"Previous administrations have been criticized for the jarls' apparent willingness to send the children of carls and thralls into combat and dangerous situations. To risk those lives, while their own children remain safe. Whether these criticisms are rightful or wrongful is not an issue to get into at this time.

"I will not be seeking volunteers. I will not be implementing a lottery or instituting a draft. I will not be subjecting our fine young men and women in uniform to this task.

"I will be sending my sons.

"Harald and Leif have accepted this obligation. They understand the importance of it, how we must show our absolute commitment to this cause. As a mother, yes, my heart is struck with dread. Yet, also as a mother, I am humbled and filled with pride.

"Let this stand as evidence; I would not request more of my people than I am willing to give of myself. Their lives are dearer to me than my own. I will do everything within my power to see this matter resolved.

"And I will personally host, within the White Hall as honored guests, the emissaries being sent from R'lyeh. No insult or action against them shall be tolerated. To this, I am hereby oathsworn before you all.

"In a moment, I'll be handing the podium over to our scientists, for a further briefing and discussion. Before I do so, I'd like to reiterate, to everyone not just here in Heimland but across and around this entire free world… we face the greatest challenge of our time, but, together, we will rise to the occasion.

"Gods bless, and goodnight."

***

At cruising altitude, the thudding ascent of *Asgard-One*'s eight rotor-engines became a steady gallop of smoother, soothing motion. The big *Sleipnir*-class aircraft leveled off, riding as easily above the clouds as a longship might skim the open seas. Beyond the round windows flitted wisps of white, and beyond that stretched blue sky and curving horizon.

All fell quiet but for the distant thrumming noise of flight, and what muffled conversation filtered in from the steerhouse at the stern. They'd refuled in Cusco, been warmly welcomed and generously hosted by the Inca, and from there embarked upon this last and most dangerous leg of their journey.

Leif Freylindesson stretched, and rolled his head, glancing over at his brother on the far side of the wide aisle. Harald, two years older, wore his flax-fair hair and beard short and neatly groomed. Leif preferred the wilder bad-boy look, himself. His own flowing mane was amber-gold, his beard reddish like their father's had been, though they both had their mother's storm-grey eyes.

They hadn't spoken much since leaving New Thingvellir. What else, really, was there to say that hadn't been said already?

"Do you think she's sending us to our deaths?" Leif had asked.

"I think she's doing what must be done," had been Harald's reply. "And who better for it?"

"True enough."

Now, here they were, leaving the last outposts of humanity further and further behind, with only the barest inkling of what awaited them. Just as their own ancestors had, centuries ago, set the prows of their ships westward, knowing it was a brave endeavor from which they might never return.

Leif grinned.

Yes, they could die, could meet some horrible and hideous un-speakable end… but if this truce and plan failed, well, the rest of the world would shortly follow. So, in the long run, their fates would hardly matter.

The success, however, of both truce and plan, would save them all. And then he and Harald would have made great name and fame for themselves for their courage! They would be remembered not only as the sons of a Lawspeaker, or by trading on their father's war-hero reputation, but by being the first men to set sane foot upon R'lyeh, and come back alive.

What a tale for the ages that would be!

With, of course, conditions. There were always conditions. Not even when staring oncoming annihilation dead in the eye were the R'lyehans about to reveal more of their secrets than they had to. No filming, no photography, no video or audio recording of any sort would be permitted… communications would be limited, and supervised… Harald and Leif would hardly have free run of the place, but neither would they be prisoners. Tourists, after a fashion.

Or, what was it Mother had said? Honored guests. Yes. Honored guests. Just as she would treat whoever—or whatever—this Spawn-priest sent in the exchange.

Their counterparts. Fellow hostages.

He was, truth be told, a little disappointed they weren't doing the swap like in the movies, some gloomy span of no-man's-land between tensely squared-off armed and armored war-bands... on one side, Heimlandr shield-tanks, and elite bear- and wolf-troops, maybe with Quetzalcoatan heart-snipers covering them from a distance... on the other, R'lyehan crawlers encrusted with sharp-edged barnacles and toxic spitting polyps, octophibian warriors, and thought-drinkers seeking psychic hints of treachery... as he and Harald were escorted out from a guarded gate, and as the chosen hostage-guests from R'lyeh likewise approached from the other... the moment of dramatic connection as they all paused, taking measure and marking in memory... then passing on, to be relinquished to their host-captors.

But, no. The reality of it was far less fraught and far more prosaic.

The reality of it was long hours as the engines thrummed, as the attendants brought ginger-mead and meals, magazines, blankets, whatever else might be requested or required for their comfort. The reality of it was droning motion, waiting, and unrestful sleep.

"Nearing Ephemera coordinates," said the steersman's voice over the intercom. "Beginning our descent. Crew prepare for anchor-dock."

Peering out every available window revealed to Leif only different views of the same vast sea-scape. This was, while not the middle of nowhere, certainly well within nowhere's borders. He saw no sign of land, no ships, no other aircraft. Even the media were, for once, obeying instructions and keeping to the agreed-upon distance.

Most of all, he certainly did not see a... what did they call it, again? A nightmare corpse-city of slimy green vaults and some-thing-or-other masonry... Harald, being the more scholarly of them, would know. Harald had tried to prepare Leif, or help Leif prepare himself, for the assault sure to beset their senses. Wiser and more learned men than they had been reduced to gibbering by the merest hint, glimpse, breath, or touch of R'lyeh.

"So... where is it?" he asked, squinting against the bright beams of the setting sun and their brilliant light-dazzle off the endless waters. "Where's the city?"

"We won't see it yet," Harald said.

"Obviously, for I don't see it now."

"Be glad. If we could, if it were visible, the steersman might tear out his own eyes and nose-dive us into the deep."

"And we're going there."

"You wanted excitement."

They gathered their belongings—what few items they were allowed to bring with them, clothing and food, personal effects, no weapons or war-gear of course—as the eight rotor-engines changed pitch and pace. *Asgard-One* banked and slowed in a gradual, descending curve, circling widely around a patch of ocean that, to Leif, looked just like every other patch of ocean.

"What about this outpost, or island, or whatever it is?" he asked.

"Ephemera? An island with an outpost."

Leif peered out a window again. "Shouldn't we be able to see that, then, at least?"

"It's ephemeral, isn't it?" Harald said, with a slight chiding tone. "It comes and goes. Sometimes there, sometimes not. Weren't you paying attention at the briefings?"

"Some," Leif said. He shrugged. "You're the brains of the family, brother-mine; I'm the good looks, dash, and charm."

"You're in for a rude shock if you're thinking to charm the R'lyehans, or win them over with your so-called good looks, and you'll likely meet disappointment—at best—if you tried."

"Oh, I know better than to hope for lissome mermaids out of ancient legends. Still, when Uncle Torvald was in Leng—"

"Uncle Torvald," Harald said, "was a drunk and a brute and a fool, and he died in a sand-pit with his guts squeezed out from both ends. I suggest you don't seek to take after him."

***

The world revolved in its constant spin. The sun set in a boiling chaos-storm of fire. The moon rose near-full, a bleak white staring eye. Planets traced their patterns against the eternal dance of stars and spheres.

And a speck, all but invisible, a pinprick among pinpricks, portended a death-knell for billions upon billions.

Y'cthiss waited.

Sensing the approaching presence of the humans. The thunder-weight of their machine, shaking the skies, whipping the waters. Electric tingling, chained-electric and life-electric, artificial, organic, sputtering signals, senseless cacophony. The stinks of metals and plastics, fuel and fumes, the poisons they called progress.

That they should have risen to dominance... *they*! When their thin crust of dry land covered not even half of the globe! And much of *that*, frozen or barren, inhospitable, worthless!

Yet, so it was.

While, in the seas, from shallows to depths to chasm-black trenches, the rightful had been passed over. Cheated. Denied. Glorious cousin-creatures of supple grace, boneless beauty, sleek of skin, shimmering of scale, myriad colors and delicate shapes... this should have been *theirs*.

Not the dominion of these... these...

Y'cthiss mind-searched their lexicon for a fitting epithet.

These *fucked-up monkeys*!

And, worst of all, to now be in *need* of them, in need of their *help*!

Could the Old Ones, in all their eons of dreaming, have come up with a more vile, insulting, abhorrent turn of events? It made the perverse obscenities of the Y'ha-nthlei deep-dwellers seem almost quaint, a mere lust-quirk.

Breeding with them. Y'cthiss shuddered, the involuntary motion causing a rippling chromatophore cascade, an oily spectrum racing outward along tapering radial limbs.

That any sentient being would even *consider*...

With such a monstrosity!

Grotesque and gangling, their stiff skeletal frameworks, their angular joints! Bony! Warm-fleshed, warm-blooded, sprouting with bristly loathsome hair! Bipedal and bilaterally symmetrical, with their ridiculous front-face binocular vision and their stupid round-hard skulls!

The machine-thunder departed, taking its barrage of noise and stink with it. Leaving behind two life-pulse-mind-signals. The two who were to be brought back to the city. To be well-treated. To be kept whole, unharmed.

Sane... might be another matter.

Sanity was far from guaranteed.

Nor was sanity guaranteed for Fthaal and Yhidd, though unharmed wholeness had been. Y'cthiss did not envy them the experience. Could not, in fact, imagine anything much worse than being a 'guest' among the humans. Except perhaps being taken captive to Carcosa, there to be displayed, tortured, and tormented for the entertainment of the court and servants of the King.

But Fthaal and Yhidd, as had these two, gone with forewarned foreknown awareness into the bargain. They had agreed. They thought themselves strong enough of mind and will to withstand whatever strangeness they would encounter.

Perhaps they could. Perhaps Y'cthiss underestimated.

It was not of immediate concern.

Of immediate concern was the charge of bringing these two to the city, looking after them as the Spawnpriest wished.

As if through a sheeting veil of water-space, Y'cthiss observed them.

They stood together on a rugged stretch of coarse, dark rock, the long-cooled remnants of a long-dead volcano's final spew. As gangling, stiff, and bony as expected... compensating for that ridiculous front-facedness by setting themselves back-to-back to permit their weak binocular fields of vision to cover more of their surroundings. Of which, at the moment, there was little to be seen from their perspective.

The humans called this place Ephemera, mistakenly thinking the island itself came and went, when in truth the island itself stayed stationary, while angles of reality came and went around it.

"I saw it with my own two eyes," one said aloud, in their weird language of breath and lips and tongue. "There was nothing as we descended, nothing, only open sea… and then, suddenly, as if in plain sight all along …"

"I told you," said the other. "And, any minute now, it'll happen again. A turning, as of a dial, or revolving door."

Reflected moonlight played pale upon glistening formations of sea-slick stone as the transition occurred. The watery veil between Y'cthiss and the humans dissolved, bringing their grotesqueness into sharper, vivid focus. Bringing the warm blood-meat scent of them, the fast heart-pulses, the churning of their brains. By a particular potent and musky tang, Y'cthiss identified their 'maleness;' both were male, one younger and far hairier than the other.

Quelling an instinctive reaction to flare out frill-fins and extrude droplets of venom, Y'cthiss drew up to an approximate matching height with them, balanced on splayed tendrils grasping surely to the coarse volcanic rock.

They whirled, the hairier one clenching arm-claw digits into knobby clubs. The other put out a limb as if to restrain him. Their inadequate eyes widened in an effort to be more useful. Their throats made awkward gulpings—so many vessels ran through such a narrow juncture, air-tubes and blood-tubes and food-tubes; it was incredible the inner workings didn't tie themselves in knots.

Y'cthiss moved toward them, undulating smoothly. The inflating and deflating pulsations of small bladder-sacs through fluted orifices allowed for a warbling, reedy approximation of their speech.

"You are the offshoots of the lander-leader."

"It talks!" said the hairier of the two.

The less-hairy one nudged him with the restraining limb, then took a hesitant step toward Y'cthiss.

How they did not fall right over... unsupported by embracing water... tottering on a single foot-leg at a time...

"We are the Heimlandr Lawspeaker's sons," he said. "I am Harald. This is my brother, Leif."

"I am Y'cthiss. To bring you to R'lyeh."

***

Harald thought he had been prepared for this. He thought he had been ready.

He'd studied the available tomes, spoken to the best scholars and occultists, attended all the meetings and briefings with his mother and her advisers. He'd watched what few surviving videos there were: jumpy panic-stricken found footage; remote military and satellite surveillance; grainy black-and-white films from old wars.

He'd been to libraries and museums and secret government vaults. He had held, in his very hand, a figurine wrought from some strange and porous green-black mineral, the hunched and malformed image of the god supposedly sleeping beneath the sea.

He'd attended lectures and demonstrations by architects, mathematicians, physicists. He'd seen sketches, paintings, attempts at model-making and computer-generated rendering.

He'd even gone to asylums, and prisons for the criminally insane. He'd spent hours listening to cackling-mad mariners relate tales of the South Pacific. He'd met with a tiny, frail old woman who had, in her younger years, worked as a nanny for a family named Marsh.

R'lyeh.

Its immensity. Its looming, monstrous skyline... pillars and towers... tilted slabs taller than mountains... stacked walls of rough-hewn stones... coated with scum and slime, draped in fingerlike stringers of kelp... slick and wet in the pallid moonlight, in the harsh white blaze of stars... the way its buildings leaned, or bent, or curved... domes that did not seem like domes... plinths and monoliths and obelisks... arches twining back upon themselves... great vast dripping doorways into cavernous gloomy blackness...

All this, yes, he had thought himself prepared for.

The stench... brine, mud, rotting sea-weeds and dead fish, the rancid tang of sharkflesh left to ferment. A stench such that permeated the nose, that was tasted on the tongue and felt upon the skin as much as smelled, and the knowledge it was this air... this dank, damp, decaying air... being drawn into his lungs...

The sounds... the eternal slosh and crash of waves against pilings, against cliff-faces, coughing hollowly into yawing caves... a low but grinding, groaning creak as if the city itself strained to move... the eerie sighing whistle of wind through gaps and crevices.

Even the physical feel of the place was a revulsion. The surface of the path *gave* in a sick and sinking, appallingly wrong way beneath his feet. When he touched some mildewed piece of masonry jutting from a crumbling wall, it was firm but also soft, spongy, reminiscent in some terrible way of pressing the bald, birth-slippery crown of a newborn infant's skull.

A nightmare corpse-city, they called it. But not because it was a city *of* the dead, no sepulcher or catacomb populated by wraiths and wights and the restless bodies of drowned men... the *city* was dead, the corpse was *of* the city... the nightmare the very fact of its existence.

Dead.

Dead, but dreaming.

Dead, but not empty, not abandoned.

Not populated by wraiths and wights and the restless bodies of drowned men... but by beings altogether inhuman. Many of them even nowhere near humanoid.

Very few of the denizens they saw, as they walked the broad slabstone thoroughfare beneath twisted bridges and overhanging fleshy lanterns like the lures of trenchfish, were what Harald had expected.

Hardly any of the froglike fishfolk of the Atlantic were in evidence, with their bulging eyes and slapping flipper-feet. Some octophibian warriors were stationed as silent, stoic guards outside a towering citadel.

Most were... other. Very, very other. Other, like the strangest, foreign, unearthly and most alien creatures ever dredged from the deep. Wavering polyps and clustered eyestalks, elongated spider-spindle legs, pincers, carapaces, underslung jaws bristling with needle-teeth. They crept, they crawled, they oozed like sea-snails with whorled shells and trails of slime.

He had thought himself prepared, braced for every mind-wrenching and soul-shattering abomination R'lyeh could throw at them.

But then there was Y'cthiss...

Their captor, guard, or guide.

Harald had not been prepared for... someone... or something... so...

So... beautiful.

The very idea, the very thought, distressed Harald to the core.

How could anything here, in this worst of all possible places, be anything but hideous?

Yet, Y'cthiss, flowing ahead of them, leading them onward toward that self-same guarded citadel, was... yes... beautiful.

Beautiful, and... and *feminine* somehow in aspect... though how, precisely, he could not say.

Perhaps it was the fluid grace of movement upon a gliding undulation of many slender, rolling limbs. Perhaps it was the iridescent sheen of colors swirling through a clear-dark amorphousness, as if the night-sky glimmer of the aurora had been captured within a smooth and living glassy sculpture.

"Mother's plan to save the world," Leif said, in a subdued, uneasy mutter, "means saving *this*. Saving *them*."

Without turning, without needing to turn, Y'cthiss brought several limpid orbs to bear on Leif—whose mutter, however subdued, had evidently not gone unheard. Myriad mouths like tiny blossoming undersea-flowers opened, issuing forth a haunting hollow whistle that took on the form of words.

"Our god," said Y'cthiss, "slept already in his house here before the furthest ancestors of you fucked-up monkeys dropped from the trees. For us, saving this world means also saving *you*."

***

The one who'd spoken blinked hair-fringed skin-flaps over his stupid binocular eyes, gaping as if to suck plankton. The other, who'd been in an odd-thought silence, broke it now with a burst of ragged sound like the barking of a seal.

Y'cthiss presumed this meant the use of words from their lexicon had been effective, and continued on. With their stiff-limbed, angle-jointed, single-footed strides, they followed.

"My brother," said the one called Harald, when he had stifled his seal-barks, "intended no offense. We are honored to be here."

"You are not welcome," Y'cthiss said. "This is of necessity, nothing more. Mistake it not. Your presence in R'lyeh is for no embassy of friendship or further alliance. Just as is the presence of two of ours among your people."

He wobbled his bulbous yellow-haired head upon his feeble-seeming neck. "Hostages to ensure the cooperation of our governments. We understand. Our mother sent us, her sons, to show her personal commitment to this common cause."

"For so like are Fthaal and Yhidd of the Spawnpriest's own brood-pods. High rank and importance."

"Are they... are you... related?"

At that, Y'cthiss could not suppress a trilling violet-flicker quiver of annoyance. "We do *not* share lineage."

"And *my* brother," Leif said, flashing non-threatening blunt white nubs in a harmless display, "meant no offense either. Did you, Harald?"

The hair-ridges above his eyes drew together as if perplexed. "No, none, of course not."

Ahead loomed the central citadel, its curled spires clawing at the moon, its mass blotting out the stars. Eldritch light spilled through its corroded, verdigris-caked gates and latticed windows. Tide-basins brimmed to either side of the entrance, seawater trickling sluggishly down mismatched travertine terraces where hagskips flopped and wallowed. A narrowing, upward-winding path between them was flanked at intervals by hulking armored guards with deadly and ornate spears gripped in suckered coils.

Thus far, both humans had made a not-unimpressive effort at keeping their wits intact and fear in check. Now, they drew together as if seeking strength. Each of their tottering steps brought them higher, R'lyeh spreading out beneath them in its convoluted geometry. Higher, and nearer to the gated archway... where the Spawnpriest awaited their arrival.

He wore a robe of bloodkelp falling from an elaborate high-ridged coral collar. Suffering-pearls studded his diadem and belt. Tiny bone-white crabs scurried, preening, among the writhing nests of thin and ropey tentacles surrounding his beaked mouth. Sycophantic remorae clung to the gill-ridged underside edges of his backswept chitinous skull.

"So," said Spawnpriest Cthlullan, not so much speaking the word as letting it roll like a heavy stone into the depths. "Harald and Leif, the Freylindessons." His slow, deliberate, and precise pronunciations of their names resonated from the ancient architecture in such a way it seemed R'lyeh itself trembled to its darkest core. "Your mother's, and your nation's, hostages to fortune for the sake of the entire planet."

They nodded almost imperceptibly. Both were shaking, and their flat faces had gone pale.

"I will not insult you, or waste any of our time, with petty threats and warnings," Cthlullan continued. "There is no need for that, don't you agree?"

Again, the humans nodded.

"I simply trust you will honor your mother's oath. After all, these next days will either see the ending of us all, or a new beginning." The palpi around his mouth writhed into a seething semblance of a smile. "Who knows? We may come out of this as… friends."

***

The chamber to which Y'cthiss led them had obviously not been constructed or furnished with the human shape in mind. It gave the impression half of an undersea cave-grotto, half of the interior of some large spiral shell, with its doorway a giant clamshell set on edge. The predominant colors were pale grey, dark blue-green, and marbled black.

There were no windows, which Leif considered in their case a bonus. He'd only barely held onto the brave marrow and courage of his forebears against the painful battering the sight of R'lyeh had already given him.

It hurt the senses.

It hurt the *mind*.

He was just as glad not to have a constant view of its scenic monstrous panorama. Bad enough to have the *feel* of it, the *knowledge* of it, the tidal groan and pulsing all around and through him.

Bad enough to have stood before that squid-headed abomination with the loathsome squirming smile. Who'd gone on to tell them—so unctuous, so magnanimous!—that they were permitted, within reason, to go more or less freely about the city, that they were not prisoners to be locked in a dungeon cell.

As if the city itself was not both prison and living nightmare! As if they could leave whenever they wished!

"You will find," the jelly-squelch blob called Y'cthiss said, "some efforts made toward your comfort and accommodation. Power sources and connections are in place. You have rain-cistern fresh water. The resting-ledges have been padded with soft lichens."

It gestured with a riffled, rippling, ribbonlike appendage at these and other various amenities. Harald paid close attention, very close, seeming almost to hang on every word and motion. Leif only half-listened, pacing like a wolf in a cage.

"The Spawnpriest," he cut in, interrupting. "You said those who went in hostage exchange for us were his children?"

"Of his brood-pod, yes."

"So they… look… like that?"

"Fthaal and Yhidd are only of the third stage since their emergence," Y'cthiss said. Murky oilslicks of color shifted weirdly within gelatinous dark flesh. Leif noticed his brother gazing at them with a strange, almost hypnotic, fascination.

"What does that mean?"

Harald cleared his throat and spoke the way he had to their tutors, as if glad to have a chance to show off what he'd learned. "They won't have yet developed the, ah, elongated skull structure or distinct facial characteristics—"

"They won't have slimy masses of face-worms?"

"Leif!" Harald spoke sharply.

As if diplomacy mattered when dealing with a sea-slug who'd referred to them as fucked-up monkeys.

"I will leave you to settle." Y'cthiss squish-oozed out and the clamshell closed.

"Why must you be so rude to her?" Harald demanded, rounding on Leif. "If we are to be kept here, it wouldn't hurt our cause to—"

"Rude? I—" Leif's jaw dropped. "Wait, *her*? What do you mean, *her*? That thing is female?"

"Of course she is!"

"How do you …" He stopped, awash in a sudden aghast and revolted horror that made everything earlier seem small. "You… by Loki, what's the *matter* with you? *That* polypy pile of sludge?"

"I don't know what you're talking about." Harald reddened.

"Don't play dumb with me, brother-mine. And you chided me about Uncle Torvald. The snake-women of Leng were at least *women*!… sort of."

"You wouldn't understand. *I* think she's beautiful."

"*I* think this place has already driven you mad."

***

The world continued its spin, unconcerned with the petty scramblings of life upon it, oblivious to the oblivion plunging headlong toward its sun.

Against the infinite glittering sweep of the skies, a speck became a streak.

The orbits of outer planets and asteroids roiled in its wake, some settling, some altered forever.

A streak became a brushstroke smearing back from a dull, baleful star. A smudged ember, a glaring and angry idiot eye, a blind and petulant striking fist.

***

"… reports coming in from all over New Thingvellir …"

"… scene of chaos and devastation…"

"… multiple fatalities …"

"… of a second explosion at the Althing Monument …"

"… widespread panic …"

"… can see behind us, smoke and flames …"

"… being advised to take cover …"

"… the White Hall has been evacuated… current whereabouts of …"

"… burning out of control, emergency response teams on the scene but …"

"… deliberate attack or …"

"… fires like nothing we've ever …"

"… soon to tell, though several groups …"

"… eyewitnesses claim to have seen …"

"... from a senior White Hall staffer that Lawspeaker Freylinde ..."

"... no closer than these police barricades ..."

"... known terrorists with links to Carcosa ..."

"... was in session at the time ..."

"... terrible burns ..."

"... which was also, as you know, serving as the guest housing for ..."

"... the glow from here ..."

"... hospitals overwhelmed ..."

"... like a war zone ..."

"... described as some sort of symbol ..."

"... on Heimlandr soil since ..."

"... already in danger of total annihilation, would ..."

"... as the Yellow Sign ..."

"... unconfirmed, we cannot stress that enough, *unconfirmed* ..."

"... the Lawspeaker and her Wittan ..."

"... in their homes, not attempt to ..."

"... on the very eve of the joint effort to avert ..."

"... nation in shock, unable to ..."

"... *do* something so heinous ..."

"... is dead, I repeat, we now have official confirmation ..."

"... to contact R'lyeh have been ..."

"... urgent meeting of the jarls from ..."

"... spoken out against ..."

"... Eibon denying any involvement in or knowledge of ..."

"... of the Lawspeaker's sons, who ..."

"... will mean for the proposed ..."

"... claiming responsibility, chanting 'the will of the King' ..."

"... directly to a live press conference, where the announcement we've all been dreading ..."

***

A heavy, palpable silence filled the chamber after Harald switched off the screen.

Leif gripped his shoulder, hard enough to hurt, but he bore it without wincing. He turned to his brother. Their eyes met—storm-grey to storm-grey, their mother's legacy.

For a moment, that shared look of stricken grief said it all, and then they clutched each other in a fierce, wordless embrace.

***

Elsewhere in the citadel, a similar silence held.

None of the attendant guards moved from their places, but appendages constricted and chromatophores blend-faded to make an instinctive and protective camouflage.

The scrypool from which the mind-oracles communicated had gone dark, its liquids still roiling and rippling from the vicious slash of the Spawnpriest's starfish claw.

R'lyeh itself, for a moment, seemed to tremble.

***

The new and nearing light loomed in the skies. Burning wormwood, baleful death, destruction, Grim-Ruin. A column of smoke by day, a pillar of fire by night.

In Eibon and Leng, the gates waited, silver keys and conduits ready. From other, further dimensions, indifferent entities watched.

And, in Carcosa, lost Carcosa, beneath the blackly-blazing Hyades, masked and robed sisters sang their paeans to the King… for there were other worlds than this.

***

The clamshell door burst open on a tidal surge of rage as the Spawnpriest stormed into the chamber. "The prime of my brood-pods!"

he bellowed.

Leif and Harald rose to face him, both strong and defiant.

"We lost our mother," Leif said. "And many more of our folk and our friends."

The writhing nest of tentacles around Cthlullan's beaked mouth lashed outward, seizing Leif by the head, face, and neck. His beak, hard-edged and sharp, snapped with menace a fraction of an inch from the tip of Leif's nose.

"If you imagine for one beat of your warm-blooded heart that your losses amount to a krill-squirt—"

"Wait!" Harald stepped toward them, hands raised as if to interpose himself. "Let me speak."

"Fear not," said Cthlullan. "I will get to you next."

"This was not their doing," Y'cthiss said.

"You defend these land-apes, you wretched mongrel of shoggoths? They came into this knowing their lives would be forfeit if any harm befell—"

In a sudden swelling of oily blackness, Y'cthiss quadrupled in size, sprouting whiplike pseudopods and bulging luminescent bladdersacs. *"Tekeli-li!"* The piping cry shrilled from several fluted orifices at once, resounding in the chamber's spiraled upper reaches as if echoed by thousands.

Again, for a moment, R'lyeh seemed to tremble.

Impossible though it was, given their biology, the humans and the Spawnpriest wore identical shocked expressions. They fell back, though Cthlullan did not relinquish his hold. Nor did Leif, whose fists had clenched bony-tight around tentacles.

"There are others," continued Y'cthiss, "enemies, who would have this truce fail and see this world fall. Perhaps you should hear the Freylindesson out."

Another moment passed, of heavy and palpable silence. R'lyeh did not so much tremble as to hold its breathless, dead breath.

Ever-so-incrementally, the gripping tentacles relaxed. So did Leif's fingers. The Spawnpriest's attention shifted to Harald.

"Give me one good reason why I shouldn't pull his brain from his head in moist pink chunks."

"Vengeance," Harald said.

Cthlullan paused, his shiny grapelike clusters of eyes narrowing. "Go on ..."

"Your mages will listen to you. The Heimlandr government—the jarls, the military—will listen to me."

"Yesssss..."

"So, we stop Grim-Ruin, we save the world ..." Harald lifted his chin, his jaw firm, his storm-grey gaze proud. "And then we *get* those Carcosan bastards."

***

As the Shuttle *Thor's-Hammer* roared into the turbulent and doom-streaked sky, its sleek hull wreathed in shifting green sigils of R'lyehan magic, a cool, smooth pseudopod twined around Harald's hand.

He glanced over, startled, and found numerous scintillating orbs shining back at him, while the colors of the aurora played through amorphous dark-glassy flesh.

"I had it mistaken," Y'cthiss said, in a voice fluting like music. "It seems you are not such... fucked-up monkeys... after all."

***

In the unsighted, unlighted, unknown beyond and between, in the outsideness encompassing and within all, mindless dirges pipe and drum. Keys turn within keys and wheels within wheels, spheres revolve within spheres, to know all and see all and care for nothing.

And *ph'nglui mglw'nafh C'thulhu R'lyeh wgah'nagl fhtagn*, not yet waking, not yet rising. A god bound to a world and bound to its fate, slumbering in dark dreams, conscious neither of danger nor hope.

SKVESHA'S SAGA

For Jeff Burk
In memory of Squishy, may she be long-remembered

So it was that, among Ygdrassil's boughs, the towering ash, the all-spanning World Tree

There dwelt many beasts both fabulous and strange, stags and squirrels, snakes and serpents

And there dwelt also Skvesha, her form a great cat, her coat wooly-thick, warm as fleece, ever-shedding

Her pelt color-brindled as of scatterings of gems, jet and dark amber, upon deep drifts of snow-white

Her weight stone-solid, her girth an immensity, claws knife-sharp, jaws of teeth needle-piercing

In battle famed for fierceness, troll-bane and rat-slayer, shatterer of shield-walls, dreaded by foes

Yet foremost in her nature a gentle affection, her purr a rumbling so as to shake the whole earth

And it was that, in time, Skvesha grew weary of the ash-tree's vast trunk and broad branches

Craving the comforts of home, hall, and hearth, she set out from Yggdrasil to explore other lands

First, came she to Asgard, where the gods gathered, Odin and Frygga, Tyr, Baldr, red-bearded Thor

On cat's-paws she treaded Valhalla's gold shingles, ate from the stew-pots, sampled the mead

The rich feasting she did find much to her liking, but the warriors at their revelry too raucous by far

The clash of sword-blades and clangor of spears a constant disturbance to her needed slumbers

Nor was Skvesha inclined to ride over war-fields, galloping with grim Valkyries, choosers of the slain

And Odin kept already two wolves and two ravens, wary at his feet and perched at his shoulders

These, he sent swift on errands across the Nine Worlds, which sounded like far too much work

In fair Freya's household there were other cats, large and grey-furred, from far-reaching forests

Who, in harness, gave pull to her bright chariot swift through sun-kissed or star-laden skies

But, for such labors, Skvesha felt herself also ill-suited, politely refusing the goddess's offer

On she went, head held high, tail raised a proud banner, barrel-full belly wagging side to side

Paws padding cat-quiet and keen whiskers twitching, to investigate further among the Nine Worlds

Niflheim proved too cold, and Surtr's kingdom too hot; the elf-lands light and dark she disdained

Next she came to Jotunnheim, realm of the giants, high crags and rock-peaks and cracked clefts

Where storm-winds howled as if from beasts' throats, where boulders rolled and stones hurled

Where, in cavern-halls hewn from mountain-hearts, sat jotunn-lords upon their huge thrones

Backs draped in bearskins, brows iron-crowned, broad-swords and war-axes ready at hand

Drinking blood-wine from hollow skull-bowls, eating roast meat and bread baked of bone-meal

The spoils of battle, men slaughtered and butchered, gutted and flayed, choice corpses plundered

As trolls capered, cackling, in cages and among the floor-rushes dire-hounds nosed for scraps

But the bonfires blazed, the milk-jugs were enormous, and the mice she saw were as big as stoats

So, Skvesha approached, mewing and inquisitive, and the cat caught the notice of the giant-king

Who bade her welcome, offering a soft deer-pelt for her seating, and a dish of herring in cream

This hospitality she accepted, dining daintily, then attending her grooming with fastidious care

She was told she could stay, if such prospect pleased her, provided she perform a small task in return

It was known to the jotunn that the thunder-god Thor had set out restless on quest for adventure

And was, in his travels, soon to be passing through mountainous reaches of high Jotunnheim

So they wished to have ready a fitting reception, to honor his visit and for their entertainment

Three tests of strength had the giant-king devised, for valor and mettle, to show Thor's fortitude

To drain dry a drink-horn, to face in wrestling a grandmother, and to lift aloft the four feet of a cat

Simple enough on the surface, but with malice beneath, so as to see the hammer-wielder humiliated

The horn would be by magic linked to the sea, which no thirst of man nor of god could diminish

The grandmother, frail-seeming, was time personified, old age itself, bester of all living things

And the cat, well, a cat such as Skvesha, surely the All-Father's son could not hope to heft—

To this, Skvesha waxed wroth, insulted beyond measure; claws-first, she leaped at the giant-king

He shrieked as her weight landed full on his crotch, shrieked again, louder, as she went for his face

Hissing and spitting, back bristled, tail bushed, a white ball of fury mottled with amber and jet

She tore his skin, dragged his cheeks bleeding furrows, and savagely bit off the tip of his nose

As the vast stone-hewn chamber rang with riotous echoes of roaring mirth, the jotunn amused

Impressed with Skvesha's audacious attack, raising no harmful hand to her as she turned to go

Head held again high, tail proudly upraised, with bold indignation she strolled from the hall

Moving on from Jotunnheim without looking back, setting her hopes next upon mortal Midgard

That some, there, might be found who were worthy of the company of a cat of such stature

It was then, though, that Skvesha's fortunes took a bleak turn, for she had come to a far-future

A Midgard made modern, busy cities cold and unfeeling, chaotic clamors of crowding and noise

There, Skvesha wandered, lost and bedraggled, her fine coat mud-matted, paws wet with rain

All too often alone, and oftener hungry, her stout stomach protesting with ravenous growls

Scrounging and scavenging, wretched, alone, until it happened her path crossed that of a skald

A young storyteller of wild exuberance, ink-skinned, tangle-haired, his voice ever-laughing

He soon won Skvesha's trust, took her in, brought her from the cruel streets to his warm, safe home

Where she could be frequently fed and well cared for, bathed and brushed, kept in great comfort

Given treats and trinkets, lavished with loving attention, petted and patted and heartily thumped

So that, once again, her rumbling purr shook the earth, and guests to the house stood awestruck

This, they said, must be the most majestic of cats, of famed reputation and legendary name

This glorious creature, this warrior brave and tenacious, Skvesha, for whom many sagas are sung.

THE SLAUGHTER: BORN OF BLOOD

Death came in the night, roaring and ravenous.

The hall's great heavy door burst inward with a splintering crash. A cold gust whirled up sparks and ash from the firepits, stirring slumbering embers into startled flickers of flame.

Men shouted. Women screamed. Dogs howled. Children shrieked. Furs, fleeces and wool blankets were flung aside as people sprang up from the long low sleeping-platforms.

Before the first sword sang from its scabbard, before the first axe could be seized from its wall-pegs, the invaders rushed in and the slaughter began.

Bones snapped and flesh tore. Blood gushed and guts spilled. Flailing, fighting bodies raged through the smoke-filled air.

A girl fell to her knees, blond braids shining like gold, imploring hands raised. One of them seized her by those very braids, ripped her scalp to the red-glistening ivory dome of her skull, then dashed her head against a beam so that it cracked apart like a clay bowl of lumpy gruel.

A brown-bearded man, naked but for coarse breeches and the bronze hammer-amulet worn around his neck on a leather cord, lunged with a short-blade made for stabbing. The blade sank deep, piercing enemy skin. He voiced a loud cry to rally the other men, rally them to battle and to victory.

The cry cut off in a gurgle as a forearm thick as a stout bough slammed across his throat, pinning him to the wall. A huge, strong hand closed over his wrist. With a twist and a crack, the stabbing blade dropped useless to the floor.

Moments later, so did the corpse of the brown-bearded man.

Another invader tore a babe from the arms of its panicked mother, swung the squalling infant by the feet, and cast it into the fire. The mother wailed and scrabbled after her child, which thrashed, screeching, burning, blistering. The invader stomped upon her spine. She fell flat, clutching feebly at the hearth-stones, legs dragging limp as she tried to pull herself forward.

Men stumbled this way and that, holding at their bellies to keep their innards from sliding out in ropy, slippery uncoils of bruise-purple intestine. A head rolled, white hair blood-matted in strings across a face still with eyes darting wild and alive. The dogs, maddened with rage and fear, bit at each other, bit at themselves, bit at anything within reach of their jaws.

Some of the hall's inhabitants fled, not for the main door where more invaders rushed in, but for the smaller side-doors that led to the animal pens, and the garden where herbs and onions grew. The lintels there were low, so low that any but a child had to stoop or bend double to pass through, and narrow besides. In their terror, the folk crowded the opening, they struggled and jostled.

The first to duck under the lintel—a stripling youth, fast and agile—paid dearly for his speed. Enemies waited there too, snatching him up as soon as he emerged. He kicked and squirmed and writhed. He almost got free. But then one gripped him by the ankles, and another by the wrists. They twisted him the way washerwomen might wring out a cloak, only what drizzled from the youth's middle was much redder and thicker than water.

Close at his heels had been a grey-haired woman leading three small, sobbing children. Seeing the youth's fate, she made to retreat, only to have her arm caught and wrenched off at the shoulder.

The sound was that of a joint of meat, a muffled wet crack and a gristly tearing. The old woman staggered backward, her remaining hand clamped to the stump, blood gouting between her fingers. It sprayed hot and sticky into the faces of the children.

The eldest of them, a stocky boy not yet eight years of age, uttered a furious warrior's roar. He flung himself at the attacker that yet held the woman's twitching arm, slashing with an antler-handled knife. The other two, a girl of six and a much younger boy, watched in horror as he was snatched up and pulled to pieces.

Axes chopped and swords hacked. Some of the men had found their shields, limewood and boar's hide reinforced with iron. Some were able to don helms, the hammered metal eyepieces and nasals glinting in the firelight. None had time to pull on their mail, so they fought bare-chested, or in their shirts and tunics.

Several women grabbed up weapons, even cook-pots and lengths of wood. Others crouched by the fallen, doing what they could to stanch the bloodflow from terrible, mortal wounds. A few cowered, weeping, huddled with their little ones or mourning their dead husbands.

The invaders did not relent. They did not slow. Injured, they pressed on all the fiercer, despite sustaining blows that should have crippled, should have killed. One took a sword-thrust to the base of the throat, the blade plunging, splitting gullet and wind-pipe, the point emerging dripping at the back of the neck, and barely seemed to feel it. The stroke of an axe cleaved another from collar-bone to waist, parting ribs at an angle, exposing laboring lung and dark liver, but it was the axe-man who found himself overpowered, whose last sight was of his foe's kill-hunger snarl.

Soon, the hall was a butcher's yard, strewn end to end with mangled bodies and severed limbs. The smoky air grew smokier, laden with the stench of blood and shit, of burning hair and charred flesh from parts that had landed in the firepits, where skin crisped and fat sizzled.

No more screams disturbed the night. No more blade-clash and battle-cry. A dog or two had escaped past them, but no men, women, or children had been so lucky.

Aside from the hiss and crackle from the firepits, there was only the smithy-bellows sound of the invaders' breaths, at once eager and labored, sated and satisfied.

That, and the slow steady plip and patter of blood, which had splashed so high it rained down from the rafter-beams. The furs and blankets piled on the sleeping platforms were soaked with it, sodden with it, oozing from trailing edges, coursing rivulets over the uneven hardpack-earth.

***

Ogvaldr came with the dawn, grim-set and grievous.

He rode through pale mists up the rocky slope, his horse iron-grey with mane and tail of black.

A frosty dew bent the silvery grass low and edged the spindly white birches with a fine patterning of ice. The sky had not yet taken on any touch of blue. The sun through veils of cold haze might have been the moon instead, a wan and shimmering glow. All the world seemed but a colorless ghost of itself.

Over mail-coat and grey leathers, Ogvaldr wore a mantle of wolf-skin held with a silver brooch. His helm hung hooked over the saddle-horn, his flax-fair hair bound back from his high, clear brow. He kept his beard trimmed to a short, neat point.

His eyes on this day had the look of distant storm-clouds as he crested the rise above the valley where Senwulf's hall lay hidden by early-autumn fog. He tugged the reins and paused there, watching, listening.

Somewhere, a doleful cow with overfull udders lowed for a milking. Somewhere, a cock gave a desultory crow. The rest was silent and still. As silent and still as Hama's hall had been, and Bodjar's before that.

A piebald donkey clopped up beside him. Ogvaldr's proud horse did not even deign to snort at the unkempt lesser beast. The donkey, for its part, nosed at a patch of withered flowers.

The donkey's rider, when Ogvaldr turned, met his inquiring gaze with a calm steadiness. She nodded. He nodded back. His jaw set grimmer than ever.

She, too, was colorless and nearly ghostlike, with skin thinner and more withered than the flowers that interested her steed. A wrap stitched together from various winter pelts swallowed up her frail, tiny frame. Strands of snowy hair straggled from under her hood. A milky rime covered most of one eye. The other was silver-flecked grey, flint and steel combined.

More hooves thumped up the slope, more horses with mounted riders, black horses and brown, roan and bay, and one fine mare the color of gold, Vann's pride, which he called Sifil. Behind them came a trio of dun-colored donkeys. They spread out into a line along the top of the rise. The horses stamped and snorted, tossing their heads, steamy plumes of vapor issuing from their nostrils. The donkeys plodded, led on a rope line by the rearmost rider.

The men, some in leather coats and others in mail, carried round shields, and swords slung across their backs or axes at their hips. Gold, silver, copper and bronze gleamed at their belt buckles, at their cloak clasps, at the arm-rings they wore. They were large men, and strong. Warriors.

Ogvaldr, their lord, their leader, was no small man himself. But, of these dozen or so of his followers, most towered over him, broader of shoulder and thicker of chest.

A lad rode with them as well, and four other women besides the crone with the milky eye. The lad, sporting no more than a fledgeling fuzz of darkish beard, had a stout boar spear and a hand-axe. He rode at the back, leading the donkeys, laden with burdens of bundled wood, food-stores and ale-jugs.

Of the women, three were tall and proud, wide-hipped, with their braided hair coiled and pinned; they kept long knives at their belts and knew well how to use them. The fourth might have been mistaken for another lad at first. She was lean and slim, her foxfur hair cropped short beneath a cap of leather. A vicious scar sliced from the corner of her mouth to her ear.

They stared down into the still and silent valley.

"Frani, Siggrim," Ogvaldr said. "Take four men apiece and ride out, check the carls' steads, the slave-hovels, the stables and byres. Be wary. Be watchful. The rest of you, with me, to Senwulf's hall."

He touched heels to flank of the iron-grey and rode ahead. Maghild, the old woman on her piebald donkey, trotted to keep up. Frani and Siggrim signaled each to four other men, one group heading left and one heading right, until they had vanished from sight into the mists. The rest followed Ogvaldr.

"You are cautious," Maghild said to him.

"Yes."

"After Bodjar's hall, and Hama's, what is it you think to find?"

"I know what I think to find," Ogvaldr said.

"A slaughter," she said.

"A slaughter."

They passed fields where rye and barley grew, and a meadow of wildflowers and bilberry. They passed untended pigs snuffling in a muddy yard. They crossed a log bridge over a creek, which further down had been dammed with stones to make a pond, and fishtraps bobbed in the water. They passed a struggling orchard, apple trees and cherry surrounded by a plank fence. They passed a thorny thicket of brambles and hazelnut, where squirrels ceased in their scampering to peer at them, bushy tails twitching, black eyes bright.

A slaughter, Maghild had said. A slaughter, Ogvaldr had agreed.

And soon enough, the smell of it wafted dank on the air.

Soon enough, they saw it too, at the carnage of Senwulf's hall. The great doors had been smashed inward, the opening there mounded with corpses. Battle might be hot, but death was cold, cold with congealed blood and stiffened limbs, and entrails slick with jellied mung.

Flies and worms had already come, as flies and worms always did. Ravens as well, flapping up black-winged from their feast to perch along the roofbeams at the approach of living men.

"Geirmund, hold back with the beasts," Ogvaldr told the lad, dismounting. He donned his helm and looped his reins around a post. "Josurr, stand guard."

They did as he ordered, while Ulrik, Eldjarn, Sigvir and Torull similarly dismounted and made ready. The women, but for Rota, would wait outside as well, and woe to anyone who thought to try attacking them or making off with the horses. As for Rota, she of the scarred face and foxfur hair, she sprang down easily from her saddle. Her eyes, though green, were as bright and avid as those of the squirrels.

Maghild pulled from within her wrap the necklace that she wore, beads of silver and glass and polished ivory, adorned with raven's feathers. She lifted it toward the birds on the roof, and touched her wizened fingertips beneath her milky eye. For ravens were Odin's birds, Odin who'd traded his eye for wisdom. They cawed at her as if in recognition.

Before entering the hall, Ogvaldr drew his sword, which had a knob of jet in its pommel and was named Helsnautr, the death-goddess's gift. Though whether the weapon had been a gift from Hel, or whether its keen killing blade made regular gifts to her, Ogvaldr had never been sure. Perhaps it was both.

A dog, hurt, whined and limped away as fast as three legs would carry it. Cats skulked, their glares baleful, their ears flat.

It had been a fine hall, with good sturdy timbers and thick-plastered walls. The structure was long and narrow, aligned to take the brunt of the winter winds along its shorter side. A ram's skull had been mounted on each cornerpost, the curved horns decorated with twined grain-sheaves.

Above the door was a curled wooden prow, intricately carved, with the rearing head of a sea-serpent. From Senwulf's favorite ship, Ogvaldr knew. The *Wave-Striker*, it had been called. Char still showed from where the prow, too, had nearly been consumed by the flames that reduced the *Wave-Striker* to so much blackened rubble on the shore by Koenigsfell.

Such a day that had been, such a battle, the banners flying above masses of men, shield-men and sword-men, archers and axers, the fortress on the mountain and the fleet of longships on the sand…

Such a day, and such a battle.

Then.

Here and now, there was only this. This slaughter.

He stepped inside, placing his boots with care so as not to trip or slip on the residues of Senwulf's people. Keeping his boots free of the blood proved instantly impossible. It was everywhere.

The coals in the firepits had burned out, leaving beds of wet ash, leaving darkness but for what little of the thin, watery morning light filtered through the mists to pierce the doorways. Ogvaldr's vision adapted enough to make out the shapes of sleeping platforms along the walls, heaped with blankets and furs over a layer of straw. The bodies upon them were in no way sleeping.

"Get a fire going," he called over his shoulder. "Bring torches."

Here was an old man's severed head, white-haired and white-bearded, the stump of the neck a ragged pulpy mess from which neck-bones poked. Here was a woman with her ribcage staved in like a broken wicker basket. Here was a man, blond beard forked and plaited and bound with gold wire, the haft of an axe still gripped in his dead hands. Here was a child, pulled apart from the ankles the way a man might pull apart the wishbone of a roast fowl.

Ulrik brought in some blazing brands, passing them around. No one spoke as they surveyed the devastation.

A slaughter, yes, a slaughter indeed.

There had been no plundering. Blood-streaked valuables gleamed in the torchlight. Rings and bracelets, arm-rings and neck-torcs… one woman wore a rich necklace of amber… the attack in the night caught them with their belts and cloaks laid aside, with the buckles, the brooches, the clasps and ivory fastenings untouched… there were inlaid boxes that might hold spices or coins or jewelry... a glass jar that had somehow survived the violence intact... not to mention whatever treasure-hoard Senwulf might have buried, the floor beneath his wooden chair a most likely spot.

Neither had there been raping. The girls and women of the hall were dead, but their clothes no more torn away than what had happened in their killing, their legs no more splayed than as they had fallen, their thighs no more bruised nor bloody than was sustained by their mortal injuries.

"There's a babe in the firepit," Torull said, stirring the cinders with his boot-toe, nudging over the small corpse. It had, in its last, drawn tucked and tight, its tiny fingers bent into rigid hooks near its gaping, toothless mouth.

The sight put Ogvaldr uncomfortably in mind of Rikva, his last wife, and the lifeless son she'd died in birthing. He turned away.

And here, he found, here was Senwulf. Shirtless and brown-bearded Senwulf, his throat crushed with such force that his bronze hammer-amulet was embedded into his flesh. His eyes, glazed now, bulged from their sockets blue and accusing, as if to demand of the gods how they could have let this misfortune descend upon his hall and house.

Senwulf's stabbing-blade, which he'd named Quick-Strike as his ship was *Wave-Striker*, lay nearby. Bloodied, Ogvaldr saw. He saw also that Senwulf's hand lay curled over the well-worn hilt.

Good. Good. He had not died weaponless. He had died as he had lived, a warrior, a fierce warrior and leader of men. That assured him a seat at Odin's long tables, where the mead flowed endless from golden mead-horns, and even those who'd met their ends as foes would meet again as friends, to feast and drink and make merry until the final battle came.

Eldjarn, who could, men said, hear a flea fart at a hundred paces and a lark sing while still in the egg, made a sudden signal of warning. His gifted ears, the rest of them had long since learned to trust. So, although they'd noticed nothing out of the ordinary, they all heeded him at once.

"Someone coming?" Ulrik asked in a whisper. "Horses? Men?"

"Not someone coming," Eldjarn said. He eased forward a stride, paused, then in a swift motion went to his knees beside a sleeping platform, flipped up the bloodsoaked furs—clammy droplets sprayed from them, spattering his nearest companions—bent down, and looked under with his sword poised to jab. "Someone here!"

***

"Wait!" cried Maghild from the doorway, her old voice cracked but sharp. "Stay your hand, Eldjarn Akisson. Mind me, now!"

He obeyed. Of course he did. They all did. They always did. As they should.

Although she was in truth mother to but one of them, she'd ever been, in a greater way, mother to them all. Whether they'd grown up gathered around her knees, listening to her tales, or whether they'd been men-of-age, made no difference. They feared and revered her, respected and honored her, and if they did not love her, that was just as well.

"Yes, Mother Maghild." Eldjarn held back his blade, still kneeling by the sleeping platform.

"A survivor?" she asked.

Ogvaldr, who *was* her true son and *did* love her, nodded. "A child."

"A child." Maghild repeated the words, letting them roll like sweet honey over her tongue. "Poor little mite. Show me."

She undid the whalebone clasps that held shut her wrap, and slid the heavy patchwork of furs from her shoulders. Tolla, who was Torull's sister and Frani's woman, took it to hold. Beneath the wrap, Maghild wore a long-sleeved dress of pale linen and a shift of grey wool, belted with silver. On her feet were warm shoes of reindeer hide. Her hair, once fairer than sunlight on clear water, hung whiter now than snow to her waist.

The nearest men offered to help, or even to lift and bear her past the heap of bodies in the door of Senwulf's hall. Maghild brushed aside their offers to pick her own way through. Her hem dragged in the death-muck. This was a grim business, this slaughter, and it was right that none of them should expect to go untouched by it, or expect to pass through it clean.

The space between the sleeping platform and the hardpacked earthen floor looked less than two handspans high. No adult could have fitted, nor youth or slender maiden without a squeeze. That cramped darkness beneath would have held only loose pebbles and debris, a place where rats scurried for food and cats hunted for rats.

Maghild hunkered down, with slow care, at the platform's edge. Her knees groaned and her spine creaked—spry for her age, she might be, but her age was venerable indeed, and her days of running and dancing were far, far behind her. She set her hand for balance on a fleece, found it clammy, still damp with blood. Not all had soaked into the floor yet either, and she felt it seep through her skirt. Her hair, falling forward as she bent her head low, trailed in it.

She heard a faint, rustling movement. She heard shallow gasping sips of breath, and a plaintive, quickly-muffled whimper.

"Light," she said, and Ogvaldr crouched to bring the glow of his torch shining into that dark space.

And there, cringing, squinting, pressed as far back as the wall would allow, was a child. No more than three years from the womb, Maghild judged, barely weaned from the tit, as steady on two legs as a new foal on four.

Filthy and terrified, that child was. With hair that looked like dirty dung-caked straw but would wash clean the color of summer grain, with a snub nose and quivering downturned bow of a mouth, smudged cheeks tracked by tear-paths.

"Child," Maghild said. "Come here, child. Come to me."

The pitiful sob would have softened any mother's heart.

"You poor little mite," she said. "Come out from there. You must be cold, and hungry."

The child looked at her, and she saw eyes as blue as the fjords, welling fresh with tears. Maghild stretched out a thin, tremulous hand.

"Shhh, now, shhh. Come to me. Come to Mother Maghild."

She sensed Ogvaldr exchanging dubious glances with his men, knew that they were wondering why she simply didn't have them upend the sleeping platform, haul the child from hiding? Never mind the kicking and screaming; it was a child, for Freya's sake, a small and harmless child, not a bear's cub or lynx, some bundle of teeth and claws.

"It is better this way," she said to them without turning her attention from those fearful blue eyes. "Kinder."

"How could anyone have survived?" Ulrik wondered. "Even a child?"

"Oh, what you must have seen, poor thing." Maghild beckoned, crooning. "Did you hide all of your own? That was very clever. Or did your mumma put you in there, tell you to hold so still and be so quiet? Come on, now. No more need to hide. No more need to be afraid. Come out. Come here."

The child sniffled, and gulped, and crept forward. One grubby, blood-smeared hand made a tentative motion toward Maghild's beringed, wrinkled one. Then, as the child shied, and made to snatch back that hand, she grasped it.

For all that they were grown men and seasoned warriors, half of them jumped at the child's piercing shriek. Maghild held on—not only spry for her age, she had a tough and wiry strength—and drew the struggling little body out from under.

A thought occurred to her then, that this was one of the stranger midwiferies she'd ever done. She laughed. It discomfited the men, and she only discomfited them further when she announced, "Ah, a boy!"

For so the child was, a boy, in baggy linen under-trousers and a loose sleep-tunic trimmed in squirrel's fur at the hem. Goodly enough garments, no slave's rags or thrall's humble clothes, hard though it was to tell what with the way they were befouled.

The boy fought her at first, frantic, but Maghild bundled him into her arms and sat on the sodden pile of furs and fleeces. She rocked back and forth, continuing to croon, cradling him to her shrunken bosom. He gave one final whooping cry of anguish and despair, then collapsed against her, limp as a cloth doll, breath hitching, blue eyes vacant.

"Shh, there, shh, now." She stroked his matted hair, rocking and rocking, aware that she sat partially on a severed leg, and that more unspeakable death-muck soaked through her dress.

"Senwulf's son?" Torull asked.

Ogvaldr shook his head. "Senwulf had two sons; I saw them at the hallmote. The elder was Geirmund's age, thin, but quick." He pointed to one of the corpses, that of an agile youth, which lay twisted like a rope not far from a low-linteled side door. "And another, a brown-haired boy. There, by the old woman."

"Ingirid," Maghild said. "Her daughter, Ingunne, was Senwulf's wife."

"And Gunnlaug, Senwulf's chief huscarl, was Ingunne's brother," said Sigvir. "I remember him from the shield-wall at Thorsvik. That was a great battle."

At the names, the child in her arms made no stir, no sign of recognition. He had gone away for a time, crossed some inner bridge. His mind walked for a while in another world, some living counterpart to chill grey Niflheim.

"Then who is he, this boy?" asked Ulrik.

"Does it matter?" Maghild dabbed the child's chin with her sleeve, wiping at the blood dried there. All that blood. Covered in it, he was. Drenched in it. But none of it seemed to be his. He was unhurt. Untouched.

Of the body, at least.

How had it been, for a child? To witness this? To see everyone he knew and loved in all the world be torn apart? To hear their agonies? To be left alone with the dead, surrounded by mangled corpses in this sea of blood?

Had he crawled out from his hiding place? Found the body of his mother, perhaps? Patted at her cheek, shaken her, begged for her to get up and care for him? Had he wandered through the hall, his wails increasing in desperation as he realized no one would answer? Had he then, broken of spirit, too young to know what else to do, retreated under the sleeping platform?

Such a thing to endure, and at such a tender age.

These years had been prosperous for Senwulf and his people. This boy-child, well-dressed, had the round face and plump limbs of one who'd not known want, or deprivation yet in his young life.

Until this.

"Do you have a name, child?" Maghild set her fingertips under the boy's chin and lifted. His vacant gaze looked past her, through her. When she removed her hand, his head thumped to her shoulder and his mouth hung slack.

His lips, and small nubs of teeth, were red-stained. As if he had been eating cherries, over-ripe, fleshy, juicy, the darkest fruit.

"Oh yes, how hungry you must have been, poor mite," she said, rocking him some more. "No one to feed you, no one to fetch you a drink. How hungry and how thirsty, how very thirsty, you must have been."

The men turned toward her again, horror rising in their eyes.

"You don't mean…" Torull moved his torch around, shining its light to play over the interior of the hall.

Which was, if not for the sprawled bodies, tidily enough kept… jugs stoppered, barrels lidded, grain-sacks tied, meats strung up, foodstuffs stored away… to keep off the rats and the dogs, of course… but also to leave nothing out for the empty, panging belly of a child unused to missing his meals.

The men—grown men and seasoned warriors all—shifted with unease. A few murmured to one another. Some touched hammer amulets or other good-luck tokens they wore, and Hroald kissed the little cross he'd been given by a Christian monk. Ulrik rapped thrice with his knuckles on a post, where some craftsman or artisan of Senwulf's had carved a symbol of Yggdrasil, the great World Tree.

It did seem a strangeness of superstition for these of all folk, given what they were, and what they had done.

Ogvaldr looked at the boy, then looked at Maghild. "Mother?"

"I want him," she said, resting her hand atop the head of matted hair. "I midwifed his new birth. I want him, I claim him, I'm keeping him. He is mine."

***

Much went on inside the hall. Much talk was made.

Geirmund from where he had been sent to wait with the beasts could hear none of it, and it rankled him to the very marrow.

Josurr, left to stand guard, fared the same. But Josurr, sometimes called Josurr the Giant, unstoppable in battle once begun, remained at other times the most patient and dutiful of men. Given a task, he kept to it, without wavering, until it was done or some counterorder came. He was likewise ever content with his lot, whatever it might be, and had no end of sayings to that effect.

"Pouch-silver jingles more than promise-gold," was one such. "Bread is not meat, but neither is it cabbage," was another, usually declared at meal-table when the fare was less than might be desired, and men wished yearningly for beef and bacon, barleywine and butter. And, "Better a plain girl in your bed than a queen seen from afar."

So, it troubled Josurr not in the least that they were excluded from what talk went on in the hall, while they stayed outside! Even the *women* were privileged to gather by the door, and peer in, and listen.

And Rota? Who might as well be no woman at all, skinny stick that she was, with her cropped hair and no tits to speak of? Rota the Fatherless, Rota the Boyish, Rota Never-Wife? *Rota* had been among the first to follow Ogvaldr within!

Geirmund sulked. He kicked the dirt. He found a stone and threw it at a cat, and missed, which further curdled his mood.

Wasn't he, Geirmund, of as much worth and right to be here as any of them? He'd slain his first—if thus far only—man in battle! He'd lain with his first—if also thus far only—woman in bed!

Wasn't he even Mother Maghild's own grandson, Ogvaldr's nephew? True, his father was no warlord, no warrior... only a craftsman and crippled as well... but his mother was the daughter and sister of jarls! With Ogvaldr unlucky as he was when it came to wives and sons, who *else* would hold the hall and lead the men after him, if not Geirmund?

Yet here he stood, waiting, while horses stamped and donkeys grazed, knowing nothing of what went on. He kicked the dirt again.

Josurr hummed to himself, placid as ever. He shifted his big weight from one foot to the other. No boredom affected him, no concerns as to what he might be missing out on so much as crossed his mind.

The great dull fool.

At the hall's door, the women fell back, then turned and hurried to various duties at the fire they'd built to make torches. A few of the men, and Rota, emerged, followed by Mother Maghild bearing a bedraggled and filthy body in her arms.

A body that moved, that flinched from the fog-bright morning. A small body. A child.

A child? Of Senwulf's folk? Found alive after the terrible bloodbath?

It did not seem possible, yet, there the child was. By the looks on the faces of men and women alike, the others shared Geirmund's astonishment. Some faces also showed pity, or discomfort that did not quite border upon fear.

Ogvaldr emerged next with the last of the men. He, too, looked unnerved, but gathered himself and summoned the others.

"Jarl Senwulf is dead," Ogvaldr said to them. "You know what to do."

And so they set about doing it… picking through the corpses to relieve them of weapons and valuables, raiding the food-stores, digging about to unearth the iron chest that held Senwulf's hoard.

When they had taken that which they could carry, that which they wanted, the best of the goods, they would turn Senwulf's hall into a great pyre, to consume the corpses of him and his folk, rather than leave them to the continued ravages of the flies, the worms, the ravens, and eventually other scavengers.

With this, at last, Geirmund was able to help. He used the butt end of his boar spear to root through furs and blankets, through chests of folded clothes. He and the other men stripped cold, stiff limbs of rings and bracelets, necklaces and amulets. They collected combs of bone and ivory, ornaments of silver and bronze, glass beads and baubles, jars of salt and pots of honey.

Hilfe and Skridda had built up a small fire in one of the outside cook-pits when Ogvaldr called for torches, and at Maghild's instruction they went to work building it higher, fetching water and readying a tub. They undressed the child as he stood unresisting, unprotesting, slack of expression, saying nothing.

Geirmund found he had to suppress a shiver whenever he went by, whenever he caught a glimpse of the empty blue eyes that seemed at once to see, and not-see, whatever passed before them. And when he heard what the men muttered, what they suspected, the shiver proved more than he could suppress.

The women washed the filth from him. Mother Maghild used one of the combs to work the tangles from and smooth his yellow hair. She sent Geirmund back into the hall to find clothes of a size to fit the boy.

She meant to keep him?

To *keep* him?

To take him home with them?

This strange, empty-eyed thing? This creature who'd witnessed the deaths of his kin, who'd huddled alone and hungry among them?

"Is it true?" Geirmund asked, when he brought the garments he'd found. "What the men say? Is it true?"

Maghild's good eye, the flint-and-steel one, fell sharp upon him. "Just what do the men say, Geirmund Thorgeirsson?"

"That he... that..."

Flame-haired Hilfe, Ulrik's young and pretty woman, laughed with a soft and pitying scorn that stung Geirmund worse than a handful of nettles.

"Can't bring yourself even to say it?" asked Rota, who sat nearby on a stump sorting through a pile of tools and utensils to see what was worth taking and what could be left behind. Her scorn was anything but soft, and not in the least pitying.

Stung worse, Geirmund glowered at her, then turned again to Mother Maghild. "That he ate of them, of their flesh, and lapped up their blood like a dog from a puddle, that he's a corpse-eater and blood-drinker."

"And if he is?" Maghild held up against the boy a tunic woven of striped brown and beechnut, worked with blue thread at the square collar and cuffs. She nodded to Skridda, who pulled it over his head and worked his arms into the sleeves.

"Then he's cursed," Geirmund said. "Cursed and bad luck. Evil-touched. Dangerous."

Rota snorted. Hilfe hid a smile. Geirmund's face burned.

"Yes, such a monster, this one, so fierce," Skridda said, straightening the boy's tunic, cinching it with a braided cord. She fluffed his hair. "You've but to look at him, how dangerous he is."

"Hush now," Mother Maghild told Skridda, selecting fawn-colored trousers and blue-dyed woolen leg wraps. "He's mine, my concern."

Soon enough, they had the boy clad, complete with laced-leather shoes and a cloak of deerskin. He made no sound through it all.

Only when Tolla brought over a chunk of bread slathered with soft cheese and some herring did he show any spark of awareness. He snatched the offered food from her, cramming it greedily into his mouth.

"Even a bite can be a bounty," Josurr said. Relieved of his guard-duty, he'd come near the fire for a mug of ale. He smiled down at the boy, who blinked up at the man's immense height.

"What are we to call him?" Tolla asked.

"And are we really to keep him?" added Skridda.

"Why not?" Rota snorted again. "Won't be the first strangeling Mother's snatched from death or taken in."

"Like you?" Geirmund spoke without meaning to.

"And you; you're to talk." Her green eyes glinted.

His face burned again. She was not *that* much older than him, two years, three at the most, but treated him as if he were no less a child than this silent, irritating boy.

He almost retorted that he, at least, had a father… but stopped himself. Half a father was what he had, and in a way that was far worse than having none at all. Half a father who was no warrior, and a mother who might have been Maghild's own daughter but who'd abandoned husband and son and kin and hall, who'd left them for her lover, left them in dishonor.

Geirmund stalked away angrily instead, around the long side of the hall, through the lasts of the lifting mist. A clear sun shone over the valley now. He settled upon a large slanting boulder, heels swinging, jabbing his spear-point into the earth.

Fine and well for Josurr to go on about being content with one's lot… Josurr with his sayings and adages, Josurr who thought it wastefulness to wish and to wonder. He had no imagination, the huge man, and no ambition. Whatsoever the gods rolled his way, good fortune or ill… whatever threads the Norns wove into his life, bright favor or dark omen… he would accept and be grateful.

Josurr was a fool.

What of wealth and pride and reputation? What of being at the helm of the ship of one's own destiny? What of being a leader of men? A giver of gifts and gold? A jarl? A king? What of being sung of by the skalds?

What of not being slighted? What of having one's due? Being fairly treated, not spurned, not set aside, not overlooked and met with injustice?

A low and plaintive whine caught his ear. Geirmund looked to see the lamed dog, which had gone limping from the hall at their approach, hunkered abject on its belly in the grass nearby. Its tail thumped. It uttered another plaintive, beseeching whine.

He slid down from the rock and went to the dog. Its hurt leg stuck out, badly broken, ends of bone jutting from puffy swellings of flesh, the fur clotted with blood and pus.

Geirmund envisioned himself picking up the animal, cradling it to his chest and carrying it back the way Mother Maghild had carried the boy. Would the women fuss to clean and tend and feed it? Would, if he announced his intention to keep the dog as his own, Ogvaldr agree?

Possibly.

Then what?

Then he would have this dog…

Its tongue licked at his boot. Its tail thumped again, and its gaze seemed at once humble and hopeful.

He would have this dog… which, even if it healed, would be forever hobbled, forever crippled. Unable to hunt, to herd, to fight. Useless.

Useless as goose-shit.

He jabbed its side with his spear. The point scraped along a rib and the dog yelped. Its gaze went reproachful, betrayed, and Geirmund jabbed it again, in the hip above the wounded leg. The dog mewled, a weak and pathetic sound that only further irritated him. It began scrabbling away. He pursued it. Again and again the spear-point punched shallowly through the dog's hide, piercing it, drawing blood. The dog wheezed and whimpered. It dragged itself, pawing at the dirt, leaving a crimson trail.

Useless, fucking useless, good for nothing—

Another dragging scrabble, another step, another jab, but this time the dog whipped its head about. Its jaws snapped, teeth catching and tearing his trousers, grazing his calf. He swore and raised the spear, meaning to drive it into the beast's guts, and stand over it to watch it die a slow, twitching death—

"Geirmund!"

The sudden voice made him all but jump out of his skin. He spun, the spear gripped in both hands. And there stood Ogvaldr, his uncle, his war-lord, Ogvaldr who wore the wolf-cloak and carried the sword Helsnautr.

Looking at him with storm-cloud eyes narrowed in suspicion, darkened in disgust.

"What are you doing, Geirmund?"

"The dog…" He gulped. "This dog… it… I… it's hurt, Uncle. Suffering."

"So you think to put it out of its misery?"

"Yes."

"By poking at it like a girl just learning to sew?" Ogvaldr shoved him aside, making him stumble. "Like some fumble-fingered drudge inept with a needle?" He went to a knee beside the dog. It growled at him, eyes rolling wildly, but he stretched out a hand just the same and set it upon the dog's head.

The muzzle sank to the ground. A mournful sighing breath issued from it. The tail thumped once more, weakly. Ogvaldr drew his boot-knife, bright silver. He patted the dog's head, scratched it behind the ear, and then slit its throat with a sure, firm stroke.

"Run with Garm," he told it as the red torrent poured out.

Geirmund felt his fists clench on the boar-spear's ash shaft. For a fleeting moment as his uncle knelt there, back to him, bowed and unprotected, he had the mad urge to plunge the steel point deep between Ogvaldr's shoulderblades.

The impulse fled so fast he wasn't sure it had been there at all.

He shuddered from it nonetheless. Men hated nothing so much as a kinslayer, unless it was an oath-breaker, and by striking down his mother's brother, his jarl, he would become both.

He passed a shaking hand over his face. When he lowered it, he found Ogvaldr's storm-cloud eyes fixed upon him again. Still narrowed. Still darkened. As if he knew what had been in Geirmund's mind.

But Ogvaldr did not speak of it. He wiped his knife on the grass, returned it to his boot, and stood.

"Go back to the women," he said. "Have one of them see to your leg."

And he again turned his back on Geirmund, walking away.

***

Frani and Siggrim rode in with their scout-parties from the nearer farm-steads and slave-hovels, meeting the rest of them at Senwulf's hall when the sun was at its highest.

They'd gained little news. If any in the valley had heard the cries in the night that accompanied the slaughter, none had wondered or worried at it enough to venture out. Neither had any been there on some errand, some business or visit with their jarl. They'd kept to their own fields and flocks, oblivious of trouble, and expecting none.

Siggrim's group had found where Senwulf's horses were stabled and brought back the best, half a dozen good mares of which two had spirited and frisky foals, and a strong young stallion with the makings of a fine war-horse.

The returning men remarked over the child found alive in the hall, and they as well as the others made much of a joke and teasing over Geirmund's dog-bitten leg.

He bore up under it with a scowling black humor, Rota observed, and never did reveal how exactly he'd happened to come by the wound. Nor would Ogvaldr do more than make briefest mention of it.

Yet, something, she was sure, something had gone between them.

She wondered what, and resolved to keep closer watch on the youth... whom she'd never liked or trusted anyway, sullen wretch that he was... never satisfied with what he had if he thought another might have more, or better... ever comparing, weighing, measuring... ever slighted, ever thinking himself to have the short end of any stick... so indignant in his certainty that another's gain must be his loss, another's fortune his detriment.

Others overlooked this, but not Rota.

Inquisitiveness and distrustfulness were in her very nature, as much so as the green of her eyes and the foxbrush hue of her hair. So too were a slyness and quickness that led some to call her Lokis-dottir, though she herself never claimed the patronymic. The gods would not take kindly to such impertinence and insolence, the presumption of making such a boast.

Being known as 'the Fatherless' was enough, insulting though it was. True, she had no father, but she needed none. She'd had her mother Hrothilde and her mother's companion Aud... she'd had the men of Ogvaldr's household, who were all as doting, rough-housing uncles to her.

She remembered once, when she'd been younger, though by no means as young as the boy Maghild had found, going to the king's Thengmote. Or, rather, to the great market festival occuring along with it. Such an assembly of jarls, lords and lawmakers drew throngs of merchants and traders, as well as beggars, whores, thieves, men looking to hire out their sword-loyalties, entertainers, and other wayfarers from far and wide.

One such wayfarer had been a traveling monk, a skinny Christian from across the sea. He'd worn a coarse mule-brown robe, with a rope belt, a wooden cross hung around his neck, with sandals on his feet and the crown of his head shaved as bare as his chin.

Standing atop a stump, gesturing with a crooked staff, he preached to the passers-by of his god in their tongue, clumsy and heavily-accented though it was. Still, the monk spoke well, in a way that caught and held the attention. He could have been a skald, reciting the sagas, instead of wasting his breath trying to convince the Norsk that their ways were pagan and wrong, their gods fanciful and false.

He had, that preacher, that monk, begun going on about the miracle of a virgin giving birth, and at that, several of Ogvaldr's men hooted and jeered. Unusual, it might be, they told the monk, but hardly unheard of. Why, this very girl here—Frani tossed Rota high and caught her again as she laughed—had likewise been born of a virgin.

By such reasoning, therefore...

The monk, Rota recalled, had been quite affronted, and the listeners vastly amused.

Her other memories of the Thengmote were more vague, memories of noise and commotion, of being awe-struck by the activity, by the sheer press and number of people, more than she'd seen in her young life, more than she'd dreamed there could be in the whole world.

She did remember holding tight to her mother's dress with one hand, and to Aud's with the other. She remembered riding high above the crowds perched on Josurr's broad shoulders, able to see all around. She remembered a curtained cabinet where cloth-and-wood puppets capered along as a white-bearded man told stories of trolls, dragons, dark aelves, and heroes. She remembered Aud sharing with her a dish of nuts and honey... and she remembered that being the day she'd first understood that Aud and Hrothilde were not just as friends or sisters but... else, other.

An else and an other, she later suspected, of which that skinny Christian monk surely would have sternly disapproved.

In addition to selecting of the corpse-jewelry and goods of Senwulf's hall, Ogvaldr bade them pick the best of the goats and pigs. These were sacrificed, their throats cut, their blood caught in bowls. The choicest portions, the men set aside as offering to the gods, and the rest the women cooked for their meal.

Mother Maghild sat apart from them in a little hut, once used for the drying of herbs. She too had washed, and changed her clothes from the blood-stained ones, and put back on her wrap stitched from the winter-pelts of many animals. In the hut, as the others did their work, she did hers. She took a flat stone that would have been used for the patting-out of bread, and sprinkled onto it handfuls of salt, ground grain and soot, watching the way the granules fell and the patterns they made.

They told her the omens, of course. Anyone could recognize the more obvious omens if they saw them. It did not take a sooth-sayer to know that an egg cracked double-yolked meant good fortune, while an egg cracked blood-yolked meant illness or ill luck… that a two-headed calf was a definite sign… as was a tree giving blossom or fruit in the depths of winter… omens all, though interpreting their exact meanings was another matter. The ways of the gods were many, and mysterious.

Maghild kept the silent boy at her side, a cord tether linking his wrist to her belt though he showed no signs of wandering off or running away. He went where he was led, stayed where he was put, ate what he was given, and gazed into nowhere with his strange and empty eyes.

"We need a name for him," Tolla said again as they ate.

"Whose son is he?" asked Frani.

"No one's son, now," Rota said, tearing at a strip of pork-crackling with her teeth, finding it crisp and greasy and tasty. "And all the better for him that way."

Several of them frowned at that, frowned at her and each other. To be without family, without kin, to be no one's son, was a dangerous thing. How was a man to seek refuge and hospitality? Who would care for him if he were struck sick, or hurt? Who would raise his children if he died in battle, or avenge him if murdered in some dispute?

It mattered more to men, Rota knew, than to women… than to

most women, regular women, women not like her. A kinless man was weak and vulnerable in the sight of the law, at the mercy of those who'd do him harm with no fear of reprisals. Such a man might as well be an outcast, or a slave-thrall. But a woman could always marry, if she was of a mind to, and join with her husband's family.

"All the better?" Ulrik echoed.

"He is ours," Ogvaldr said.

"You mean," said Geirmund, scowling, "he's to be *your* son?"

There was a hush as men paused in their eating and drinking, as women held their breath. Perhaps they expected Ogvaldr to rise and smite a furious backhand blow across his nephew's petulant mouth. Rota did not expect it, but she did hope for it.

"No," Maghild said before anyone moved. Neither she nor the boy had appeared to be listening, her lost in the omens and him lost in the mind-shadows. But her gaze flicked over them now, the milky eye more daunting than the flint-and-steel one. "We will foster and raise him as we would any orphan of our own folk. He will be fed, clothed, taught, and trained. His old life is dead. Gone. Washed away like a twig on the river. He is new-living now, new-living to us."

"Kvigr, then." Ogvaldr looked at the boy. "We shall call him Kvigr Neingrsson, for he lives but is the son of no lineage."

"Kvigr." Maghild nodded, smiling, pleased. She touched the child's cheek and turned his face toward hers. "Kvigr. You are Kvigr."

He only blinked at her, but that was acknowledgment enough to satisfy Maghild. She kissed his smooth young brow with her thin old lips, then gave him a piece of bread soaked in milk and honey.

"Let us be done here," said Ogvaldr, draining his drinking-horn of the last drops of mead. "Put torch to the hall to be their pyre, and we go. I want to be well away by dusk."

***

When they were done with their meal, they packed up all that they would take with them, loaded the panniers, and roped together the spare horses. They mounted—Maghild once more riding the piebald donkey, with Kvigr held before her half-swaddled in her winter-fur cloak.

The boy made no protest as they left the place that must have been the only home and world he'd ever known. If anything, the further they went from the blazing, smoke-pillar pyre of the hall, the more his sturdy little body eased, until he not only relaxed into her embrace but dozed off. Lulled perhaps by the rock and sway of the donkey's pace, or simply overwhelmed with exhaustion from his ordeal.

Poor mite. Poor thing.

She caught side-glances from several of the others.

Some—Skridda's, Torull's—were fond, hopeful, even affectionate. They had always liked children, and there'd been so few who lived past infancy in their forest-hold fastness since the plague years.

For similar reason, no doubt, Hilfe's look was more wistful, and Ulrik's soft with sympathy as he reached across the gap between their horses to gently squeeze her hand. She wanted a babe of her own so very much, but not even the most potent of Maghild's medicines had so far let her carry one to term.

Tolla had been luckier; she and Frani had lost their infant daughter but had two surviving sons waiting at home in the capable care of their kinsfolk. She took enjoyment in Kvigr's company, for their boys were getting too grown for play and motherly cuddling.

Of the others, some seemed more wary, more dubious. Sworn and loyal men of Ogvaldr's, they had faith in his leadership, but they also knew well the duties and value of kinship, and what fate might hold for this child once he was grown. Josurr had already accepted the addition to their company with the equanimity he did all things. The younger warriors shrugged it off as women's-matters, in which they had no interest whatsoever.

Geirmund of course was sulky, his leg paining him despite the salve and bandage. He rode at the back, leading the line of other donkeys, laden as they were with fleeces and firewood, furs and other goods. He seemed to regard Kvigr's presence as some personal slight to himself, perhaps resenting the attention given the younger boy for all that he often claimed he wished to be treated as a man grown.

Maghild had just to look at him and see how he resembled Miglin, brown-haired and pout-lipped Miglin, his mother, her daughter. Miglin, for whom nothing had ever been good enough... her clothes that should have been dyed richer colors, trimmed with better fur, sewn with finer thread... who demanded the whitest bread, the tenderest meat, the sweetest mead and apple-wine... given a piece of jewelry, she would be delighted for a day, until deciding the metal was too poorly worked, the design less than ideally suitable... who'd married for silver and adultered for gold... and gone off in search of some even better life, leaving her only child to her lame-legged husband.

And Ogvaldr? Maghild's son?

Already, his mind would be turning ahead to Einar Yngvarsson. Jarl Einar, whose hall they'd come to next. And to the fortress of Hallbjorn Halfshield after that... what news, what dark and bloody news, this would bring!

Rota, who normally showed no more interest in children than she did spinning, weaving, sewing, cooking, or other women's-work, nudged her horse alongside Maghild's donkey and looked on the sleeping boy as if taking curious notice of him.

"How did he survive the slaughter at Senwulf's hall?" Rota asked now, peering at Kvigr.

Maghild brushed her hand over the boy's head, letting blond locks curl around her wizened fingers. "Perhaps the gods protected him. Perhaps it was fate. Perhaps nothing more than a simple twist of luck."

"Do you think he saw them die?"

"Saw them, heard them, smelled them, all," she said.

"And do you think he ate of their corpses?"

"I think he did what he must do, as his need made him."

"Trolls eat the flesh and gnaw the bones of men," Rota said.

"Christians eat the flesh and drink the blood of their god, so I've heard," Maghild replied, shrugging.

"He could hardly be a Christian."

"Well, but does he look a troll to you?"

"No."

"Then be it of no mind." She shifted Kvigr's weight so that his head cradled in the crook of her arm. He smacked his lips, murmured, and sighed.

They rode on. Up from the valley and into the high hills, which soon rose higher and steeper yet, the path cutting a pass between rearing mountains whose topmost peaks were snow-dusted, wreathed in cloud. The fading day's shadows spread, the sun lowering in the west until it made a coin of gleaming gold.

There were secret crevices here, tucked away and hidden, like the lush folds of womanly parts. There were welling springs and waterfalls, dottings of tiny flowers sweet and fragrant, mosses and rambling berry-vines. Sure-footed mountain goats sprang among the crags, and, somewhere, an eagle voiced its cry.

In her arms, Kvigr twitched and echoed it with a cry of his own. Behind closed lids, his eyes moved in a dreaming. His mouth went downturned, his chin quivered.

"Shh, now, shh, my boy," Maghild crooned, drawing her wrap more warmly about him. "Shh, sleep, sleep and let it fall away. Sleep, and when you wake, wake to this, your new life."

***

Screams.

Screams in his dreams.

Sudden and shocking.

Screams in the night, screams and a cracking like thunder.

Thunder... Thor's hammer splitting the skulls of frost-giants, that was what Senmark said when he sat with them by the hearth and told them tales of gods and battle and war-glory.

Only this closer than any sky-thunder ever, and the screams!

The screams and the shouts! Flurries of spark-light and flame, shapes looming large, shadows leaping, the howl of dogs and the shining brightness of sword-steel, axe-steel!

Caught in the furs, in a tangle of the furs, knocked one way and another, spilling to the floor, crying, crying from confusion...

...then a wet splatter, a wet dark splatter, warm and thick, sticky...

...wiping at it and his hand coming away from his face red...

...blood, bleeding, he was bleeding, he was hurt, he didn't feel hurt but he must be because here was the blood, the blood came out, like when he'd tripped and hurt his knee on a rock, blood like when they cut up squirrels and fish and eels for the stewpot...

Shrieking now, the blood, the blood, couldn't find where it hurt but terrified—

—don't be a baby don't blubber like a girl, that's what Ingwulf would say, older, not older like Senmark but older than Gunnlith, older than him, and he wasn't a baby, he wasn't a girl, he wasn't he wasn't he wasn't! Gunnlith was the girl, and Hobrik was the baby, not him!

But the blood!

And someone fell down, fell down right in front of him, fell down hard with a heavy, meaty smack like when the men killed a pig, pig was good, pig made smoked hams and boiled pork and salty bacon and smack it would go, smack, but it wasn't a pig it was a man a man with the blood running from his head, his head crushed like an egg crushed and leaking and one eye bulging out a frog's eye about to pop...

More blood and more bodies and a woman with her arm all dripping rags of skin holding together a bundle of bone and a man with his beard and jaw wrenched from his face his tongue flapping lolling flapping from under his teeth—

A roaring there was a bear no a man no a troll no a bear no a giant no a man a giant bear-troll of a man with rune-marks black on his chest and arms and legs, rune-marks under shining sweat and blood, a scrap of bearskin knotted around his waist and a bear's skull where his head should be!

And then Omma was there, Omma who looked after them when Mother was busy. But this was Omma frightened and pale when Omma had never been frightened and pale, Omma was laughing and kind! Her grey braids swung and she was pushing him, pulling him by the hand, pushing and pulling Gunnlith and Ingwulf, and they were crying too, even Ingwulf—don't be a baby don't blubber like a girl—but Ingwulf was being a baby, blubbering like a girl, blubbering as much as Gunnlith or more!

"This way!" Senmark's voice and Omma led them and Senmark shoved aside Huppa who just stood there, stood there staring with his mouth gaping open and the big hands he used for hauling firewood and fish traps dangled limp at his side and they called him Clever Huppa but that was a joke, and Senmark shoved him aside from where he stood blocking the way of the door that went out to the garden where the cabbages grew and the hut where the hens made their eggs...

...that was Gunnlith's chore, getting the eggs, and she'd slapped his hand once for taking one when he'd only been trying to help...

He would let her slap him all she wanted if they could go get the eggs and have everything be the way it was supposed to be, not this way, this screaming roaring horrible way with so much blood!

Senmark ducked through the little door and Omma ran to follow but then Omma screamed his name and leaped back and a hand shot through the gap, through the gap to grab her arm, a grab and a hard twist, a hard cracking snapping twist and a ripping noise like wet cloth and her arm was gone, she stumbled and her arm was gone and there came more blood, spurting over them like rain, like warm red rain!

Then Ingwulf stopped crying like a baby blubbering like a girl, stopped crying and made a war-shout, the way he did when the bigger boys, the boys not little boys but not big enough like Senmark to be with the men, the way he did when the boys had their own battles in the field, battles with wood-swords and play-shields and Ingwulf always got to lead the charge because his father, he said, was better than anyone else's.

So he made a war-shout and went with his knife, went at another man half-naked and rune-marked, another man with a bearskin around his waist and a bear's skull for a head, the man who had Omma's arm, only he let it drop to snatch up Ingwulf instead and—

—then they were clambering over someone's body, somebody broken and dead, clambering over skidding and slipping and slopping in the blood, blood everywhere, and his knee hit a lumpy round thing and it rolled and it was Old-Afi's head, they all called him Old-Afi though he wasn't anyone's *real* Afi, the way Omma was their real Omma.

"Get under!" Gunnlith threw him flat on the floor, nudging him with her foot, kicking him, thrusting him beneath the sleeping-platform's edge.

He bumped his head on the wood and it hurt and he cried again but he wormed his way as far back as he could, wormed his way and wormed around and looked back at Gunnlith through a hanging dripping mess of furs and blankets and she stuck her arms under but then went backward as if yanked by the legs and her wide blue eyes met his, scared, so scared, and then she was gone.

Finally, the screaming stopped.

Quiet. He had to be quiet, oh so very quiet! He huddled in his dark hiding-place, sure that they would find him, they'd hear him or smell him, they'd seen Gunnlith push him under.

There was only breathing, a heavy snorting kind of breathing the way boars and bull-oxes did. And movement, the squishing squelching movement of feet as if through thick mud.

But then that, too, stopped.

And they, too, were gone.

Still, he dared not budge.

Dared not, and dared not.

Until he did.

Until he had to.

Until he saw the birds, the black birds, the great Afi All-Father's black birds… and the rats, bad rats, rats got into the grain or nested in the thatch, rats stole their food and bit Hobrik once when Disa was supposed to be watching him and she got a terrible scolding, but now the rats found Disa too… and the dogs, some dogs were dead too, dead, but some weren't and they slinked in low and shamed to lick at the blood…

Because they were hungry and thirsty.

They were hungry and thirsty and there was no other food or drink for them.

Or for him.

So he had…

No… no… no.

Bad. Bad like a rat, like a raven, like a dog slinking and shameful.

It went away.

He made it go away.

Made everything go away, away into the dark. Into the cold, lost dark.

As the new Omma wanted… the different other Omma, with white hair and not grey… the new-different-other Omma who brought him out from the dark, made him clean and warm, fed him good food, held him so that he knew he was safe.

Who called him Kvigr.

COPYRIGHT ACKNOWLEDGMENTS

"…an excellent read for those who enjoy myths and legends of all kinds." —*Publishers Weekly* (starred review)

For a decade, author Christine Morgan's Viking stories have delighted readers and critics alike, standing apart from the anthologies they appeared in. Now, Word Horde brings you *The Raven's Table*, the first-ever collection of Christine Morgan's Vikings, from "The Barrow-Maid" to "Aerkheim's Horror" and beyond. These tales of adventure, fantasy, and horror will rouse your inner Viking.

"…stories that will make you want to don your helm, sword and shield before riding off into battle." —*The Grim Reader*

Format: Trade Paperback, 306 pp, $16.99

ISBN-13: 978-1-939905-68-0

http://www.wordhorde.com

WINNER OF THE BRAM STOKER AWARD FOR SUPERIOR ACHIEVEMENT IN A NOVEL.

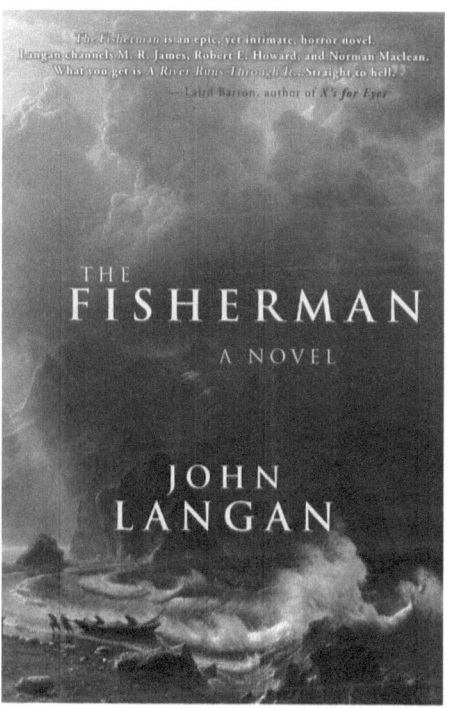

THIS IS HORROR NOVEL OF THE YEAR 2016

In upstate New York, in the woods around Woodstock, Dutchman's Creek flows out of the Ashokan Reservoir. Steep-banked, fast-moving, it offers the promise of fine fishing, and of something more, a possibility too fantastic to be true. When Abe and Dan, two widowers who have found solace in each other's company and a shared passion for fishing, hear rumors of the Creek, and what might be found there, the remedy to both their losses, they dismiss it as just another fish story. Soon, though, the men find themselves drawn into a tale as deep and old as the Reservoir. It's a tale of dark pacts, of long-buried secrets, and of a mysterious figure known as Der Fisher: the Fisherman. It will bring Abe and Dan face to face with all that they have lost, and with the price they must pay to regain it.

Trade Paperback, 282 pp, $16.99

ISBN-13: 978-1-939905-21-5

http://www.wordhorde.com

ABOUT THE AUTHOR

Christine Morgan recently bade farewell to the cool and cloudy Pacific Northwest to return to her ancestral roots and reconnect with family in sunny Southern California. After thirty years working in residential psych facilities, usually on the overnight shift, she's decided to take the plunge as a full-time writer. She also edits, reviews, makes weird crafts, bakes cookies, gets bossed around by her cats, and is probably way too into dinosaurs for a woman her age.

www.ingramcontent.com/pod-product-compliance
Lightning Source LLC
Chambersburg PA
CBHW031342070726
47496CB00017B/1436

* 9 7 8 1 9 3 9 9 0 5 5 8 1 *